HOSTILE GROUND

L.A. WITT
ALEKSANDR VOINOV

RIPTIDE
PUBLISHING

D0924146

Riptide Publishing
PO Box 6652
Hillsborough, NJ 08844
www.riptidepublishing.com

Hostile Ground

Cover Art by L.C. Chase, lcchase.com/design.htm
Editor: Gordon Warnock
Layout: L.C. Chase, lcchase.com/design.htm

ISBN: 978-1-62649-124-3

First edition
May, 2014

Also available in ebook:
ISBN: 978-1-62649-125-0

HOSTILE GROUND

L.A. WITT
ALEKSANDR VOINOV

RIPTIDE
PUBLISHING

TABLE OF CONTENTS

CHAPTER ONE

The bass vibrated through Mahir's bones as a pair of bouncers led him along the staff-only corridor in the nightclub. He caught a line of the rock lyrics—*tough luck, tough guy*—and thought it ridiculously fitting. He was already seeking conclusions and grasping at nothing, like that meth head from last week who had received messages through the TV, convinced that God spoke to him on the shopping channel.

He walked between two goons who'd hopefully soon be his colleagues, trying not to appear too eager or too relaxed. Saeed, his cover identity, would be alert, but he also needed to radiate competence. He must've done a good job of it to have made it this far.

The goon on his left rapped on the last door of the corridor. The door opened, and the goon waved him in.

The room was half supply cabinet, half office. Boxes piled high against the wall. A water cooler looked out of place between the Formica table and cheap folding chairs. There was only one man in the room, and he stood off to the side.

He was taller than Mahir, though not by much. Just enough that he'd have to look up a little if they were ever standing face-to-face, which Mahir hoped didn't happen anytime soon. That wasn't to say the guy was unattractive. Well dressed, well groomed, dark hair arranged perfectly, and tailored shirt and slacks crisp and smooth. He was slimmer than most of the guys working in this ring but certainly not lacking. His white sleeves were rolled to the elbows, showing off strong, sinewy muscle. And if his forearms were that cut, Mahir could only imagine what the man was hiding under the rest of his clothes.

It didn't help that Mahir knew this guy played for his team. If he was the head of Lombardi's security, he was gay. They all were. That was how Lombardi kept his men from fucking with his girls.

Yeah, he was gay and he was attractive, but there was an air about him that made Mahir more than happy to stay on the opposite side of the room. The guy radiated a menacing intensity. A focused, predatory aura that pulled all of Mahir's nerves taut.

The room was dim, lit only by a single weak bulb over their heads, but the still, silent man wore sunglasses. Dark ones. The slightest motion of his eyebrows said he was looking Mahir up and down. Mahir had seen guys like this before. Some were just douche bags who wanted to look like gangster badasses or action-movie leads, but then there was this kind: the guy who didn't like people looking him in the eye. It probably unnerved the shit out of most people, and Mahir had a feeling that effect was *not* accidental.

Question was, how much of this was a test? Was Mahir supposed to be intimidated and unsettled or look this guy straight in the eyes—well, lenses—and not back down?

The butt of a high-caliber handgun stuck out of a shoulder holster beneath the man's arm. He didn't play around. Working for a notorious pimp who was likely also a high-powered drug dealer meant he didn't have to play by the same rules Mahir did. Passing whatever test he was currently taking wasn't optional.

Deep, even breaths. "You must be David Ridley."

"And who the fuck are you?"

Mahir swallowed. The guy's voice was smooth but sharp at the same time. He'd probably sound sexy as hell if every word wasn't laced with *give me a reason not to shoot you.*

"I was told you were expecting me."

"I'm expecting someone." The guy raised his chin, drawing Mahir's attention to the flawless lines of his jaw and throat. "You might want to introduce yourself before you start asking questions."

"I'm Saeed." Social protocol suggested he should extend a hand, but he didn't. Probably best to let this guy call the shots. "I was hired by—"

"You Arab?"

Mahir gritted his teeth. That didn't take long. "Syrian."

"I see." The guy paused. "You don't have an accent."

Mahir resisted the urge to roll his eyes. He'd played this game enough times. "My family came here before I was born."

The guy responded with a subtle nod and a quiet grunt of acknowledgment. He pulled off his sunglasses, and when he looked

Mahir in the eye, Mahir caught himself wishing the man had left the glasses on. His clear blue eyes? Piercing. And enough so to make Mahir tongue-tied and off guard.

The guy slid his sunglasses into the collar of his shirt, which had the top button open, and then extended his hand. "To answer your question, yes. I am David Ridley."

Mahir took the hand and shook it. No point showing even a moment's hesitation, and Ridley had one thing going for him already: no jokes about the virgins awaiting him in heaven. Maybe he wouldn't joke about that. "Saeed Hayaz."

The man held on to his hand longer than was polite among straight Western men and kept their eyes locked. Mahir did his best to relax under the challenge. Not give anything away. Levelheadedness usually got him out of tight spots. This would be no different.

"Tell me why you're here." Ridley's grip was strong and dry. Rough skin, like that of an honest worker—or a fighter.

"I need a job. I was told this is a good place for me, considering my skill set."

"By whom?"

"Word on the street." Mahir could see that wasn't enough. "A guy I met in another club. We compared notes, and he said I should come here."

"Who?" He still kept his hand, as if that touch were some kind of lie detector.

"Tommy. Tall, blond, tattooed."

"Tattoos where?"

"Pretty much all over. Two sleeves, one on the neck. Rip tattoo along his left side, looked like the flesh was torn away and you could see the organs below. Pretty gross but a good piece of work."

"Anywhere else?"

"He did have a Prince Albert," Mahir mentioned as if in afterthought.

"Too bad Tommy can't vouch for you. He's dead."

"Damn." Mahir looked down, pretending he had to gather his thoughts. "He did drive like an idiot, but . . ."

"Bullet." Ridley finally let go of his hand, but didn't step back. "That kind of thing happens when guys talk to cops."

Ice trickled down the length of Mahir's spine. "I wouldn't expect any less."

Ridley gave a small nod. His eyes were still locked on Mahir's. "So I don't have to worry about you taking his place as their narc."

Was that a question? A statement? A threat? This guy was impossible to read.

"I don't care for cops," Mahir said. "I just need a paycheck."

Ridley laughed, which was more unnerving than anything else he'd done so far. Any guy who could make a single, quiet sound—and look—that cold was not someone Mahir wanted to spend more time with than necessary. "Well, you'll get a paycheck." He clapped Mahir's shoulder. "As long as you do your job and know what's good for you." He stepped away, allowing Mahir to breathe. Reaching for the door, Ridley added, "Let's go someplace more comfortable."

He pulled open the door, and Mahir followed him into the hallway back toward the nightclub's lounge area. At the edge of the lounge, where the painted concrete floor met plush red carpet, Ridley pulled his sunglasses from his collar and put them back over his eyes. Mahir couldn't blame him. The flickering lights were a migraine waiting to happen.

As they crossed the lounge, Ridley seemed to make a point of taking a winding path that led them right by all three of the round stages where girls danced for sweating, liquored-up patrons. The walls were almost entirely mirrored, and when Mahir glanced at one of the many reflective surfaces, he thought he caught Ridley looking at him. Impossible to say for sure, though, thanks to those damned sunglasses. Mahir had been warned that the pimp didn't play around with making sure all of his security guards were gay, and he had no doubt he was being tested again.

He didn't have to fake being uninterested in the ladies, but he made sure to give a male bartender an exaggerated double take as he went by. And just before they left the red carpet and stepped into another hallway, he exchanged grins with one of the other security guards. Hopefully that would be the extent of his tests in that department.

Out in the hallway, Ridley took off his sunglasses again and hooked them in his collar. He opened another door and gestured for Mahir to go ahead of him.

This room was closer to what Mahir had expected in a place like this. Lavishly appointed with the same rich, red carpet as the lounge and furniture that probably didn't contain a trace of particleboard.

Ridley went around behind a broad desk and lowered himself into a red leather chair. Then he gestured at one of the two smaller chairs in front of the desk. "Have a seat. Relax."

Yeah. Relax. Right.

Mahir sat down, leaned back, but kept his legs uncrossed. With his back to the door, he was vulnerable, and he glanced over his shoulder. Showing that it made him uneasy would only show he knew his job.

"Who used to sign your paychecks?"

Mahir's focus returned to Ridley. "Uncle Sam. I did my four years and got out in 2004. Did security ever since then. Odd jobs. Drove deliveries across the country, bounced in bars. Didn't really get settled anywhere."

"Ten years of drifting?"

Mahir shrugged. "They tried to get me to reenlist, so I just stayed on the move."

Ridley steepled his fingers on his belly. Flat, trim, powerful. "Iraq?"

"Yes." Mahir met his gaze. "Fallujah was the last big thing I was involved in."

Why are you working for the infidels, brother?

But the question of which side he worked on was never that easy. "Where do you live?"

Mahir balked. "I've house-sat recently, slept on couches. Looking at a couple crash pads once I know I can afford them."

"I guess that means you'll need a sign-on bonus?"

"Certainly wouldn't hurt."

"Family?"

"Nobody I still speak to." Making him disposable and vulnerable. Nobody who'd start asking questions if he vanished for good.

"Right." Ridley sat up straighter. "Take off your jacket."

Mahir took off his jacket and folded it over the back of the other small chair. He was wearing a dark, tight T-shirt and jeans he could actually move in but were still well cut. Apart from the heavy steel-toed boots, this was what he wore when he drove to a club to score. It was nothing special, though people told him he wore it well. He showed off what he had, and that was usually enough.

Ridley stood, walked around the desk, and then sat down on it in front of him, the grip of the pistol almost touching Mahir's face. "Shirt off too."

Mahir didn't hesitate. He wasn't wearing a wire so there was nothing for the man to see. He laid the T-shirt over his jacket and sat back, arms on the armrests so Ridley could see his exposed chest.

"Stand up."

Mahir obeyed, a little unnerved. Not because he thought Ridley might find something damning, but because the two of them were, in spite of the abundance of space in the room, close together. If Ridley so much as pushed out a breath with a little more force than usual, it would probably brush Mahir's chest, and that thought made his flesh prickle with goose bumps.

Focus, Mahir. No point in getting a hard-on.

Though if he did, and Ridley felt inclined to do something about—

Mahir.

"Turn around." Ridley sounded amused. As close to amused as someone like him could, anyway.

Mahir slowly turned so Ridley could see every inch of his torso. Every place he might've hidden a wire. And it dawned on him—he always wore these jeans to clubs because they sat just right on his hips. He wondered if Ridley noticed.

When they were facing each other again, Ridley grinned.

But faint as it was, the grin quickly disappeared. Ridley's expression was carved in ice again, and so was his voice. "How do I know you're not a cop?"

Mahir didn't bat an eye. "You've got a guy running background checks, don't you?"

"Of course."

"Is he good at what he does?"

Ridley's eyes narrowed. "Are you suggesting I hire incompetent fucks around here?"

"No. Quite the contrary."

"What?"

"If he's good at what he does," Mahir said, "then he'd have found anything linking me to the cops. If he didn't, then . . ."

Ridley pursed his lips. After a long moment, he nodded. "All right." Then he put his hands on the edge of the desk and slowly—extra slowly, as if he was doing it deliberately to fuck with Mahir's head—pushed himself to his feet. When he was fully upright, he stood *maybe* a couple of inches from Mahir. Normally, he would be thrilled to be this close to someone so attractive, but the tightness in his chest had nothing to do with arousal.

"There've been some cops through here," Ridley said. "Undercovers and whatnot."

"They made it past your—"

"*Yes*, they made it past," Ridley snapped. "They're crafty sons of bitches sometimes. And if you're a cop, if you've ever even dreamed of being a cop in your wildest, most fucked-up fantasies, then I would suggest you turn around and walk out. Right now."

Mahir didn't move. "I'm not a cop."

"So you say." Ridley inclined his head, drawing them just a little closer. "The last three undercovers left this place in body bags."

Mahir didn't let himself gulp or show even the slightest hint of nerves. He also didn't let himself curl his hands into fists as he wondered if the man in front of him had pulled the trigger on any one of them. The memory of their funerals—grieving widows, confused children asking where Daddy was, Mahir himself trying to keep it together in his dress uniform—was still fresh, still raw. The only things keeping him composed now were a shitload of undercover training and the desire to see this investigation through so his colleagues wouldn't have died for nothing.

"I've had enough of serving Uncle Sam. I have my grudges, Ridley, and I don't think ten years is enough to let them go." Planting the suggestion strongly in the man's mind. Fallujah. Massacre. Trauma. Death. Cover-up. Showing him a figment of the truth, making it sound so easy and natural.

He looked up into Ridley's eyes again. "If you believe I'm a cop, tell me to go. I need to work with people who trust me." A gamble. Ridley'd likely not keep him around for his nice torso. "I get enough shit in the rest of my life."

Ridley held his position. Mahir could feel heat radiating through Ridley's shirt. No response to the dare, though. Another test? Something for Ridley's own amusement?

Beads of cold sweat materialized on the back of Mahir's neck, and he gritted his teeth to appear calmer than he was. He was getting irritated, too. Of course, this was part of getting into the organization, but headfucks got old. Fast.

"You *might* be a good fit here," Ridley said.

"Oh yeah?" Mahir refused to break eye contact. "What else do you need to know?"

Ridley's eyes narrowed again, and Mahir didn't have to look to know that the corners of the man's mouth had lifted. He could *feel* that fucking smirk.

Mahir lifted an eyebrow. "Is it true what they say about you, Ridley?"

To his immense satisfaction, that prompted the slightest startle out of Ridley. For this man it was probably the equivalent of a sharp gasp. His voice was steady and even as he said, "I suppose that depends. What do they say about me, Saeed?"

Mahir shrugged. "I've just heard you handpick every man on the security team." He added a smirk to match Ridley's, and Ridley folded his arms across his chest.

"Meaning?"

"Meaning I've heard you personally screen all the men," Mahir said. "To make sure they fit *all* the requirements."

Ridley laughed. "And don't you wish that rumor were true?"

Now that you mention it . . . "Don't flatter yourself."

Ridley's brow creased.

Mahir made a dismissive gesture. "Though I admit I was looking forward to finding out if you're as good a cocksucker as Tommy said you were."

Ridley threw his head back and really laughed this time. "Oh, Saeed." He put a hand on Mahir's shoulder, patting it hard and then pressing down heavily. When he looked Mahir in the eyes again, the challenge was back and stronger than ever. "Do you really think I'd suck your cock to prove you are who you say you are?" Never letting his eyes leave Mahir's, he shook his head slowly. "Other way around, my friend."

"Is that an invitation?"

Ridley's breath caught just enough to suggest that wasn't the response he was expecting, but he recovered quickly. "You aren't the first cocky SOB to walk through here, you know. I guarantee you won't be the last."

"You didn't answer my question."

Ridley held his gaze. He was off guard. Uncertain. Considering the question? Or how to outsmart Mahir and bring the conversation back into his control?

"Well?" Mahir folded his arms, mirroring Ridley. "Was that an invitation or not?"

Maybe he felt a bit smug when Ridley uncrossed his arms and one hand went to his groin to adjust himself. While Mahir was trapped being Saeed, he might as well get something out of it. And if it proved he wasn't a cop, even better. But it had to come from Ridley. The man appeared to respond best when Mahir challenged him. At the same time, though, it should be easiest to bend the man to his will if he allowed Ridley to think it had really been *his* idea all along.

What Ridley did then surprised Mahir enough to make him jump. He grabbed Mahir's neck and *kissed* him—one of those open-mouthed, passionate kisses that were all about *let's fuck.* It caught him by surprise, but his body responded immediately, opened up under the onslaught. Every time Ridley tried to invade his mouth, he countered and tried to claim Ridley's instead. He pushed forward, backed Ridley against the desk, and ground their hips together.

Ridley gasped into the kiss and held Mahir's neck tighter. He put his other hand on Mahir's ass, pressing him closer. Mahir felt naked without his usual stubble. Clean-shaven against clean-shaven was a totally different feeling. He dug his fingers into Ridley's shoulders, keeping the man pinned against the desk with his weight and grinding touch. He could pretend the man wasn't a criminal, just one of his bar conquests, and that helped. Ridley was also incredibly hot—tall, muscular, and smart. Mahir would love to see how he responded to a dick up his ass. Whether he managed to be bossy then, too.

Ridley's hand left Mahir's neck and went up into his hair. He grabbed it, pulled back, and they were suddenly eye to eye and breathless, staring each other down. Okay, this was getting out of control quickly.

Ridley didn't let go of Mahir's hair. His other hand, though, moved between them, nudging Mahir's hips back. Eyes locked, neither of them looked away, but when Ridley's belt buckle jingled, they both pulled in sharp breaths.

Then came the zipper. *Oh fuck.*

"To answer your question—" Ridley paused to lick his lips. "—yes. That *was* an invitation." He tightened his grasp on Mahir's hair and shoved downward, but Mahir was pretty sure his own knees dropped out from under him a split second before that pressure came. Whoever's idea it was, the end result was the same: Mahir was on his knees, and he had Ridley's dick between his lips.

Ridley's aggression was as unrelenting as it was hot. He forced himself deep into Mahir's mouth, fists pulling at his hair, which unnerved Mahir because it was so different. Most of his adult life, his hair had been too short to be pulled, but Saeed wore it longer to distinguish him from Mahir. And getting grabbed and having his head controlled did funny things to Mahir, especially in this position.

The man wasn't small by any means, bigger than a lot of guys Mahir had been with, but Mahir didn't let it show that his jaw ached or that Ridley pushed the limit of his well-trained gag reflex. Mahir's own erection pressed against his zipper. How long had he been itching for a man who'd fuck his face like this? Just one split-second mental image of Ridley fucking his ass and Mahir damn near came.

He put a hand on Ridley's hip just to steady himself and wrapped the other around the base of Ridley's cock. Ridley groaned. His other hand hit the desk beside him with a sharp *smack*, and Mahir stole a glance just to confirm that, yes, Ridley's knuckles really were turning white as he gripped the edge of the desk. The ones in Mahir's hair were probably just as pale if the painfully tight grasp was any indication.

In spite of the way Ridley tried to force Mahir to stay still, Mahir managed to bob his head up and down, taking control of the depth and speed. He stroked with his hand, teased the head and slit and underside with his tongue whenever he had enough space to do so, and he shivered as Ridley rewarded him with a low, throaty groan.

"Oh fuck," Ridley murmured, fingers loosening and tightening in Mahir's hair. "Oh God . . ." His hips fought against Mahir's hand, so Mahir put his arm across Ridley's belly, pinning him in place, and the groan turned to a faint whimper. Mahir couldn't tell if the man was frustrated as Mahir kept eroding his control over the situation or if Ridley was just too far gone to give a fuck. All he knew was that he couldn't remember the last time he'd been this turned on, and he stroked and sucked Ridley's cock like it was the last time he'd ever touch a man.

The whimper became a low growl. Ridley's hips trembled, his fingers twitched in Mahir's hair, and Mahir squeezed Ridley's dick just right. Ridley swore once under his breath before he came hard, nearly choking Mahir, but Mahir recovered and swallowed everything the man gave him.

"St-stop. Fuck. Stop."

Mahir glanced up and pulled off Ridley's dick slowly with a teasing *pop*. The suction and release made Ridley shudder from head to toe. Seemed he was the type who got oversensitive just after orgasm, the type who'd likely try to shake Mahir off if he came first while fucking. Mahir clambered to his feet again and licked his lips. "Your turn."

Ridley stared at him as if not comprehending, mind still blown from the orgasm, and he tucked himself in, struggling a little to close the zipper over his still mostly hard dick. "Only polite, eh?"

"I'd say." Mahir grinned at him, tasting the man on his tongue, in his throat. He shouldn't have swallowed, but damn, he liked it, and he didn't want to smell of cum when he left this place.

"Fair enough." Ridley grabbed him by the hair and kissed him again, as deeply and passionately as before, likely tasting himself, too. Mahir pressed his groin against Ridley's hip, desperate for some kind of relief. Ridley pushed him toward the desk. "Down. Facedown."

He can't possibly fuck me. Mahir allowed Ridley to bend him over the desk. Ridley was working on Mahir's belt and fly to free him, pressed close and keeping him in place.

Ridley spat in his palm, and Mahir expected the spit-slicked fingers in his ass. Wrong. Ridley's hand closed around his dick, and he pushed up against him from behind, the denim rough against Mahir's bare ass as Ridley began to jerk him off.

Mahir pushed against the desk, not to escape, just to not lie there like a dead fish while that hand tortured him. Ridley was thrusting his hips forward, mimicking fucking, and at that moment, Mahir wished he hadn't gotten him off yet.

"I knew you were a bottom," Ridley whispered low into Mahir's ear, the tickle of breath making every hair on his body stand up. "Imagined I'd fuck you the moment you entered the room, didn't you?"

Mahir shook his head because he hadn't. And calling *him* a bottom— Now, that was almost funny. "Just get me off." He thrust into Ridley's hand, tried to fuck it, but his range of movement was restricted by Ridley behind him. Unless he pushed back much more, fucking anything was wishful thinking. Not that he needed to. Ridley's strong, wet hand gripped him just right—slow, intense strokes robbing him slowly of breath and control, squeezing the head of his cock with just a spike of pain, the other hand working his balls.

"I'll get you off," Ridley growled, letting his lips and his breath brush Mahir's ear. But then his hands slowed down. "When I'm damn good and ready, that is."

Mahir closed his eyes tight and couldn't quite stop himself from releasing a frustrated groan.

Ridley laughed. He kissed the side of Mahir's neck. "You'd do anything I told you to, wouldn't you?"

That comment from any other man would've made Mahir laugh, but he just bit his lip.

Ridley went on. "If I wanted to fuck you, you'd bend over and lube yourself up before I even took my dick out, wouldn't you?"

He would. Fuck, as much as he'd always thought of himself as a top with the *occasional* tendency to bottom just for grins, Mahir couldn't argue.

Ridley's hand slowed even more, nearly stopping. "I asked you a question."

Mahir moistened his lips. "Yes. I would."

A chuckle against Mahir's neck, and Ridley's hand picked up speed, stroking him just fast enough to blur Mahir's vision. "I want you to remember that," Ridley whispered. "That no matter what, you'll do anything I tell you to. Because you will. Won't you?"

Mahir nodded. He tried again to fuck Ridley's hand, but the desk and Ridley's weight still kept him from moving.

"I could stop right now." Ridley bit Mahir's neck just hard enough to make him yelp and then shiver. "I could stop, walk away, and leave you to this"—he squeezed Mahir's dick for emphasis—"and you'd thank me for it. Isn't that right? I could fuck you, not finish the job, and you'd be grateful."

Mahir's knees shook. He grabbed the opposite edge of the desk, just for something to hold on to. A power top with all other men, Mahir whimpered a soft, unsteady plea to the man on top of him for the first time in his life. "Please. Fuck, please . . ."

Ridley gave a soft laugh just maniacal enough to make Mahir cringe. Ridley was going to stop. Any second now, he'd stop. Walk away. Leave Mahir with semen on his tongue and an unresolved erection. And if he came back and ordered Mahir to his knees for another blowjob, Mahir would drop to the floor and thank him for the privilege. What the fuck?

"I won't do that to you this time," Ridley murmured, and he stroked Mahir faster. Mahir's whole body tensed, every muscle tightening with the energy of his impending orgasm, and he silently begged Ridley to be true to his word and not leave him hanging.

Ridley kissed beneath his ear again. Then he whispered so softly Mahir barely heard him. "Come."

And damn if Mahir's body didn't respond immediately. He came hard, unable to even exhale never mind make a sound, and shuddered between Ridley and the desk. His grasp on the edge slipped, so he just let go. He didn't have far to collapse, but as his orgasm subsided, he sank onto the desk and felt like he'd just dropped out of the damn sky.

Before Mahir had even caught his breath, Ridley nipped his earlobe and then let him go. He pushed himself up off Mahir. "You're in, Saeed. Be back here tomorrow night at nine o'clock sharp."

Footsteps. The door opened. Closed.

And Mahir was alone. He straightened, heart pounding in his throat, confused as all hell about what the fuck had just happened. He managed to tuck himself back in, then spotted a door leading to a small bathroom where he washed his hands and belly and rubbed the semen out of his jeans. It was invisible, but he knew it was there. Then he pulled his T-shirt on and, looking around, resisted the urge to search this place. He doubted very much that anybody would take a prospect into a room that kept any important papers. The best thing he could do was be "in," gather information, and then make the whole thing collapse.

You're in.

Well, he'd definitely passed the gay test, and quite spectacularly. Even by his own standards, this had been one of the hottest encounters of his life.

He took his jacket and slipped into it, then left the office. He wove his way back through the Friday-night crowd and resisted the impulse to sit for a moment and have a drink to calm down. He'd have to sleep this off, get into the mind-set and stay there while he was Saeed. This leg of the investigation would likely take weeks, if not months, so he'd better get used to it.

Now, whether to drive to his—Saeed's—crash pad or go home. No competition, really. He would likely spend quite a few nights in that one-bedroom shithole that the department kept for him close-by, so for tonight, he'd take the opportunity to sleep in his own bed while he could.

CHAPTER TWO

He walked to the ferry terminal and got on the next boat to Bremerton. Studying the dark water as the ferry made the crossing, he calmed himself with the thought that he could always tell people he'd done what he'd had to do to pass the test. Saeed wasn't him. Not entirely. Saeed was more resentful. Angrier. Mahir, on the other hand, had made his peace. Was a productive member of society. A decent cop, even if he sometimes wondered why he put up with all the shit. Saeed had simply made one decision differently. Taken a different path at a certain fork in the road. He could easily imagine what it would have meant for him.

On the other side of Puget Sound, he made sure he wasn't being followed before going to his car. Another short drive through town took him into his neighborhood, a pleasant, unremarkable cul-de-sac in an area that had held up decently even in this economy. Cops, state employees, a few sailors and contractors from the nearby shipyard, some low-level IT people who'd raised their families here since it was pretty green and quiet. Three- or four-bedroom houses with two-car garages.

Mahir only owned one car, and his other bedrooms were pretty much empty. He'd bought all that space as an investment and had nothing to fill it with. Sometimes, when he spied families having a barbecue or carrying the shopping in, he felt the lack astutely. Maybe it was a cultural thing, but part of him hated being alone.

Still, it was better than that awful crash pad.

He pulled into the driveway and turned off the car.

When he got out, he spotted something on the porch next to his front door. Somebody.

"Mahir?" The boy's voice sounded sleepy.

Kinza. He hurried toward his nephew, then almost lost a beat when he saw him get up. Damn, he'd grown up in the last year. Kinza displayed that odd grace some teenaged boys had. Pale, smooth skin, unruly hair, and dark, wide-set eyes with long lashes—the kind that made Persian poets speak of gazelles. He was tall and gangly, but by no means a child anymore. Give it two or more years, and he'd be absolutely stunning.

"What happen—"

Kinza crossed the distance and hugged him, just threw himself at Mahir as if he had no doubt even for a moment that his uncle would catch him. Mahir's heart broke a little as he hugged the boy back. Kinza held him too tight for Mahir to believe this was just a surprise visit, and he whispered a silent skyward thank-you that he hadn't gone to his crash pad tonight.

He patted Kinza's back. "What's wrong? What happened?"

Kinza loosened his embrace. As he stepped back, the floodlights caught a hint of a shine in his eyes, but teenaged pride kept anything more than that from showing. The boy set his shoulders back and tightened his jaw. "I didn't know where else to go." He held Mahir's gaze, and those slightly wet eyes begged Mahir not to push. Not yet.

Mahir swallowed and gestured at the front door. "Let's go inside. Have you eaten?"

Kinza's shoulders relaxed a little. "Not . . . recently."

"How long ago is 'not recently'?"

"Couple days."

Mahir raised a disapproving eyebrow. "And why is that?"

That look again. The *please don't ask* one. Mahir ground his teeth. He'd have words with his brother over this. And his sister-in-law. This wasn't the first time Kinza had shown up on his doorstep, and it was usually for the same reason.

As Mahir unlocked the door, Kinza reached into the shadows on the side of the porch and picked up a backpack. Then a duffel bag.

Mahir eyed him. The kid was planning on staying awhile, apparently.

And for the third time in as many minutes, Kinza's eyes begged him not to ask. Of course, Kinza knew they'd have that conversation before the night was over, but first, get in the house and get some food into the boy.

Inside, Kinza dropped his bags on the couch and followed Mahir into the kitchen. Mahir didn't have a hell of a lot of food lying around.

His long hours, not to mention his bitch of a commute, meant he ate out on the Seattle side a lot more often than he cooked at home. So it was nothing but convenience-store food and beer.

He dumped a bag of frozen pasta and vegetables into a skillet, and while it warmed up, he grabbed a beer out of the fridge.

"Can I have one?" Kinza asked.

"No." Mahir popped the top.

"Why not?"

"Because you aren't old enough."

"And you're a Muslim, so we'd both be breaking rules."

Mahir took a long swallow of the ice-cold beer. "You are, too, so you'd be breaking two rules. And, you know, do as I say, not as I do, et cetera." He took another drink just for emphasis.

Kinza huffed as he slouched against the counter. His gaze drifted toward the skillet, where the heat was slowly turning frozen chunks into something edible. Mahir swore he could *hear* the kid's mouth watering.

"You know, there's a McDonald's right up the road." Mahir tilted his beer bottle in the general direction. "You could've gotten something to tide you over."

Kinza scowled but didn't look at Mahir. "Don't have any money."

Mahir blinked. "Not even a dollar or two for—"

"I don't have any money, okay?" Kinza snapped.

Mahir put up a hand. "Okay, okay." What the hell? Seventeen years old, out on his ass without a dime to his name? Adil would definitely be hearing about this, the fucker. Adil had strong opinions, and as a brilliant cardiac surgeon, he was used to having his orders followed inside and outside of the operating theater. But his big-brother power stopped exactly where it impeded Kinza's well-being, and Mahir would see to that.

"Does he know where you are?"

"He's at a conference in . . . I don't know. Somewhere in Europe."

"Your mother?"

Kinza prodded at the pasta with a wooden spoon. Mahir got the impression the kid would eat the food in this state, not quite warm yet, just no longer frozen.

"You know what, why don't you go grab a shower? By the time you're done, dinner will be ready."

Kinza hesitated as if giving that a real thought or two, then nodded and headed down the hall with his duffel bag.

Mahir reached for the phone on the breakfast bar and speed-dialed his sister-in-law. Khalisah sounded distressed, and he told her Kinza was with him, in one piece, and that he would be staying awhile. He didn't prod her for the reason of the fight this time, just reassured her that he'd look after the boy for the time being and talk to his brother when he returned from Europe.

When Kinza came back, black hair tousled and wet, Mahir was just serving the food onto two plates. Kinza sat down and dug in immediately, pausing every now and then to make happy noises and drink a mouthful of water.

"I told your mother you'll be staying for the moment."

Kinza stared at his plate, then kept eating. Mahir knew the boy thought that his mother always sided with his father. But once that teenaged resentment wore off, he might appreciate that his mother would otherwise have been worried sick.

"I'll set the guest room up for you."

"Do you have to work tomorrow?"

"Yeah, but not until late." Hopefully Kinza's newest spat with his father would be resolved before the undercover job got too intense.

How much more intense could it get than being bent over that desk?

He cleared his throat. "I'll be working a lot of nights for a while."

"Really? I thought you were on days now."

"It's a . . . temporary thing." Mahir chased a carrot chunk around his plate with his fork. "I'll probably be staying on the Seattle side a lot, too."

"Temporary? Like how long?"

As long as it takes. "Don't know yet. Just depends on what the captain tells me I have to do." Not quite true but good enough. He looked at his nephew. "But I can probably get you back to your folks' house before—"

"*No.*" The word came out sharply, angrily, but the look in Kinza's eyes wasn't one of fury. His eyebrows rose, his eyes widened, and Mahir was sure the boy was . . . *scared*? Kinza shook his head. "I'm not going back."

"Kinza, your mother is—"

"I don't fucking care." Kinza pushed his mostly empty plate away. "I'm not going back."

Mahir watched him for a moment, trying to make sense of Kinza's outburst. He slid his own plate aside and folded his arms on the table. "What happened?"

Kinza dropped his gaze, staring intently at his hands as he wrung them in his lap. Mahir wished he'd never bought that clock hanging above the doorway because its *scratch-tick, scratch-tick, scratch-tick* was about as unnerving as the silence that had hung between him and Ridley earlier that evening.

Nearly a minute passed. Finally, Kinza looked at him across the table. "Mom found out I'm gay. And she . . . she told Dad."

Mahir let out a breath and rubbed his forehead with the heel of his hand. If there was one brother in their family who didn't need to be the father of a gay child, it was Adil. He'd barely accepted Mahir was gay, and it had taken a few years before the two of them were able to speak again without nearly coming to blows. Mahir had suspected about Kinza—as had his folks since Mahir was the uncle Kinza always ran to when shit flew between him and his father—but he'd hoped to Allah the boy would wait until he was out of the house and on his feet before he came out.

"Dad'll kill me," Kinza said.

Not literally—Adil was a dick, but he wasn't a monster. Still, the fallout would be bad.

Mahir rested his hand on the table and took a deep breath. "Maybe it's best you stay here, then. Until this blows over."

Kinza exhaled. "Thanks."

"What about school?"

"I can get there from here," Kinza said. "It isn't far."

Mahir chewed the inside of his cheek. "You're still a minor, though. If your parents want you back, there's nothing I can do. Legally, I mean. And . . ." He tapped his fingers on the table. "Shit. I don't know if we can do this."

Kinza sat straighter, panic widening his eyes again. "What? Why not?"

"I won't be here most of the time," Mahir said. "I'll be in Seattle. I can't . . . I can't just *leave* you here."

"I'm not a kid anymore," Kinza snapped. "I can take care of myself."

"The law says that unless you're emancipated, you need to be under the care of an adult."

"Then I'll get emancipated."

Mahir eyed him. "You'll be eighteen in six months. There's no point."

"It's either that or go back to my parents." Kinza shook his head slowly. "And I'm not going back. So either I stay with you or I go out on my own."

"And take care of yourself how?" Mahir leaned forward. "You couldn't even feed yourself tonight."

He couldn't tell if Kinza's expression was angry, scared, or both, but the voice was definitely desperate when Kinza whispered, "Please, Mahir. I don't have anywhere else to go. I mean, can't you just take me to your place in Seattle?"

"No." The word was sharper than Mahir had intended it to be. "I mean, it's not . . ." He blew out a breath. How to explain this . . .

Kinza's expression hardened. "If you don't want to help me out just say so."

And that, too, wasn't an option. He'd always loved the kid. Had feared for him when Kinza just seemed softer and gentler than his brothers. He remembered Adil's spiteful look when they'd sat together, breaking fast during Ramadan one evening, and Kinza had dressed up his sister's Barbie dolls. When Adil had ordered Kinza to return them to his sister, Kinza flat-out refused, and the whole situation escalated into a crying fit on one side and shouting on the other. He'd never gotten his own Barbies—of course not. Like giving dolls to a son *made him gay*. Mahir couldn't shake the impression that Adil blamed him, as if his sheer existence was a corrupting influence.

"I'll do what I can," Mahir said. "Maybe I can talk some sense into your father." He couldn't work out any alternative. Ask to be pulled off the case? Not after he'd managed to get in. He owed that much to the men who'd died trying.

Six months seemed like an eternity, but maybe Kinza could put teenaged rebellion aside until he was on safe ground. And then he'd get out on his own and discover all the freedoms that came with being an adult. Go to college, get a job, and break free from that family just like Mahir had when he made his escape via the Army.

Kinza smiled at him, reached across the table, and took Mahir's hand. Mahir hadn't known how such a simple gesture could express so many things and mean so much. It spoke of trust and love and *family*—both rainbow and blood.

"You'll have to work with me on this, Kinza. If anybody gives anybody else the idea you're not properly cared for, I'm in a lot of trouble, and I can't afford that."

"I promise."

"Good. I'll hold you to it."

Kinza relaxed, and Mahir pulled away. "I'll set up the guest room. Put the dishes in the washer and tomorrow we'll get whatever you need to stay here."

He headed down the hall, grabbed sheets and a spare comforter that got very little play in his house—he only kept those around for guests, and so far, only Kinza'd used them—and set up the bed in the guest room. The room was pretty bare at this point, mostly furnished with boxes that Mahir hadn't bothered to take down to the garage, but if Kinza was going to stay for so long, he might as well set it up properly with a desk and wardrobe. He did have the space, and it wouldn't take much. For the moment, Kinza could cope.

The kid came back from the bathroom, wearing a T-shirt and boxers, and slid into bed, all bony legs and shoulders, which triggered every instinct in Mahir's body to protect and care for his nephew.

"Thanks. You're the best."

Mahir ran his hand over the boy's forehead, then bent down to kiss his brow. "Sleep as long as you need. We'll get some breakfast tomorrow."

"Okay." Kinza smiled at him and pulled the pillow closer. "Night."

"Good night." Mahir switched on a reading lamp and dimmed it down to almost nothing, then switched off the rest of the lights.

CHAPTER THREE

The next night, Mahir stood outside on the upper passenger deck, watching Bremerton's lights fade into the distance. If not for the persistent radiance of the shipyard, the city would have disappeared into the night by now. It stayed visible until the ferry rounded a bend, and even then, the faintest glow remained.

But for all intents and purposes, he couldn't see it anymore, so he turned around and walked inside. It was weird, leaving Kinza alone. He'd be safe, Mahir reminded himself. Bremerton was a quiet town. As long as Kinza didn't sneak off to one of the bars where the sailors and shipyard workers went to blow off steam, he'd be fine, and Mahir was pretty sure the kid was smarter than that. Maybe that was a silver lining to Adil's reliance on stereotypes. He'd pounded it into all of his kids' minds that every member of the military would jump at the opportunity to beat the snot out of someone of Middle Eastern descent. Though things occasionally happened, the only military-on-Arab incidents Mahir had been involved in were *quite* consensual.

"I've got homework," Kinza had said before Mahir left. "That'll keep me busy."

Between that and the contents of Mahir's DVR, he was probably right.

Mahir walked the length of the boat to the doors on the opposite end and out onto the deck. The night was chilly, and some of that typical Seattle drizzle mingled with the pungent sea spray, so there was no one else out here. Considering he probably wouldn't have another moment to himself for a while, Mahir could deal with the wet and the cold.

He zipped up his jacket and nestled his face into the collar. Folding his arms over the metal railing, he looked ahead for the lights of the city where he spent the other half of his life. Hell, more than that. For the foreseeable future, he'd be in Seattle more often than not.

He shivered, telling himself it was the mist clinging to the back of his neck that did it. He loved Seattle, he really did. The city was beautiful. But he was a cop. He'd seen its underbelly, its expansive network of crime and cruelty. As the postcard-perfect skyline came into view, the Space Needle glittering off to the left of the skyscrapers and waterfront, he was glad he had this expanse of water between his house—and nephew—and the Emerald City. Kinza had enough to worry about without getting robbed, stabbed, shot, or—

Don't think about that. Just don't.

The ferry's engines fell silent, and the boat coasted toward the dock. A recorded voice came over the loudspeaker, advising drivers to return to their vehicles and walk-on passengers to gather their things.

Mahir's stomach twisted, and his heart pounded. He took a few deep breaths, mentally running through the dossier of his cover ID a few more times. He knew every detail of Saeed's life by heart—his military history, his alienated family, the fictional girlfriend he'd left for some Green Beret, the time he was arrested for public intoxication and precisely how long he'd been clean and sober since that incident—but he ran through it anyway. That made it easier to slip into Saeed's mind. It made it easier to *become* Saeed.

Another piece of that puzzle was the hole that Saeed lived in, so he took a moment to go there, sit on a chair, and look at the mess of his fictional life. A pair of military-issue footlockers holding his few possessions. An empty bed, which he'd mussed. He imagined coldhearted fucks there, fierce and lonely, meaningless and skilled. Saeed fucking men, getting fucked, and kicking the other guy out of the door before falling asleep, exhausted. No books in this place apart from a lonely, weathered Quran, but there was a weight-lifting bench, a yoga mat for stretching, a cheap little carpet for prayer. A mirror—frameless, polished steel tiles just bolted to the wall. This was the place of a man who had nothing to lose. Somebody who'd imprisoned himself in his own toughness and strength years ago.

He stood and inhaled, absorbing the vibe of Saeed's world and slipping into that persona. Then he was ready, grabbed the keys, and left.

This time, the bouncers at the staff entrance gave him just a cursory pat down. Still not quite a member of the team but they seemed friendlier when they told him that Ridley was waiting for him in the lounge. He slipped between the guys and entered the club. It was just starting to get crowded, but he spotted Ridley from far away, sunglasses on, sitting in one of the booths and playing idly with a coaster.

Mahir made his way to him and was measured and weighed again.

"On time," Ridley remarked.

"Disappointed?"

Ridley grinned briefly. "No. I was rather hoping you'd be back."

Mahir opened his hands in a *what can I say* gesture.

"I'll show you the club and introduce you." Ridley stood. He took one last drink, then pushed the empty glass away and waved for Mahir to follow him.

They left the lounge area for one of the quieter, darker hallways. As they walked, Mahir watched him from behind, wondering which Ridley this was: the one who'd threatened him from behind dark sunglasses in a cramped office or the one who'd bent him over a desk and jerked him off. The dangerous one or the dominant one.

Once they were a ways down the hall and didn't have to shout over the music, Ridley took off his sunglasses. "The boss will be in later. You'll get to meet him." He glanced back at Mahir, and when he spoke, his expression and voice were completely devoid of humor. "He'll be the one to decide for sure if you stay here."

Ridley didn't wait for a reaction. Just faced forward and kept walking. Definitely the dangerous Ridley. Mahir wondered if yesterday had been a fluke or a test or the simple impulse of a madman. Whatever it had been, Ridley seemed to have left it behind, and aside from some brief pleasantness when he saw Mahir come into the lounge, he'd reverted back to ice cold and unreadable.

Ridley took him into a back room where some suited-and-booted bouncers played cards over a small table.

"Hey, boss," one said.

The other two grunted something that more or less resembled a greeting. All three looked at Mahir, eyeing him with considerably less subtlety than Ridley had last night. The tight lips and twisted sneers were unmistakable, though he couldn't be sure if it was because he was new blood or because he was the wrong blood. Wouldn't be the first time Mahir saw *a fucking Arab?* written across someone's face.

"You boys clocking back in soon?" Ridley asked with just a hint of malice. "Or fucking off back here all night?"

One looked at his watch. "Ten more minutes, boss. Then we're all yours."

"I'll hold you to that." Ridley gestured at Mahir. "And Gray, you'll be showing Saeed here the ropes."

Gray flexed his pecs, scowled up at Mahir, then muttered, "Yeah, boss," before returning to his hand. He pulled two cards free and slammed them down hard enough to wobble the table.

Ridley glared at him, which didn't do a thing to melt the guy's icy exterior. Shaking his head, Ridley gestured for Mahir to follow him.

Once outside the door, someone grumbled, "Since when does durka durka work here?"

Mahir rolled his eyes and kept walking. Just once, couldn't someone come up with an *original* insult?

When they were well out of earshot, Mahir said, "I get the feeling your boys don't like my kind."

"It's not that." Ridley looked at him, expression completely blank. "They don't like you."

So much for the fabled *gay conspiracy.* Mahir lifted an eyebrow. "And I don't imagine bringing cookies into work will get me anywhere."

Ridley shrugged. "They'll get over it. Everybody's doing his job here. The boss won't have it any other way."

Working with racist pricks was nothing new, but cops at least had to follow the laws and tended not to kill their own. These people—he wasn't so sure.

Ridley showed him the exits and the layout of the place, and it was a fair bit larger than Mahir had imagined, even after studying the blueprints in his office. Several of the rooms he'd pegged as empty were in use, though Ridley didn't open every door for him, just made cryptic comments about "storage," and Mahir nodded, asking questions only about the security of the bar area. Saeed would think of this mostly as a bar to protect from unruly customers. Only Mahir knew it was more than that.

Something buzzed, and Ridley pulled his phone out. "Time to meet the boss." He herded Mahir back into the lounge and then up a Plexiglas staircase that glowed light blue in the black light.

Upstairs, another goon patted Mahir down, devoting more time to Mahir's ass than was necessary. He grinned. "So you're Falafel Boy."

Now, that was one he didn't hear often.

Ridley nodded at the goon. "Falafels from Fallujah, Mitchell."

Mahir drew a deep breath.

"After you." Ridley pushed him through the door.

The room was vast and well insulated against the noise. Only some of the vibration made it through. On one side, a glass desk with an open laptop and a large leather chair. On the other, a dancing pole and a couch so large it could host an orgy.

Gene Lombardi waved a naked girl in high heels out of the room, her skin sparkling with glitter, perfect breasts and perfect legs. Not that Mahir looked for longer than a second before focusing on the ultimate boss of this place. Early fifties, stubble jawed, pale, and he looked like he worked too hard. Whatever Mahir had interrupted, it hadn't been sex—the man didn't look relaxed at all.

"Saeed, is it?"

"Yes, sir." Saeed would likely be tempted to stand at attention, so Mahir straightened but didn't actually go through with it.

"You know we only hire faggots in this place? They keep their dicks out of the merchandise. There was a rather unpleasant 'incident' involving my girls a while ago. Since then, I've not hired a single straight man."

"Works for me, sir."

"Why did you leave the Army?"

"My time was up, and I didn't reenlist. I didn't want to shoot more people like myself."

Lombardi regarded him coolly. "Wasn't the war nearly over then?"

"The war will never be over, sir. America relies on having an enemy, and right now that's us."

"Us?"

"Muslims, sir."

Lombardi grunted. "If you think we'll only serve kosher stuff, you're mistaken."

Halal, you idiot.

"So, you have a hard-on for Uncle Sam." The pimp walked around him. "What about prostitution?"

"As long as it's not our women."

"Drugs?"

Mahir scoffed. "Leave the shit to Americans."

"Alcohol?"

"I don't drink."

Lombardi eyed him. "You don't drink? At all?"

Mahir set his jaw and narrowed his eyes. "No. I don't."

"Huh. Is that right?" The pimp gave a sharp nod and grinned. "You know, I could use a few more of your type on my payroll."

"A few more . . .?"

"Queer sand niggers."

Mahir stiffened, grinding his teeth. "I'm touched."

"You're perfect for my needs." Lombardi shrugged. "You won't drink, snort, or touch my merchandise."

Saeed glared at the pimp while Mahir quietly tucked that into the back of his mind. The subtle acknowledgment that there was more than booze and sex being sold here.

Lombardi put a heavy hand on Mahir's shoulder. "So if your, whatever it is, that book you all follow—"

It's called the Quran, motherfucker.

"—says you can't drink, and you're an honest enough man to abstain from that, can I assume you're an honest enough man not to steal from me?" Before Mahir could answer, the hand on his shoulder got heavier, and the pimp looked him straight in the eyes. "Oh, I don't even need to ask, do I? You skim off my profits or stick your dick in anything I own without paying for it, I'll kill you. It's that simple."

Mahir deliberately let his nerves show just then, raising his eyebrows and gulping. Let the man know he'd made his point and didn't have to worry about Saeed fucking up. "Understood, sir."

"Good." The hand moved from Mahir's shoulder to the back of his neck. Mahir's heart leaped when Lombardi's thumb materialized on the side of his throat, dangerously close to his jugular.

"And since you're obviously a fast learner"—Lombardi let his thumb rest right on top of Mahir's racing pulse—"I don't need to explain to you what happens if you talk to the cops, do I?"

Mahir wanted to shake his head but wasn't sure he could move. "No, sir, you don't."

"I've had an awful lot of cops trying to get into my organization, Saeed." Lombardi's thumb traced small arcs that were halfway between a caress and . . . not. "Some of them try to get my men to talk. Some of them come wandering in here undercover and don't think I'm smart enough to notice. And the consequences . . ." His thumb stopped, and now it pressed harder. Not quite enough to cut off the circulation but just the threat sufficed to darken the edges of Mahir's vision. "The consequences of that are never pleasant for anyone." He leaned closer, eyes boring right into Mahir's. "Am I clear?"

Mahir moistened his lips. "Very, sir."

"Good."

Lombardi released his neck, and Mahir swore the rush of blood nearly knocked him out cold. He absently rubbed his throat and looked at Ridley.

Ridley's expression revealed nothing. He wasn't surprised. Wasn't horrified. If anything, he looked a little bored. *Blah, blah, blah, don't fuck with my shit, blah, blah, blah, I'll fucking kill you, yawn, is it lunchtime yet?* Mahir couldn't help wondering which of these two men was the bigger sociopath.

Lombardi was the type to beat a man to death with a baseball bat to make an example. Ridley was the man who'd walk toward somebody, pull a gun, and put three in the hot square without breaking his stride. Mahir wondered briefly how the other cops had dealt with this situation. Whether they'd wavered for a moment and then trusted their own cold blood and competence and experience. Like he did.

"One question, sir."

"Oh yeah?"

"If I do spot a cop, and somebody approaches me like you said, who do I report to? Him or you direct?"

"Ridley will be adequate. He'll decide."

So Ridley took the fall for any cop murders. This was just a verbal instruction, perfectly deniable when he dragged this slimy bastard into court.

"Understood, sir. Thank you."

"Ridley said you're hard up."

"That's correct, sir."

Lombardi walked to his desk, opened a drawer, and pulled a slim bundle of hundred dollar bills out. He tossed them on the ground in front of Mahir. "Signing bonus. If you quit too soon, I'll take this money out of your flesh."

Exactly how soon is too soon?

"Understood, sir. Thank you." Mahir picked up the money and pocketed it without looking at it.

"Ridley, get him out. I have *work* to do."

So this was fun rather than work? Or perhaps just a distraction from making money. Mahir was often surprised at how business savvy criminals were. As focused as legitimate CEOs sometimes. A sobering thought—wasted talent for the real economy, only that the services and goods were illegal and people killed each other over turf. Or *market share.*

Ridley took him by the shoulder and led him out. "That ought to cover your rent," he said low near Mahir's ear.

The way his breath caressed Mahir's skin made him think of yesterday, of the man's strong hand getting him off, and he swallowed hard. He emphatically did not work here to get laid. In fact, getting laid here was absolutely the worst thing he could do. First time had been to prove he was gay. A second time was a habit forming.

"Better put you to work."

That tone was the closest thing to a leer. Mahir was glad he was off the staircase now and shot Ridley a glance. The man didn't bat an eyelash.

"We'll put you near one of the stages."

Mahir settled in and did his best to blend into the background. He kept an eye on the patrons who went up to Lombardi's office and noted how long they spent up there. He had to learn the players quickly, who knew what, who had access to the boss, and the dynamics and hierarchy.

He was relieved after four hours for half an hour and went backstage into one of the staff rooms. People here still didn't like him, but at least they didn't make a move. He pulled a free coffee from a vending machine and sat there, sipping the stuff, ears ringing from the din outside. Tomorrow, he'd get some earplugs.

The half hour passed without incident, and he returned to his post. He could see the entrance, and he tensed when a couple of policemen strolled in like they owned the place. A few patrons looked around warily, another one or two left. Everyone noticed. Even the strippers. On the bright side, for once it wasn't Mahir getting the *Is he wearing a dynamite undershirt?* looks.

"Couldn't get more conspicuous if they tried," Ridley commented close to Mahir's ear.

He almost jumped out of his skin, then turned to Ridley. "What are they doing here? Isn't the boss paying them off?"

Ridley drew closer. "Stage trick. Walk in like that and they draw attention. Get people looking at one hand and do the important, covert stuff with the other."

Which was exactly what the boys in blue were doing. Helping Mahir cover his tracks. He just hated that Ridley had noticed. And why the fuck was he telling him? To flush him out? Had Ridley seen something odd? Or was he just gauging how Saeed responded to pressure?

"Well, the blond one is kind of cute," Mahir said. *There's a redirect for you.* Pretend he was a shallow fucking asshole who saw all men only as meat.

Ridley glanced at him, an odd expression on his face. Eyes a little narrow, lips a little tight. Was that . . . *jealousy*? Ridley shook his head and watched the cops again. Why wasn't he wearing his sunglasses? "I'm not into blonds."

"I am if they have a uniform that needs ripping off."

Ridley jumped, but so did Mahir. Where the fuck that had come from, he didn't know, but he ran with it, grinning when Ridley looked at him.

"Why do you think I joined the Army?"

"Ah." Ridley gave a single nod. "That makes sense. Though if I were going to enlist on the basis of uniforms, I wouldn't have gone with the Army."

They glanced at each other. Then, in unison, "Marines."

Ridley laughed. "I wouldn't mind tearing a set of those dress blues apart."

Mahir shivered. "Hell yeah."

Ridley casually cupped his elbow in one hand and chewed his thumbnail. Mahir barely heard him over the thumping music as he said, possibly more to himself, "One button at a time."

Added to the bucket list, that's for sure.

Ridley shifted his weight. He rolled one shoulder. Then the other. Then both. As if he couldn't get comfortable. His gaze was fixed on the two cops, who were whispering back and forth, turning their heads just right so Ridley and Mahir couldn't read their lips if they tried. And Ridley kept fidgeting.

"You all right?" Mahir asked.

Ridley nodded. "Yeah." He turned his head toward Mahir and conspicuously held up a hand to cover his mouth from the cops' view. "They're here to make us nervous. Keep us from noticing the guys in plainclothes."

A chill ran down Mahir's spine. Of course Ridley had figured this out. He was far too intelligent to let a little act of diversion draw his attention away from the more important—and more dangerous—activities going on.

Ridley turned around, showing his back to the cops. "If they think a few boys in blue are enough to keep me from noticing the undercovers, they're idiots."

"How long's it been since they've sent in an undercover?"

Ridley looked him in the eyes. "There's three in here right now."

It took everything Mahir had not to show his nerves, and what little he did show, he disguised as surprise. "What? Now?"

Ridley nodded. "Up at the bar. Third stool from the right. Red shirt."

Mahir looked at one of the mirrored walls and found the guy in question. He didn't recognize him, but the guy seemed a little too aware of—and interested in—his surroundings to be some sorry loser searching for a drink and a fuck.

"Stage two," Ridley said. "Seat on the end. Sweaty guy with the Mariners jersey."

Still using the mirror, Mahir found him. Though this guy stood out from the crowd in his excessively casual attire, it actually camouflaged him, too. He wasn't subtle enough to be a cop, sitting there getting drunk and waving twenties around in his pudgy fingers.

"And the third one?"

Ridley shifted beside Mahir. When Mahir looked at him again, they were even closer together. Too close together. Ridley's eyes were as unreadable as they'd be if he'd still been wearing the sunglasses hooked in his collar, and Mahir's blood turned cold even as his body temperature rose from an entirely different effect.

Ridley's eyes darted to the left, looking past Mahir. He furrowed his brow. Turned away. Scanned the crowd. "He was just . . ."

Relief swept through Mahir. Ridley may have lost sight of whomever he was looking at, but thank fuck, it wasn't *him*. He didn't feel the need to taste the barrel of that pistol underneath Ridley's coat.

"There." Ridley faced away from the crowd again. "Last booth on the right. Getting a lap dance."

Mahir found him easily enough. That must be a tough job. Go into a strip club. Get drinks. Get lap dances. Maybe collect some intel in between the tits and tonic.

"So what are you going to do?" he asked.

"What am I going to do?" Ridley looked at him like he'd lost his mind. "Let them sit here and pour tax dollars into Lombardi's wallet, of course."

"You're not worried about them finding anything?"

"Hell no. Not out here." He chuckled and clapped Mahir's arm. "This place keeps them busy, and they don't notice a thing." He held Mahir's gaze.

And after a moment, Mahir realized Ridley was still holding on to his arm.

Apparently Ridley had forgotten, too, because he looked down and then yanked his hand back. "I . . . Sorry."

Sorry? Mahir shook his head. So Ridley only fucked the guys to test them? It would probably be the professional thing to do. And Saeed wouldn't care either way. He opened his legs, then positioned one to press against Ridley's thigh. "And here I thought yesterday you'd fuck me today. As promised."

Ridley stared at him.

"Maybe off duty," Mahir offered. "I have a place five minutes from here. Unless you have a boyfriend or already promised your big cock to one of the other guys." A deliberate tease, punctuated with adjusting himself in his trousers. There was something about Ridley's badassness that turned him on. It wasn't about building a rapport with him, wasn't a seduction game. It was something Saeed would do to relieve stress. And if Mahir was going to be a bad guy, at least he could collect some of the perks.

"Or would I have to pay Lombardi? I don't really want to get shot in some back alley for putting my dick in you."

Ridley gave a short laugh. "My ass is mine. And I don't think you'll ever get into that position."

"Try me?"

Ridley placed his hand on the side of Mahir's neck, exactly where Lombardi had threatened him with a touch. "I top."

"You promised you would."

Ridley glanced at his watch. "Keep the thought." He pushed away, and Mahir caught his breath. Maybe he shouldn't have teased him. He should go home, look after Kinza. But he was making excellent progress, and this would allow him to blow off some steam so he had his head clear for the rest of his life. And it would get him in closer with Ridley, even if it was sex and nothing more. It was for the sake of the investigation. Nothing more.

Sure it is, Mahir.

Thankfully, the uniforms left after another stroll through the club, and two of the undercovers left about an hour later. Soon it was nearly two o'clock, that weary time when Mahir and the rest of humanity were at their worst. The bar closed down around then, and the boss left at half past. The dancers left. The bartenders left. The customers were long gone.

Until Ridley decided to give the word and relieve them, only security remained.

CHAPTER FOUR

Ridley finally released most of the security staff but kept Mahir back. They checked the club for anybody left behind, hiding, or passed out, then closed up. Mahir was dead tired, though a nervous current ran through his gut when Ridley waved him to a car. He got in, gave Ridley the address of his crash pad, and directed him there.

Ridley parked down the street, then followed Mahir to his door, up the stairs, and through the next door. He looked around briefly.

Mahir shrugged his jacket off. "I'd offer you a drink, but I don't have any."

"You really don't drink, eh?"

"Of course not." *I could so go for a beer right now . . .*

"Well"—Ridley reached for Mahir's shirt—"that just means you'll be completely alert, doesn't it?"

Mahir swallowed. He was exhausted, but one whiff of Ridley's light cologne woke him right the hell up. "Yeah. I'm wide-awake."

Ridley grinned. "I should hope so." He pulled Mahir to him and kissed him. Not as aggressively as he had last night, but he certainly wasn't passive, either. He assumed complete access to Mahir's mouth, and Mahir let him because he'd been dying for this all damned day.

Mahir wrapped his arms around Ridley. There was no desk to hold them up this time, so he had to rely on their legs to keep them from crumpling to the floor. And if they did, then they'd just fuck right here. He didn't care.

Ridley released Mahir's shirt and slowly wrapped his arms around him, too. Mahir's arm grazed Ridley's shoulder holster, and the thrill that rushed through him made him unbearably hard. Yes, Ridley was fucking dangerous, but for tonight, he was Mahir's. Or Mahir was his. One of the two. Mahir would take it either way.

Ridley broke the kiss. A few strands of dark hair slipped out of place and fell down over his eyes, giving him a slightly disheveled and incredibly primal look. He licked his lips. "Where's your bed?"

Not nearly close enough.

Mahir couldn't remember how to speak so he slipped a hand into Ridley's and led him across the living room and into his bedroom.

"Clothes." Ridley halted and freed his hand. "Off."

Mahir faced him. Ridley unhooked his sunglasses from his collar and dropped them onto the secondhand dresser beside the door. Then he went for the first open button of his own shirt.

"Clothes off," he ordered again and freed the button with a little excessive force.

Mahir didn't have to be told a third time. He stripped, aware of Ridley's constant scrutiny with every motion. And the more Ridley removed, the less Mahir could concentrate on simple tasks like unzipping his pants or pushing them over his hips.

The man was insanely sexy. Just as Mahir had suspected, the rest of his body matched those toned forearms. His abs were lean and ridged, and the harsh overhead light threw shadows that played on all the grooves and contours every time Ridley moved. He had a tattoo on his rib cage, right beneath where that shoulder holster had been. Mahir couldn't make out the details from here, only the presence of sharp black lines and a few hints of color.

He'd already seen Ridley's impressive dick, but it seemed even bigger against the backdrop of such a smooth, powerful body. Those legs were absolutely made for fucking. All muscle. Built to thrust hard enough to make a grown man cry.

Ridley smirked. "Like what you see?"

And that was when Mahir realized he'd been staring. He cleared his throat and looked away. "I do. Yes."

"So do I." Ridley once again closed the distance between them. "I'm especially looking forward to seeing how you look from behind."

A doggy-style fuck, then. Mahir couldn't say he objected to the idea, except that it meant he'd only feel, not see, and this was a body he wanted to see in action. But feeling it would be more than enough to get him off. Hell, he'd never believed in fucking a colleague—so ironic that he'd start with that kind of complication during an undercover mission. Why was that? Because it was easy, because he knew that Ridley was gay and interested? Maybe because the danger—of having his cover blown and getting murdered like the others before him—made him reckless about sex. A way to deal with the tension. A way to play his role, the one of an angry man who'd consider sex nothing but stress relief.

He got on the bed and dug for condoms and lube. "Get suited up." He tossed the strip to Ridley, and his breath stuttered when Ridley stroked the condom down his length. Those strong rough hands touching his large dick—it was incredibly erotic how Ridley concentrated on making sure the latex sat just right.

Mahir took the lube and squeezed some of it into his hand, warmed it, then lay back and opened his legs, sliding two fingers into himself. He remembered what Ridley had said—*You'll do what I say*—and decided to not let the man remember giving him orders. Preemptive obedience. He groaned at the stretch, self-inflicted as it was. And not only the burn from the stretch but the way Ridley watched him, watched his hand, wrist, fingers, his asshole. He'd never considered himself an exhibitionist, but then, Saeed just didn't give a fuck what people thought of him.

Ridley grabbed the lube, too, and smeared some over his condom. Then he climbed on top of Mahir, a full-body touch that caught Mahir completely by surprise. Another hungry kiss, and he took control of Mahir's wrist, pushed his fingers deeper. At Mahir's groan, Ridley grinned sharply. "Add another."

"I . . ."

"Do it."

Mahir added a third finger, arched when the burn intensified. He pressed against it, the pressure, the stretch, and half resented that Ridley controlled the speed and depth. He also loved it. He normally wasn't into this kind of game, but with Ridley he could be.

"Enough." Ridley grabbed Mahir's hip and pushed. "Turn around. Legs open."

Mahir did as Ridley commanded, sliding his body against Ridley's as much as he could during the turn, and pushed his ass back against Ridley when he'd settled on his knees and elbows. "Okay. Do it."

A quiet chuckle told Mahir that Ridley wasn't done fucking with him yet.

"Saeed, you silly boy." Ridley ran a hand up the length of Mahir's spine. "Did you forget who's in charge here?"

Mahir groaned, closing his eyes. "Just . . . fuck me."

Ridley's weight shifted. His slick cock pressed near—but not into—Mahir's ass, and a second later, his chest warmed Mahir's back. One hand snaked around Mahir's waist, and Mahir sucked in a breath through his teeth as Ridley closed his fingers around Mahir's cock. Last night flashed through his mind, that scorching hot handjob while Ridley'd had him pinned and immobile over a desk.

"Seems like you're in a rush," Ridley murmured in his ear, stroking him slowly. "What's your hurry?"

"Hurry?" Mahir rocked his hips, trying to simultaneously fuck Ridley's hand and work them into position so Ridley's dick slid into him. "I've been . . . wanting this since . . . *Fuck.*"

Ridley laughed and kissed the side of Mahir's neck. "Something the matter?" He squeezed Mahir, stroked him faster, and pressed against him so Mahir felt his cock but couldn't do a damned thing to get it inside him. "Am I frustrating you?"

"You should be fucking me," Mahir growled.

"Should I?" Ridley taunted. "That sounds an awful lot like you think you're in charge." His hand stopped, but he kept squeezing and releasing so Mahir could barely think. "Do you think you're in charge here?"

"No." Mahir pressed against Ridley's cock. "No, I just want you."

"Mmm, do you?" Ridley pulled back. "You want me to fuck you? Right now?"

"*Please.*"

"Except I'm so damned turned on." Ridley's whisper was hoarse now, borderline breathless, lifting the veil on his own tenuous grasp on control. "If I fuck you, I'll lose it. And this will be all over." He pressed his lips beneath Mahir's ear. "And you don't want that, do you?"

Mahir licked his lips. "We have more condoms."

"Hmm, yes, we do."

"If you come, you can fuck me again."

Ridley moved his hips from side to side, grinding his lubricated dick against Mahir's ass. "You're already inviting me for a second fuck? You don't even know if I'm any good." The devilishness in his voice said Ridley knew damned well he was more than "any good." Any man in his right mind would want that cock more than once.

"Just fuck me," Mahir growled. "No . . . no games."

Ridley laughed again. "The games are half the fun." Ridley let go of Mahir's dick, making Mahir's head spin. Still holding himself up on one hand, Ridley shifted his body to one side, his torso lifting just slightly as if he'd moved his free hand. Then his fingertips drifted over Mahir's ass, and Mahir held his breath as Ridley adjusted his position.

"I have to confess," Ridley murmured, pressing just the head of his cock against Mahir's well-prepped asshole. "I've been wanting to fuck you since you walked into the club."

Speech was lost on Mahir. He whimpered, hoping that translated to something in the ballpark of "likewise."

"Isn't very often we get guys in that I want to fuck." Ridley pushed in slightly, giving Mahir only the first inch or so of his dick, but it was enough to make Mahir's whole body shake. "And it's definitely not often we get guys who are so . . . *submissive.*"

The word zinged along the outer edges of Mahir's senses. Somewhere in the back of his mind, objections like "fuck, no" and "what the hell?" tried to crowd his consciousness, but he was too focused on that thick cock gradually pressing in a little deeper, stretching him farther than he'd already stretched himself.

"I like men like you," Ridley slurred and withdrew slowly. "So willing." He slid back in, taking what seemed like forever to push himself all the way into Mahir, and when he was buried to the hilt, he whispered, "So *obedient.*"

It shouldn't have been so hot. He'd never thought of himself as submissive. And obedience to a criminal? Seriously disturbing. Behind the protection of the fake identity, though, he could sink into that shell Ridley saw. Submissive. Somebody who barked and never really bit. Truth was, he did want to fuck Ridley one day, too. Take his fill of that chiseled, powerful body, make him beg and maybe scream, fuck him like an animal. Give and take. And definitely take everything he could get from him before Ridley went to prison. Because he wouldn't come out for a very, very long time, if ever, and once he knew what "Saeed" was, there'd be no chance of a repeat performance.

All thought fled when Ridley began to move inside him—slow, teasing, controlled, though Mahir could feel him tremble with the strain. Mahir gasped, his breath labored with arousal. "Oh fuck."

Ridley seemed to have reached the end of his tether. He began to thrust, the pleasure searing every nerve in Mahir's body. Damn, more than he'd expected, and he'd expected a lot. What really turned him on was feeling how much Ridley wanted, needed. Not necessarily *him*. No doubt Mahir was just a convenient fuck, but Ridley turned on and taking what he wanted was fucking hot.

One hand grabbed Mahir's shoulder for stability, the other reached for his dick.

"I like men who stay hard," Ridley panted.

Mahir chuckled, but that soon became a groan as Ridley went for it, unleashing his strength on him, their flesh slapping together hard, and with every thrust, pleasure exploded in Mahir's body. He struggled to keep a modicum of control, but then it just ceased to matter. He moved in unison with Ridley's thrusts, and he reached for his own dick, grabbed Ridley's hand, and jerked himself off because it was getting unbearable and he was so close.

He could have sworn they came at the same time. Clenching muscles, erratic thrusts, and he felt the enormous relief of orgasm, spurting over his and Ridley's fingers while he felt Ridley pulse inside him. He slid forward onto his belly, hand coated in semen and fingers still entwined with Ridley's.

Ridley stayed inside him and lay down on him, breathing hard and coordinated with Mahir's own harsh breaths. "Too short. Too fucking keyed up."

Mahir chuckled. "It's okay. I'd have strangled you if it had gone on for much longer. I fucking needed this."

Ridley laughed softly and kissed the back of Mahir's neck. "Me too." He lifted himself up, and they both gasped as he withdrew.

They were still out of breath as Ridley got up to get rid of the condom, and Mahir slowly sat up. He cleaned off his hand, and when Ridley came back, they both dropped onto the narrow bed. Just a mattress and box spring on the floor; the department hadn't sprung for much. It fit Saeed's persona—broke, drifter, very few fucks given about anything—but conveniently fit the department's budget, too. Of course.

Ridley rested one hand behind his head on the pillow and stared up at the water-stained ceiling. His chest still rose and fell rapidly, but as he caught his breath, his colder side came back. That wasn't someone Mahir necessarily wanted to be in bed with. The man made of ice who hired, fired, and when ordered to, executed.

Mahir lifted himself up onto his elbow and resisted the urge to playfully or affectionately run his fingers down the center of Ridley's smooth, almost hairless chest. It hadn't been five minutes since this man was balls deep inside him and whispering filthy things in his ear, and now he seemed too dangerous to touch.

Slowly, Ridley turned his head toward Mahir. As their eyes met, the hairs on Mahir's neck stood on end. He felt oddly like he was looking down the barrel of a pistol.

But then Ridley's expression softened as much as it ever could. His lips curled into a slight but seemingly genuine smile, and when he reached for Mahir's face, his touch was gentle. No warning pressure on his jugular, no tight grasp to imply how easily he could snap Mahir's neck. The backs of his fingers trailed down Mahir's stubbled cheek and onto his neck, then back up. It was a tender gesture, even a kind one, and still brought to mind an image of Ridley drawing the flat side of a razor-sharp blade across Mahir's flesh.

"This is dangerous," Ridley whispered.

Said the lion to the lamb.

"I know," Mahir said. "I'm . . . assuming we shouldn't talk about it. At the club."

"We shouldn't do it." Matter-of-fact and blunt, but tinged with an unusual hint of regret. "If Lombardi finds out—"

"He doesn't have to."

"We shouldn't take the risk. Gene has a lot of places to hide bodies, and he wouldn't hesitate to add us to the cache."

Mahir swallowed. "Just for sleeping together?"

"Lovers can be more loyal to each other than they are to employers." Ridley caressed Mahir's face again. "*No fucking* is not a hard-and-fast rule, but Gene can't risk disloyalty. Which means . . ." He trailed off, looking at his fingers on Mahir's skin.

"Which means we can't do this."

Ridley didn't speak. He just nodded slowly and sighed. And then, in spite of everything, he lifted his head off the pillow and drew Mahir into a kiss that said absolutely *nothing* about not doing this again.

The word Ridley had used was disturbing: *lovers*. Not fuck buddies. Not . . . any other term. It implied much more than Mahir had expected to find here, and he wasn't sure if he wanted to consider Ridley his *lover*. He'd had one-night stands. He'd had a couple of boyfriends who eventually worked out that dating a cop was just a recipe for disaster and heartbreak. That, in many ways, the job came first.

And Mahir had an uncanny talent for finding the type of man who did not easily accept being number two in his life. Others had been uneasy about never meeting the family: It spoke of a lack of commitment, of playing things safe, of staying in the closet, and, again, the strongheaded, independent type that Mahir liked so much didn't take that kind of stuff lying down. Sometimes he'd thought dating another cop might be the solution to at least one of the problems, but that went against his aversion to fucking his colleagues.

Ridley's kiss was too damned heartfelt, too tender, too intense. Maybe it would be good if they didn't take this any further. So Mahir could focus on his job. So they were both safe. So he wouldn't spend more time in this hole, away from Kinza, than necessary.

"Well, we've done it," Mahir said. "We can do it again, and maybe again, and then drop it. Or one of us leaves the club and we do . . . things outside."

"You need the paycheck. And I'm in too deep." Ridley lay back, stretched out, and stared at the ceiling. "Pointless."

CHAPTER FIVE

idley left not long after the sun came up. Mahir was exhausted, not to mention sore as hell from two more go-arounds with a man that rough. By all rights, he should've slept until tonight's shift at the nightclub.

And he would have, except he had a meeting across town.

Saeed didn't own a car, which left Mahir at the mercy of Seattle's abysmal public transit system. And calling a cab was out of the question, at least until Saeed had pulled in enough money from this new job to cough up twenty dollars to get across town.

So, a little past noon, he shuffled out of the apartment and down the street to a bus stop. The brisk, drizzly air shook him out of his half-comatose state, and just inhaling the fumes from one of the many espresso carts and coffee shops was enough to wake him up.

A bus took him from the waterfront out to the U District, where he walked the last half block to the vintage record store. Inside, he immediately spotted Lieutenant James standing beside a row of milk crates that had been stacked on top of cinder blocks. Mahir didn't go straight to him, though. He thumbed through a few stacks, perused the posters on the wall announcing concerts from no-name bands at hole-in-the-wall venues.

There was no one else in the store besides the clerk, a girl in her twenties with camouflage pants and hot-pink hair. She leaned over the counter beside the aged register, sighing as she flipped through some rock magazine.

Mahir slowly made his way to the row where James looked through a crate full of sixties-era vinyl.

"See anything good?" he asked.

James didn't look at him. "Nothing worth buying."

Good. That was their code for *I haven't been followed.* Mahir started going through the next crate, this one full of seventies crap.

James pulled Hawkwind's "Silver Machine" single out of the crate and looked over the back of the sleeve. "Heard anything interesting lately?"

"Still learning the ropes." Mahir feigned interest in a Sex Pistols record. "Some of your buddies showed up last night. Didn't quite fit in with the crowd."

James slid the Hawkwind record back into the crate and continued thumbing through the vinyl. "They didn't need to."

"Yeah, well, people notice." Mahir glanced at James. "Even the ones who *did* fit in."

James's fingers stopped. He didn't turn toward Mahir, but Mahir definitely had his attention. "What's that supposed to mean?"

"It means they should be careful," Mahir said, "because they're not blending in as well as they think they are."

"You telling me how to run my shit?"

"You're risking a fourth funeral, that's all." Mahir was fed up with people constantly jerking his chain. Not without coffee, breakfast, or even some decent sleep first. They could give him all the shit they wanted for his race. After twelve years, he was pretty much used to it. But he was a damn good cop, and he was taking this one for the team.

James glared at a Motörhead record, almost visibly counting to ten. "Really? You think they were spotted?"

"Three suits. Two in blue."

James's jaw tightened. "What do you suggest? Pull them?"

"That'll tip Lombardi's people off." Ridley was too fucking clever. He would be keeping track of the opposition. "I do think this angle'll work."

"How are you getting on? Any results?"

Mahir blew out a breath, turned a Deep Purple record in his hands as if trying to decide whether to buy it. He wished he knew more about this age of music, but his conscious appreciation for rock music started in the late eighties—or at least five boxes down that way. "I got the *welcome to the team* speech twice. They're on edge, paranoid. It'll be a while until I'm accepted. And they aren't exactly Osama bin Laden fans, either." Making jokes about it was one way to deal with the pressure.

"Yeah. That." James straightened and moved toward the eighties. "Well, do what you gotta do to win their trust. Chances are, they'll test you."

Passed the gay test, but I'll spare you the details.

"Nothing new there." Mahir shrugged. "Napalm Death? Really?"

"The eighties were crazy," James muttered. "No better way to sell records than offend everybody's sensibilities with some swastikas and demons and shit." He put the record back. "Keep me updated." He started to walk away but paused. "Watch yourself with their head of security, by the way."

The Deep Purple album almost tumbled out of Mahir's hands. "Oh yeah? Why's that?"

"Guy's a lunatic. There's no proof yet but he may have been the one who . . . *retired* our boys."

Mahir gulped. "I'll . . . um . . . I'll keep an eye on him."

James nodded sharply and strolled out.

Mahir kept staring at the record in his hands. He could swallow the idea of Ridley killing someone in cold blood. Maybe even a cop. As long as he kept thinking of the Ridley he first met and not the one who bent him over a desk and, more recently, Saeed's bed. The guy with the icy stare behind dark sunglasses—he could shoot a cop and not blink. The one who'd left Mahir aching all over, and who had seemed just as unhappy as Mahir that they couldn't continue things, wasn't a murderer. He couldn't be. Could he?

Mahir shoved the album back into the crate, slid his hands into his pockets, and headed out of the shop. Maybe it was hard to stomach, but he knew damn well there was no rationalizing away the truth: If Ridley was head of security for someone like Lombardi, then he wasn't just a nice guy who happened to be good at keeping a nightclub secure. He was a criminal. Likely a hardened one. He'd probably worked his way up through the ranks, and in an organization like Lombardi's, that meant leaving a few bodies in his wake. Especially if Mahir's investigation proved what several other investigators, including the three dead ones, had believed all along—that pimping was just a front for a massive drug ring.

"*You won't drink, snort, or touch my merchandise,*" Lombardi had said.

Great in bed didn't negate guilty as hell.

Mahir walked a few blocks and found one of the last remaining pay phones in Seattle. He dropped in a few quarters and called Kinza's cell phone. It occurred to him Adil might have cut off the kid's phone, but within seconds, it started ringing.

"Hello?"

"Hey, it's Mahir."

"Oh, hey," Kinza said. "You on your way home?"

"No, I— I have to work again tonight."

"Oh." The disappointment was palpable. "When *are* you coming back?"

Mahir scrubbed a hand over his face and sighed. "It's tough to say. I'm working weird hours right now. I just wanted to check up on you. Make sure you were doing okay."

"Yeah. I am."

"Talk to your parents?"

"No." Kinza sighed. "My mom keeps calling, but I haven't answered. Thought you might be her, so you're lucky I answered your call."

Mahir laughed. "Well, glad you did. Listen, I have to get back to work, but I just wanted to check in." He paused. "If you need to get in touch with me, call my chief, all right?"

"Your chief? Don't you have a cell phone?"

"It's— I can't use it. Not while I'm working. But my chief can reach me if necessary."

"You really don't mind me calling your boss?"

"Well, don't do it if you just want to shoot the shit," Mahir said with a soft chuckle. "But, you know, emergencies, or if things go south with your folks."

"Okay. Good to know."

After they'd hung up, Mahir headed toward the nearest bus stop. He hated leaving his nephew hanging like that, but he didn't have much choice. Kinza's timing could not have been worse. But what could he do? He'd left him money in an envelope in the kitchen and told the neighbors that Kinza would be around, but other than that he had to hope that Kinza went to school unprompted—and unsupervised.

Hopefully all this would be over soon. He'd find the evidence he needed, the information, maybe even a witness willing to throw everyone under the bus, and he could go home. The case wouldn't last six months. If he didn't dig something out in the next few weeks, he was doing something wrong. He had to trust his nephew to cope on his own for the time being.

He wished he could be so flippant and tell himself that teenagers these days were happy as long as they had minutes on their phones and high-speed internet. Kinza struck him as needing more than that. Somebody who listened, possibly hugged him when things were rough. They'd always been fairly affectionate with each other—something Adil really didn't like.

I didn't turn him gay. I was just there for him.

The bus pulled up, and he stepped on, drew up his hoodie, and settled on a bench, half-dozing with his head against the window while the drizzle outside turned to rain and slapped against the bus.

Being Saeed might be easier than being Mahir when it came to restrictions he placed on himself. But it also meant not having much of anything. No connections, no family. Whenever he felt lonely, he'd remember this sense of desolation. Being nobody in a city where nobody gave a fuck, at the mercy of criminals, about ready to slip from petty crime to the heavy stuff. Murder. Drug-running. Saeed was on his way to hell and possibly didn't even know it. Or care.

Mahir arrived at the apartment, locked the door, and stripped out of his wet layers, then pulled off his shoes and fell onto the bed, face-first. He pulled the pillow closer, burrowed his face into it. He caught a whiff of Ridley's cologne and was almost immediately hard again. He remembered getting pressed into the mattress just like that, one of Ridley's hands in his hair, the other digging into his shoulder, strong thighs opening his legs wide, keeping him pinned and passive. *Obedient*, Ridley called it, ready to back up his demands with violence and power.

He'd even appreciated the added bite, being sore after the second harsh fuck. And the third was almost more than he could take. Mahir reached down, opened his jeans, and quickly finished himself off, still on his belly, still feeling the echo of Ridley's strength in his body, his savage need. He should've been appalled, but he just couldn't muster the energy afterward.

He couldn't muster the energy for anything except sleep.

A few hours of orgasm-induced sleep were enough to bring Mahir back to the land of the living. His muscles still ached, but by the time he headed to the club that night, he was awake, alert, and refreshed.

Ridley was nowhere in sight. Mahir still felt out of place here, but Ridley acted as an anchor of sorts. Someone he could look at and remind himself he knew—sort of—in this crowd of dangerous strangers.

His shift didn't start for another fifteen minutes, so he went back into the break room for some coffee. Again, a few of the guys were cursing and grumbling over a card table.

"Hey, look who's here," one of them said. "You're early."

Another chuckled. "Trying to stay in the boss's good graces?"

"Or make the rest of us look bad," said a third.

Mahir rolled his eyes while his back was toward them but plastered on a smile as he turned around. "Just wanted to make sure I didn't get stuck in traffic." He brought his Styrofoam cup to his lips, and just before he sipped, added, "Too many cars and my camel gets spooked."

All three men went from smirking to glancing uneasily at each other. *Did he just say that? Are we supposed to laugh?*

Their expressions nearly caused Mahir to choke on his coffee. Beating guys to the racist punch always resulted in some amusing reactions. And generally shut them up, which was what he was going for.

He swallowed. "Ridley around?"

"Why?" The first guy's eyebrow rose. "Need a dick in your mouth?"

"No." Mahir finished his coffee and tossed the cup onto an overflowing trash bin. "Your mother took care of me already."

The guy started to stand, his face contorting into a snarl, but the other two laughed and shoved him back down.

"Easy, killer," one said, still snickering. He looked at Mahir. "He's out on an errand for the big boss."

"Oh. So do I just"—he gestured toward the lounge area—"stand by one of the stages again?"

The men looked at each other. The one who'd told him Ridley was out tapped the edges of his cards on the table. Something unreadable passed between the three of them, something spoken through subtle nods and head tilts.

The second guy set his cards down and pushed his chair back. "Ridley show you around? Downstairs, I mean?"

Mahir shook his head. "Just here and the big boss's office."

"Come with me."

Mahir hesitated. He eyed the other two, watching for any tell that might indicate this was dangerous, or some sort of hazing. Either there was nothing untoward going on or both men were damn good at keeping straight faces, so Mahir took a breath and followed their companion out of the room.

"Name's Pete, by the way," the guy said. "Those idiots back there are Keith and Mike." He turned around and lowered his voice to a conspiratorial whisper. "They're both fuckups and morons. You want to get somewhere in this place?" He pointed with his thumb at his chest. "You talk to me. Got it?"

Mahir nodded.

Pete kept walking and led him through a labyrinth of dim hallways to a steel door across from another door marked "Exit." He glanced back, craning his neck as he looked past Mahir. Then he pulled a card out of his pocket and swiped it through a reader.

Card readers? That was some high-end security for a nightclub.

Oh no, nothing shady going on in *this* building.

The LED above the reader turned green, and the latch on the door clicked. Pete pulled it open and gestured.

"After you."

The door led into a dark stairwell, and he could hear voices down below. If there was a reader on the door and he didn't have an access card, this wasn't a place he wanted to be caught alone.

He cleared his throat. "Why don't you go ahead?"

Pete raised an eyebrow. "Paranoid?"

"Cautious."

"Smart man." Pete walked past him and started down the stairs. Mahir glanced down the hall again, then followed him.

At the bottom of the stairs, another hallway led into what Mahir assumed was a larger room; he couldn't see it, but he could hear the voices and activity just beyond the corner.

Pete leaned in close. "Listen, I ain't supposed to bring you down here. But if you're going to be working that shit upstairs when there's cops running around, you ought to know what's really going on."

Mahir swallowed. "If I'm not supposed to see it, then—"

"You need to know why there's cops crawling all over this place," Pete snapped. "They ever come in here guns blazing—and they will—it won't be because of the girls upstairs. Those cops? This is—"

Right then, two guys came out of the other room. No, not guys. *Boys*. They couldn't have been older than Kinza. Fifteen? Sixteen?

Mahir watched, slack-jawed, as the boys made their way past and up the stairs. The door banged shut behind them, and he looked at Pete. "What the fuck? Those are *kids*."

Pete waved a hand. "They're just couriers. Don't worry about them."

"Just couriers?" Mahir hissed. "You just told me you're worried about the cops coming in here with guns blazing, and there are"—he gestured at the stairs—"fucking *kids* working here."

Pete gave a half shrug. "They're good at what they do. But they're just running errands and shit. The part the cops are interested in? That's—" He turned toward the other room and froze. Some color left his face.

Mahir turned in the same direction, and his heart dropped into his feet.

Arms folded, lips tight, Ridley glared at them from behind his sunglasses. "What the fuck are you two doing down here?"

Pete cleared his throat. "I was just . . . I brought him down to—"

Ridley's lips thinned into a bleached line. "Saeed. Go back upstairs."

This was the cold version of Ridley, and that one brooked no argument. Though abandoning Pete could have dire consequences. He couldn't just depend on his lead with Ridley—what little there was. Somehow Ridley didn't strike him as a man who'd let a couple of fucks rule his brain. "With all due respect, I've seen nothing."

Ridley stared at him. "I gave you an order."

Mahir grimaced, glanced at Pete with what he hoped would read as *I tried, buddy,* and headed back upstairs. Disobeying meant Ridley would never add him to the very short list of men he trusted, yet he couldn't be seen as the man's pet any more than he apparently already was. Damn this.

He stepped through the door but didn't let it close, just gave it a long look—not quite a bank-vault door but also not something SWAT could just kick down. Noted.

He let the door close and waited in the corridor, shoulders against the wall.

The last two undercovers had mentioned something shady going on in the basement, but to his knowledge—and according to the reports they'd submitted before their investigations had abruptly ended—no one had made it past this point. Still, he was sure James could dig up the construction plans, see if there was a different entry or exit. Slim hope, but better than sucking cock until somebody here fucking trusted him.

Stings and floor plans aside, the important thing was finding out what was going on down there. They needed probable cause to raid the place, and he suspected SWAT would be appreciative of some warning about meth labs or explosives before they came in with C-4 and flashbangs.

Maybe ten minutes later, the door opened, and Pete stepped out, looking rattled but unharmed. "Fucker's in a mood," he grumbled.

Mahir pushed away from the wall. "You all right?"

Pete nodded. "Told me to not get too friendly with you."

Mahir choked on a laugh. Jealousy? From Mr. Fuck and Run?

Pete glanced down the corridor. "Gotta work. See you around." He marched off, the response of a man who intended to heed a stern warning and yet tried to save face as much as possible.

Mahir waited another five minutes until the door opened again. Ridley. The cold one, too. Mahir didn't expect to meet the other version of him in the club ever again. And outside was unlikely, too, after the talk they'd had. Though he had a case for seduction. Distract him, undermine his position, neutralize the man in increments.

That part will make fantastic reading in the report: I fucked his brains out for Uncle Sam.

"You're not supposed to know about this," Ridley said.

"Well, *pardon me.*" Mahir blew out a breath. "You think all I'm good for is bashing a couple of skulls together when they grope the dancers? I can handle more than that." Petty criminal begging—*Use me*—in so many words. *Put me in, coach.*

"You are good for more than that." Ridley moved his hand in front of his groin, then cupped himself.

Gee, thanks.

Mahir rolled his eyes. "Can we talk *business*? If you have a meth lab down there . . . Shit, I know meth. I don't take it, but I know how that shit works." *And for fuck's sake, I want to know if I'm working on top of a goddamned lab.*

Ridley folded his arms tightly across his chest. "A meth lab?" The muscles in his brow twitched, implying he'd narrowed his eyes behind the dark lenses. "How much *did* Pete tell you?"

"He didn't tell me anything," Mahir said. "Just brought me down there, said there was some shit going on." He swallowed. "And I saw a couple of boys walk out of there."

Ridley's lips tightened. For that matter, every muscle in his body seemed to tighten. "What did he tell you? About the boys?"

Mahir glanced at the door. "Said they were couriers."

"Couriers." Something flickered across Ridley's expression, something there and gone so fast Mahir couldn't quite make sense of it, but he swore he'd caught a glimpse of the other Ridley. Then Ridley cleared his throat, and the ice returned to his expression. "Well, you weren't supposed to know about any of this. Not yet. But now you do."

"Except I don't really know anything."

Ridley reached up and pulled off his sunglasses. Those clear blue eyes drilled right into Mahir's. "You've been downstairs. As far as I'm concerned, that means you know too much."

Mahir gulped. "I don't. I swear. Ask Pete."

Ridley gave a dry laugh. "You think I trust that son of a bitch any further than I can throw him?" He didn't wait for a response and started down the hall, gesturing with his sunglasses for Mahir to come with him.

Mahir fell into step beside him. "So, um, what now?"

"I don't take anyone down there until I'm absolutely certain I can trust him." Ridley slid his sunglasses into his collar. "Until I have no doubt at all he's not a fucking cop." He turned his head toward Mahir, giving him an icy look. "And I'm not there with you. Not yet."

You've been eight inches up my ass, but you still think I'm a goddamned cop. Great.

Ridley faced forward again. "I need to know for sure I can trust you."

"And if I can't convince you to trust me?"

Ridley glanced at him just before they stepped into the lounge. "Then the only ones who will ever find your body are some ambitious archaeologists that aren't even born yet."

From anyone else, it would have sounded like a joke. From Ridley, Mahir wasn't so sure.

CHAPTER SIX

They crossed the lounge. Mahir didn't dare make eye contact with any of the undercovers—only two this time—no matter how much he wanted to flag one of them down. *Get me the fuck out of here*, he wanted to say, but there was no undercover semaphore he could use to communicate with them without inviting an intimate moment with the pistol under Ridley's arm.

They passed through the hallway again. Ridley pushed open his office door and waved Mahir in ahead of him. Mahir's heart pounded. Being alone with Ridley could be hot or it could be dangerous, and right now, it was definitely the latter.

"Sit."

At least that gave him a reason to be off his shaking knees. Mahir eased into one of the chairs in front of Ridley's desk.

Ridley took a slow, deliberate path around the side of his desk, and he paused with his hand on the back of his own chair. He looked down at Mahir. Stared at him. Let a few long, *long* seconds grind past. Then he sat and folded his hands on top of the bare hardwood.

"It's not that hard to pick out cops," he said. "Especially the idiots who aren't so subtle." He laughed humorlessly. "You'd be amazed how many try to work their way onto Lombardi's payroll."

Mahir managed a nervous laugh. "I can imagine."

Ridley's expression hardened again. Mahir wished the man would put his sunglasses back on. Not being able to see Ridley's eyes was decidedly easier on the blood pressure than looking right into them.

"Every once in a while," Ridley said, "one slips past me."

"Do they?"

Ridley nodded slowly. Fuck, that man could make any gesture look menacing. "They always get caught eventually, though." A chilling grin spread across his lips.

Mahir shook his head. Considering one of the undercovers who'd been killed recently had been shot execution-style, he wasn't about to call Ridley's bluff on this.

"Care to guess how?" Ridley's tone brought to mind a spider fucking with an insect already caught in its web.

Mahir coughed into his fist. "I . . . I wouldn't know how. How you'd catch one, I mean."

Ridley leaned back and swung one foot, then the other, onto his desk. He crossed them at the ankles and folded his hands across his flat stomach. Now he looked entirely too relaxed. "The easiest way is to tell him to shoot a man. A cop won't do it."

Mahir's heart pounded harder. A sick, acidic feeling burned in his gut. *I had sex with this psycho?*

"But that method is so"—Ridley waved a hand and shook his head—"expensive." He looked Mahir in the eyes. "And messy." Rolling his eyes, he gave an exasperated sigh. "Hiding bodies is *such* a pain in the ass sometimes."

"I can imagine," Mahir murmured.

"Especially around here." Ridley clicked his tongue. "Ground's wet all the time. That clay is a bitch to dig in." He shrugged, holding Mahir's gaze as if he was scrutinizing every response. Searching for a tell. Something.

Mahir rested an elbow on the armrest and stroked his chin with his thumb. "Seems like you could just dump them in the mountains somewhere."

The faintest upward flick of Ridley's eyebrows suggested he hadn't expected that. "Go on."

"Well, the mountains are full of service roads and logging roads. Toss someone out there, a grizzly will get to him before anyone else ever finds him."

Ridley stared at him. Then he laughed and smacked his palm on his desk. "Oh, Saeed. You never cease to surprise me." But just as Mahir was ready to relax, glad that Ridley's icy composure had cracked, all humor drained from Ridley's face so fast and so completely Mahir would have sworn it had never existed. "I might have to take you with me next time I have to dump someone."

No. Hell no.

"Found a . . . a few good places out there hiking."

"Good, good." Ridley couldn't possibly be the same man who'd been in Mahir's bed a few hours ago. "I still have a few other techniques for weeding out the badges that keep trying to sneak in here."

"Such as?"

Feet still up, Ridley reached down behind his desk. A drawer slid open, and something plastic crinkled. "There are certain things cops won't do." He brought his hand up and set a mirror on the desk. Then a razor blade.

Mahir's throat tightened. Ridley didn't need to know that undercovers could do whatever it took not to blow their covers. One of his buddies was still taking penicillin after he'd fucked a couple of prostitutes to keep himself from getting caught. Mahir could do whatever Ridley told him to, short of killing someone. He'd never done more than weed, and he'd never really enjoyed that. Coke? That shit scared him.

The plastic bag full of white powder landed on top of the mirror. Mahir's pulse shot up as if he'd already snorted half the bag.

Ridley sat up. He slid the mirror, razor, and bag toward Mahir. "Go on."

Mahir sat up, too, but eyed the stuff warily. "I've . . . never done it."

"Never?" Ridley smirked. "Don't tell me you're a virgin."

"When it comes to anything stronger than weed, yes."

"This from the man who doesn't drink."

Mahir gulped. "I tried it when I was a kid. Was a mistake."

"Well, now you get to try coke." Ridley pulled a hundred dollar bill out of his wallet and set it beside the mirror. "Unless you're a cop."

"I'm not a cop." Mahir glared at him. "I'm a Muslim."

"You can take it up with Allah later." Ridley didn't break eye contact as he reached for the pistol in his shoulder holster. He drew it, clicked off the safety, and set the weapon on the desk, finger hooked loosely over the trigger. "Or sooner. Your call."

Mahir reached for the mirror and stared at the drugs, psyching himself up. He opened the bag, shook a little onto the mirror, deliberately pouring out an amount that would likely kill him. Saeed would have no clue how much to use. An eighth of a gram would look the same to him as a gram. White powder, unless you had junkie eyes.

He assumed the stuff was pure, too, though there was no way to check. It could be half rat poison, which would save a bullet, but it wouldn't be very cost-effective.

He picked up the razor blade and ground the coke to a finer powder, separated the gram into two uneven lines and picked up the hundred, rolled it.

Ridley leaned forward, an odd twist to his lips.

Mahir bent down over the lines and was about to pull the powder through his nose when Ridley spoke. "Don't take all of that. That's a lot."

So you do have a conscience, motherfucker.

Mahir looked up. "How much? Half?"

"A fourth each."

Each. Bastard.

Mahir kept an eye on the mirror and inhaled. The powder hit the inside of his nose, his sinuses, then his whole face went numb. Holy shit. He barely managed to take the roll out and put it into his other nostril while the numbness spread through his body. He wanted to rub his face, wipe his eyes, but he still had to complete the order. He snorted the stuff up the other nostril and dropped the bill on the table.

Heart pounding. Brain pounding. The effect was pretty much immediate. His body started to feel warm and tingly all over, a pleasant glow that intensified with his racing heartbeat. Worse, though, was the feeling of happiness. Confidence. Suddenly, nothing mattered. It was like the earth was spinning around him, with him its natural center, and he itched to do something. His nose was still completely numb, and Mahir touched it. Ridley reached over, offering him a handkerchief. Mahir noticed his nose was running. He took the handkerchief and dabbed at it. This felt spectacular—warmth, power, confidence, pure happiness. Wide-awake, too. Raring to go.

"Nice, isn't it?"

Mahir nodded. "Yes. Didn't think . . . never thought so clear. So light."

Ridley came around the desk and placed a hand on Mahir's shoulder. "What do you think your department would say if they could see you now?"

Mahir opened his mouth, then shook his head. "I'm not a cop." He looked up at Ridley, felt the heat in his body and the tingle all over his skin. It made him think of what they'd done last night. He wanted more of that. "I'm a Muslim." He laughed, like that was suddenly funny. Hell, right now, it was. "Flying sand nigger, right?"

Ridley's lips twitched, and he leaned closer. "Allah doesn't like faggots either, does he? What kind of Muslim is that?"

"Muslim light?" Mahir laughed harder. Shit, this was hilarious. He felt invincible, despite the gun on the table, despite the man touching him. Touching him on the shoulder, the chest, running fingers down his throat. "One day I'll figure it out. Why he's made me that way."

Ridley ran his fingers up to Mahir's jaw. "Why are you here, Saeed?"

Who? Mahir blinked. "I want to fuck you."

Ridley inhaled sharply. "I asked—"

"Fuck, man." Mahir turned fully toward Ridley, searching with half-numb, half-tingling lips for Ridley's mouth. "I want—"

"Not now."

"Yes, now." Mahir found Ridley's leg, and he slid his hand up Ridley's inner thigh.

Ridley gasped. "Saeed, I need you to—"

"Suck your dick?" Mahir cupped Ridley's crotch through the front of his slacks, and Ridley's quiet groan made Mahir's already pounding heart beat even faster. "Don't mind if I do." He was distantly aware of some residual fear, like the echoes of something he'd felt when he'd walked into this room, but right now he was ten feet tall, bulletproof, and hornier than he'd ever been in his life.

"Saeed." Why the hell did Ridley keep saying that name? "Don't . . ." He trailed off as Mahir tugged at his belt.

"Don't what?" Mahir looked up at Ridley, and an odd sense of raw vulnerability crept in. Not like he was afraid of being harmed, but he was terrified Ridley would deny him this outlet he wanted. Needed. Coveted. Mahir rubbed his cheek against Ridley's bulge.

Ridley swept his tongue across his lips. Why was *he* so out of breath? "Don't—" He swallowed. Then he swore softly and ran his fingers through Mahir's hair. "Don't stop."

Mahir's relief rivaled what he'd felt after powerful orgasms in the past. He fumbled with Ridley's belt and zipper, but his hands were shaking. Shaking badly. Why? He didn't get it. Zippers were easy.

He knew that. But this one wouldn't move. Or Mahir couldn't focus enough to make it move.

Ridley's hands were rock steady as he gently nudged Mahir's out of the way, and with a few effortless motions, he had his belt and slacks undone. He freed his very erect dick and stroked it once before Mahir shoved his hands out of the way and took over.

Mahir took as much of Ridley's thick cock into his mouth as he could, groaning as he stroked and sucked and teased with his tongue.

Ridley grasped Mahir's hair in both hands, gripping it tightly enough to sting his scalp even though his skin was still somewhat numb. He thrust into Mahir's mouth, and Mahir took him easily, eagerly. Any other time he might have been afraid he'd choke and resisted for the sake of not pushing too hard against his gag reflex, but this time he wasn't afraid of anything. Ridley could've picked up the gun and pushed it against Mahir's temple, and Mahir wouldn't have missed a beat.

The rush was intoxicating, exhilarating, and the more Ridley's cock pushed the limits of his throat, the dizzier Mahir became. He was flying high. In absolute ecstasy. He couldn't have been more turned on and blissed out if Ridley had bent him over and fucked him good and hard. Just thinking about that made him groan and stroke Ridley even faster.

"Holy *fuck*, Saeed," Ridley moaned.

Stop calling me that, Mahir wanted to say, but his lips and tongue and throat were all occupied. *Who the fuck is Saeed?*

Ridley's cock stiffened even more in Mahir's mouth. His moans turned to soft whimpers and gasps for breath, and he held Mahir's hair tight. Mahir could barely breathe, but he couldn't stop either, and that first hint of salty sweetness on his tongue almost made him come in his pants. Ridley sucked in a breath. Swore. Shuddered. He came on Mahir's tongue and in his throat, very nearly choking him this time, but Mahir managed to swallow it and keep going until Ridley ordered him to stop.

Mahir sank back in his chair, smiling and floating as if he'd been the one who'd been blown.

Ridley slumped against the desk. His hands weren't so steady now, shaking as he tucked himself back in and fixed his clothes. "Shit. That wasn't . . . what I expected."

"What *did* you expect?"

Ridley held his gaze, eyelids heavy but eyes still intense as ever. "I thought you were going to tell me you were a cop."

I am a cop. The thought startled Mahir halfway back to sobriety, especially as he realized how close he'd come to actually saying it. Wait, had he said it? He stared up at Ridley, begging the man's expression to tell him whether or not he had said it. And what was weird was not just the horniness, the clarity, the feeling he could deal with anything, but the strange affection for Ridley. He wanted to take care of the man, wanted to touch him more, talk to him, was just so fucking glad he was here with him and that he had somebody to talk to.

Ridley walked back around the desk and was still a little unsteady as he lowered himself into his chair. He didn't say anything as he collected the coke and paraphernalia from the desk.

"So did I pass?" Mahir asked. His heart was still racing, and he had to fight to stay completely focused. "Am I not a cop?"

Ridley didn't look at him. "You're on duty in the lounge. Go."

Mahir blinked. "Like . . . like this?" He held up a shaking hand.

Ridley glanced at him but quickly averted his eyes. "It'll wear off. Just stand there and look scary. That'll keep people in line."

Confused as hell, Mahir rose. He started toward the door but stopped. "So, to be clear, you know I'm not a cop now, right?"

Ridley finally met his eyes. "I don't know what the fuck you are."

Mahir shook his head. "I need the paycheck. Say the word and I fuck off to where I came from." It didn't make any sense, but he couldn't keep himself from speaking. "But I want to keep fucking you, whatever the fuck *you* are."

Ridley seemed to jump in his chair, then settled that ice into place. "Go. Work."

Mahir managed to get to the lounge and locate his position for the night, to the side of the bar. The flashing lights assaulting him from all sides, the beat of the music like a solid wall pressing against his brain from the inside. He wanted to get on the dance floor; this was the silly, invincible mood of a teenager rocking his air guitar for all he was worth. Ridiculousness wasn't even a consideration.

His heart seemed to have slowed down, or at least didn't race like mad anymore, just faster than usual, as if he were jogging. Not out of control, not scary, just fast. And the warmth suffused him still, though his skin felt clammy to the touch. He watched the patrons, finding them all attractive in their own ways, precious human beings all of them. Nothing despicable about pushing dollar bills on a mostly naked dancer. This club, normally cheap and loud and dark and pathetic, now seemed overwhelmingly erotic and tempting. Cozy. Home. Perfect.

He rubbed his face, astonished by how powerful these emotions were. He'd never had much respect for a junkie, how they debased themselves—the rapid physical deterioration should put anybody off—but these sensations were real, and they felt damn good. He couldn't remember when he'd felt so happy, like he had everything under control, his whole life, everybody around him. Nothing was too hard. He'd find a way to deal with his family and Kinza.

A barkeep leaned over and pushed a large glass of water across to Mahir, small ice cubes floating in the glass.

He looked up. His throat was still numb, but his mouth now felt dry. He downed two thirds of the glass in a couple of swallows. He still felt parched, so he finished it and gestured at the bartender for another.

The bartender scowled and shook his head but pulled a glass out from under the bar and filled it. He pushed it over to Mahir, but when he tried to take the glass, the bartender held on to it.

"Don't let the boss catch you like this." His voice was barely audible over the pulsing music. "He'll have a fit."

Then he released the glass and was gone before Mahir could ask what he meant.

Mahir took this one a little slower. He sucked an ice cube into his mouth and let that keep the dryness at bay for the moment. An inkling of panic crept under his skin, a chill to disrupt the pleasant warmth. He scanned the crowd, patrons and employees alike, wondering who else had caught on. Who might say something to Lombardi. A minute ago, this whole place had been teeming with love and humanity, but suddenly he was suspicious of every soul, from the dancers to the panting patrons waving twenties.

His gaze drifted along the bar, and he caught the eye of one of the guys hunched over the barstools. Ridley had pointed him out as an undercover last night. He eyed Mahir, brow furrowed, then returned his attention to the glass in front of him. He played with the lime wedge on the rim and looked at something else.

The mirror behind the bar.

Which likely gave him an unobstructed view of Mahir.

Something in Mahir wanted to stand up, stomp over, and ask what the fuck he was looking at. That would be a bad idea. Dangerous. Couldn't draw attention to a cop. Didn't dare draw attention to himself. Not even if it was the kind of *See? I'm not a cop* attention that would come from grabbing that son of a bitch by the shirt and roughing him up a bit.

Still, some part of him wanted to.

Saeed. It was Saeed who wanted to do that.

The hairs on the back of Mahir's neck stood on end. *Saeed.* The name Ridley had repeated over and over while Mahir was lost in that horny haze.

What do you think your department would say if they could see you now?

Mahir split the ice cube in two with his molars. That son of a bitch. He hadn't made him snort coke to see if a cop would snort coke. He'd gotten him high so he could catch him off guard and make him talk. Cunning, manipulative motherfucker. And Mahir had even felt affection for him. Oh, hell, he'd felt affection for everyone within a ten-mile radius. That was the coke. It had to be. No way in hell would he, in a sober state of mind, feel a damned thing for a man who casually talked about what a pain in the ass it was to bury bodies and then drugged someone to get him to incriminate himself.

An image flickered through his mind of Ridley's hand on the pistol, finger on the trigger. Mahir's heart was still pounding, but the high was gone. All the happy, floaty feelings were a distant memory now, and it was panic that had his pulse racing. What if he'd answered that question wrong? Told Ridley his department head would disapprove of him snorting coke, but you do what you have to do when you're undercover? Two to the chest and one to the head? Or just one to the back of the skull? Or neatly between his eyes right there in this office. No wonder the carpet in this place was red.

A rattling sound, followed by a cold, damp sensation, brought Mahir out of his thoughts, and when he looked down, he realized some of the water had sloshed out onto his shaking hand. He set the glass down, dried his hand, and mopped up what had spilled on the bar.

Then he looked at the undercover cop. At the other security guards. At the vacant hallway leading toward the office where Ridley had head-fucked and then face-fucked him.

His mouth was dry again. It wasn't the coke this time.

He was in way, way over his head.

Maybe he should pull out and walk away while he still could. Ridley had *expected* him to confess he was a cop. The man might not be able to put a finger on it, but something gave Mahir away, and did he really want to stick around until he tripped up? Despite all his training, despite all his dedication—despite the three dead cops, even—he *wasn't* Saeed. This little test, if he confessed it to his superior, would allow him to pull out. And then? They'd send in somebody who was likely even less capable of dealing with it. Force him to shoot somebody, make him take drugs. Ridley would spot it, though. Another dead body. Another grieving wife. Kids without a father.

How had Adil put it so eloquently and so often? *You'll never have family of your own. You'll never have a wife who loves you, children you'll teach how to be good people.*

Thanks, brother. I knew that.

Mahir did have the advantage of having gotten under Ridley's skin. Even if the man was a sociopath, he responded to Mahir. It might not save his life in the end, but it was a hell of a lot more than his predecessors had had to work with.

He may have been in over his head, but he was *in*, and he would see this through.

CHAPTER SEVEN

He was unspeakably relieved when the club closed. Time was different on coke, too. Twitchier. Regardless, Ridley kept him back just like last night, the bastard.

Mahir just wanted to get home and rest. His brain still felt like a rat was ricocheting off the insides of his skull, like he'd drunk a gallon of espresso mixed with a kilo of white sugar. He was itching to get out the door. Run home, maybe. He still hadn't managed to get rid of the nervous energy.

"I'll drive you home," Ridley said from behind, startling him.

Mahir stared at him. "Want to fuck?"

Ridley just took him by the arm and pushed him toward the car. "You're still not quite clear."

And how would you know?

Mahir tried to shrug him off and balled his fists when Ridley wouldn't let him, but managed to not punch him. "The fuck?"

"I made you take it; I'll get you home."

Conscience? Or just angling to blow another load? Trouble was, his body didn't care. Getting home with Ridley meant getting fucked into the mattress, which was exactly what he needed right then, though he was less frantically aroused this time.

Shit, Saeed urgently needed a boyfriend. One less dangerous than his fucking boss.

Ridley pushed him into the car like he was a criminal—just the handcuffs missing—then got in.

They were both silent as Ridley drove. Mahir because it was less risky. Ridley because he wore that icy facade again. Professional. Mahir couldn't sit still. Nerves? Coke? Fuck, he couldn't tell the difference anymore. It occurred to him more than once that he could just open the door and jump out. Tuck and roll. Some broken bones would suck, but he'd be out of this car. And probably off this goddamned job.

You're out of your mind.

Ridley stopped outside Mahir's building and looked at him. "The next few hours are going to be . . . unpleasant."

"As opposed to the last few?" Mahir muttered.

Ridley cocked his head. "You don't enjoy it?"

A dozen snappy retorts danced on the tip of Mahir's tongue. He bit them all back, wondering for a moment if Saeed was becoming a real person, a different side of him. His own personal Tyler Durden. He shook the thought away and looked Ridley in the eye. "I'm going inside now."

Ridley put a hand on his arm. "You probably shouldn't be alone."

Mahir shrugged off Ridley's grasp. "I'll just jerk off. I don't need any help."

"Saeed."

Mahir almost snapped back *Stop calling me that!* Instead, he just glared at Ridley.

"This job is even more dangerous for me than it is for you," Ridley said. "If a cop gets past me, I get a hot-lead injection." He reached for Mahir's arm again. "I had to be sure."

"Are you sure now?" Mahir asked through his teeth. "Or do I need to do a few more fucking tricks for you?"

He couldn't be completely certain, but Mahir thought Ridley winced.

Sighing, Ridley took his hand off Mahir's arm, put the car in park, and killed the engine. "Come on. We're going inside."

Mahir didn't move. "I don't recall extending the invitation."

"Is that an invitation?" he heard himself asking Ridley a lifetime ago.

"You need someone to keep an eye on you." Ridley got out of the car and came around to the passenger side. He opened the door. "Let's go."

Mahir swore under his breath but then unbuckled his seat belt and got out. The sooner he went up to his apartment and settled in, the sooner Ridley would leave.

The walk up to the third floor was . . . strange. Not just because of the tense silence between him and Ridley but because his body didn't feel like his anymore. He felt like he had the energy to run up a hundred flights of stairs, and if he didn't release that energy in the next five minutes, his entire body would come apart at the seams. At the same time, he was exhausted. Heavy. Dragging his twitching legs up one step after the other.

His fingers weren't much better. Partly twitchy, partly numb, and somehow disembodied. Like he was remotely controlling someone else's hands.

Ridley gently grasped his wrist and freed Mahir's keys. Without a word, he unlocked the door, pushed it open, and gestured for him to go inside. A set of motions that was strangely parallel to when Ridley had taken him into his office earlier. When Mahir had been scared and uncertain and Ridley had been cold and quite possibly on the verge of something more dangerous than Mahir could imagine. And now, hours later, Mahir was the cold one, while Ridley seemed . . . different. Not quite meek or subservient, but more pliant. Gentle, if the man was capable of such a thing.

Ridley followed him into the apartment. When he closed the door, he turned the dead bolt. The *click* of the lock was amplified, echoing in Mahir's head, and he glared at Ridley.

"Exactly how long are you planning on staying?"

"Once you've come down, I'll leave."

"And how long is that going to take?"

"Depends. You'll be fine tomorrow. You got any painkillers?"

"Not here." Mahir stopped himself from saying *at home.* "In the gym. Signed up this morning, got the locker stocked."

Oh fuck. To have passed all these fucking tests only to slip up now because he was irritable and itchy and struggling to control his temper . . .

"Taking painkillers before exercise increases your chances of tearing muscles."

"Know what? I don't give a fuck. Zero fucks given."

"Irritability." Ridley crossed his arms in front of his chest. "Go on."

"It just fucking grates, you know? You fucking with my head like that."

Ridley herded him into the bedroom. "Undress."

"Fuck you."

Mahir sat down on the bed, torn between the buzzing energy and a sense of depletion and hollowness. Comedown time. With it, the strong urge to take another hit—only to fend off what he expected to come next. Restore his equilibrium. Feel good again.

Ridley was undressing him. It took real effort to not punch him as he took off Mahir's jacket, then his shoes. He unlatched Mahir's belt, and there was another surge of pleasure. Desire. Sex was at the forefront of Mahir's brain—again. He lay back when Ridley opened his fly. He was getting hard again, pretty much in Ridley's face.

"You'll have to sleep. I'll get you some painkillers. They'll help. Weed would help with the agitation."

"Or just blow me."

Ridley quirked an eyebrow. "In this state, you could last half an hour. I'd get bored by that point."

"Oh."

Ridley grinned at him. "Your best bet is trying to sleep."

"With you in the room?"

"With me in the room." Ridley pulled Mahir's pants down and removed his socks, hands sure on his skin. "You're clammy."

"I feel good."

"Well, yeah, let's hope it stays that way."

Mahir pushed himself up onto his elbows. "*Hope* it stays that way?"

Ridley avoided his eyes, carefully folding Mahir's clothes and setting them on the floor beside the bed. "It's worse for some people than others."

That knowledge was tucked somewhere inside Mahir's head. Everything about illicit substances and their effects had been hammered into him since his academy days. But knowing them well enough to pass tests and identify what was causing some idiot to come unglued during a call was entirely different than this. This was *him*. His body. And all the information he'd long ago memorized deserted him.

"How bad does it get?" He sniffed sharply. Swallowed. Sniffed again. Fuck, he needed something to drink. He started to sit up, but Ridley caught his shoulder.

"Just relax. What do you need?" His eyebrow quirked again. "Water?"

Mahir nodded.

"Don't move." Ridley left the room, leaving Mahir to his thoughts and his running nose and his parched mouth.

And don't move? Not a chance. He rubbed one foot against the other. It didn't itch per se, but he couldn't stop moving it. Needed to move it. He ran his fingers back and forth across a wrinkle in the sheet, and even after that wrinkle was smooth he kept moving his fingers. Holy fuck, he didn't like this feeling. This restlessness. Sleep? He was supposed to sleep like this?

Ridley returned with a glass of water. "This will hold you for a few minutes. I'm going to run out and get you some painkillers and bottles of water. I'll be back in, I don't know, twenty minutes."

Mahir drank heavily but didn't finish the water. If Ridley was going to be gone, Mahir might as well make this glass last for— Oh, fuck it. He downed the rest of it and sat up.

"I'll be back as soon as I can. Just . . . try to relax." He turned to go.

"Ridley."

Ridley turned around.

Mahir ran his dry tongue across his lips. "You didn't answer my question."

"Which one?"

"How bad can this get?"

"It's not pleasant." Ridley shrugged. "But it's not dangerous. If you were going to have a bad reaction, you would've had it before you left my office."

They locked eyes.

Before I sucked you off. Mahir didn't say it, but he was pretty sure they were both thinking it.

Ridley swallowed, then muttered, "I'll be back," and left.

The dead bolt turned, loud and ominous enough to make Mahir jump.

He walked naked from the bedroom to the tiny kitchen. He filled the water glass twice, and then went back into the bedroom. That had to be the worst thing—this damned dry mouth. No. That wasn't the worst. The worst was not having a goddamned outlet for all this fucking energy.

Like fucking Ridley. That would be fitting. *You did this to me, and now I'm going to do this to you so I can finally sleep, you son of a bitch.*

He lay across the bed. The room was cool, and he was tempted to pull the sheet over him, but his skin was so itchy, he didn't want anything else touching him. The longer he lay there, though, the hotter he felt. He knew the air around him was cool, but his skin was superheated. Not quite feverish, but . . . close.

He shifted. Again. There was no getting comfortable when just trying to stay still was uncomfortable as fuck.

He sat up against the wall, and as the sheets brushed his bare legs, he remembered Ridley quickly and carefully undressing him.

Or just blow me.

In this state, you could last half an hour. I'd get bored by that point.

Bored? Mahir closed his eyes and slowly released a breath as his dick hardened. He couldn't imagine getting bored sucking Ridley off. And he'd done that a couple of times. Seemed only polite for Ridley to return the favor, and to hell with him if he got bored. Mahir couldn't imagine lasting that long anyway. One touch from Ridley's mouth and he'd be done.

But Ridley wasn't here. How long did he say he'd be gone? Fuck it.

Mahir reached down and closed his fingers around his erection. The friction was pleasant, and maybe he'd manage to get off and finally sleep. And fuck Ridley—he could take care of himself. Though without him, he felt keenly that he had nobody to talk to. Alone. He was completely alone. He worked his dick, felt arousal build quickly . . . and then it plateaued. He gritted his teeth, played through his favorite fantasies, discarding one after the other as none managed to get him higher, not even the slightly weirder ones, the ones involving force and violence. So this was the famous sex drug; though, wasn't it used to numb stuff? Drugs 101—fail.

That agitation wasn't what he'd expected. Why would anybody want this? He'd once overdosed on vodka and Red Bull at a party—before he knew what vile stuff vodka was—and the effect had been similar. Exhausted, restless, running up the walls. Once he'd vomited, he'd felt a great deal better. Though that had pretty much ended his alcohol career, apart from the occasional beer, usually to wash down the grease and salt of a take-out dinner.

He fished for the lube and slicked up his hand, tried again to get off. Went slow and intense, then hard and fast, and didn't quite manage to get there, whatever he did.

Bored.

He kept trying, but it felt like climbing Mount Everest. Slow, steady, exhausting.

The door unlocked with a couple of *clicks*. He groaned in frustration—*almost there*. Or at least a hell of a lot closer than he'd been fifteen minutes or so ago.

When Ridley walked in, Mahir didn't bother to cover up. The man was carrying a paper bag and lifted an eyebrow at him. "You had to test the theory, right?"

"I'm just trying to fucking sleep." *Now let's see how bored either of us gets with your dick in my ass.*

"Right." Ridley took the paper bag outside and came back empty-handed. He sat down on the bed and pulled Mahir into one of those mind-bending kisses. Without warning, he moved and sat high on Mahir's legs, effectively pinning them. He took the lube and poured some into his right hand, then batted Mahir's hand away.

Mahir arched when the man touched him, took his dick, but that wasn't even most of it. Straddling him, the other hand firmly around Mahir's shoulder. Blue eyes bored into him, clear, intense, and—Mahir swore—getting off on the power. He shuddered, couldn't push into the strong grip, could only gasp when the man ran a thumb over his glans. He normally almost hated that touch but not now. Right now, it might even get him off.

Ridley gripped him even more tightly. "I was thinking of shoving a couple of fingers up your ass, but you'd be moving too much."

Mahir groaned, felt the tension build. Traitorous fucking body—obeying Ridley but not him. "You're a fucking bastard."

"Yeah, that's right. And you're not far off, either."

Petty thug getting a forceful handjob from his boss. Not a cop. He wasn't a cop. Right now he was a criminal graduating to junkie. And shit, but cocaine was nice. Despite the jittery feeling.

"Look at me," Ridley said through gritted teeth.

Mahir blinked his eyes into focus and looked up at him. Ridley moistened his lips. He tightened his grip on Mahir's cock, and the jerking motion of his arm made his whole torso move almost like he was fucking Mahir in short, sharp thrusts.

Mahir bit his lip and groaned. "Oh, fuck . . ."

"You wish I would," Ridley growled. "Bet you wish you were fucking me right now, don't you?"

Mahir's eyes rolled back. His back arched off the bed, and he thought he heard himself moaning and swearing.

"Yeah, you would like that," Ridley said. "But I like being in control." His hand slid from Mahir's shoulder to the side of his neck. Not quite grabbing on, just touching. That wasn't usually Mahir's thing, but he pressed against Ridley's hand, and Ridley took the cue, putting his whole hand over Mahir's throat.

Mahir swore in his native tongue. In English. In Arabic again. Ridley's hand was a firm and unspeakably erotic presence, and Mahir's pulse raced against Ridley's fingers.

"Fucking hell, you look hot like that," Ridley breathed. "I'll have to do this next time . . . next time I fuck you."

And that was all Mahir could take. He cried out something even he didn't understand, and hot semen landed on his stomach and his chest as his whole body tensed, shuddered, and—*finally*—relaxed.

The hand on his dick stopped and let go. The one on his throat loosened and slid up to Mahir's face. Caressed his sweaty skin. That hand was so steady, so calm. A weird contrast to Mahir's entire body, which wouldn't stop trembling.

Ridley's weight shifted, and his lips pressed against Mahir's. Lightly, briefly.

"Now," Ridley murmured, "you can sleep."

CHAPTER EIGHT

Ridley was gone the next morning. Mahir turned in bed, but nothing betrayed whether Ridley had stayed around or left immediately after he'd fallen asleep. He might even have dreamed the night before, if not for that sore ache all over and the taste from the painkillers. The comforter felt heavy and damp. He must have sweated out all the water he'd drunk because he didn't need to piss. At all.

He was listless but no worse than those days when a glance out the window only revealed rain and a gray sky that had forgotten the purpose of a sun. That kind of dejected downer but with none of the dreaded cocaine depression. He figured he'd gotten off lightly, all things considered.

Gotten off? You certainly did that.

Slowly the evening began to filter back into his mind—the sex and that he'd talked, possibly too much. He only hoped Ridley hadn't asked him any more questions when he was tweaked off his ass.

Though would he have woken up at all if he'd betrayed himself?

Likely not.

He pried his body out of bed. A shower. That was what he needed. As he stretched his stiff, creaking joints, a piece of paper on top of his folded clothes caught his eye.

He picked it up, blinked a few times, and read the neat, angular handwriting:

Come in when you feel like it tonight. If you need the night off, call. But pls check in. R.

He cocked his head, eyeing the note like it might offer up some more information. He was lucky he could read the words, never mind anything that might be hidden between those lines, but at least he didn't have to worry about dragging his battered carcass into the club on time tonight.

He set the note on his bed and went into the bathroom for a shower.

His memories of the previous evening were surreal. Clear, but somehow not. Like a dream he'd managed to remember. And it wasn't just the cocaine. That had added a filter of weirdness to everything but his entire world had been off and fucking bizarre since the moment Ridley had confronted Saeed and Pete downstairs. And from there it had just gotten weirder. Every step took him deeper into the rabbit hole.

And somehow they'd ended up here. He'd hated Ridley. Fucking hated him. What kind of jackass did this to someone? But then Ridley had been gentle and almost affectionate, taking care of him, which may have been the result of a guilty conscience more than anything. The guilty conscience of a man who thought Pacific Northwest clay was an inconvenience because it was a bitch to dig into.

All of that before he'd pinned Mahir down by the legs and the throat and jerked him off. So he could sleep? Yeah, right. Fucker was enjoying that, and Mahir would never believe him if he said otherwise.

I'll have to do this next time . . . next time I fuck you.

Mahir ran a hand through his wet hair and then let the hot water rush over his face. Next time? There would be a next time? What the hell kind of Jekyll and Hyde was he working for, anyway? If he spent enough time working for this nut job, Mahir could easily see himself begging for an orgasm and for his life on the same damned day. Quite possibly at the same time.

Which could be hot.

What the fuck? He shook his head and then rubbed both hands over his face. *Please tell me that was the cocaine aftermath talking.*

Whatever it was, he needed to be careful around Ridley. James was right. He was a fucking lunatic. Mahir should probably go in and work. Except this kind of job required some investment in terms of concentration. This wasn't a job where he could drill deep down into files to cover up the fact he'd slept badly or not at all. And the last thing he needed was everybody knowing he'd been using and that he couldn't fill his role. He could actually take a day off, go home, maybe do some gentle exercise to smooth out his muscles, fill up the fridge for the ravenous teenager in his care—hell, maybe spend a couple hours like a civilized human being. The thought was just way too tempting.

He reached for his cell phone and dialed Ridley's number.

"Yeah?"

"Saeed here. I just woke up."

"Good. How are you doing?"

"I just need to locate the house I've ripped down with my bare hands."

Ridley snorted. "I kept you from throwing cars at least, though that tends to happen on some of the stronger stuff."

Mahir huffed. "I'm quitting that shit now."

"Keep hydrated. You going to come in?"

"No. I think I'll just sleep a bit more. Maybe head to the gym for half an hour or so. Stretch."

"All right." No indication if he was disappointed or relieved. "I'll get one of the others to cover for you. See you tomorrow night."

"Thanks." He really wasn't the type to take a sick day, but he did want to be at one hundred percent, and looking after Kinza would at least calm one of those worries. Just check in with him, see how he was getting on, put some more money on the table. Relax, possibly sleep in his own bed that night.

Maybe regain some of the sanity that had been rapidly slipping away since he'd taken on this case.

He locked up Saeed's apartment and headed for the ferry dock. Since it was mid-afternoon on a Sunday, there weren't a lot of cars waiting to get on board and just a few walk-on passengers. Once he was on board, he settled onto one of the cracked fake leather seats and rested an elbow beneath the window.

The one-hour ride felt like it took three times that long. Kind of like the handful of times he'd taken the ferry when he was hungover. He got a little queasy thanks to the boat's gentle rocking, but that wore off when he was finally able to hurry down the ramp and onto dry land. The more he walked, the more his muscles loosened up, and the fresh air didn't hurt, either.

He drove home and keyed himself inside. "Kinza? You here?"

"Upstairs." Typical teenaged disinterest, but there was a note of relief there, too. Like he was glad Mahir was home but didn't want to show it.

Mahir went upstairs and found Kinza on the couch, a textbook propped up on his bent knees. "How's it going?"

Kinza shrugged. He slid a note card between the pages, closed the book, and set it on the floor. Clasping his fingers together, he stretched like a cat, finding additional inches hidden somewhere. "You look like ass."

Mahir laughed. "Gee, thanks."

Kinza chuckled. He dropped his hands onto his lap. "You been working this whole time?"

"Well, and sleeping some."

His nephew arched an eyebrow. "You sure don't look like you've slept recently."

"Didn't say I'd slept very much or very well." Mahir started toward the kitchen and asked over his shoulder, "You eaten today?"

"Like seven times."

Mahir halted. "It's not even mid-afternoon."

Kinza shrugged and hoisted himself up off the couch. "Boy's gotta eat, yo."

"Then I guess we're hitting the grocery store before I leave."

"Which is when?"

Mahir pulled a bag of coffee grounds from the cabinet. "Not until tomorrow. I'm taking tonight off."

"And staying here?"

"Yeah."

"Oh. Good." The boy sounded genuinely relieved.

As he poured water into the coffeemaker, Mahir glanced at his nephew. "You been doing okay here? On your own, I mean?"

"Yeah." Kinza shifted, keeping his gaze fixed on the linoleum at his feet. "Yeah. Been okay."

Mahir faced him. "Something wrong?"

Kinza didn't answer.

Mahir set the coffeepot aside and reached for his nephew, but the boy recoiled. Cold dread shot through Mahir. "What's going on?"

Kinza swallowed. "My dad. He, um, he came by."

Mahir's breath caught. "He came here?"

His nephew nodded. "I didn't answer the door. Pretended I wasn't here. But it was definitely him." He slowly lifted his gaze and met Mahir's. "And he was mad."

"Shit," Mahir whispered. His brother wasn't prone to violence, but he wasn't above it, either. "All right, listen. I'm going to talk to Mrs. Blunt, the neighbor. Let her know what's going on." He put a hand on Kinza's shoulder. "If your dad comes back, don't answer the door. Go out the back and go next door. Got it?"

Kinza nodded, avoiding his uncle's eyes. "You're going to be in Seattle a lot, aren't you?"

Mahir's heart sank. Kinza always put on a tough teenaged front, and there were few things more heartbreaking than when he lowered that front and showed the scared kid underneath. Because that was all he was. A kid. A boy.

Just like the two who'd brushed past him at the club last night. *Couriers. They're just couriers.*

Couriers who had access to a place even Mahir couldn't go until Ridley trusted him? With the kind of trust that was earned with guns, sex, and cocaine?

Mahir pulled Kinza to him and hugged him. He had to protect this kid. Yeah, he had a job to do that was an hour away by boat, but he had to fucking protect this kid. And Kinza, for all his occasional bluster and weird gangsta speech, held him tight and rested his head on his shoulder. How his brother couldn't see how precious that was was beyond Mahir.

And how he was going to protect Kinza . . . Mahir had no idea.

They were carrying bags into the house when Mrs. Blunt appeared in her driveway. He'd gone over to visit her before they went to the shop, but she'd been out.

She was a short-haired black woman who'd fostered like ten kids with her husband since Mahir had known her. He didn't know much about the husband—Mahir couldn't remember having exchanged more than a nod and a vague greeting with him—but over the years, his relationship with May had gone beyond acquaintance and was approaching something like friendship. She'd asked him questions regarding criminology on numerous occasions, and from the complexity of her scenarios, he assumed she might be writing crime novels.

"Planning a party, Mahir?"

Mahir glanced back at his car. "That would involve more drinks." He put the bag down. "I've acquired a teenager for a few days. Short of feeding him wallpaper, a shop was inevitable."

She looked Kinza up and down, seemed to decide she liked him, and smiled at him. "Family?"

"Yeah." Mahir didn't see any suspicion in her eyes. Single man living with a teenaged boy—now, that could have looked very wrong. And despite her writing material, she didn't seem to assume the worst. "Kinza, this is May Blunt."

"Hi."

"Hi." She looked back at Mahir. "Same eyes. Brother or sister?"

"My older brother's. We're both the youngest in the family, so we had some immediate bonding."

"Getting picked on?" She chuckled. "Older brothers have strange ways of showing love."

"Well, you could say that." That was the extent of Mahir's diplomacy when it came to his brother after he'd threatened Kinza. He nodded to Kinza. "Anyway, he's going to stay with me for a while."

Kinza, seemingly bored with the conversation, grabbed a couple of the grocery bags and trudged on into the house.

"And—" Mahir lowered his voice. "—if you have a moment, I might need to ask a favor."

She came closer. "Trouble?"

"Yeah. His . . . his father's giving him issues. Not that I expect him to take any extreme measures, but just in case. I'm working some weird hours at the moment. I might not be here as much as I should, but I can't send him back. It'll all blow over eventually, but for the moment I'd be glad if somebody kept half an eye on him."

"Is his father violent . . . ?"

"No. But he can be loud. And unpleasant." Mahir took a deep breath. "I'll talk to him next. It's just that it's hard to reach me at the moment."

"A difficult case?"

"Yeah. Quite." She loved cops. Adored them, in fact. One of those people who told him (or any other policeman) she was grateful for their service, if in less cheesy words. She'd also never made a comment about his faith or looks—the foster kids had been all kinds of colors, too.

"Tell me when it's in the newspapers," she said, touching his arm.

"I'll do that."

"Is there anything I should do if the father does show up?"

"You can tell him you'll call the cops. He'd hate losing face like that." And Adil always assumed any members of law enforcement were Mahir's buddies—from traffic cops to the FBI.

"I'll do that." She patted his arm. "You'll have to come to dinner sometime. I have more questions for you, but they're complicated."

"Sure. No problem."

"Human trafficking," she said. "The research is really messy."

"Depressing as anything." He looked back at the house where Kinza had just shown up in the door. "I better get some food into him. Thank you so much, May."

He took his jacket from the car and went inside. "She's nice. Invited me for dinner sometime. If you need anything, don't hesitate to ask her."

"Good to know." Kinza emptied grocery bags onto the counters, and the two of them had everything put away within a few minutes.

Mahir was about to suggest they make something for lunch, but his cell phone vibrated on the counter. He picked it up and . . . nothing. "I think that might've been your phone."

"Was it?" Kinza leaned across the kitchen table and picked up his buzzing phone. "Aw, crap."

"What? Who is it?"

Kinza turned the phone around so Mahir could see the screen.

Incoming Call: Dad

Mahir held out his hand, and Kinza handed him the phone.

"Adil?" Mahir said.

"He is with you, isn't he?" his brother snarled on the other end. "I'm coming over there and taking my son—"

"No, you're not." Mahir kept his voice calm and level. "Now settle down and let's talk."

"Talk? You're keeping my son from me."

Mahir glanced over at Kinza, who still looked nervous but was diving into a tub of potato salad that *was* going to go with dinner tonight. "Seems to me you and Khalisah chased him out. I'm not holding him here against his will."

Kinza stopped chewing, gave a quiet sound of amusement, and took another bite.

"He is a child," Adil said. "It isn't up to him where he stays."

"It is when he doesn't feel safe," Mahir snapped, and Kinza jumped. Mahir held up a hand and mouthed, *Sorry.* The boy relaxed and continued demolishing the potato salad.

"Safe?" Adil snorted. "He just doesn't want to face consequences."

"And what consequences does he need to face? He hasn't done anything wrong."

"His mother found pornography in his room. Pornography with *men* in it."

"So that's what this is about? Some magazines?"

Kinza lowered his chin, some color flooding his cheeks. Mahir squeezed his arm gently, and when the boy raised his eyes, offered a reassuring smile. Kinza returned the smile halfheartedly, then turned away and put the lid back on the potato salad.

On the other end of the line, Adil huffed sharply. "Magazines? No. I don't allow pornography in this house. You know that. But *men*, Mahir. Men!"

"So what?" Mahir snarled. "So the kid's gay. Get over it."

His brother was silent for a moment, fuming on the other end. Mahir watched Kinza put the tub back in the refrigerator and then slink out of the kitchen as quickly and silently as he could, as if he was afraid his father would hear him and then blow a gasket.

"You knew about this," Adil said. "You knew he was . . . one of them."

"One of us?" Mahir leaned against the counter and let every bit of his exasperation into his voice as he said, "I had my suspicions, yes."

"And you said nothing?"

"What was I supposed to say? 'Hey, Adil, I think your kid is gay, so why don't you get on the ball and beat the shit out of him?' Fuck you."

A low growl reverberated down the line, and Mahir could almost see his brother's face turning purple with fury. Comical sometimes, but not when it was directed at this poor kid.

"Listen," Mahir said. "He's staying here until you have a chance to calm the fuck down."

"You're holding him hostage? Kidnapping him?"

"Keeping him safe," Mahir snapped. "Until his father is rational enough to—"

The line went dead.

Mahir sighed and set the phone on the counter. He pressed his fingers into his temples and muttered a few curses in his native tongue. He had visions of Adil jumping in the car and coming over to confront him face-to-face, but in spite of the man's irrational volatility, he respected cops. Respected their authority and the force they had at their disposal for defusing situations. Even if the cop in question was his own "faggot brother," as he'd so affectionately called him once.

Kinza appeared in the doorway, peeking in and looking around like he thought Adil might have materialized in the room. "So what did he say?"

"I guess nothing you haven't heard." Mahir shook his head. "As a medical professional, you'd think he's seen weirder things than gay people. Or even porn. I mean, you're old enough that they should respect your privacy a little." *And next time, maybe use the internet for that and clear your browser history.*

Kinza relaxed somewhat.

"Anyway, you're not going anywhere." Not until he'd found a solution, at least. Maybe he should get in the car and talk to Adil, beat him to the punch. And quite literally show that his brother stood no chance if he pressed the matter. Mahir had been the runt of the litter as a kid, but that had only meant he'd faced his physical weakness and then piled on a lot of muscle once his hormones cooperated.

And I've faced Ridley. A heart surgeon has nothing on him.

"Thanks. I sometimes wish you were my dad."

Ouch. "I love you, too, Kinza." He couldn't really defend his brother, say he wasn't so bad. Or tell Kinza that his life had never included the thought of kids. Or that having a cop for a father could be worse heartbreak. At least Adil didn't run the risk of getting shot on a normal workday, assuming he didn't run off at the mouth to the wrong person.

"Now if you've left me some of that salad, we'll put something proper together."

He could follow simple instructions when it came to food—defrost this, heat that in the pan—and make it all presentable on the table. Not that Kinza likely cared, but it did give Mahir a sense of civilization. And after spending time among criminals, he wanted to sit at home and do something normal and nice like have a proper meal with his nephew. It was something Saeed didn't have, and might not even miss, but something Mahir needed.

Especially since there was no telling when he'd be able to do this again.

CHAPTER NINE

S tepping back into Saeed's world was nearly as strange and jarring as coming off the cocaine the other night. He recognized the shithole building where the department had decided Saeed would live, but it seemed weird to actually be here. Almost like he'd seen it in a movie rather than spent time here—slept here, fucked here.

He still had an hour or so before he needed to report to the club. Plenty of time to immerse himself and become Saeed again before he had to perform for all the men who didn't know Mahir existed.

On his way up the stairs, he ran through the mental checklist of things he needed to do this week. The delivery for Kinza's desk and assorted small items of furniture on Monday evening. He had to report to James again soon. Tuesday, wasn't it? He'd have to check. And the brass was getting impatient; they'd want some sort of progress.

As he put the key in the door and turned it, he wondered if he should mention the basement and the "couriers" or wait until he had something more concrete. A better explanation than just a mysterious room and some kids wandering through.

Something to look into tonight. He pushed open the door. *Maybe Pete will—*

He stopped dead, hand instinctively flying to his hip where he usually kept his weapon.

On the other side of the small room, sitting cross-legged in his one wooden chair with his fingers loosely intertwined in his lap was Ridley. Cold, stoic Ridley. Sunglasses and all.

Moving slowly, Mahir stepped into the room and toed the door shut. His heart pounded harder than it had during the cocaine's peak. He leaned against the door. "What the hell are you doing in my apartment?"

Ridley was so still he may as well have been a mannequin. "Where the hell have you been for the last—" He made a slow, deliberate gesture of pulling up his sleeve to check his watch. "—twenty-four hours?"

Mahir blinked. "You've been sitting in my apartment for twenty-four hours?"

"No." Ridley folded his hands again. "I had some of the boys keep an eye on it. In case you came back." Something in the ballpark of a smile formed on his lips. "But I figured someone as punctual as you would be getting ready for work soon. So I thought I'd come by."

"How did you get in here?"

Ridley reached into his pocket and then held up a key between two fingers.

Mahir's lips parted. "What the fuck?"

The quasi-smile turned into a disturbing grin. "I took the liberty of having one made the other night. You know, in case of—" He closed his hand, palming the key. "—emergency."

The bastard. All that bullshit—*I'll just run out and get you some painkillers*—for the purpose of gaining more control over Saeed. So no altruism at all. It hadn't fit into Ridley's character, anyway, but Mahir had been too fucked up to notice.

Attack is the best defense.

"Fucked the rest of the coke out of my system." Mahir shrugged. "Crashed with one of the guys. And his partner. The party went on at their place." Let him think Saeed had been the center of an orgy.

Ridley twitched. *So what, you thought you were special?* "That's not exactly resting up to be ready to *work*, Saeed."

"I slept. I'm rested. I just needed to blow off some steam." He turned to his wardrobe and pulled his shirt over his head, sniffed his armpits, and made a face. "I have time for a shower."

And . . . retreat into the bathroom. He showered, stayed under the lukewarm spray to clear the adrenaline from his head, that jolt of panic at seeing Ridley before he was ready for him. The nasty version of him, too. Mahir'd just have to stick to the story. Maybe older men. Rich men who'd invited some fresh meat from the bar into their house. Drink, food, drugs—quite possibly—and Saeed in the middle of it all, unable to resist another hit of coke. Though by the standards of the gay scene, Mahir wasn't quite young enough for that. Past thirty, though he was sometimes told he didn't look it. Whatever. Maybe pickings had been slim.

He was just rinsing his hair when he became aware of another body moving closer. He jolted very nearly out of his skin, turned, and saw Ridley just stepping into the shower. What the hell?

He opened his mouth to tell him to fuck off, but Ridley grabbed him and kissed him again. Funny, how the man kissed him even when he fucking jumped him. Like accepting the kiss meant accepting everything else. Ridley broke the kiss before Mahir could do it and pushed him back by an elbow across the throat. "How many fucked you?"

Oh damn.

Mahir glared at him. "Maybe I fucked them?"

"I don't think you did." Ridley's jaw tensed.

"I lost track."

Ridley stared at him, and Mahir didn't manage to hold that gaze, not with water still running in his face. "That doesn't fit you."

"*Fit* me just fucking fine," Mahir snarled. "Get the fuck off me."

Ridley ignored him. "Drugs again, right? They offered you drugs, and you were craving. Get another hit to chase that first one. Telling you a secret, here: it's never coming back. First time is always the best by a mile."

Mahir clenched his teeth. "You fucking started me on it. Wasn't as pure as yours, either." He could play that role. He'd just needed to kick that psychological dependency very quickly or get fired.

Ridley gripped him by the throat. "I can't use a junkie."

"I'll be fine. I was fucking fine before I met you. I'll be fine." The pleading again, that cringing *I'll obey. I'll please you, you'll see. Give me one more chance.* Mahir could easily imagine Saeed like that—never taking responsibility for his own actions, turning from cool superiority to groveling when his girlfriend had kicked him out, too.

"If I ever see you drugged up again, I'll fucking kill you."

Mahir glared at him. "And you'd have killed me if I hadn't gotten drugged up in the first place." He pulled away from Ridley's grasp and showed his palms. "So why don't you just get it over with, since you obviously want me dead?"

Ridley swallowed. Off guard, apparently. "Saeed, I don't . . ." His gaze drifted down. Way down. Back up. Meeting Mahir's eyes, he said, "I don't want to kill you. But I can't have junkies on my staff."

"Then don't fucking turn your staff into junkies." The water on Mahir's shoulders was getting cold, so he reached back and turned it off. Without the shower's white noise, the silence between their two wet, naked bodies was intense. And no matter how much he willed it not to, Mahir's body responded to Ridley's presence. He turned away to grab a towel, but Ridley caught his arm.

"We have to get to the club," Mahir muttered and jerked his arm away.

"And if we're late?" Ridley reached for him again, this time sliding a warm hand over Mahir's waist. "What am I going to do? Fire myself?" He didn't give Mahir a chance to respond and kissed him instead.

Damn the son of a bitch. Mahir couldn't help drawing him closer and returning the kiss with equal fervor. Ridley's building erection pressed against Mahir's, slid back and forth whenever Ridley moved his hips. Fuck, there was no getting out of this apartment without at least two orgasms between them.

Ridley pulled back. He looked down, letting his gaze slide over Mahir's naked body. Trailing his palm down the center of Mahir's chest, he said, "So the other men, they fucked you to get it out of your system?"

Oh shit. Mahir swallowed. "Yes. They did."

"Three of them? Four?" Ridley raised an eyebrow, and the smirk teetered strangely between menacing and playful.

"Something like that."

Ridley clicked his tongue and shook his head. "And yet"—his hand drifted over Mahir's belly, then onto his hip—"not one of them left a *single* mark."

Shit. Oh shit. "I don't . . . I don't bruise easily."

Ridley laughed so softly the sound would've been lost if the shower had still been running. "What a pity. Coming down off a coke binge, with three or four men at your disposal, and not one of them"—he ran a finger back up the middle of Mahir's chest—"could leave even a single mark." His hand curved around the back of Mahir's neck, and he drew him closer. "Fucking amateurs."

A fierce bolt of arousal jolted through Mahir. Ridley was the kind that left bruises? Sick fuck. And yet, the thought thrilled him, made him harder, if that was possible. "You won't do that to me."

"Won't I?" Ridley's eyes glittered. "Turn around." He pushed at Mahir's shoulder.

"Fuck off." Mahir didn't budge. "I'm sore. And I'm not in the mood for your STDs, either."

Ridley's features hardened. "I'm clean."

"Fuck. Off." Mahir pushed back.

Ridley looked surprised; getting rebuffed was clearly not what he'd expected. Why was he pushing for it, anyway? Some kind of revenge that Saeed had chosen to fuck other men? Jealousy? Pure narcissism? Like they were lovers or something.

Yet, Mahir almost liked him when he wasn't that ice-cold asshole. There was another dimension to it, but he couldn't really decipher it. It wasn't that the cold bastard was an act. It seemed like one that'd be hard to keep up, anyway. Maybe simply a different strategy to get what he wanted.

"All right," Ridley muttered and went to his knees.

Mahir braced himself with a hand against the wet fake tile wall, staring in disbelief and . . . Holy fuck, he really was sucking Mahir's cock. No reluctance, no hesitation. Ridley went for it like he wanted this more than anything in the world. One hand steadied the base, the other slid up and down along with Ridley's mouth. Ridley's insanely *talented* mouth.

Ridley's eyes flicked up and met Mahir's. The cold borderline sociopath was completely out of the picture now. Those were the eyes Mahir had looked up into when he'd knelt in front of Ridley just like this. Not quite warm, nothing terribly affectionate, but there was no mistaking the raw sexual desire looking back at him.

Ridley dropped his gaze and focused on what he was doing. Shaking, barely breathing, Mahir felt around blindly for something to hold on to with one hand, something resembling support. He reached down and slid his fingers through Ridley's wet, dark hair, and Ridley groaned against Mahir's cock.

Mahir closed his eyes and exhaled. Thought he heard himself cursing but wasn't sure. Wasn't even sure what language he'd used, if he'd spoken at all. His head was light, his legs unsteady, and he gripped Ridley's hair more tightly, which only seemed to encourage him.

"Fuck," Mahir whispered. He opened his eyes, blinked them into focus, and stared down at Ridley, who'd added a subtle twist to his slow, tight strokes. "Fuck. I'm gonna . . . I'm—"

That was apparently all Ridley needed. Both hands stroked now. His tongue did incredible things—rapid, fluttering, swirling, harder, lighter—to the head of Mahir's cock, and his hands tightened, loosened, twisted just enough to make Mahir lose his ever-loving mind. Mahir held on tight. Clawed at the wall. Thrust against Ridley's face like Ridley had done to him in the past, and Ridley's helpless moans sent him right over the edge.

He swore. Gasped. Shuddered. Mahir came, and even as his orgasm reached its peak and started to slowly taper, Ridley didn't fucking stop. Mahir winced at a touch of teeth just then, as if Ridley needed to remind him just who was in control, but that moment of fear just spiked his orgasm further, and he pushed deeper, coming down Ridley's throat. Ridley didn't pull off immediately, kept stimulating him and stroking, sucking, until Mahir had to withdraw, dizzy with relief.

He tried to pull Ridley up, but the man stood and pushed Mahir's hand away when he tried to jerk him off in turn. That grin said *I got this*, and Mahir watched Ridley stroke himself, a fierce movement that tightened Mahir's balls in sympathy. The man pleasuring himself was unspeakably hot—flushed skin, straining shoulder, legs braced in a rock-solid stance. Primal and strangely proud, like he needed nobody, didn't accept any help, but liked Mahir watching him.

Mahir reached out and pulled him into a kiss—it just seemed the right thing to do. Or maybe he'd gotten used to it. Ridley was the kisser. Whatever he did to Mahir, he usually started by kissing him. And that held so much potential trouble that Mahir didn't dare think about it too much.

Maybe Ridley simply liked kissing; it meant nothing more than that.

Mahir pulled him closer, felt the tension thrum through Ridley, felt it translate into his own body, and thought Ridley was leaning into him for support. When the man came, it was with a choked sound that lost itself in Mahir's mouth. He stroked Ridley's slick skin, the cool wetness of damp skin in competition with the man's body heat, the heat where they touched. He murmured into Ridley's ear. "That was hot. I'd like to see that again."

Ridley smirked and rubbed his still-hard dick against Mahir's skin. "After work."

Promise? Suggestion? Order? Fuck if Mahir knew. All he knew was it was going to happen. It had to. He'd lose his fucking mind otherwise. Would probably lose it anyway at this rate.

After they'd showered—again—and dressed, Ridley drove them both toward the club. A few blocks away, as they crawled through downtown traffic, Ridley glanced at Mahir.

"This stays between us." He was part icy-cold Ridley, part . . . the other version. Like some bizarre hybrid of the two. "Say a word about it to anyone, and—"

"I'm not going to say anything. Far as I'm concerned, this only exists outside of work."

Ridley nodded, the ice melting a little, and he loosened his death grip on the steering wheel. "Good. Good. That's . . . how it should be."

Mahir watched Ridley out of the corner of his eye as he drove on in silence. The man was tense. Nervous? Did he know about some consequences for this relationship—such as it was—that Mahir didn't? Probably best not to ask. If it made Ridley nervous, it would keep Mahir awake for days.

At the club, they went in through the back door as security usually did.

Gray was waiting for them right inside the door. "Hey, Ridley." He nodded sharply toward the stairwell. "Boss man wants to see you right away." Inclining his head and lifting one eyebrow, he added, "He said it's . . . *urgent*."

Mahir's stomach twisted. It didn't help when Ridley's expression tightened, especially since Mahir couldn't tell if he was nervous, irritated, or both.

"All right," Ridley said. "Thanks for the heads-up." He glanced at Mahir. "Come up with me. Wouldn't hurt for you to see how the boss handles situations."

Situations? That couldn't be good.

He followed Ridley up the blue-lit stairs toward Lombardi's lavish office. Already, Mahir's heart was pounding like he'd run here all the way from his crash pad. How bad could Lombardi get when he *wasn't* conducting a job interview?

Two guys were posted outside the boss's door. Typical bouncer types. Gorillas in suits. One of them tapped the door with his knuckle, then called through it, "Ridley's here, boss."

"Send him in," came the sharp response.

The gorillas moved aside, letting Ridley open the door and walk into the office with Mahir on his heels.

As soon as they were in the office, Mahir's racing heart stopped dead. Lombardi looked furious. Arms folded across his broad chest. Pulsing vein sticking up from the side of his forehead. Jaw clenched. But he wasn't the one who really scared the shit out of Mahir.

It was Pete. Sitting in a chair in front of Lombardi's desk, hands bound together with duct tape, and another strip over his mouth. One eye was black. Blood trickled from his nose and along the edge of the tape.

So this was a "situation." Oh fuck.

"Ah, the cavalry." Lombardi opened and closed his right hand irritably, and Mahir noticed the knuckles were raw and beginning to bruise. "Pete here has been running his mouth off, isn't that right, Pete?"

Ridley's attention focused on Pete's face like the red dot from a gun sight. "I fucking warned you, didn't I?" No hint of surprise in his voice. Mahir's stomach roiled at the thought that maybe Pete showing him downstairs had been the proverbial straw that broke the camel's back. But holding a grudge for two days?

Pete said something, muffled and apologetic.

"I don't want to hear it," Lombardi shot back. "If you're too fucking stupid to follow a direct order, then there's no fucking place for you. The fucking bimbos on stage can follow orders. But you think you're smarter than that, right? Smarter than my orders. Smart-ass!" He slapped Pete hard enough to rock the chair—an impressive feat with a bruised hand.

Pete called out against the duct tape, nostrils flaring.

"Ridley, you know what you gotta do. Take Mustafa there and show him exactly what happens to men who fuck around when they shouldn't."

Fuck around.

Ridley casually stepped up beside Pete and looked at Lombardi. "Who did he talk to?"

"The couriers. Nobody talks to the fucking couriers." Lombardi glared at Pete. "Don't talk to them, don't fuck them, just stay the fuck away from them. It's not fucking rocket science!"

"I'd put some frozen peas on those knuckles, boss," Ridley said.

"Get me some on the way back, then," Lombardi huffed.

Ridley nodded and grabbed Pete by the arm. He jerked him to his feet, then shoved him toward Mahir. "Come on. About time you saw what happens to dumb fucks in this organization."

Pete stumbled, and Mahir caught his arm. Pete looked up at him, eyes wide—even the swollen one—in *please help me* fashion.

Mahir hesitated. How far did he go to avoid blowing his cover? He couldn't just let Ridley beat the fuck out of this guy. Or worse. What the hell was he supposed to—

"Hey. Haji." The pimp snapped his fingers at Mahir. "There a problem?"

"No, sir." Mahir swallowed. He glanced at Ridley and wasn't at all surprised to see the cold version glaring back at him. He refused to look at Pete, tightened his grasp on the man's arm, and followed Ridley out of the office.

They went downstairs and out the back to a car parked beside Ridley's. Just a nondescript silver sedan, one Mahir had thought belonged to one of the other employees. Ridley had a key, though, and popped the trunk. He gestured for Mahir to put Pete inside.

Fuck, really?

Mahir shoved the whimpering man into the trunk. As he did, a grungy blanket shifted, and the distinct sounds of wood and metal clattering against each other turned Mahir's blood cold. Especially when Pete squirmed just right to dislodge a corner of the blanket. The rounded handle was unmistakable: a gardening tool. Likely a shovel.

Oh. Shit.

Ridley slammed the trunk and ordered Mahir into the passenger seat. Heart pounding, Mahir obeyed. There were few things that unsettled him more than apathy in the face of murder, and Ridley was the very picture of it now. He put on a pair of gloves, started the car, adjusted the heater, turned down the radio, and may as well have started whistling as he backed the car out of the parking space. He was completely relaxed now. No nerves. No tension. Business as usual.

"Where exactly are we going?"

Ridley glanced at him, lips peeling back across his teeth in an icy grin. "Terminating an employee."

Mahir gulped. "And it has to be like this? You really have to—"

"Oh. I have to make a call. Excuse me for a second." Ridley casually pulled his cell phone out of his pocket and speed-dialed someone. One hand on the wheel, one on his phone, he looked like any other middle-class guy on his way to somewhere other than a crime-scene-to-be.

"Hey, Jason? It's Ridley. Listen, I have to bail on that round of golf tomorrow. I need to reschedule. Tuesday at three work for you? No, I hate that course. Make it Echo Falls this time. Yes. Tuesday at three. I'll see you then." He hung up and set the phone on the console. "Sorry. Wanted to catch him before he turned off his phone for the night."

Mahir didn't say anything. His skin crawled, wanted to turn inside out. Against his better judgment, he glanced at the clock on the dash. It had been less than an hour and a half since he and Ridley had been naked and fucking around.

There was no way to contact the other officers. Ridley was armed, Mahir was not, and any move he made would get him killed. His best bet was to try to intervene when they reached their destination. And even then, could he intervene without making things worse? The man driving this car was a fucking sociopath. He'd kill Mahir without batting an eye. And then there'd be four dead cops on this investigation.

Ridley drove them out of town and beyond the Eastside, into the foothills of the Cascade Mountains. Mahir got queasier with every mile, recalling his own comments about the mountains being the better choice for hiding bodies. Apparently Ridley had taken that advice to heart.

Ridley stopped the car in a gravel parking lot at a trailhead leading up into the hills. There were no other cars around. With the sun setting, no one in his right mind would be hiking right now.

They pulled Pete and the shovel out of the trunk. Mahir had the dubious honor of carrying that shovel while Ridley half led, half dragged Pete by the arm. After a good half mile of trudging up the steep trail, Ridley turned off the beaten path, and they continued through the soft, wet dirt until they reached a clearing. Ridley let go of Pete and pulled a flashlight out of his jacket pocket.

"Give him the shovel," Ridley said.

Mahir swallowed hard, then did as he was told.

Pete held the shovel in both hands. Eyed it. Eyed them.

"I know what you're thinking." Ridley drew a weapon from his waistband. Not his usual pistol but a larger one. Aiming it at Pete, he said, "I would suggest you start using that to dig instead."

Pete didn't move.

Ridley rolled his eyes and clicked his tongue. "Look, you know how this shit ends. Now you can either dig yourself a nice, comfortable hole, or I can show you how long it takes for a man to die from a gunshot wound to the gut. Either way"—he tilted the gun toward the ground at Pete's feet—"you're sleeping there tonight." Then he pointed the weapon at Pete's face again.

Pete's eyes flicked toward Mahir.

Mahir's pulse was pounding in his temples. His eyes darted to the gun. Unless he could overpower Ridley and get the gun from him, there wasn't a hell of a lot he could do.

Ridley stared at him, eyes cold and narrow, jaw tight. Ridley shook his head slowly. *Don't even think about it.*

Ridley's gaze slid toward Pete again. "Start digging, fucker. Now."

Pete took in as deep a breath as he could with duct tape over his mouth and his nose partially swollen. He put the tip of the shovel in the dirt, set his foot on top, and started digging.

Mahir had to stop this. There were things an undercover cop could let happen in order to maintain his cover, but this was the limit. Problem was, Ridley had two guns and the only cell phone. He had all the weapons and all the cards.

Mahir beckoned to Ridley. Weapon still trained on Pete, Ridley stepped closer, eyebrows raised.

Mahir whispered, "Is this really necessary? We can't just beat the shit out of him and call it a day?"

Ridley shook his head again. "No."

"Why the hell—"

"Because if Lombardi so much as catches this fucker's scent on the wind after this," Ridley snarled, "you and I will both be dead. Quite possibly every man on the security team along with us. It's either him"—he nodded sharply at Pete—"or all of us." The slightest undercurrent of fear vibrated in Ridley's tone. If even Ridley thought the situation was hopeless, that this was the only possible way, then Pete was well and truly fucked.

Ridley's eyes narrowed. "If you'd like to join him, just say so."

"No. I . . . no, thanks."

"Good." Ridley turned to Pete. "I didn't tell you to stop digging, motherfucker." To Mahir, he said, "Go back down to the trailhead. Wait for me there and make sure no one comes down this way."

Mahir hesitated.

"I don't like witnesses." Ridley teased the back of Pete's neck with the muzzle of his gun. "Makes me nervous. I might—" He ran the weapon along the doomed man's collar. "—miss something vital."

Mahir glanced at Pete. He'd probably take five or ten minutes to dig a deep enough hole, which bought Mahir a little time as long as Ridley didn't get impatient.

And as long as Mahir didn't stall.

So he turned and headed back down toward the trail.

CHAPTER TEN

Mahir could overpower Ridley. Physically, they were more or less evenly matched, and Mahir had learned a thing or two about hand-to-hand combat over the years. As long as he had the element of surprise and didn't wind up on the wrong end of Ridley's gun. He'd sort out explanations for Lombardi later, after Ridley was either dead or in jail and Pete was safely . . . well, probably in jail, too.

He walked about fifty yards from the soon-to-be crime scene, and then turned around and backtracked, picking his way carefully toward the clearing, squinting in the deepening darkness to avoid stepping on a stick or otherwise giving himself away. He was maybe ten yards away when he stopped.

Wait. What the hell?

Pete was on his feet. Ridley stood eye to eye with him, one hand around the back of Pete's neck, the other gesturing sharply toward the woods on the opposite side of the clearing. The gun was back in Ridley's waistband.

Then Ridley let go of Pete. And to Mahir's surprise, Pete dropped the shovel and took off into the woods. Ridley pulled out his weapon again, aimed it at the ground, and squeezed off two shots. He slid the gun back into his waistband, picked up the shovel, and started filling in the empty hole.

What . . . in the fuck . . . ?

Mahir shook his head and blinked a few times, but when he looked again, the scene in front of him hadn't changed. Pete was gone—and alive—and Ridley was carefully filling what was supposed to be Pete's grave.

He couldn't linger. He turned away and, setting each step carefully, picked his way back to the trail. Once he'd jogged down to the trailhead, he waited beside the car, pacing back and forth on the gravel as he tried to make sense of what the fuck he'd just witnessed. Or . . . not witnessed.

The sound of an engine caught his attention, and he glanced at the road beside the parking lot. A sleek black car with tinted windows sped by.

Mahir glanced back at the trail. Then at the road where the car had just passed. This was getting weird. Very fucking weird.

Ridley returned maybe five minutes later. He dropped the shovel into the trunk, pulled out a small kit, and handed it to Mahir. Once they were in the car, he also pulled out his pistol. He dropped the magazine and cleared the chamber, then handed Mahir the empty weapon. Mahir hoped the heat he was feeling in the metal was just from being pressed against Ridley's body, not from the gunshots he was *supposed* to believe had killed Pete.

"Kit's got everything you need." Ridley casually started the engine. "I want it cleaned and oiled by the time we get back to the club."

Giving him something to do was a small mercy, even if it hadn't been meant that way. Ridley was clever, but the fact that he felt it necessary to do this pointed in two different directions. The odd phone call beforehand? Coded and hence not about golf at all? It meant Ridley didn't trust Mahir. Fine.

It also meant that Ridley was a mole or an informer or, possibly, even another law enforcement agent. DEA? FBI? With the size of the operation and the marriage of drugs and prostitution, multiple agencies could be involved. Maybe they'd forgotten to brief each other or were working it from different angles, unaware that the other guys weren't asleep on watch when it came to Lombardi and his crew.

If Ridley was cop or a fed, *someone* who was being paid to help bring the organization down, then he was Mahir's natural ally. And if so, he might welcome some backup. Even if he was just an informer, they were on the same team. For the first time, he felt a little optimistic about this fucking mess. It felt good to not be alone. *But if he fails and his cover gets blown before the job's done, you'll still be deep undercover.*

There was that. If one of them failed, it could bring the other down, too. Either when he stepped in to protect a fellow officer or if one was caught and tortured. Or drugged. Lombardi could pull that coke trick, too.

The case is too important.

As long as they were both independent, the law had two different shots at bringing Lombardi down. Revealing himself would only negate that advantage.

Or, knowing the other branches, especially if Ridley was a spook, he could get territorial. He'd find out Mahir was a cop, and within twenty-four hours, Mahir would mysteriously be yanked from the case and reassigned someplace else. Fucking feds didn't like local cops getting in on their parties.

Better to just keep what he knew on the down low until Ridley needed to know. And he fought a smug grin at that thought—nothing like withholding something from a fed on a need-to-know basis.

Mahir finished cleaning the gun around the time they were on the floating bridge, crossing Lake Washington and heading back into Seattle.

Ridley put one hand on top of the wheel and rested the other in his lap. He kept his eyes on the road as he broke the lengthy silence. "That was all a test, by the way."

"Was it?"

Ridley nodded. "You were waiting by the car like I asked. No cops in sight." He glanced at Mahir, streetlights glinting off his eyes. "Means I can trust you."

"Oh. Good." Mahir set the gun-cleaning kit on the floor by his feet. "Because I'd just as soon not sleep in a hole in the ground."

Ridley laughed, which would have disturbed the fuck out of Mahir if Ridley had actually killed Pete. The reaction seemed a bit more normal—and decidedly less psycho—coming from someone who *hadn't* put a bullet through another man's head within the last hour.

"I don't think that'll be an issue." Ridley's tone and expression both turned serious, and he threw another glance toward Mahir. "But watch your step. Lombardi's going to be paranoid for a while. Any time something like this happens, he watches every one of us like a hawk. For all he knows, we were all working with Pete, and we're all potential snitches."

"So what do we do?"

"Business as usual," Ridley said. "Keep the customers in line in the lounge, and stay the fuck out of the basement and away from the couriers unless Lombardi or I tell you otherwise. Clear?"

"Yes."

"Good."

This late in the evening, traffic was light, so it didn't take them long to get back to the club. Ridley parked and started to get out.

"Wait," Mahir said.

Ridley turned. "Hmm?"

Mahir pointed at the gun in his lap. "Forgetting something?"

"Oh. Right." Ridley picked up the magazine and handed it to Mahir. "Take all this to Gray. He'll show you where the safe is."

With that, Ridley left Mahir to the freshly cleaned gun. Mahir swore and tucked the weapon into his waistband, then pulled his shirt over it. Not many people around, especially in a dark alley behind a club, but there was no such thing as being too careful.

He followed Ridley inside. Ridley went left, toward his office, and instructed Mahir to go right to find Gray.

Halfway down the hall, Mahir stopped in his tracks. The gun was suddenly cold against his skin, and the hair on the back of his neck stood up. Ridley was wearing gloves. Had been since they left the club earlier. And he hadn't touched the weapon since he'd handed it off to Mahir in the car.

Which meant the gun—the weapon for a murder everyone was supposed to think had actually happened—only had one set of fingerprints on it.

Mahir's.

Fucking bastard.

There was no fucking way Saeed would allow anybody to frame him for murder—not for a paycheck. He seemed like the kind of person who'd weasel out of a burning building just in time when he smelled smoke. Even if Mahir knew he was safe, Saeed didn't. So he had to work from that angle.

He took his position near the lounge, the lump of metal heavy in his waistband. He had the distinct sense that the other security guys were agitated—they seemed to huddle together just that little bit closer, and the way they exchanged glances and short sentences didn't seem like lighthearted banter at all. He couldn't ask Ridley what any of this meant because the man didn't show his face even once during Mahir's shift. Likely he was busy with Lombardi, replacing the man they'd just "fired." For once, Mahir was among the first security goons to go home, so he sauntered out of the building and then broke into a run a few blocks down, racing as quickly as he could to the waterfront. He frantically scanned the dark water for a good place to toss the gun. It wasn't evidence—it was absolutely nothing to Mahir—but to Saeed, it was a ticket to jail.

He strolled down to the end of the waterfront, down by the tracks where it was completely deserted at this hour. He flung the weapon out into the Sound, watching it spin like a Frisbee through the darkness before it dropped into the deep water with a satisfying *plunk*.

Once the pistol had sunk, he felt tension recede from his body, that nervous agitation that was partly due to the case and partly because of Ridley.

After work. Shit.

Ridley would be on his way to Saeed's place—to fuck and ask questions, likely in that order. Mahir jogged back to his crash pad, considered getting a taxi to keep from being so late, but then just jogged the rest of the way. He ran up the stairs and was surprised that Ridley was not waiting for him.

Still dealing with Pete issues?

Mahir dropped his jacket and changed into a more comfortable T-shirt, then settled on his only chair, which he'd turned toward the door.

Ridley didn't even bother to knock. He had the key, and that clearly gave him the right to just waltz into Saeed's apartment whenever he damn well pleased. He closed the door behind him and crossed his arms. "You didn't talk to Gray."

"He was busy."

Ridley's eyes narrowed. "Really. Where's the gun?"

"Got rid of it." Mahir looked up. "I'm not taking your fucking fall, you bastard."

"So you're choosing when my orders are orders and when they're just suggestions?"

"When you're telling me what to do with a gun that has my fucking fingerprints on it?" Mahir shrugged. "Yeah. I am."

"You were given an order."

Mahir pushed himself to his feet. "I was given a gun that could put me in prison for the rest of my life. I'm not handing that off to someone just to stroke your ego."

Ridley's eyebrows rose, *The fuck did you just say to me?* written all over his face.

"You heard me." Mahir brushed past him and went into the cramped kitchenette. Damn, he wished Saeed wasn't such a devout Muslim. A beer would have done him some good right about now.

Ridley exhaled sharply. "Lombardi wants every weapon accounted for."

"So he collects murder weapons? What kind of fucking idiot is—"

"You have *no idea* who you're fucking dealing with," Ridley snapped, shifting from cold and irritated to furious in a heartbeat. "We don't hang on to murder weapons. Lombardi's not stupid. He is, however, more than happy to get rid of people who don't follow his rules. As you quite clearly saw this evening."

Mahir swallowed. "Then what would've happened to the weapon?"

"It would have been cleaned again and disposed of *properly*. What the fuck do you think would've happened to it? Lombardi would frame it and hang it on the goddamned wall?"

"Then why the fuck was I cleaning it all the way back to the club?" Mahir growled. "Putting my fingerprints on it and making sure all the other evidence was gone."

"So that it could be handed off—clean—to someone who would get rid of it," Ridley said. "Otherwise it would have to be cleaned before it left the club, which meant keeping it *in* the goddamned club that much longer." He stepped toward Mahir, stabbing a finger at him. "And because you couldn't trust me to know how the fuck to handle this simple situation, now I have to answer questions from the big boss. And if you think *you* don't want to sleep in a hole in the ground?" He laughed dryly and shook his head. "Pull something like this again, and you'll be sleeping in one before I will, I guarantee it."

Before tonight, that threat would have stopped Mahir's heart. This time, he just held Ridley's gaze and narrowed his eyes. "Is that right?"

"You're damn right it is."

"I'll keep that in mind." Mahir glared at him. "Despite my allotted amount of virgins, I'm not eager to check out just yet." He pulled his shirt over his head and turned his back on Ridley. "See you tomorrow."

"What the fuck is that supposed to mean?"

"It means what I said. I'll see you tomorrow at the club." Mahir popped the first button of his pants and glanced over his shoulder at Ridley. "I'm not going to fuck a guy who still doesn't trust me and is a finger snap away from throwing me under the bus. Any fucking bus. You hate me, you want to kill me, then fucking do it. *Try* it." Mahir turned around again. "But don't think I'll let you fuck me before you pull the trigger. I got that in the Army, and I don't need it from you. Good enough to do the dirty work but never trusted. Never a fucking part of anything. If you think I'll just roll over and take your dick then you're wrong. I'm not that fucking desperate. You can't use me like fucking toilet paper."

Odd that the little rant made his heart race. Because, dammit, it was too close to home. Saeed wasn't that different a man. He was just angrier about it.

Ridley's jaw muscles tightened. Loosened. Tightened.

Part of Mahir expected to be punched. An attack. A laugh. Being mocked. Shit, normally, deflecting any penetrating blow by sarcasm was much better, much cleverer, much easier, but Saeed was hurt, and he had to show a weakness.

He couldn't read what was going on in Ridley, half expected to be pushed for sex regardless, and, hell, Mahir knew he'd accept it. He seemed to enjoy getting pushed, as long as Ridley did the pushing. That was all kinds of screwed up, too. Mahir shook his head. "Ah, shit." He sat down on the bed.

Ridley pressed his shoulder against the doorway. Seemed to sag a little, like the doorframe was all that was holding him upright. "Saeed."

Mahir rubbed his forehead, then looked up. "What?"

Ridley wasn't looking at him. He kept his gaze fixed on the floor between them and chewed his lower lip. After a moment, he took a deep breath and finally met Mahir's eyes. "For the record, I do trust you."

Mahir gave a quiet sniff of amusement that came out more like a derisive snort. "Yeah. Okay."

"We're all in a bad spot," Ridley said softly. "Everyone working for Lombardi. We're just . . . trying to stay alive."

"Alive or employed?" Mahir snapped.

Ridley held his gaze. "Once you're on Lombardi's payroll, there's no difference between the two. You saw what happened."

Mahir shifted on the mattress. He saw something, but he still wasn't quite sure what to make of it.

Ridley pushed himself off the doorframe and started toward Mahir but stopped when Mahir sat up and recoiled. Ridley took a half step back. "You're angry that I don't trust you, but aren't you the one who got rid of the weapon because you didn't trust me?"

Mahir forced himself to maintain eye contact. "You gave me a gun covered in my fingerprints after it was used in a murder. You want to talk about trying to stay alive? I got rid of that gun because I want to fucking stay alive."

"I know," Ridley said with a slow nod. "But I wouldn't have given you those instructions if they would've gotten you killed. Or arrested."

"How do I know that?" Mahir cursed the shaky, timid sound of his voice. The vulnerability that he hated revealing to anyone.

It was Ridley who finally broke eye contact, and Mahir was sure the man winced as he looked away. Ridley took another step, but it wasn't toward Mahir.

He pulled his car keys out of his pocket and gestured at the door. "I'm . . . I'm gonna go."

Mahir blinked. "Oh."

Ridley chewed his lip, alternately looking at Mahir and the floor. Turning away, he said, "I'm sorry."

Mahir couldn't make sense of the two simple words in time to stop Ridley from walking out. Even as the key turned the dead bolt, sealing Mahir safely within the confines of his apartment, his mind raced, and he couldn't comprehend that he'd now seen a third side of Ridley. An almost painfully human side.

He jumped up and hurried to the door. He unlocked the dead bolt and stepped out into the hall just as Ridley was about to disappear around the corner.

Ridley faced him, eyes wide. For a long moment, they just stared at each other, nothing but space and silence hanging between them in the short, barely lit hallway. Someone needed to say something. Or do something. End this weird standoff.

Ridley's eyebrows knitted together, and he didn't move. If Mahir wasn't mistaken, that expression—so far removed from anything he'd ever imagined seeing on Ridley's face—said *Tell me what to do because I have no idea.*

Finally, Mahir said the only thing he could think of. "I don't want you to go." It wasn't just about not loading more shit onto a fellow cop's shoulders. He couldn't imagine the strain that Ridley was under but dealing with what his neighbor would have called "man trouble," on top of being so deep undercover that Ridley likely barely saw the light of day anymore, seemed like too much.

It was because Ridley's presence made his blood sing, turned him on, sped up his thoughts. Made him feel real and anchored in the present. He liked Ridley and could admit it now that he knew the man wasn't actually a psychopath.

Ridley looked in his eyes. "You sure?"

Mahir nodded and pulled back into the apartment, waiting breathlessly for Ridley to join him. The man did, eventually, like entering the den of a lion, and Mahir smiled at the image. He closed and locked the door behind Ridley, then turned and leaned his shoulders against the door. "Don't leave." He felt stupid for repeating it.

Ridley arched an eyebrow. "You just locked the door."

Mahir laughed softly. "Yeah. And you almost ruined my stress relief."

Ridley's eyebrow climbed higher. "*I* ruined it? You didn't follow an explicit order." His voice was soft, but the exchange clearly allowed him to find his feet again. "I didn't mean to use you."

"That's a dance for two." Mahir pushed off the door. "I got off on it, too." He stepped closer to Ridley, relieved to see him relax a bit, look less deflated and . . . *hurt*?

Mahir placed a hand against the side of Ridley's face and kissed him. That worked every time. Once they touched and kissed, instinct took over, and they were pulling at each other's clothes before long, grinding together, and that was a strange kind of bliss.

He didn't have to worry that he was fucking a murderer, for one. And that had a weird effect. It wasn't like that made Ridley any less exciting and new and surprising in so many ways, but it was such a relief to know the other man was even the same species. Proper human. Being bossed around by another man was very different than getting controlled and humiliated by a heartless criminal. So, strangely, touching Ridley now felt completely different. The same hot skin, the same powerful muscles, the chiseled features—yet Mahir could have happily drowned in him, accepted just about everything Ridley wanted from him.

Ridley broke the mad kiss. "You still sore?"

He felt almost guilty for the lie now. "I . . ."

Ridley grinned and ran his fingers through Mahir's hair. "If you are, we can always . . ."

"Switch?"

Ridley licked his lips. "You want to fuck me?"

Since the day I fucking met you.

Mahir grabbed the back of Ridley's neck and kissed him again, demanding control, and Ridley surrendered without hesitation. He wrapped his arms around Mahir and let him decide how deep they kissed, how hard, even how much Ridley could breathe. This whole different side of him confused the hell out of Mahir. And turned him on like nothing else.

He guided Ridley backward onto the bed, and this time, some of the dominant Ridley surfaced, dragging Mahir down onto the mattress with him. Making out and tangling up on top of Mahir's comforter, they alternated between desperate grinding and something slower. He couldn't even describe it as gentle. He was fairly certain the two of them were incapable of anything gentle when they were in this state. But sometimes, in between the groaning and the clawing, they were more . . . subdued. Touching to feel rather than to force.

Ridley combed his fingers through Mahir's hair and pulled it just enough to make Mahir break the kiss with a gasp.

"Fuck me," Ridley whispered, his voice shaking. "There's . . . You have condoms and . . ."

"Lube, yes." Mahir kissed him again. "I thought you didn't bottom."

Ridley squirmed under him. "Hurry up and fuck me before I change my mind."

Mahir reached for the box beside the bed, and with Ridley's help, got a condom on and lubricated. He started to put some lube on his fingers, but Ridley grabbed his wrist and looked him straight in the eyes with a wild degree of lust Mahir didn't think he'd ever seen before.

"Just. Fuck me. *Now.*"

"I don't want—"

"Now."

Mahir dropped the bottle of lube beside the bed. He thought about ordering Ridley onto his knees, but he liked him like this. On his back, vulnerable, looking up at the man who was fucking him.

Ridley spread his legs far more willingly than such a bossy top ever had in Mahir's experience, and he closed his eyes and bit his lip as Mahir guided himself to him. Ridley was incredibly tight and winced as Mahir tried to press in, so Mahir backed off.

"What part . . ." Ridley licked his lips and then opened his eyes. "What part of 'fuck me now' wasn't clear?"

"I just don't want to hurt you."

Ridley grinned. "Do I have to get on top and show you how—*Fuck.*" He gasped as Mahir pressed harder, and he swore under his breath as the head of Mahir's dick made it past the tight muscle.

"Careful what you wish for," Mahir growled through clenched teeth. He withdrew a little, then pushed in deeper. "I do follow orders when they make sense."

"I know you do." Ridley reached back and held on to the pillow with both hands, arching under Mahir. "That's why I told you to do it."

"So you figure you're in control now?"

"You know I am," Ridley shot back, grinning.

"If your ego needs that. Yes, you're the boss." Mahir pushed forward, forcing a couple more inches into Ridley's tight body. He had to pause, gave Ridley a moment to get used to it, because this was fucking unpleasant for both of them, and even on top, Mahir was loath to see anybody hurt. Not even in the throes of passion, as it were.

Besides, if Ridley enjoyed this one, there might be more. He leaned down to kiss him again, thrilled when Ridley arched and met him halfway, one hand reaching down to stroke himself, and he relaxed somewhat around Mahir. Enough to move in little, even, sliding strokes—nearly out, then just a bit further in.

Mahir would have gritted his teeth if his mouth hadn't been full of Ridley's tongue. He rolled his hips, finding a natural movement that Ridley seemed to enjoy, judging by his moans, the breathless tension building between them, and the way Ridley stroked himself in time with Mahir's movements. That might be the little bit of control Ridley desperately needed, so he let him—to help himself get off or to work against the discomfort. Likely both.

He pulled back and broke the kiss, took a long moment of watching Ridley squirm underneath him, legs wide open, chest gleaming with sweat, eyes glowing with fierce desire, and somehow, that triggered another raw feeling, vulnerable and deep. They were crossing a line, possibly knocking down a wall or three in Ridley's case, and Mahir realized it had been a long time since he'd fucked a man he actually liked.

The more he moved, the more Ridley relaxed, and the mildly unpleasant strokes became deep, hard thrusts. If Ridley was even the slightest bit uncomfortable now, he didn't let it show, moving his hips to complement Mahir's and whispering little slurred pleas for more. Not that Mahir needed any encouragement. He was beyond aroused now and fucked Ridley hard, as hard as he could, as if it were possible for him to get just a *little bit* deeper. His whole body ached from the exertion, but he didn't stop, didn't back off.

"Oh God," Ridley moaned, dropping back onto the pillow. He shut his eyes tight, jerked his own cock faster, and sounded on the verge of tears. "Holy fuck, just like . . . just like that."

Mahir gritted his teeth and kept going, struggling to keep the rhythm that Ridley wanted. Ridley sucked in a breath. His entire body tensed, and he tightened so hard it made Mahir's eyes water. Mahir silently begged him to hurry up and fucking come because there was *no* holding back anymore, and the instant the first jet of semen hit Ridley's abs, Mahir fell apart. To hell with rhythm, to hell with anything. The pressure crested, and all he could do was fuck Ridley in shallow, uneven thrusts as orgasm hit him, blacking out everything else.

Holding himself up on his forearms, he dropped a light kiss on Ridley's mouth, then pulled out and rolled onto his back.

"*Fuck*, that was hot."

"Uh-huh." Ridley wiped sweat from his face. He reached for the tissues beside the bed and cleaned off his chest and abs. "Won't be able to walk . . . tomorrow. But so fucking worth it."

"Sorry 'bout that."

Ridley laughed softly. "Don't be."

They both got up on unsteady legs and cleaned themselves. Mahir wanted to get a shower, but they were both still out of breath, and he was a bit lightheaded, so that would have to wait. They crawled back into bed, lying close together on the small mattress.

Now that the dust was settling, an uneasy feeling crept into Mahir's gut. Things had changed between them tonight. Several times, for that matter, but especially in the last hour or so. Ridley trusted him enough for this. Maybe it was time Mahir showed a few cards.

He turned onto his side, facing Ridley, who was lying on his back.

Ridley looked at him, and his brow furrowed. He reached for Mahir's face. "You all right?"

"Yeah, yeah." Mahir moistened his lips. "But I think there's something you should know. Now that I . . ." He paused. "Now that I think we can trust each other."

Ridley's eyebrows rose a little. "You have my attention."

Mahir took a deep breath. "I think we can work together."

"We already do."

Looking him in the eye, Mahir said, "No, I mean we can *work together*."

Ridley regarded him silently, then lifted himself up onto his elbows so they were eye to eye. "What exactly are you getting at?"

"You didn't kill Pete."

Ridley's lips parted, and Mahir thought he paled a little. "What the hell—"

"Relax." Mahir put a hand on his arm. "I think . . . I think we're on the same team here."

"What are—" Ridley's eyes widened. "You are a cop."

Hoping he wasn't wrong, pretending his heart wasn't pounding so hard Ridley could probably hear it, Mahir nodded. "And judging by how this evening went down, I think you are too."

Ridley stared at him. "Which part?"

"You told me there's a way to flush out cops. Make them shoot people. When you didn't order me to shoot Pete, I knew you trusted me. Because I would . . . have failed that test. You let him go and fired two shots in the ground. The call before that? The golf appointment? Code. Moving the location for the pickup. But above all, you're not the asshole you're playing. You're a good guy, Ridley. You showed that. If you were the man you're playing, you wouldn't have reacted the way you did." He exhaled, kept his hand on Ridley's arm. "And what you said? You're in too deep? Well, quite literally, right?"

Ridley blew out a breath. "You're a good observer."

"Well, that is part of the job." Mahir smiled. "Though you had me fooled for a while."

"Uh-huh." Ridley shook his head. "Guess Lombardi's dislike for fucking on the team makes sense in that light."

"It does." Mahir trailed his hand down to Ridley's and squeezed his fingers. Ridley threaded his with Mahir's. "I was considering not telling you. So in case one of our covers gets blown, the other can still go on and bring the bastard down. But maybe we're stronger together. If I don't have to devote half my attention to keeping my lies straight and being terrified of you, I can concentrate more on what's going on in that organization."

"Terrified?"

"Yep. That other Ridley is a mean motherfucker."

Ridley nodded. "I had issues using you for sex. Too easy to fall into that trap, I guess. Just couldn't resist. And you just kept blowing my mind."

"Likewise." Mahir looked down at their hands. "We should probably stick with our covers. I don't want to know your real name."

"Agreed. Too easy to slip up." Ridley's thumb ran back and forth along Mahir's. "But I think you're right. We can work together. Now that I know you're on the same team, I can put you in places that'll be more advantageous to both of us."

"Such as?"

"The basement." Ridley eased himself back down onto the pillows but still held on to Mahir's hand. "That's where the crazy shit's going on."

"Care to fill me in?"

"How much do you already know?"

Mahir shrugged. "That Lombardi's using a prostitution ring and a strip club as a front for a drug ring."

Ridley nodded. He closed his eyes and ran his free hand through his hair. "It goes deeper than that, though."

"I'm listening."

Ridley put his hand behind his head on the pillow. "If it were as simple as the coke and hookers, we'd have busted him a long time ago. Problem is, the books aren't adding up."

Mahir raised an eyebrow. "What do you mean? Crooks being dishonest about where their money goes?"

Ridley gave a quiet laugh. "It's not that. But the merchandise going out and the money coming in . . . It doesn't line up."

"So someone's skimming?"

"No, you don't understand." Ridley pushed himself up again. "There's more money coming in than merchandise going out."

"How the fuck does that work?"

Ridley shook his head. "I don't know. I've been trying to work it out for, fuck, a year and a half now and—"

"You've been 'Ridley' for a year and a half?"

"I've been Ridley for longer than that," he said. "I was almost ready to crack this case about six months ago, but then I started getting a look at the books. And it wasn't adding up, so I've stayed undercover until I can figure out what the hell is going on." He paused. "As far as I know, it's still going on, but I haven't seen the books in a while."

"Why not?"

"Because the one guy who showed them to me ended up in a hole somewhere on the Olympic Peninsula."

Mahir swallowed. "Like Pete? Or for real?"

"For real, unfortunately." Ridley sighed and scrubbed a hand over his face. "Lombardi took care of that one personally, that cunt. Made an example out of him. Only upside is I managed to drop a GPS transmitter at the burial site, and my guys were able to find him. At least he got a proper funeral."

Mahir's stomach flipped. "How . . . how long ago was that?"

"About four months ago."

Mahir exhaled hard and shivered.

"Why?"

"I went to his funeral," Mahir said softly. "He was a cop."

"Shit." Ridley turned toward him, freed his hand, and pulled Mahir closer. How odd, to be held against a guy's shoulder and comforted. Those two parts of his life had never—or rarely—intersected. His boyfriends usually had no clue how to deal with the strain on Mahir, those cop-specific things that most outsiders never caught a whiff of. The last one had assumed that Mahir was indestructible. He'd told him as much. As if being tall and strong meant he didn't get hurt at all. But being held like this, knowing that the other man understood and didn't recoil from the things that he carried around with him, was an enormous, mind-boggling relief.

"A friend?"

"Not close, no."

"How did you get on this case?"

"My partner got injured—took a crowbar to the back. The boss put me on this case because it's something for one cop, and a gay one. And my boss . . . knows about me. The others don't, though I assume after this they will. Sordid shit like this travels fast."

"They can't know you're fucking the head of security."

"Maybe not. I still expect the closet door to be blown off with a breaching charge."

Ridley snickered. "Well, for what it's worth, you're doing a good job. Keeping it together on coke—I'm very impressed." He paused, eyeing Mahir. "And after you took the blow, I figured you couldn't be a cop. Surprise, surprise."

Mahir laughed. "You know, you didn't leave me a hell of a lot of choice. That whole *you can take it up with Allah sooner or later* thing didn't leave much room for debate."

At least Ridley had the decency to look sheepish. "Sorry. When I saw you down there with Pete, I had to make sure you could still be trusted. I've had some close calls since I've been on this case. Can't be too careful."

"Just promise you won't make me snort that shit again."

Ridley gave a halfhearted laugh. "I'd like to, but I think you know as well as I do we have to roll with the punches on this. And I may even have to 'test' you just to keep up appearances." He smoothed Mahir's hair. "But if I can help it, I won't put you in a position like that again."

"Thank you."

"I'll probably move you to a different post tomorrow. See if you can sniff anything out."

Mahir nodded. "And we shouldn't discuss anything like this while we're there."

"Right." Ridley smiled again. "Guess that just gives us another reason to meet—" His finger drifted down the side of Mahir's neck. "—privately."

Mahir shivered. "Twist my arm."

"I have a feeling you'd like that."

"I—" Mahir blinked. "What?"

Ridley laughed. "Oh, come on. You like it rough, don't you?"

"With you, absolutely."

"That's what I thought." Ridley pulled Mahir down to him, and just before he kissed him, murmured, "Hope you still have a little left for me tonight."

Even if Mahir didn't have anything left, that kiss recharged the hell out of him. Not an hour ago, he'd been eager to throw Ridley out of here and preferably never see him again.

Now?

They'd be lucky if they fell asleep before sunrise.

CHAPTER ELEVEN

He was sore and tired when he made it to the club that evening. His sleep-wake rhythm was shot. Besides, danger was a hell of an aphrodisiac. They'd eventually fallen asleep, then gone out to grab some food, and returned for more sex and more sleep. There was something decadent about just sleeping, fucking, and eating. It definitely took care of the tension and was a huge amount of fun besides. Ridley looked similarly relaxed, by his standards at least, when he met him in the club. They'd gone in at different times to cover their tracks, of course.

Regardless of how they'd spent the last sixteen hours, in the club, Ridley was all business. More so, even, than usual. Before, they'd crossed the line several times, with those hungry kisses or even a quick blowjob. But that particular tension had changed into something else. It was tamer, less primal and crazy. Less dangerous. Yet there was another shift, too. Mahir was a lot better at reading the man. A lifted eyebrow. A glance. A brush of his hand against his own chest or a fleeting pat on the shoulder. All of that said more than he had. Or maybe the signal was less scrambled now due to the lack of fear and tension. And Mahir found he could concentrate more on the job at hand now that he didn't have to be afraid of Ridley anymore.

"Saeed," Ridley called when Mahir was just about to take his usual position near the lounge. He pointed upward. "Come."

They climbed the staircase and passed the usual meathead guarding the office.

Lombardi turned in his high-backed leather chair to study them both.

"Boss. The replacement." Ridley put a hand between Mahir's shoulder blades and pushed him a step forward.

"Him?" Lombardi eyed them. "He's the greenest of the lot."

Ridley shrugged. "One of the more reliable, too."

Lombardi smoothed his tie. "How do you know he's not a cop?"

"Well, he shot Pete. A cop would have blown his cover to save him."

Mahir glanced at Ridley.

"So, how did that make you feel, Saeed?" Lombardi leaned forward. "Ever killed a man?"

"Not in cold blood, sir. Not like that."

"How was it?"

"Didn't like it much, sir."

"Ha," Lombardi said. "He didn't *like* it."

"Who likes taking out the trash?" Mahir shrugged. "It had to be done. Traitors put us all at risk. If it's him or me, I know who I'm choosing."

Lombardi eyed him. "You'll get used to it. Guys like Pete are just roaches, crawling all over your things, shitting everywhere."

Mahir nodded. "I did make a mistake though, sir. I disposed of the gun myself."

Ridley stiffened.

The boss's eyes narrowed. "I beg your pardon, son?"

Mahir pulled in a deep breath. "I was . . ." He thought quickly. "Pete made some noise about cops trying to get into the organization. Sounded like a bunch of paranoid bullshit, but I had a murder weapon on my hands. Figured it'd be better to get rid of it before a cop could get near it."

Lombardi leaned back in his chair, folding his hands in his lap. The relaxed posture only highlighted the barely contained rage in his expression. "You *figured*? Am I paying you to make decisions, camel jockey?"

Mahir shook his head. "No, sir. But if the weapon was found here, then you and your organization would be tied to the murder. If it's found now? It's only got my fingerprints on it."

Something in Lombardi's face relaxed but only slightly. "And who would find it here? Are you telling me you think I'm an idiot who hires cops?"

"No, sir," Mahir said. "But the uniforms keep floating around the lounge. Just seemed like a good idea to play it safe. Now if anyone finds that gun, it's my ass. No one else's."

"And *will* anyone find it?"

"If he's fool enough to scuba dive in the Sound this time of year, then I suppose he deserves to find it."

Lombardi regarded him silently, face blank. No twitch, no blink, no movement anywhere. The emotionless, hyperalert regard of a sniper scope or a gun turret. Far, far away, music thrummed, more vibration than sound, like a distant thunderstorm. Ridley didn't move, didn't even seem to breathe. Mahir certainly held his breath, hoping the little bit of humor would be enough to break the tension in the room. Lombardi laughed. Ridley barely made a sound, but the long breath he released shook some tightness out of Mahir's shoulders.

"A scuba diver. This time of year." Shaking his head, Lombardi wagged a finger at Mahir. "I like you, son. Might have to keep you around after all."

Mahir allowed himself a quiet, relieved laugh.

Ridley cleared his throat. "We could use someone like him downstairs." He nodded toward Mahir. "Fucker would probably turn in his own mother before he ratted out someone here. That's the kind of—"

"Yes, I'm aware of what we need down there," Lombardi snapped. He waved a hand. "I know exactly what I need, thank you."

"Sorry, sir," Ridley muttered. "Should I keep him in the lounge or take him downstairs?"

Lombardi's chair creaked as he leaned forward. He kept his hands folded and placed his elbows on the desk. Mahir was used to the piercing scrutiny of Ridley's eyes, but the way Lombardi was staring him down now was a different thing altogether. He'd once heard an undercover say he thought some of the crime bosses had telepathy mixed with X-ray vision. They could look right into you and see everything you were hiding, from the line of blow you stole to the badge tucked under your bed at the apartment they weren't supposed to know about. As a sick feeling meandered up his spine like a spark on a long fuse, Mahir wondered if that was true. If Lombardi could see that Mahir was a cop, Pete was still alive, and Ridley had left a few marks on Mahir's flesh.

"Let me make one thing clear." Lombardi's tone was cool and even like Ridley's often was. "If you fuck up working in my lounge, you'll be out of a job and never work in this town again except maybe as a back-alley discount whore." His eyes narrowed. "If you fuck up working downstairs? You'll get to watch me hang your balls from the rafters as an example to everyone else, and then I will fucking kill you. Personally. Am I understood?"

"Yes, sir," Mahir breathed. "Understood."

Lombardi gave Ridley a curt nod and turned his chair back around.

Ridley tapped Mahir on the shoulder to follow him. They left the pimp's office and started down the stairs to the club's main level.

"Hanging balls from rafters?" Mahir said. "He make a habit of that?"

Ridley laughed, but it was a dry, humorless sound. He stopped at the bottom of the stairs. "Trust me. If he finds out you're not trustworthy . . ." In his face, there was a mixture of cold, sociopathic Ridley and raw, vulnerable Ridley. "He'll do far worse than that. To both of us."

Mahir swallowed. "Duly noted."

"Also, good save on the pistol."

"Can't let you take the fall for my mistake," Mahir said in a low tone. "You're in deeper."

Ridley glanced at him and gave a tiny nod, ending the conversation as they stepped down into the lounge. As much as Mahir wanted to bring Lombardi down, Ridley had seniority. Being that asshole's enforcer for *that* long required a good payoff, and if that meant playing backup for Ridley, fine.

"I'll get you a pass." Ridley walked him to his office and picked up a security pass from a drawer—a basic magnetic strip card on a black lanyard. "Don't lose it. As far as the boss is concerned, losing that card is like losing a gun. He fucking hates that. Lose it, and divers will be finding *you*."

"Gotcha." Mahir put the lanyard on and slipped the card under his shirt. Ridley pulled open another drawer, picked up a bundle, and put it down on the desk between them. A pistol and a holster. "Security downstairs is a lot tighter. Trespassers are shot."

Mahir grimaced and pulled the cold, heavy weight toward him. "Again, I make a mistake and I'm dead?"

Ridley nodded. "There's a positive."

"Really?"

"A fifteen-percent pay raise."

"Hell, I'll take it," Mahir muttered. "Maybe I can afford a better place to sleep."

Ridley leered at him. "Or not sleep."

Mahir rubbed his wrists, remembering Ridley holding him down while he fucked him, rattling the rickety box spring with every thrust. "Wouldn't mind that." He grinned, assuming that was a date for after work.

He slipped the gun into the holster. "Okay, I'm ready." Ridley stepped behind him and adjusted it, possibly an excuse to touch him. Mahir rolled his shoulders and glanced back at Ridley. "Get me downstairs?"

Ridley led him back to the door, cool and collected. They keyed in, then headed down the stairs. Mahir briefly wondered about Pete but figured being told to dig your own grave had crushed the man's ill-conceived loyalty to the whole enterprise. One more witness for the prosecution. The big thing now was to understand what was going on, what kind of racket was being run here, and then stop all of it. Like ivy, this shit needed untangling, and all roots would have to be dug up or the whole thing would just regenerate. Then all the deaths would have been for nothing.

Ridley stopped in almost the exact same place Pete had stopped yesterday and faced Mahir. He almost stumbled when he met Ridley's eyes; in spite of the low light in this hallway, Ridley's face was stoic and cold, the sociopath clearly presented.

Ridley's voice echoed the hard expression. "Once you go through there"—he gestured at the doorway, beyond which were voices and some quiet activity—"there's no going back. This is your last chance to turn around and stick with lounge detail."

Mahir's eyes flicked toward the doorway. Meeting Ridley's eyes again, he nodded. "Let's go."

Ridley pulled his sunglasses from his collar, slid them on, and turned on his heel. Heart pounding, Mahir followed him across that threshold. That point of no return.

In the mostly quiet room, there were a few boys sitting around. Teenagers, all of them.

Couriers, he reminded himself.

They were mostly listening to their iPods and playing on tablets or handheld video game devices. Expensive equipment for teens. Ditto with the high-end sneakers, North Face jackets, and—was that kid really wearing a TAG Heuer watch? These must have been the rebellious children of yuppies working at Microsoft or Boeing or something on the other side of the lake. That or they were some of the most well-paid couriers Mahir had ever seen.

The room resembled a waiting room in a doctor's office. That is, if any doctor ever decked out his waiting room in bare concrete walls, a couple of bulbs hanging from the ceiling, and mismatched folding chairs with dents that looked like leftovers from a traveling wrestling show.

A few of the kids glanced up. Their eyes immediately went to Ridley, then to Mahir, then back to their various devices.

The door on the other side of the room opened, and two more boys entered. They were equally well-appointed—expensive jackets, white earbuds, and it was anyone's guess what toys they had in the backpacks slung over their shoulders—but they both looked pale. One had that unfocused look of someone concentrating really hard on not puking.

Mahir swallowed. Couriers. Something told him whatever they were transporting wasn't in their backpacks. The previous officers hadn't mentioned that in their reports. Probably hadn't had a chance to report it before their investigations were cut short.

Which meant if they'd gotten this far, they hadn't lasted long after this point. After crossing into this room.

Mahir pulled in a deep breath. Shit just got real.

The pair walked past Mahir and Ridley and continued out of the room. Without seeming even a little disturbed by the boys carrying and waiting to carry cocaine out of the building, Ridley led Mahir deeper into the underground operation.

He swiped his card through a reader and opened the door for Mahir. They continued down a long hall—amazing how these small-looking buildings downtown were so much bigger on the inside than they seemed from the street—and past several doors.

The doors all had card readers, and more than one had a well-armed goon posted outside. They looked like Secret Service with their suits, earpieces, and sunglasses—just like the ones Ridley wore. Some of them were probably ex-Special Forces, judging by their bulk, a few visible scars, and that vaguely aggressive stance. Special Forces guys were almost incapable of standing passively. They always looked like they were coiled and ready to pounce at the slightest provocation.

Ridley strolled down the hall without giving any of the guys a second look while Mahir kept his eyes down and tried not to think about the fact that he was walking through a gauntlet of dormant violence. When this case finally broke, and the force—or DEA—raided the club, they were going to have to bring out their best, brightest, and most heavily armed because this was like Fort Knox staffed by steroid-addicted psychopaths.

Ridley stopped at one of the doors that had suited grunts parked on either side of it. He looked at neither of them as he swiped his card. Both men eyed Mahir but said nothing when Ridley waved him through the door.

Once they were in the next room, Mahir stopped and looked around.

And caught himself wishing he was back out in the hallway.

The lab. Two guys wore filter masks and gloves; this was where the merchandise was weighed and packed. Considering how much stuff was lying around—plastic bags filled with powder, electric precision scales, cartons of condoms that were filled for the couriers—this was a huge operation, and well run, too. Everything was neat and tidy. The men worked diligently and mostly in silence. There was a clear sense of purpose in all details, all movements. No wonder there was so much money around to pay the couriers and security. An operation like this was like printing money. Lombardi would be happy to kill to keep it that way.

And that explained why Ridley had struggled to add up the numbers in the books. Lots of transactions, huge sums. A million more or less would barely register.

Mahir blew out a breath. This had to stop, and soon. He could only guess how Ridley dealt with watching this happen and being unable to stop it. It was a deal with the devil. Stop it and worry about missing something. Not stop it and watch this poison wash into the city. He didn't envy the man. Mahir wouldn't have had the nerves to pull this off. Just his first encounter with Lombardi had made him want to shoot the fucker.

"You'll keep an eye on this door," Ridley told him. "You'll get rotated through the basement over the next couple of weeks."

"Okay."

"You're not allowed to talk to anybody about anything that isn't directly related to the job. Talking to the couriers? Out, unless one of them smokes or gives you trouble. That's how Pete got himself fucked up. Anybody asks you a question, answer only when it's related to security. Nothing more."

"Okay." Mahir straightened.

"And absolutely no touching the merchandise. Lombardi wasn't joking about that, either."

Mahir nodded. "All right. Thanks for the reminder."

Ridley slapped him hard on the shoulder, then left him there.

In spite of the constant sense of danger and the knowledge that he was witnessing the distribution—by way of young boys—of cocaine into the streets of Seattle, standing guard for hours at a time was boring as fuck. At least the lounge was mildly entertaining. He couldn't drink and the music was too loud, but there weren't a lot of dull moments. Idiot drunks needing to be subdued. Panting, drooling men making asses of themselves at the feet of a particularly attractive dancer. The occasional suggestive glance passing between him and one of the other security guys. Grating, but bearable.

Down here? He was either bored out of his skull or fighting some serious nausea while struggling to stay in character. The cold, hard security goon was a tough persona to maintain when a boy no older than Kinza was collecting condoms filled with cocaine, bobbing his head to whatever music was coming from his iPod, and not seeming remotely concerned about what he was doing. Some of these kids probably didn't even have learner's permits and they were swallowing enough blow to get them in serious trouble if they were caught—and kill them if their stomach acid ate through the thin latex.

A prostitution ring. A drug ring. Minors as couriers. Mahir couldn't decide if he hoped Lombardi lived to be an old, old man so he could suffer through as many years of a life sentence as possible or if he hoped SWAT "accidentally" put a few bullets through him when they finally busted this place. Maybe a few nonlethal but incredibly painful shots, followed by a few decades as someone's bitch at the maximum-security pen in Walla Walla. Wouldn't take much to let the other inmates know Lombardi was using kids, too. Even the most violent criminals didn't tolerate the fuckers who hurt kids.

Prison will be hell for you, you son of a bitch, Mahir thought as he watched a couple of boys walk out after swallowing some coke pellets. *And I will see to it personally that's where you end up.*

As the pair of couriers from the doctor's office left the lab, the technicians continued cutting, weighing, and packing the drugs, and boredom set in again. Mahir's mind drifted to his nephew on the other side of the water. He shifted uncomfortably. Rationally, he knew Kinza was safe in Bremerton, miles and a ferry ride away from this hideous operation, but hour after hour, the itch to see the kid worsened. He needed to see Kinza with his own eyes and be *certain* he was all right. He needed to get home. Ridley could wait, and so could he, but . . . Kinza.

Another guard—one of those quietly angry ex-Special Forces grunts—relieved him after a few hours.

On his way out, Mahir turned to one of the other guards in the hall, "Hey, you seen Ridley?"

The guy's upper lip curled into a *Who the fuck are you?* snarl.

Mahir rolled his eyes and left. The club was small enough. He'd find him.

Upstairs, he bumped into Gray in the hall.

"Hey, man," he said. "You seen Ridley?"

Gray gestured over his shoulder. "Was in his office ripping Keith a new one, last I heard."

Mind out of the gutter.

"Yeah, he seems to enjoy that." Mahir thanked Gray and headed to Ridley's office. The place would forever remind him of coke and a blowjob. He listened at the door, then knocked when he heard no shouting inside.

Ridley was bent over at his desk, as if collecting himself. He looked up at Mahir but didn't protest when Mahir came in and shut the door behind him.

"Rough night?"

Ridley nodded. "It's a full moon or something. Sometimes it feels like half the guys are were-idiots."

Mahir bit back a laugh.

"What's up?"

Mahir moved closer. "I need to go *home* tonight." He raised his eyebrows in a meaningful kind of way. "Family stuff."

Ridley arched an eyebrow. "Don't tell me you're married."

"No. Nephew." Mahir glanced at the door. "I'd hate to move our next date, but . . ."

Ridley straightened and gestured dismissively. "You gotta go, you gotta go. Back tomorrow?"

"Yeah." This double life would kill him one day, no doubt about it. Without Kinza to take care of and Adil threatening in the distance, he could have just blended into this life, fully embracing Saeed and his fucked-up existence. But Kinza reminded Mahir of what he stood to lose—besides Ridley, though that was still very much in the air—and he'd promised the kid he'd look after him. He couldn't take responsibility and then abandon him. Right now, he was no better than Adil. Negligence was just a softer form of abuse.

"Good," Ridley said. "Take care."

Mahir approached and touched Ridley on the arm, then pulled him closer by the shoulder. The kiss was gentle, tentative by their standards, and Ridley didn't push for more. Still risky, still dangerous, but one way to say *be careful*, and *see you soon*. He was getting closer to Ridley, and it wasn't just the sex. He couldn't really afford to think about what would happen once the case was closed.

Which meant, of course, that he thought about it on the ferry home. Standing outside on the upper passenger deck, looking out at the Sound—and deliberately avoiding even a glance in the direction of the place where he'd buried a gun under twenty feet of ice-cold saltwater—he kept thinking about Ridley. And Kinza. And Ridley again.

It was just sex. And business. Whatever connection they had beyond that was the kind of bond two men shared when they were fighting in a trench together. And anything stronger was probably due to the fact that they'd thought they were in opposite trenches. Discovering they were on the same side brought a powerful sense of relief. The comfort of having an ally where he'd thought an enemy was lurking.

That was all it was.

Mahir blew out a cloud of breath into the crisp late-night air and rubbed the back of his neck with both hands. Just sex and business. Sure. That totally explained why spending a night away from Ridley left a deep ache inside his chest, one that wasn't even a little bit sexual.

Shit. It wasn't unusual for undercover cops to get in too deep, but this wasn't what Mahir had in mind.

Up ahead, the glow of the shipyard came into view, backlighting the massive ships lined up against the pier to the left of the ferry dock. Mahir's heart beat a little faster. Almost home.

He knew damn well Kinza would be in, probably sound asleep this time of night or doing homework—or grazing his way through the refrigerator—and nowhere near the lab full of condom-wrapped coke. He knew that, but he needed to *see* it.

The boat docked, and Mahir was the first passenger off. He hurried down the ramp and to the parking lot. There was a ticket on his windshield, but thank God, they hadn't booted his tire. He'd have to find someplace else to park if he was going to be gone for a couple of days at a time.

He broke more than a few traffic laws on the way home. Irrational, maybe, but to hell with it. If he got pulled over, he could use his badge to get out of it. Not an ethical thing, not something he'd ever allowed himself to do, but tonight? He didn't give a damn.

The house was dark when he pulled into the garage. He told himself not to panic. This time of night—creeping up on five thirty in the morning, actually—Kinza would be asleep. That was all.

He unlocked the door and moved as quietly as possible so he didn't wake the boy.

From somewhere in the house, something thudded. Crashed. Then hushed voices.

Mahir's hand went to his hip, and he mouthed a curse as he realized he didn't have his gun on him.

Something else clattered. Someone swore.

It was definitely coming from the direction of Kinza's room. Mahir knelt beside the couch and felt around for the pistol he kept hidden underneath the end table. He found it, freed it, and clicked off the safety.

Moving quickly and quietly, keeping the muzzle aimed at the floor and his finger near the trigger, he slipped toward the hallway.

"This way," someone whispered.

"Are you sure?" someone else replied just as quietly.

"Yes, I'm sure!"

Recognizing the voice, Mahir flicked on the light switch and found himself face-to-face with Kinza and another boy of roughly the same age.

Kinza's eyes were huge. So were the other kid's. Considering Kinza was in his boxers, and the other kid looked pretty disheveled, Mahir didn't have to ask if they'd been studying.

He clicked the safety back on. "What the fuck is going on here?"

"I . . . uh . . ." Kinza glanced at the other boy. "We . . ."

Mahir looked at Kinza's . . . friend. "You need a lift home?"

The boy blinked. "What?"

Mahir tucked his gun into his waistband. "I'm not going to kick you out at this time of night." He gestured over his shoulder. "You can either sleep on the couch, or I'll take you home."

"Oh. Um." The boy glanced at Kinza. "The couch is, um, probably fine."

Mahir moved aside. Without giving Kinza a second look, the boy brushed past them and went into the living room.

Mahir eyed his nephew, who looked embarrassed, terrified, and pissed off, all at the same time. "You want to get your friend a blanket and pillow?"

Kinza nodded. "Okay. Uh, good night."

"Good night?" Mahir laughed dryly. "I don't think so. Get your friend set up, and then we're going to have a talk."

"At this hour?"

"Or we can do it over breakfast and make it a three-way conversation."

Kinza's eyebrows jumped. "Okay. Give me a minute."

Kinza got his friend—Tyson, his name turned out to be—settled in the living room. Then he joined Mahir at the other end of the hall in Mahir's office.

Mahir almost took a seat in his desk chair, but that reminded him too much of the conversation he'd had with Lombardi earlier. The idea of putting Kinza in that unnerving position was nauseating. Instead, he sat on the windowsill, arms folded across his chest and one ankle crossed over the other.

Kinza leaned against the door on the opposite side of the room. "So, are you going to kick me out?"

Mahir shook his head. "No. But I can't let you have him over."

Fear immediately turned to anger. "Why the fuck not?"

"Because you're both minors," Mahir threw back. "Do you have any idea how much trouble I could get into for leaving you two alone here if I know you're . . ."

Kinza quirked an eyebrow. "Know we're what?"

Mahir blew out a breath. "If I *suspect* you're intimate with him."

"Well, you left me alone here." Kinza folded his arms and raised his chin, glaring at him. "Was I just supposed to stay here all by myself all the fucking time?"

"Is that really the only reason he's here? For some company?" Mahir regretted it as soon as he'd said it. Of course the kid was lonely. Maybe even scared, being here by himself.

"Does it matter?" Kinza's anger deflated. He lowered his gaze and shifted his weight. "He's my boyfriend. At least he can come here without us worrying about my dad, you know?"

"It's not that simple, Kinza." The day's events flashed through Mahir's mind, reminding him why he'd been so eager to come back here rather than . . . well, rather than spending the night with his own boyfriend, for lack of a better word. This little parallel between Saeed's world and Mahir's—lonely gay men hooking up in places that weren't home while danger lurked outside—turned his gut. Too close to home.

He pushed himself away from the window and crossed the room. "I know you don't like being here alone." He put a hand on Kinza's shoulder. "You know I'm just trying to keep you safe, right?"

"Or keep anyone from knowing about me." Kinza jerked his shoulder away from Mahir's hand. "Don't want anyone to know your little faggot nephew is staying with you?"

Mahir stepped back. "What the hell?"

Kinza tightened his arms across his chest. "If you really gave a shit about me, you wouldn't hide me over here."

"Where else would I take you?" Mahir asked. "I told you, I'm working, so—"

"So let me stay with you over there. You said yourself you've got a crash pad. Why can't I stay there?"

"You wouldn't see me there any more than you do here. And you probably wouldn't see Tyson at all."

"My dad wouldn't find me."

Holy hell. The fear in the boy's voice, and the way he hugged himself like he was folding in on himself, broke Mahir's heart.

"Has he contacted you again?"

Kinza shrugged. "He's called. Hasn't come over, though." He met Mahir's eyes. "Can't you take me to Seattle with you?"

"You've got school," Mahir said quickly, and the excuse sounded even weaker when he said it, although it *was* true.

"I can take the ferry back and forth. I just want to stay with someone who doesn't kick me out or can't keep me over even if he wants to"—he gestured toward the living room to indicate Tyson—"or, you know, someone who actually comes around once in a while."

"Kinza." He touched Kinza's arm again. But nonverbal reassurance wouldn't cut it. He needed Kinza to understand, needed Kinza to trust him. Maybe show, in turn, that he trusted Kinza. "I'm not working in the office. I'm undercover, and I'm spending the nights with some extremely bad people. People who kill on a whim or as little as a suspicion. If they ever doubt that I'm the person they think I am, they'll shoot me, and Allah alone knows what they'll do to my family if my cover's blown. The pad belongs to somebody else, somebody without family, somebody with a very deep grudge, somebody who'll steal or kill at an order. I can't take you there, as much as I want to spend time with you."

Kinza watched him, no doubt reading his face. "What is it?"

"I really can't tell you. I'm hoping to finish this very soon, though it might be a few weeks. Then I'm all yours. I'll take some days off. We could go somewhere and talk."

"I wouldn't tell anybody."

Anybody but Tyson, probably.

"It's against the rules, Kinza. I'm a cop; I have to follow the rules. Undercover means exactly that. Nobody's supposed to know. I'm really not even supposed to be here. And with these people involved . . ." He shuddered at the thought of the bored kids waiting for their turn in the lab. "Seattle is going to be a much safer place once we've taken those guys off the streets."

"How . . . Are you okay?"

"Yeah, I'm okay. Getting to this point in the investigation has taken a huge amount of sacrifice—I can't blow it. I owe it to my friends, and I've made very good progress. But as much as I love you, I can't have you anywhere near me while I'm working. If those guys knew about you, they wouldn't be above using you as leverage."

"Wow." Kinza looked half-intrigued and half-worried. "That's so cool."

"Not when you're stuck in it, it's not."

"I want to be a cop, too."

"With your smarts, the FBI will be happy to have you."

"Can you be gay there?"

"Best place for it in law enforcement, from what I've heard. They can't lose qualified people just because they're sexual minorities. With your fluent Arabic, you can pretty much choose whichever agency you want to work for. But it does mean you have to keep your nose clean and not get into any kind of trouble. They do background checks, you know."

And his brother would absolutely blow a gasket if Kinza went into such a badly paid profession.

He patted Kinza's shoulder. "For now, though, why don't you get some sleep? I'll take Tyson home in a few hours."

Kinza swallowed. "When are you going back? To Seattle, I mean?"

"Tomorrow night."

"Do you know when you'll be back?"

Mahir shook his head. "Hopefully soon."

Kinza avoided his eyes. This was such a tough age. He could flip back and forth so easily between looking like a young man and a boy. Just like most of those kids at the nightclub, looking much too young for their flashy electronics and expensive clothes. And much, *much* too young to be swallowing cocaine by the gram.

The thought alone made Mahir pull Kinza into a tight hug. Kinza stiffened a little, probably startled, but then hugged Mahir back.

"I'll be home as soon as I can," Mahir whispered. "I promise."

CHAPTER TWELVE

Night after night, Mahir stood watch over the illicit operations going on below Lombardi's nightclub. The monotony still drove him insane, but within a few days, he'd learned the rhythm of the organization. Who did what. Which rooms were used for which purposes. He staved off boredom by watching for patterns and anomalies, observing every move every person made.

Places like this ran with such well-oiled mechanical efficiency, they'd make most factories and corporations weep with envy. Each worker had one task that they focused on like robots on an assembly line. The scenery rarely changed. Security guards rotated posts, but for the most part, it was the same crew. Though he couldn't see much of the technicians except for their eyes—and even those were partially obscured by safety glasses—he learned the "faces" of that group, too. New faces were rare.

With one notable exception.

Leaning against the wall in the lab late one night, Mahir watched a pair of couriers gathering the pellets they'd be swallowing and transporting. The blond kid was new. Not unusual—none of the couriers lasted long.

The black Mohawk on the other kid was distinctive enough to catch Mahir's eye. That kid had been here two times previously. The first night, he'd come in with one of the other boys, and he'd eyed the pellets warily. A week later, he'd been back, looking less nervous but a hell of a lot better dressed. He'd traded his well-worn jeans and faded Seahawks T-shirt for some pre-ripped jeans that were, if Mahir wasn't mistaken, three or four hundred dollars a pair. The Under Armour shirt wasn't cheap, and neither was the thick gold chain disappearing under its collar.

Tonight, he was back for the third time and quietly explaining something to the wide-eyed, nervous blond boy. Mahir watched them, stomach twisting as the Mohawked kid made a gesture toward his throat, lifting his chin a little, as if giving the other kid pointers on how to get the cocaine pellets down more easily. No sixteen-year-old should know a goddamned thing about that shit.

After they left for destination unknown—no one in security, including Ridley, had any information about where the boys went after they left the club—Mahir stared at the closed door, shifting on his feet. He kept replaying the Mohawked kid's three visits to the lab over and over in his head. Something didn't sit right.

An hour or so later, another pair of boys came in.

One had his head shaved and a thin gold hoop in his nose. The other . . .

Mahir's heart jumped.

He'd seen this one three times, also. Once as a terrified boy in plain street clothes. Once as a less nervous kid in decidedly more expensive clothes and a cocky grin. And now, dressed like a pimp in training, guiding another terrified boy in plain street clothes through the motions of swallowing the pellets.

"It's easy as hell," the familiar kid told the new one. "Trust me, it's no big deal. And the money kicks ass." He grinned, revealing a gold tooth. "A few more runs, and I can buy me a sweet ride."

A few more runs.

A piece fell into place in Mahir's head. He ran through all the other boys he'd watched come through here and focused on the ones who, for whatever reason, stuck out in his mind. The same pattern. Three visits. Inexperienced, then more confident, and finally mentoring another inexperienced mule before leaving and never coming back.

Interesting. Maybe they were only used for three runs, and then sent packing, although it seemed counterintuitive to train them and then let them go. Whatever the case, Mahir tucked that thought into the back of his mind. He'd run it by Ridley later and see what he made of it.

He breathed a sigh of relief when the shift was over. There was a bit of camaraderie upstairs, as dysfunctional as it was, but down here, it was every man for himself.

Mahir was sitting on the edge of the bed, massaging a sore foot, groaning as he worked every toe and felt the joints pop, when Ridley showed up.

He locked the door and stripped out of his jacket.

"Hurting?"

"The concrete floor is hell on my ankles."

"Yeah. At least I get to move around." Ridley sat down next to him. "Got anything?"

"Yeah, but I have no clue what it means." Mahir moved from his toes to his heel. "Every mule gets three runs. They're also exceedingly well paid. That doesn't seem very efficient to me. I get the idea the boys are better paid than us."

"Well, their job is riskier, but yeah. The kids sure flash a lot of expensive stuff around."

"Which attracts their peers. Third go, they tend to bring a newbie. But I don't think I've seen anybody make a fourth run."

"Well, it means it's all very much under the surface—parents and grown-ups won't spot it going on. It's proliferating through the kids' networks. Like shit they do on Facebook these days."

Mahir put his foot down and pulled the shoe off the other. "We need to find out who the kids are. Do they just go back to their normal lives when they're done here? Do they graduate to a different organization? Lombardi likes the puzzle-box approach. He could be feeding another racket that none of us have any idea about. We might be missing the most vital part yet."

"Well, whatever it is, it's worth millions."

"I'll take it to my superior. I'll have them look at missing-kids reports." Mahir wiggled his toes and grimaced. "Who knew there were so many things in a foot that can hurt?"

"Bad construction," Ridley said. "Same with the spine. We haven't been bipedal long enough for evolution to iron out the last kinks from the design."

Mahir looked at him and grinned. "I don't want my kinks ironed out."

Ridley laughed. "I walked into that. As it were." He pulled Mahir close and kissed him. "Talk to your superior tomorrow. Tonight your ass is mine, officer."

Thank God everybody in the city who owned a coffee machine opened a coffee shop. This place had four tables and maybe room for nine customers total, but it was perfect to meet James.

Mahir kept his voice down as he told the lieutenant of his progress, hoping that, even if things went south, the bit about the couriers and the business downstairs would help.

"I need you guys to look into missing kids—teenagers, all boys. It worries me that these mules have such short careers, and it's not because they're fucking up, as far as I can tell. There's a method to it. Everything is planned to the detail." He paused, thumbing the handle of his coffee cup. "Plus, if these kids were quitting or getting canned, sooner or later, one of them would talk. Word would get out."

James gnawed his lower lip, glancing around as if to check for eavesdroppers. Facing Mahir again, he said, "I'll check around. But if there were that many going missing, there would be red flags. The number of mules you're talking about, that would be hundreds of missing kids. Possibly into the thousands by now, depending on how long this has been going on. It would've been all over the media months ago."

Mahir rested his arm on the table. "Expand the search beyond Seattle and King County, then. Oregon, Idaho, British Columbia. Maybe even Montana and Alberta. Hell, west of the Mississippi, north and south of the border."

"You really think Lombardi would be recruiting that far out?"

Mahir shrugged. "If he needs to bring in that many boys without rousing suspicion. A handful of missing kids from Seattle, Tacoma, Vancouver"—*Bremerton*, he thought with a shudder—"wouldn't really raise any eyebrows. If we can connect them all . . ."

James nodded. "I'll see what I can find out."

They finished their coffee over chitchat about the Seahawks, something "normal" in case anyone was listening in. Then Mahir headed home to Bremerton for a much-needed night in his own bed.

It was early for once when he got home. Past sundown but before midnight.

Kinza was still up, lounging on the couch with a textbook and a sandwich constructed from probably three-quarters of the refrigerator's contents.

Mahir eyed the sandwich. "Do I need to go grocery shopping?"

Kinza threw him a look over the top of his book. "Just leave some cash."

Great. A surly teenager was totally what he'd wanted to come home to.

But at least Kinza was *here*.

"I'm going to make myself something to eat." He paused. "You mind joining me?"

"I'm good." Kinza focused on his book and still managed to cram a bite of sandwich into his mouth without spilling anything.

"Maybe you didn't understand me," Mahir said. "I want to talk."

"So call someone who cares."

Mahir gritted his teeth. And he wondered why most of the parents in the department were gray beyond their years. Forcing himself not to look irritated, he took a breath. "Ten minutes. Then you can get back to studying."

No one could sigh as melodramatically as an annoyed teenager, and Kinza had the sound down to a science. He dropped his textbook beside the couch, letting it fall facedown, hauled himself up, grabbed his plate, and sauntered into the kitchen.

The plate clattered onto the table, and Kinza dropped into one of the chairs. "Fine. What do you want?"

Mahir kept his motions relaxed and casual, not offering a single hint that he was irritated. Especially since he was more amused than anything, and that would only piss off Kinza. No quicker way under a kid's skin than to laugh at him when he was annoyed.

Mahir took a beer out of the fridge. He leaned against the counter and opened the bottle. After he'd taken a long drink—fuck, but he'd needed that all damned week—he looked at Kinza. "I'm curious. Has anyone . . . left your school recently? I mean, besides moving away or something."

Kinza tried to keep up his surly front, but what looked like curiosity and a bit of concern pulled his eyebrows together. "Like, dropping out?"

"Sure." Mahir shrugged and took another sip of beer. "Dropping out. Leaving. Just . . . showing up one day and not the next?"

Kinza was quiet for a moment, eyes losing focus. "One of the stoners quit showing up a few months ago."

"Any idea where he went?"

Kinza shook his head.

"Did you know this guy? Like, would you have noticed if his behavior changed or if he'd started dressing differently?"

"Changed, how?"

Mahir shrugged again. "At all. Anything."

"I don't know. I guess. I didn't really pay attention to him. I just remember he was at school one day and then he was gone, but I never heard why."

Mahir tapped his beer bottle against the edge of the counter, wondering how far he should tip his hand on this. "Have you noticed any of the guys going from dressing like—"

Kinza snorted. "What? Gotta ask the gay kid if he notices how everyone's dressing?"

Mahir laughed. "That's not what I meant. But seriously, has anyone suddenly started dressing like they've got more money?"

"What? Like, wearing a bunch of jewelry and shit?"

Mahir shivered at the memory of the gold chains, the TAG Heuers, and even the odd Rolex. "That or more expensive brands. Shoes, whatever. Maybe driving nicer cars."

"No, not really." Kinza cocked his head. "Why? Is this part of your investigation?"

"Mine? No. It's, um, there's been some missing kids recently. In this area. Just wondered if you'd heard anything."

"What the fuck do their clothes have to do with it?"

Mahir waved a hand. "Not something I can discuss."

Kinza narrowed his eyes, definitely annoyed and curious. Especially since Mahir had shut him down. Kinza would likely make one of the more annoying feds if he did go down that route. "That why you're so weird? Kids went missing and now you think I'll get into trouble?"

Yup, fed material. Mahir took another pull from the bottle. "It's no secret that queer kids are more at risk of homelessness and violence than straight ones. Of course I'm worried about you."

Kinza didn't buy it. "I'm not a child. You can trust me."

"I do."

"Really." That sarcastic tone grated on Mahir's nerves. "I can't be with Tyson, you can't take me to Seattle, you can't tell me anything, and I'm just supposed to sit here and wait and hope that all's fine."

"You're a minor, and that's the extent of it."

"For another five months," Kinza shot back. "Is there some magic space ray that turns my brain 'adult' on my birthday?"

Mahir chuckled. "If you ask the law, yup. Magic space ray and *poof*, you're allowed to have sex and vote. And three years after that, another magic ray hits and suddenly you can drink and buy a handgun."

Kinza rolled his eyes. "The law sucks."

"Hey, at least you get to look forward to something. My age, all I'll get is more gray hair and wrinkles."

Kinza rolled his eyes. "Yeah, but you're *old*."

"Careful, you." Mahir raised a finger in mock threat. Still, he didn't think he could remember Kinza bantering like this with his father. With his brothers, probably, but Adil would have nothing of it. Part of Adil's issues with homosexuality were medical—mental health, AIDS, and overall statistics that said that being gay meant you were more miserable, unstable, and practically an STD magnet. The others were moral and cultural, of course, never mind that there existed a large body of homoerotic poetry and a long history that backed Mahir up when he'd told his brother that being gay wasn't a Western invention. Religion was another big issue—though he'd come across gay Muslims who managed to heal the rift between how Islam was commonly interpreted and their own hearts. But he was optimistic, overall, that every generation made a small step toward tolerance and understanding. And, who knew, next generation, it might not be a big deal at all.

Whatever the case, it was still a big deal these days, especially with Adil, which left Mahir taking care of a kid who didn't quite qualify as a scared little boy anymore but wasn't yet the tough man he thought he was.

Mahir cleared his throat and brought his beer bottle up again. "Anyway. That's all I wanted to ask you about. You should finish studying."

"Didn't you say something about going grocery shopping?"

Mahir lowered his drink and looked at the microwave. "At this time of night?"

"Why not?"

"There enough food left for breakfast?" Mahir crossed the kitchen and opened the fridge. Well, supplies were running a bit low. "Are you going to start chewing through the furniture if I don't get something before morning?"

Kinza laughed. "There's enough left."

"Good." He finally took that swallow of beer, then tilted the bottle in the direction of the living room. "Get your homework done. I'll hit up the grocery store while you're at school."

"You going to tell me about these kids that are—"

"No." Another bottle tilt. "Homework."

Kinza stood with a dramatic huff that was considerably more good-natured than the earlier one. Mahir couldn't help chuckling, but the humor faded as Kinza took his sandwich and went back into the living room.

His questions were relevant to the investigation, but he'd have been lying if he'd said he hadn't been just trying to feel Kinza out and see if Lombardi's recruiting tentacles had made it to this side of the Sound. Maybe they had but didn't have a noticeable presence at Kinza's school. Not yet, at least.

There was no way in hell Lombardi could go through that many couriers without at least one of them blabbing to the wrong person. A parent would have caught on by now. The police would have gotten at least one hysterical phone call about some man giving kids money to transport drugs. Which meant these couriers weren't going anywhere they could talk.

Mahir's blood went colder than the beer in his hand. With cell phones and social networking—on things like the tablets those boys all seemed to have—the kids would be able to contact someone. All it would take was one cocky Facebook status, and the whole thing would blow open. But that hadn't happened. Which meant these kids were either scared shitless of saying anything or—and Mahir didn't want to admit this was more likely—they were *unable* to say anything.

"We shouldn't take the risk," Ridley had said. *"Gene has a lot of places to hide bodies, and he wouldn't hesitate to add us to the cache."*

Oh. Fuck.

Mahir swallowed the last of the beer in one go and pushed himself off the counter to get another. Whatever was going on, he and Ridley needed to figure it out fast. Before any more boys—and one boy in particular—disappeared.

CHAPTER THIRTEEN

Mahir was at the grocery store when James called the next morning.

"Hey, what's up?"

"I did some checking," James said. "Into the missing kids."

"And?" Mahir continued pushing his cart up the aisle, no longer captivated by the rows of cereal and crackers. "Anything interesting?"

"Well, possibly. There's been a very slight uptick in reports of runaways, specifically males in the fifteen to seventeen range, over the last fifteen months or so. In Seattle, King County in general, but also Snohomish and Skagit counties. I'm still waiting to hear back from a few other jurisdictions, but there's definitely an increase."

Mahir stopped his cart. Shit. Good for the investigation, not so good for these boys. He would've given his right arm to have been wrong on this one. "All right. Thanks. I'm going back into the club tonight, so I won't have my phone on me for a while."

"It'll take me a few days to hear back from everyone I've contacted," James said. "Just give me a call toward the end of the week, and I'll update you."

"You got it."

After he hung up, Mahir closed his eyes and let out a long breath. His gut told him James would get the same information from all of those other jurisdictions. And . . . *fifteen months*? He didn't even want to calculate how many kids that could entail.

He finished stocking up on groceries, deliberately getting a few extra packages of some of Kinza's favorites—Barq's Root Beer, that appalling store-brand potato salad, some of those frozen jalapeño poppers—and headed home.

Right around the time he'd finished putting everything away, the kid came in through the front door. Kinza dropped his backpack and trotted up the stairs. "Get anything good?"

Mahir smiled in spite of the sick worry that he knew would remain knotted just below his ribs until this investigation was over. "Just a bunch of that horrific crap you call food."

"Did you get any more of the jalapeño things?" Kinza opened the freezer, the door blocking his face from Mahir's view. "Ooh, you're awesome."

Mahir laughed. "They're all yours. And there's some more soda in the garage."

"Awesome." Kinza closed the freezer, and his smile fell. "You're heading out soon, aren't you?"

Mahir nodded. "I have to go. There are some ... new developments I need to check out."

"Oh yeah? Like what?"

"Like stuff I can't tell you about until the investigation is over."

Kinza rolled his eyes and huffed. "You and your Secret Squirrel crap."

Chuckling, Mahir shrugged. "It's part of the job, I'm afraid. And you'll be all right here for the next couple of nights?"

Kinza's shoulders sank. "The next *couple* of nights?" He didn't sound surprised, just disappointed. And irritated.

"Quite possibly a few more than that." Mahir grimaced. "I'm sorry, kid. But you know you can call my boss if you need—"

"Whatever. I'm getting a soda." Kinza stomped downstairs toward the garage.

Mahir watched him go, and when he was alone again, he pinched the bridge of his nose and sighed. Between his nephew and this investigation, his hair was going to be snow white by the end of the fucking year. And that didn't even cover the weird thing he had with Ridley. All in all, it would cost him something like ten years of his life.

He left Kinza some cash in the kitchen—just in case. It was likely a guilt thing; he wanted the kid to be all right and able to feed himself if the job kept Mahir tied up in Seattle. And hopefully that would also keep his nephew away from strangers offering money for dubious jobs. But phone minutes and food cost money, too. At least now he could talk to Tyson.

Though if you were him, you'd take the "couple of nights" as an invitation to get the boyfriend back in.

He remembered when a colleague had broken the news that his teenaged son was becoming a father: *Teenagers are horny creatures. What can you really do?*

And now he was guilt-tripping himself. Ultimately, he had to trust Kinza to do the right thing and Adil not to strangle him dead if he didn't.

A little over an hour later, Mahir stepped off the ferry and wandered back toward the club. Funny, how it had all turned into a routine, like this was the life he was living and not the other one. It would be seriously weird to get back to the office, sleeping at night and working during the day like the rest of the law-abiding population.

He was half an hour early, so he walked up to the bar where one of the bartenders was setting up his station. "Where's Ridley?"

"Office."

"Thanks."

He made his way to the back of the club, and knocked on Ridley's office door before he entered. Ridley sat there with a big mug of coffee, just finishing off an apple.

Mahir locked the door and came up to the desk. "Kids are going missing—have been for fifteen months. More than normal, my colleague said. We're onto something."

Ridley wiped his fingers on his trousers. "Damn."

"That's what I thought." Mahir plunked down on the chair. "This is messing with my head. Drugs, sex—I get that. That's adult shit. Grown-ups make some horrifying decisions about what to do to themselves, but kids . . ."

Ridley glanced at the door. Then he sighed. "Fuck. I can't . . . This is so fucked up."

"I know. I don't know what the fuck to do."

"I know what I'd like to do to you."

"Uh." That came out of nowhere. Holding Ridley's gaze, Mahir swallowed. There was a hint of desperation in Ridley's expression. Not desperation for sex but an unspoken *I need to get the fuck out of here. I need to get away from all of this.*

"We can't leave," Mahir said.

"No." Ridley glanced at the door. "I don't know about you, but I need . . . I need to turn all this off."

Relieved he wasn't the only one, Mahir managed a grin. "So you'd rather turn each other on instead?"

Ridley's wink was almost a physical tug. Jerking his chain—their chains in this place. Not the smartest thing to do. But truth was, he needed the relief that Ridley offered him. Whichever way he turned, the potential for major disaster stared him in the face, and compared to that, fucking Ridley was a simple thing that allowed him to keep going without losing his mind in the process.

Ridley stood and came around the desk. "Strictly speaking, the shift hasn't even started."

"Uh. Fifteen minutes."

"Plenty of time." Ridley grabbed his face and kissed him soundly. He tasted of apple and coffee, and Mahir groaned into the kiss. Dammit.

Ridley tried to pull Mahir to his feet, but Mahir grabbed Ridley's shirt and pulled him down. The chair was small, but with a knee between Mahir's and a hand on the back of Mahir's neck, Ridley was able to support himself.

Mahir ran a hand up the inside of Ridley's leg. Ridley shivered, then groaned softly as Mahir pressed his palm against Ridley's hardening cock. Mahir stroked gently, alternately cupping Ridley and sliding his hand up and down the clothed ridge.

With a gasp, Ridley broke the kiss but didn't pull away. "Fuck . . ."

"Should—" Mahir murmured, squeezing him again. "Should we be doing this here?"

"Absolutely not." Ridley kissed Mahir even harder than before, forcing his tongue past Mahir's lips and gripping his neck more tightly as if to keep Mahir from pulling away. His mouth left Mahir's just long enough to allow him to whisper, "I'd sell my soul to be able to fuck you right now."

Mahir shivered. Of course they couldn't. Not here. Ridley probably had all the necessities in his desk drawer—no way in hell they'd risk stealing a condom from downstairs—but there wasn't enough time. And there was too much risk of getting caught.

But to hell with it. Mahir kissed Ridley again and drew down Ridley's zipper. As he stroked Ridley, his own erection pushed uncomfortably against his trousers. They'd have to do something about that, and soon, but first . . .

He shoved Ridley back. With one foot off the floor from half-kneeling on the chair, Ridley stumbled but caught himself. He grabbed the edge of the desk, regained his balance, and had just started to slur something like *What the fuck?* when Mahir dropped to his knees in front of him, shoving the chair backward.

And wasn't this where it had all begun? Mahir on his knees with Ridley's cock in his mouth and hand in his hair? Their world had just turned by 180 degrees since then. Neither of them was the tough-guy badass they'd pretended to be, nor the washed-out criminal with nothing better to hope for than to get rich before dying or being locked away for good.

He sucked Ridley down like his life depended on it—and it did, because he'd *better* be fast—forced himself to take Ridley quickly and deeply, aching jaw and sore throat be damned, and urged Ridley on to fuck his face. By now, they knew roughly how much the other could take, and Ridley took full advantage of that.

Their movements were practiced, just on the verge of what Mahir could deal with, if with watering eyes. He craved the sensation of Ridley's big cock fucking in and out, though, tracing saltiness over his tongue when he slipped out just enough to let him breathe. He hungered for all of it, the heat and taste, the sheer power they had over each other. If he could have spoken, he'd have told Ridley he needed him, right now. That need wasn't purely visceral either—it had as much to do with physical, pent-up desire as not wanting to be alone in a dark place.

Ridley groaned softly, a barely contained sound that probably wanted to be a loud, throaty roar but couldn't be. Not here, not now. The reminder of how aroused they both were, about how easily somebody could walk in, drove Mahir on, and Ridley shuddered, the desk creaking as he tried to thrust within the narrow space between it and Mahir. His curses came as softly as that somehow-restrained groan, and his fingers tightened in Mahir's hair just the way they always did when he was close. Closer. *There.*

Ridley gasped, then went silent, shaking as he held on to the desk and to Mahir, and Mahir was sure he'd come himself as he almost—*almost*—choked. After a moment, Ridley gently pushed him back with an unsteady hand as he whispered, "That's enough."

Oh no, it's not even close to enough, Mahir wanted to say, but he obediently sat back on his heels and wiped his lips.

Ridley was shaking like hell now as he tucked himself back in. He gestured at the chair behind Mahir, and Mahir pushed himself up into it, knees aching a little from the hard floor. Back to business, then. Let the man catch his breath, assuming his legs didn't collapse under him first, and they could get back to what they were—

Ridley's legs did collapse.

On second thought, they didn't. They buckled, no, bent, and Ridley was kneeling in front of Mahir. Mahir's heart pounded even harder now, dizzying him. It had been an entirely deliberate set of motions, calculated and executed with as much grace as any man could muster in Ridley's state.

"We really shouldn't be doing this here," Ridley murmured, struggling with Mahir's zipper.

Mahir stroked his hair. "I know."

"I mean . . ." Ridley shook his head. "If they—" Instead of finishing the sentence, Ridley leaned forward and went down on Mahir's very erect dick.

So much for back to business. Mahir groaned and pushed back against the chair, making the wood creak. He opened his legs wider, to fit Ridley all the way between them, and closed his eyes, fully in the moment, the sensations of wet, sucking heat.

He gritted his teeth, tried to be as quiet as possible, but it was hard with Ridley sucking and stroking like that. He wanted more than this, more than the fleeting, quick releases in the face of getting caught. He wanted to take his time, try out what Ridley liked, play at that odd power current between them. He didn't want to do that in Saeed's bed, though. He wanted a place where he felt more human than that.

Thoughts blanked when he got closer, Ridley's free hand squeezing his balls in a near-painful grip. Bastard. But it triggered Mahir as surely as if Ridley had ordered him to come, like he had that first time. Mahir bit back a curse as Ridley swallowed, and managed to touch the side of the man's neck once he was coherent enough to have any intention at all.

Ridley pulled away, and that sight just destroyed any last vestige of job-related sanity.

Locking eyes with Ridley, Mahir said, "We *really* need to do this elsewhere."

Ridley's eyebrows rose. "Already thinking about after work?"

Mahir paused for a moment, straightening his clothes and, with them, his thoughts. "No. Sort of. I mean away from here." He glanced at Ridley, and though a hint of confusion tightened Ridley's brow, he didn't push. He may not have been able to read Mahir's mind, but he obviously picked up the *that's all I should say here.*

They always met after work for sex. They both needed to relieve the tension and compare notes, and Mahir just now realized how foolish that had been. Them slipping out of their roles in a place where the other goons knew to expect Saeed. They knew where his crash pad was. Ridley had seen to that personally. Anybody walking in on them presented a danger, and they'd both been too keyed up to realize it. "We should get more distance between us and the rest. Where they don't already know to find me."

Ridley's eyes widened, and he nodded. "Good call." Another glance at the door. A slight shift of his weight. "Take the rest of the night off. Leave me a time and an address, and I'll meet you." One more glance. "Probably better if we don't leave the club together."

Mahir hesitated. He didn't like the idea of Saeed giving out Mahir's information inside this hellhole, but this was Ridley. He could trust him.

He hoped.

Mahir told himself time and again he absolutely trusted Ridley, perhaps more than he should have. The reason he'd given him the location of a generic parking lot a few blocks from the ferry dock wasn't distrust or the fear that the piece of paper with his address might wind up in the wrong hands. His house was just . . . hard to find. Lots of turns. Streets that looked the same, signs that were hard to see.

Fidgeting in the driver's seat, he watched for Ridley. The ferry had pulled in a few minutes earlier, and the steady stream of cars and walk-on passengers crept past.

Was this really a good idea? Bringing Ridley into Mahir's world? His car? His *bedroom*?

Kinza wouldn't be home. He'd gone to his sister's for the weekend; apparently she was attempting to mediate the bullshit between father and son.

Mahir and Ridley would be alone. Nothing about this seemed remotely like a good idea, but as it was, they were both going out of their minds. The stress of the club kept driving them to take bigger risks, so they needed to blow off some steam and just relax for a goddamned night. Make sure they were on the same page.

Mahir kept watching the road.

And there he was. A sharp tingle accompanied the sight of Ridley in his jeans and tight T-shirt, a backpack balanced on one shoulder. Mahir swallowed. His two realities just ripped and began humping each other.

He rolled the window down and waved, and Ridley's sunglassed face turned toward him. And, dammit, but that was a smile tugging at the man's lips. Butterflies in his stomach? More like a horde of red-assed apes going berserk in there. Damn. Ridley should not have this much of an effect on him, but it seemed the cat was out of the bag. No chance of containment now. And he couldn't just drive away, either.

Calm. It'll be fine.

Ridley pulled open the door and swung his fine ass inside. Mahir stared at him for a moment too long, then scanned the parking lot and any people still left on the ferry who might be watching. But nothing. For all anyone else knew—or cared—they were just a couple of guys meeting up for a booty call. Though that would've likely included a kiss hello.

Mahir started the car. "All good on your end?" He started the engine and looked over his shoulder before he pulled out.

"Yeah. Made up a bullshit excuse."

Mahir lifted an eyebrow, wondering again if they weren't taking too much of a risk being away from the club at the same time. Well, as long as they didn't establish a pattern, it should look inconspicuous. Though Lombardi *was* smart. You really couldn't be a crime lord without having a sense for people. "I guess even the boss can't have you working 24-7."

Ridley gave a quiet laugh. "Not unless he wants me falling asleep on the job and missing important shit." Ridley looked out the passenger-side window and murmured, "Like cops on the payroll."

Mahir wove into traffic, glad for the distraction of driving, before they stopped at a red light. He put a hand on Ridley's leg. "You weren't getting sloppy with me."

Ridley stared out the windshield. "I have to wonder, to be honest. I don't think I was as vigilant as I could have been." He swallowed and looked at Mahir. In the shadows, Ridley's hand slid over the top of Mahir's. "I didn't want you to be a cop."

"You didn't want to play on the same team?"

"You weren't supposed to know I was on that team." Ridley gave a sharp, bitter laugh. "See? Not being so vigilant."

"It's done." Mahir turned his hand and laced their fingers together, a strangely affectionate gesture considering the two of them had been either desperate fuck buddies or dangerous adversaries at various points in this game. "Let's just use tonight to catch our breath. In the morning, maybe we can make some sense of what's going on at that club."

Ridley said nothing.

Mahir's house wasn't far from the docks, but the drive seemed to take all night. In part because Mahir wanted out of this car and these clothes and into bed with Ridley, and in part because of the lingering silence.

But eventually, they arrived, and the garage door rumbled down behind the car, sealing them inside the garage that Mahir fully intended to organize at some point. It felt weird, having Ridley see these scattered, cluttered pieces of his other life. Like Ridley might be able to pick up more information than he ought to from the dusty pair of skis above the freezer or the mountain bike with the broken tire.

But did it matter? As he unlocked the door between the garage and the kitchen, he chastised himself for even worrying. It would have been different if Ridley was still, well, Ridley, but he wasn't. They were on the same team, as he had reminded Ridley in the car.

Inside, he flipped on the hall light. He turned to ask Ridley if he wanted a beer or something, but the faint light from the hallway highlighted a gleam in Ridley's eyes that said a cold drink was not on his agenda this evening.

So, without a word, Mahir led Ridley down the hall. Past the framed photos of the life Ridley wasn't supposed to know about. Past the closed door of the guest room where his nephew slept most nights. Past the office full of all the papers and pictures from the existence he had to keep firmly up his sleeve for the foreseeable future.

And into his bedroom. He closed the door and flipped the switch, which brought to life the small lamp beside the bed.

The room had always seemed huge. Far too big for one man and whomever he brought home from time to time. Facing Ridley, though, Mahir had the distinct sensation of the walls creeping in from all directions, like Ridley had his own gravitational pull and nothing—least of all Mahir—could resist the powerful need to get closer to him.

Mahir didn't even remember taking a step toward Ridley, or Ridley taking a step toward him. Only that they had been apart, and now they weren't, and Ridley's hand was warm, soft, and uncharacteristically gentle on Mahir's cheek.

Their eyes met. Mahir forced himself to take a breath if only so he could stay conscious and not miss a thing.

"This is so dangerous," Ridley whispered. His eyes narrowed a little, and he grinned. God, but he was the most enticing, unnerving combination of the two sides of the man Mahir had come to know. The hand on Mahir's cheek slid into his hair. Tightened. Pulled. Mahir surrendered, letting himself be drawn in, and just before their lips met, Ridley said, "I like it dangerous."

Talk about delivering a gut punch just before robbing the last bit of his breath. No trace of the bitterness he'd spied in the car, no trace of anything but Ridley at his sexiest, most dangerous. And yes, those two things did go hand in hand, damn them both: Mahir for happily jumping off the cliff, and Ridley for getting him close to the edge and whispering, *Jump*.

Mahir pulled at Ridley's clothes, desperate for touch, skin, heat, sex, while he surrendered his mouth to Ridley's tongue and lips and teeth. All he could do was provoke Ridley into letting go of that control, too. He ground against Ridley's groin, their chests moving with harsh breaths as the desire intensified.

"Lucky I like it dangerous, too," Mahir managed to get out between biting kisses. "And that I have a weak spot for dominant assholes."

Ridley laughed, apparently catching that Mahir was teasing.

"I know exactly what spot that is," Ridley growled.

Okay, he'd walked into that one. Mahir blew out a breath of laughter, then undid Ridley's belt and slid it from the loops. Before he could cast it aside, though, Ridley took it from his hand. "Might need this later."

Mahir's balls tightened, though there was no way on earth he'd let Ridley beat him with that. He didn't mind a slap on the ass during sex, but that heavy leather would be a step too far.

Ridley looked deep into his eyes. "Trust me." Dammit. He did.

The belt landed on the bed. Ridley lay down beside it and drew Mahir down on top of him. Mahir couldn't remember moving from where they'd stood to where they now lay, but he didn't stop to try to recollect the steps, and followed Ridley's lead into a long, sensuous kiss. Every kiss was languid with the knowledge that they had all night and no one was going to find them here, but each touch was still laced with the crackling hunger of two men who knew this might be the only night they'd ever have like this.

Ridley tugged Mahir's shirt free from his waistband, and Mahir moaned into their kiss as warm hands slid up each side of his spine. Ridley's fingers curled, kneading the muscles and pulling Mahir's body against his. As much as Mahir wanted every stitch of clothing on the floor where it belonged, he didn't want to stop, and even the clothes didn't temper the heat of their bodies as they pressed together.

Mahir dipped his head to explore Ridley's throat. Ridley tilted his head back as much as the firm mattress allowed, spine arching beneath them as Mahir kissed his way from jaw to collarbone.

"Jesus," Ridley whispered, shuddering beneath him. He lifted his hips a little, grinding his clothed erection against Mahir's, and when Mahir released a ragged breath against Ridley's neck, they both shivered. "So much I want to do. No idea where to start. Fuck."

"You could start by getting out of those clothes," Mahir growled, and they both startled a little, as if neither had expected that boldness from his lips. He raised his head and looked down at Ridley, and yes,

Ridley did look surprised, his eyes wide. Mahir moistened his lips, sat up, and started pulling off his own shirt.

Without lifting off the bed more than he absolutely had to, Ridley took off his shirt. As they both started on their zippers, their eyes met again, and Mahir's heart should have been going a million miles an hour by then. Adrenaline coursing through his veins, arousal turning him into a shaking mess.

But his pulse pounded steadily in his ears. His hands maneuvered the belt buckle, the button, the zipper pull without difficulty. It was as if he'd transcended shaky nervousness and given himself over completely to the idea that this was happening, that they were both in control. He was no longer afraid of the jump because he'd already jumped, and there was nothing left to do but enjoy the ride all the way to the end.

He slid down his jeans and his boxers, left them in a pile on the floor next to "his" side of the bed. They weren't nearly at the stage in their relationship where one of them would be assigned a side, but the thought niggled in Mahir's head anyway.

The mattress shifted, and he glanced at Ridley, who was now naked, too, and utterly fucking gorgeous like that, hard and intent and in Mahir's bed. And there, he managed to pinpoint the strangeness. Ridley was going to have sex with Mahir, not Saeed. And those were still two different men, if from similar backgrounds.

Mahir ran his tongue along his lips and turned fully on the bed until they were lying side by side, both naked on top of the covers. Aroused and unashamed, the hunger now more mellow. They were going to savor this, share as much as they could.

Kissing, brushing skin against skin seemed such an indulgence under the circumstances, though Mahir realized just how much he'd craved being alone and safe with this guy. He wanted to know who Ridley truly was, if he could be lured out of that hard shell—if he could afford to let his guard down and show Mahir who he was. They couldn't even share their real names, though maybe Ridley already knew, given it might have been written on a bill or award around the house.

That, of course, assumed Ridley had had the presence of mind to notice such things on the way to the bedroom. He might see something tomorrow before they returned to the world of Saeed and the club, but at least tonight, Mahir was fairly certain his identity was safe.

Safe in name, anyway. Lying like this, wrapped up and entangled with Ridley, Mahir couldn't begin to pretend he was Saeed. All his defenses had fallen. Ridley drew back a little and met Mahir's eyes. For a fleeting second, Mahir thought the moment would come to a screeching halt with words that had no place in an encounter like this, but Ridley just grinned. "You have condoms, right?"

Mahir exhaled, then returned the grin. "Of course." Full of confidence, not a shred of doubt. Not a single hint of the fact that Mahir had checked the drawer five—okay, seven—times before he'd gone to pick up Ridley.

Ridley licked his lips. "Get one."

Mahir nodded past him. "They're on your side. *You* get one."

Ridley's eyebrows flicked up. In the beginning, Mahir would've taken that as a dangerous *The fuck did you just say to me?* look, but now the upturned corner of his mouth offered an entirely different response. As did the fact that, without a word, Ridley rolled over and reached for the drawer.

Maybe it was the sudden separation from his skin, or maybe it was because he kind of liked the way boldness tasted when he was in bed with Ridley, but Mahir slid toward him and molded his body to Ridley's.

Ridley froze, hand still in the drawer, as Mahir kissed the back of his shoulder. "Fuck, Saeed . . ."

Don't say that name. Please, don't say that name.

"Weren't you getting something?" Mahir murmured, kissing Ridley's neck.

"I . . ." Ridley leaned toward the drawer, and foil rustled quietly. He swore under his breath, as if Mahir's soft kisses were turning that simple task into something akin to cracking a safe. And so just to fuck with him a little more, Mahir bit the back of Ridley's neck. Ridley shivered violently against him. "*Fuck.*"

Mahir paused to kiss the spot he'd just nipped. "Problem?"

"Problem? I, uh . . ." Ridley squirmed as much as he could in this position. "I'm just— *Christ.*"

"Something wrong?" Mahir squeezed Ridley's hard dick and then stroked it slowly. "You're not usually so . . . flustered."

Ridley growled something, but any protest he might have made died on his tongue as Mahir continued stroking him. Ridley pressed back against Mahir, his ass right against Mahir's own erection. Touching his forehead to Ridley's shoulder, Mahir closed his eyes. He could see himself fucking Ridley like this, holding their bodies together and just moving slowly, smoothly, savoring every stroke until someone finally gave in and took over, increasing the tempo until an orgasm became possible, and then probable, and finally inevitable. He could just hold on to Ridley like this as they both came unglued.

Ridley swore, the sound taut like it was through clenched teeth, and foil rustled again. He closed the drawer hard enough to make the lamp wobble and held the condom over his shoulder. "On. Now."

This time it was Mahir who froze. "You want me—"

"Please."

Unexpected, to say the least. Ridley had only let him do this once, and even that had seemed way out of character.

Mahir took the condom and kissed Ridley's neck and powerful shoulder while he stroked the condom down over his length. He made completely sure it sat right, though he couldn't help but wonder what it would be like to feel Ridley naked, but that was getting way ahead of everything so he banished the thought.

He stretched over Ridley to get his hands on the lube. He poured some in his palm, then put the tube down to focus on prep. He wouldn't rush this, either. He wanted to feel all of Ridley's responses, didn't want to miss a single gasp or curse. He slipped his fingers into Ridley's crack, slid over the pucker a few times to wake up the nerve endings there, felt a tingle of pleasure when Ridley pushed back against his hand. He obliged, changing the angle to rub the muscle there, circle it, then apply a bit more pressure, nearly breaching Ridley.

Ridley pulled a knee up, easing access as he pushed his ass out more. Yes, he was ready, saying so without a single word, but Mahir was still going to get him slicked up well. He pushed two fingers inside Ridley, kissing his neck while he slicked the passage.

"Christ," Ridley muttered and let his head fall back. "You're doing this on purpose."

"No, total accident."

"Fucking tease."

Mahir laughed, letting his breath brush Ridley's neck. "You're enjoying it, though, aren't you?"

Ridley groaned, pressing back against Mahir's hand again. "Just fuck me, for God's sake."

"You didn't answer my question." Mahir lifted his head a little and nibbled Ridley's earlobe. "Are you enjoying this?"

Another string of quiet curses. Mahir nipped his ear harder, and the cursing turned into a helpless whimper.

"Please." Ridley's voice was brittle. "I've been . . . all day . . ."

"Hmm?" Mahir slipped his fingers deeper. "You've been what all day?" His only regret just then was that he couldn't see Ridley's face, couldn't watch his eyes screw shut or his lips contort with frustration, but it was a small price to pay to feel the man squirming and hear him getting so flustered.

"I *need* this," Ridley finally said. "I need . . . I need you."

The words lodged Mahir's breath in his throat. He kissed the side of Ridley's neck. "Tell me."

"I did."

Slowly withdrawing his fingers, Mahir said, "Tell me again."

Ridley shivered against him. "I need you. To fuck me. Now."

As much as Mahir wanted to tease him and make him beg, the raw desperation in Ridley's voice stopped him. Mahir slid his fingers all the way out and grabbed the lube. He stroked some onto his cock, making sure he was good and slick, and when he capped the lube and set it aside, Ridley murmured something that may have been *Oh, thank God* . . .

Both still on their sides, Mahir guided himself to Ridley, and they both groaned as the head of his cock slid in. He steadied himself with a hand on Ridley's hip and pushed in slowly. Ridley pressed back, taking him deeper, and Mahir closed his eyes and buried his face against Ridley's neck as their bodies found a slow, steady rhythm. This position didn't offer much range of motion or allow him to fuck Ridley deep and hard, but he was inside Ridley, inside him and moving deliciously slowly, and he couldn't have asked for anything better.

Ridley arched off his chest. He felt around blindly, and when he found Mahir's hand, he grabbed his wrist and pulled his arm around him. Mahir expected to be guided to Ridley's cock, but instead, Ridley clasped their fingers together against his chest, and now their bodies were even closer, locked together, and that turned Mahir on even more than fucking Ridley.

He kissed his way up to Ridley's ear. "Is this what you wanted?" He moistened his suddenly dry lips. "This what you've been thinking about all day?"

"N-no." The answer startled Mahir, almost cost him his rhythm, but he recovered a second before Ridley said, "So much better."

Balls deep in such a hot man, it was hard to think of anything else but the sensation, keeping himself in check so he could wring as much pleasure from this as he could. But something about those words twinged in Mahir's chest.

It felt as if Ridley was letting his guard down, and quite spectacularly so—touching him rather than trying to get off, admitting to his own vulnerability—something Mahir was sure Ridley'd never do with a one-night stand.

Mahir rocked his hips, focused on the pleasure, the powerful, shuddering man in his arms. If there had been any way, he would have pushed deeper inside Ridley, stripped more of him away. They both needed this. It didn't hurt to admit that, too. Give Ridley something more to cling to, show him he appreciated the gesture, the openness, even if it unnerved him slightly. This was running deep—much deeper than Mahir was used to.

"In terms of blowing . . . my mind, coke's got nothing on you," he murmured near Ridley's ear. "You should be illegal. Hell, you probably are, in several states."

Ridley chuckled, but it ended in a choked sound of pleasure when Mahir changed the angle of his hips. They rocked together, a grinding and clinging in small, focused thrusts that drove them both insane. Damn, but spooning was a hell of a lot more intimate than Mahir had calculated. That full-body contact was even more intense than fucking face-to-face, despite not being able to share more than an awkward glance over Ridley's shoulder. "Least I can do is try to blow yours, too," he added.

Ridley gripped his hand harder. "'s working."

Damn. How had they come so far, so fast? The danger? The shared job? Both jobs?

Hell, he didn't know. All he knew was they *had* come this far, this fast, and with much more of this, he'd also be coming hard and fast.

"Oh God . . ." He buried his face in Ridley's neck again. "Fuck . . ."

Ridley's hips moved, as if he wanted to take over and control the cadence and the depth. Damn his body, but Mahir's followed suit, helplessly adapting to Ridley's tempo. Slightly faster, just a little harder, putting Ridley in control with just the right amount of urgency. He closed his eyes, breathing faster, every breath tasting like Ridley's scent, and he gripped Ridley's hand tighter as, one erratic thrust at a time, he unraveled.

"Don't think for a second," Ridley panted, "that I'll be done with you anytime soon."

And Mahir let go. He forced himself as deep as Ridley would take him, shuddered, and came. Just as in his fantasy earlier, he kept holding on to Ridley even as his orgasm peaked and tapered, stayed tangled in him as the dust settled, but he hadn't imagined how electrified the air would be or how turned on Ridley would still be. Ridley hadn't come yet.

Don't think for a second that I'll be done with you anytime soon.

Holy fuck. He'd worried the night they'd met that Ridley might kill him. Wouldn't it just be poetic if the man reduced him to smoldering ashes before this night was over?

When he was sure he could trust his body not to fall to pieces, he let go of Ridley's hand. Slowly and unsteadily he pulled out and managed to get up long enough to dispose of the condom before collapsing on his back beside Ridley.

Ridley didn't miss a beat. He slid up next to Mahir, and either didn't notice or didn't give a damn that Mahir hadn't caught his breath enough for a kiss like that. Mahir didn't protest, though. If he passed out, he passed out, but he wasn't stopping this long, deep kiss for something as trivial as oxygen.

He wasn't stopping for anything.

CHAPTER FOURTEEN

I t was Ridley who finally broke away, and now he was just as out of breath as Mahir. "I hope you realize I was serious. I'm not done with you."

Mahir's body was still floating in that hypersensitive post-orgasmic state, but he grinned anyway. "Whatever you've got, I can handle."

One eyebrow slid upward. Mahir realized a comment like that with someone like Ridley was as good as a throwing down a gauntlet, and that eyebrow was Ridley picking it up and telling him to be careful what he wished for.

"I'm going to get another condom." Ridley's lips grazed Mahir's. "And I'm going to fuck you. Especially after you teased me like that."

"You liked it."

Ridley laughed and kissed Mahir full on. Before Mahir was ready for that kiss to end, Ridley pulled back and leaned toward the nightstand again. Condom in hand, he rolled onto his back and put it on.

Mahir grinned to himself, watching Ridley pour some lube into his hand. "I want you on your—"

Mahir straddled him. Surprise always looked so goddamned good on that man's face, his lips apart and his eyebrows up, and his eyes widened a little more when Mahir took the lube from him.

Mahir grinned. "You were saying?"

"Knees, I think. What are you doing?"

"Didn't get to see your face last time. I intend to fix that." Mahir scooted upward a little. He kept some tension on his thighs, warning Ridley that even if he started bucking, he'd put up a fight to stay on top. It was just a show of intention, though. The man looked like he knew any number of dirty tricks. Which meant lots of potential for games.

Mahir took Ridley's hand, scraped the lube off with his own palm, and slicked up Ridley's very erect cock. Ridley gazed down at himself, then back up to Mahir. "You know, all the 'camel jockey' jokes were actually just jokes."

"You're quite pretty for a camel," Mahir conceded with a straight face.

Ridley laughed. "I spit less, I imagine."

Mahir raised an eyebrow. "I've only seen you swallow."

Ridley rolled his eyes. "Just put on the damned lube and get on."

Mahir squeezed more lube into his hand and lifted up enough to prepare himself. He was tempted to turn around into a sixty-nine position and make Ridley rim him, but while that was a great idea, it was one for another day. He wasn't going to ruin the easy banter and chemistry they were having by making a somewhat risky proposition. Besides, he liked the amount of control he had right now, with Ridley staring up at him as if he were starving. It had a certain effect on him. Being wanted like this was a heady drug, and even if he didn't manage to come again in such short order, he was determined to fuck Ridley and his mind some more.

Mahir took Ridley's cock and positioned himself a little higher up; let the hot, thick length trace his crack; and kept it there as he moved against it, sliding, pushing, tightening his cheeks around that gorgeous cock. Ridley cursed and grabbed his hips, pushed a little in an attempt to get Mahir to change position enough to finally sit down on him, but Mahir just circled his hips, teasing him some more.

"You fucking . . ." Ridley shut his eyes tight, arching his back and squirming under Mahir.

"Hmm?" Mahir circled his hips the other way. "Something you want to say?"

Ridley's lips moved soundlessly, but Mahir could make out the shape of several not *quite* spoken curses.

Mahir grinned. "Do you have any idea how hot you are when you're frustrated?"

Ridley glared up at him, just enough playfulness in his eyes to keep him from edging into that unnerving *if looks could kill* realm. "Son of a bitch."

Mahir laughed, lowering himself just enough to make Ridley press against him.

"*God.*" Ridley closed his eyes again. "You fucking tease."

"Mmm hmm." Mahir leaned down to kiss him. He paused, fully intending to make some smart-assed remark, but then Ridley grabbed both sides of his neck and kissed him hard. His tongue forced Mahir's lips apart, and he demanded unhindered access to Mahir's mouth. Mahir was caught so off guard he had no choice but to give Ridley everything he wanted.

One hand left Mahir's neck, though the other remained there with an unrelenting grip, and Mahir moaned softly as he felt Ridley's dick press against his ass. Ridley wanted to fuck him. He wanted to be inside him. He wanted it now, and everything about his touch, his kiss, even the heat radiating off his body said he would have Mahir now and that was final.

Lost in Ridley's ironfisted embrace, Mahir let himself be guided onto Ridley's cock, and they both sighed into their breathless kiss as Mahir came down and Ridley breached him. Ridley pushed deeper, pulling Mahir down onto him. Then he thrust upward, forcing himself in hard enough to make Mahir's eyes water, and in spite of Ridley's grasp on his neck, Mahir broke the kiss with a whimper.

He let his head fall beside Ridley's, and just like their bodies had earlier, they found a rhythm—Mahir rising and falling over Ridley, and Ridley's hips complementing every motion, lifting off the bed just right to drive himself all the way inside Mahir over and over and over again.

Ridley was in control, reclaiming that which Mahir had playfully taken earlier. But Mahir had had a taste of that control, and all it took was that one taste. He was hooked, just like he was hooked on Ridley himself.

He brushed Ridley's hand off his neck, wondering when that steel grip had become nothing more than a gentle, kneading presence. He did the same with the hand on his hip and pinned Ridley's wrists to the pillow on either side of his head. Now Mahir was more than just on top, he was *on top*. And he didn't know which of them was more surprised at the sudden, effortless shift in control.

Ridley's surprise quickly faded in favor of fierce determination, and he thrust upward, as if he intended to use his hips to reclaim the control his hands had failed to keep.

Mahir lowered his hips and leaned back just enough to pin Ridley's lower body. Ridley's wrists twitched in Mahir's hands, and he tried to thrust again, but he couldn't move. He was completely immobile. Completely at Mahir's mercy.

After just a few panting breaths, their eyes met, and Mahir was taken aback even now at the power behind Ridley's stare, but he didn't back down, not an inch, not a thought. Between them, they could probably melt steel right now, but it wasn't a threatening or dangerous feeling. More like a challenge, a promise, a tingling flow of electricity racing along every nerve. In terms of size, they were evenly matched. Weight, too. Dirty tricks, most likely. Mahir was tempted to kiss Ridley again, but that would mean shifting his balance and giving up control.

You want me, you'll take me on my terms.

Mahir smiled and winked. Then he moved, grinding, circling, gasping at the sensation of Ridley's cock and knowing it couldn't possibly go any deeper. The fullness just spiked the pleasure of having Ridley at his mercy, and it sparked desire and more arousal. Who'd have known control and power could make things so intense?

Mahir slid upward, then bore down on Ridley's dick, gasping at the sensation, feeling the man tense underneath him, clearly trying again to thrust. "If we go slow, I might get off again," he whispered. "Let me have it." *Control. You. Your cock.*

Ridley's eyes narrowed, but he didn't struggle. He flexed his fingers a few times but didn't look upset, just determined as all hell. Mahir figured he couldn't blame him. "Because I'm not nearly finished with you, either."

That did it—Ridley relaxed a bit, allowing Mahir to loosen the grip on his wrists and move a little faster, fucking himself on Ridley, and in some odd way, fucking Ridley as surely as if *he* were inside him. Maybe he'd come again, maybe he wouldn't, but damn, this felt amazing either way.

Ridley closed his eyes. His hands tightened into fists, relaxed, tightened into fists again. He wasn't fighting Mahir now, wasn't trying to regain control or being bossy and demanding, but for a man like him, giving in and being ridden, being fucked, was probably alien. Something he didn't quite know what to do with.

Though it meant giving Ridley the chance to turn the tables again, Mahir leaned down and kissed him. Ridley startled at first but relaxed and opened to Mahir's kiss. He wasn't the one demanding access now but the one granting it. For that matter, granting it so willingly and easily, Mahir couldn't help thinking Ridley was silently begging him to take full advantage.

Mahir pushed Ridley's lips further apart and deepened the kiss into one that was almost violent, completely incongruous to the slow, steady way their hips moved together. As if anything about this encounter made sense, though. So Mahir embraced it all, fucking Ridley like they had all night while kissing him like they were both starved for each other.

Beneath Mahir, Ridley shivered. His hips lifted a little, pushing his cock deeper into Mahir, but he wasn't trying to regain control. Complementing Mahir's movements, if anything, like Mahir often rocked his hips when he bottomed.

Ridley tugged away with one of his arms, like he was trying to get free. Mahir hesitated but released Ridley's wrist, curious to see if the newfound freedom would lead to another power struggle.

Instead, Ridley's hand materialized in Mahir's hair, grasping it gently, stroking it, combing through it, a gesture so much less demanding than when he'd gripped Mahir's hair during one of those frantic office-floor blowjobs. Confident Ridley wasn't going to fight him, Mahir let go of his other wrist. He held himself up on his forearms, and Ridley wrapped his now-free arm around Mahir.

The power had undeniably shifted, and Ridley didn't fight it. More so than Mahir had ever imagined he would, he'd surrendered to his powerlessness. Maybe even embraced it. As they kissed and held on and moved together, Mahir was completely in control. And Ridley—though he could certainly have turned the tables at any moment if he'd wanted to—made no effort to change things. As if he wasn't just humoring Mahir this time but actually liked it this way.

Ridley broke the kiss and exhaled hard as his head fell back to the pillow. "Oh fuck. Oh . . . God, Saeed, don't stop . . ."

The whispered mention of his alter ego nearly jolted Mahir out of the moment, but he forced himself to focus, and he rode Ridley harder, watching the man's muscles tense and body shake as he started falling apart piece by piece.

"Like that?" he asked just to encourage Ridley to speak again.

"Yes," Ridley breathed. "Fuck, that is so . . ." He looked up at Mahir, eyes heavy lidded and expression blissed out to *just* this side of total oblivion. "You're amazing."

Mahir grinned and came down for another kiss.

Their lips had barely touched when Ridley sucked in a breath. His whole body arched and tensed beneath Mahir's, and he thrust upward in short, jerky movements. Not a demand for control, just the desperate last-second need to get in a few more deep, hard strokes before succumbing to the inevitable. His fingers dug into Mahir's shoulders, and Mahir felt more than heard the warm, whispered curses across Ridley's lips just before every muscle in his body seized up, and with a soft moan, Ridley took one last deep thrust and shuddered.

Mahir tensed around him, felt Ridley's cock pump into the condom between them, and ran his fingers over Ridley's sweaty, glowing face, kissing him tenderly until Ridley relaxed in that post-orgasm haze. Only then did he move again, sliding off Ridley's cock while securing the condom. He pulled it off then and dealt with it in the bathroom before he returned to bed, lying down next to Ridley.

Ridley lazily turned his head, face relaxed and eyelids drooping. "Need anything?" he slurred.

"I'm good." Mahir smiled and kissed him. "More than good, actually."

Ridley nodded and pushed closer. His head on Mahir's shoulder, arm slung over his belly, they rested, still on top of the covers. Mahir appreciated being able to study Ridley, the lines of his muscles, the small details—hairs, scars, and blemishes that every body had. He idly ran his hand along Ridley's shoulder, then rested it on his back, feeling the man breathe deeply and evenly. It wasn't quite sleep, just that bone-deep calm that came from exhaustion and having absolutely nothing to fear.

He turned his head and closed his eyes. No rush. "Wake me when you can go again," he said in a low voice, but Ridley didn't respond, and it really didn't matter either way. This was as close to bliss as he'd gotten in years.

After a few minutes, Ridley spoke. "I guess this is as safe a place as any to talk."

So much for basking in that postcoital bliss.

Mahir sighed, scrubbing a hand over his face. "Yeah. I guess it is."

"Much as I'd like to just shut everything out for a while"—Ridley shifted onto his side and propped himself up on his elbow—"we can't ignore it."

Mahir nodded. "I know."

Ridley ran his other hand up and down Mahir's arm, as if his body was oblivious to the conversation and conscious only of the things they'd done and still had left to do before sunrise. "You said there's been an uptick in reports of missing boys."

"Yeah. Eastern and western Washington, Oregon, Idaho, British Columbia." Heavy guilt settled in on his shoulders: how dare the two of them take a little time out for sex? He moistened his lips. "We're expanding the search into Montana, Northern California, and Nevada. Trying to find a pattern."

"And how many of these boys are being recovered?"

Mahir held his gaze.

Ridley exhaled hard. "Shit."

"Yeah."

Ridley ran a hand through his hair and then rested it on Mahir's arm. "So the question is, what's happening to them?"

"Think Lombardi's the type to execute his couriers?"

"No," Ridley said without hesitation. "He's a bastard who deserves to be raped by a horse, but I don't think he's having kids killed." He chewed his lip. "Though knowing him, and judging by the unexplained surpluses in the club's books, it might be something worse."

Mahir furrowed his brow. "Worse? How can— *Oh.*" His stomach turned. "Where the hell could he sell teenaged boys, especially in those numbers, without being noticed?"

"I'm not really sure I want to know." Ridley's words had a weird edge to them, almost like he had the same acidic feeling in the back of his throat that Mahir did. "But the sooner we do know, the sooner he'll be stopped."

Mahir's skin crawled. "Let's hope so. Now, how do we figure it out? The couriers are always unescorted, and I doubt we'll be able to get one to talk without sending him running to Lombardi. They all worship him."

Ridley scowled. "Fucker's a charmer. That and he showers them with money. We'd be hard-pressed to convince them we're on their side and he's not."

"Ever put a GPS on one of the couriers?"

"Yep. First one led me to a Dumpster in Portland. Second wound up two hundred miles away at the bottom of Lake Chelan."

Mahir raised an eyebrow. "Dumped bodies?"

Ridley shook his head. "Just the transmitters. I don't know if the boys found them or what, but the transmitters were ditched, and I'd rather not risk one of Lombardi's assholes finding one and punishing a boy for it."

"There goes that, then."

"Yeah. Any other ideas?"

Mahir shook his head. "Using an innocent as bait is out. We can't deliberately put a minor at risk." They were still cops, still bound by law and common decency. It did mean playing with a deck stacked against them most days, especially if the opposition was as ruthless as Lombardi.

But everybody gets careless. He was bound to slip up eventually. Though how wise it was to wait while more boys got involved and vanished—or how moral—was another question, one that made for uneasy sleep. It all was just too close to home, but at least he could try to keep Kinza safe.

Mahir idly ran a hand down Ridley's arm. "We might have enough on him already. Maybe he'll crack and tell the whole story when his lawyer is trying to get a deal."

Ridley snorted. "Won't keep others from taking over and copying the business model."

"No." Mahir sighed. "We'll just keep digging. Something's bound to crop up."

"Not sure what else we can do." Ridley slid a little closer and touched Mahir's face. "I don't know how much experience you have with undercover work, but you have to remind yourself over and over that you aren't the one responsible for all of this. Lombardi is the criminal, not us."

"I know." Mahir put his hand over Ridley's, turned, and kissed Ridley's palm. "I just want to bring him down *now* before more boys get hurt."

"We both do. But the shitty part of staying on the right side of the law is that we have to let bad things happen while we accumulate enough evidence to stop it." His eyes lost focus, and he sighed. "Believe me, I've been watching this go on for a year and a half."

"This isn't your first undercover case, is it?"

Eyes still unfocused, Ridley shook his head slowly. "No. It's my third deep-cover op." Finally, he met Mahir's eyes. "And I think it'll be my last."

"Really? You're good at what you do." Mahir smiled cautiously. "You had me fooled."

Ridley returned the smile halfheartedly, but it didn't last. "Maybe, but being even a little bit complicit, regardless of why, is hell."

Something twisted in Mahir's chest. He hadn't thought about how this must affect Ridley, that it had crawled just as deep under his skin, too.

Ridley grabbed his pillow and pulled it closer, then rolled onto his back.

"What were the other ops like?" Mahir lifted himself up on one arm. "Compared to this one, I mean?"

Ridley swallowed, staring straight up at the ceiling. "Same shit, different day. Drug rings as fronts for prostitution rings, prostitution rings as fronts for drug rings." He exhaled. "This is the first one that involved kids, though. Some underaged prostitutes showed up in the last one, but they were the exception. Not the rule." He was silent for a moment. Then he turned toward Mahir, and the haunted, downright terrified look in his eyes made Mahir's heart skip. "You know what scares me the most about this op?"

Mahir couldn't speak, so he just shook his head.

"That it's going to end the way the last one did."

Mahir cleared his throat. "How . . . how did that one end?"

Ridley returned his gaze to the ceiling. "Badly."

"I gathered that."

Closing his eyes, Ridley brushed a few strands of hair out of his face. "I'm sure they warned you about all the worst-case scenarios if a drug dealer finds out there's a cop sniffing around his operation."

"Yeah. Every possible ugly outcome."

"Yeah, well." Ridley swallowed hard. "This one was a massive clusterfuck of pretty much all of them."

Mahir blinked. He'd heard the stories enough times: cops executed in cold blood and left in shallow, unmarked graves. Innocent people being framed and going down for bullshit charges, only to meet "unfortunate accidents" while awaiting trial. Car bombs. Families kidnapped. Families murdered. The list went on. It had never occurred to Mahir that pissed-off criminals didn't just pick one option and leave it at that. He'd never thought there might be an "all of the above."

And if that had happened to him, would he be able to cope? As a gay single man, he didn't have much close family to worry about—aside from Kinza—but the funerals in the department were hard to bear even if it wasn't his wife, his children, his parents crying and struggling to put on a brave face while out in public. Would it have broken him enough to stay away from undercover work, or would he have gathered enough resolve to return to the fray?

That, right there, told him exactly what Ridley was made of, and he admired the hell out of that strength.

"This is my first," Mahir said. "Not sure if I'd want to make it a habit, either, though I was all for it when the opportunity came up. Proving myself, I guess."

"Proving what?" Ridley asked, looking maybe a little grateful that Mahir didn't pry.

"That I belong." The words were easy, at least with Ridley. With everybody else, he might have said, *to prove how good I am*, but Ridley didn't need the macho bullshit. At the end of the day, the opportunity had fit Mahir too well to pass up, and maybe there were some guilty feelings about Grant, his partner, getting hurt.

Come to think of it, it was a stupid dare, like when the other kids made you do stupid things when you're about eight to prove to the group you belonged. As adults, this kind of thing had much higher stakes.

"Because of your faith, your ethnicity, or because you're gay?"

Put that way, his ready-made answer blurred, too. It was all about who he was, and all three characteristics formed a kind of hellish triangle with no corner weaker than the other, trapping him forever in a state of *different*.

Maybe part of his attraction to Ridley was that he was different, too.

"Interesting question. All three?"

"You ready for being out at work after this?"

"Uh." Again, the ready-made answer didn't quite survive that inquiring gaze. He'd end up being the *queer sand nigger* even in his real job, no doubt. "Damn late for second thoughts on that. Maybe I'm hoping they'll forgive me if being gay is actually useful for something."

Forgive?

"Forgive for what? There's nothing wrong with you, Saeed."

The name made Mahir flinch. It was the one barrier left standing between them, the one thing keeping them from really diving headlong into whatever it was they were doing. Seemed like such a basic thing—a name—something so simple and not a big deal until it had to be kept a secret.

He looked Ridley in the eyes. "You think we'll ever know each other's real names?"

Ridley startled at the question. "I . . ."

"Obviously not now." Mahir put a hand over Ridley's. "Safety reasons, of course."

"Right." Ridley swallowed again. He looked at Mahir, eyes narrowed slightly like he was searching for an answer in Mahir's expression. "Do you want to know my real name?"

Mahir bit back a *Yes, I do*, and it was his turn to search Ridley's expression for something hidden between the lines. A deeper meaning to the question.

Do you want this to continue once everything else is over?

How far does this go?

How much do you want from me?

Mahir briefly squeezed Ridley's hand. "Do you want to know mine?"

"I asked you first." Ridley's tone wasn't defensive, but it wasn't quite playful, either. There was a note of uncertainty that sounded so out of place coming from him. As if he really was hanging on that question, and the answer might make or break something in him.

"Yes. I do want to know your name."

Ridley's body relaxed just a little, some tension Mahir hadn't even noticed before melting away. He smiled, though still seemed a bit nervous. "Then I guess we'd both better make it to the end of this, right?"

That thought tore at Mahir's insides. The subtle nod to the fact that they were in much too deep to have any illusions that their lives wouldn't be in danger—weren't already in danger, even. Fuck. It was one thing when he'd only wanted to get in and out alive. Now there was someone else whose safety he intended to protect as much as his own.

So Ridley was even more right than Mahir had realized: this *was* dangerous.

Ridley's fingertips brushed Mahir's cheek, startling him back out of his thoughts. "We should sleep. Tomorrow night's going to be a long one."

"I had a feeling tonight would be a long one," Mahir said.

Ridley locked eyes with him, and a grin slowly came to life on his lips. "Is that an offer?"

Mahir couldn't help returning the grin, his icy apprehension melting beneath the heat of the hunger in Ridley's eyes. "That depends. Are you accepting?"

Ridley gave a single, soft breath of laughter and pulled Mahir into a kiss.

And Mahir was right: it was a long, *long* night.

CHAPTER FIFTEEN

Mahir's life had been in various states of bizarre and surreal ever since he'd agreed to take this case. Sometimes he'd wondered if he was the unsuspecting star of some hidden-camera reality show and the production team was just fucking with him to see what he'd do.

So far, no cameras or crew or wisecracking host. Just weirder and weirder shit.

Like, say, seeing Ridley standing in Mahir's own kitchen, shirt off and low-slung jeans hugging his hips just right as he sipped coffee from a faded US Army mug. Talk about worlds colliding.

Mahir leaned against the opposite counter, cradling his coffee cup. His body ached in far too many places for him to have any illusions that last night had been a dream. Hell, when Ridley had finally let him sleep, Mahir had even been sore *in* his dreams. After sex like that, though? He had no complaints.

He started to say something, but a key in the front door turned his head.

Ridley stiffened.

"Relax." Mahir put up a hand. "It's my nephew."

"Your . . ." Ridley looked at him, then in the direction of the front door, which opened, then closed. "Oh."

"Yeah." Mahir cringed a little more with every step Kinza took toward the kitchen. This was going to get awkward. "I'll explain later."

Ridley gave a nod and peered down the hall.

Kinza stopped in the doorframe, looked at Ridley first, frowning, then at Mahir, then back at Ridley. The state of their undress—the whole positively domestic scene—really left no room for interpretation, though Mahir had to fight the impulse to lie or make excuses. Kinza wasn't eight and couldn't be so easily fooled even at that age. Right now? Next to impossible. Especially since they probably looked as relaxed as people only looked after sex.

"Morning, Kinza," Mahir said when Kinza didn't seem able to decide what he was going to say. If he defused the situation right away, maybe he could manage—

"You said you were working!" Kinza said. "He doesn't look like work!"

"Actually . . ." Mahir exchanged glances with Ridley, torn between admitting that Ridley was a colleague and not wanting to blow the man's cover.

Ever the calm and collected one, Ridley jumped in. "We work together." He set his coffee cup down and extended his hand to Kinza. "David."

Kinza eyed his hand with something between wariness and revulsion. He glared at Mahir. "You could have just told me."

Mahir sighed. "I didn't lie to you. I have been working, and—"

"Uh-huh." Kinza snorted, narrow-eyed gaze sliding back toward Ridley. "So he's just something you picked up on the ferry and—"

"He just told you we work together," Mahir said through gritted teeth. "Look, I'm sorry I've had to leave you here a few nights by yourself, but it hasn't been so I could spend time with him." Well, not entirely. Not in any way he could explain to Kinza. "I've been working."

"Whatever." Kinza waved a hand. Turning on his heel, he growled, "I'm not a fucking idiot, Mahir."

Mahir's heart dropped. He stared at the now-empty doorway, listening to Kinza stomp down the hall toward his room. The door opened, slammed shut, and Mahir slumped against the counter.

"Great. That went well."

Ridley cleared his throat. "You, um, didn't mention . . . I thought you lived alone."

"I do. Most of the time. He's . . ." And deeper still, his heart sank. "Long story. Family problems. He was supposed to be gone this weekend to deal with that, so if he's back now, things didn't go well."

Ridley glanced at the doorway, then back at Mahir, eyebrows up. "Should I go?"

"No." Mahir scowled into his coffee but forced himself to calm down, look at things more rationally. Kinza had every right to be a temperamental teenager. On the other side, *he* had every right to be an adult with a sex life and take a few hours of downtime. It would, in the end, keep him on an even keel and help him see this through. He couldn't constantly bend over backward to please everybody else. "He's a teenager; he'll get over it. It might involve some bribes in the shape of food, but . . ." Yeah, that attempt at banter fell flat. "He's in the same place I was at his age, I just didn't have a supportive gay uncle who'd give me a safe space."

Ridley's eyebrows climbed higher. "What did you do?"

"Joined the Army. I do speak Arabic."

"Sounds like a barrel of laughs."

"Fallujah was certainly interesting. That part about me, that's real. I just want for him . . ." He glanced down the hall toward Kinza's room. "For him to fit in better than I did. He's smart, much smarter than I was. I want to make sure he doesn't have to run away to eventually find his place. With every generation, we'll fit in better, make a bigger contribution. It'll take a while, but maybe he could have it easier than I did."

"I'm curious." Ridley put his mug down. "Do you ever hate America?"

"These days, who doesn't?" Mahir muttered. Ridley cocked his head like he wasn't sure how to take that. Mahir waved a hand. "No, I don't hate America. I was born here. I'd rather be gay in America than anywhere in the Middle East, let me tell you that much. Bad enough being gay in a Muslim family, I don't need to be illegal, too. At least in America, religious nut jobs seem to be in the minority." It wasn't exactly fair, and he knew it, but neither did the Middle East score very well in terms of gay rights. In the US, things were at least moving in the right direction. "Also, there's a civil war going on in Syria at the moment."

"So your family, they're . . ." Ridley hesitated. "They don't accept you?"

"For the most part, they do now." Mahir picked up his coffee again and took a sip, grimacing. He fucking hated cold coffee. "My dad's still not quite sure about it. My mother figures as long as I'm a productive member of society who doesn't have any skeletons in my closet, she can live with me being gay. Really, everyone has more or less accepted it except for my oldest brother." He sighed. "Who is, unfortunately, Kinza's father."

Ridley winced like he'd been the one who'd swallowed the ruined coffee. "Isn't that always how it works?"

"Mmm hmm." Mahir pushed the cup away and folded his arms loosely across his chest. "What about your family?"

Ridley stared into his own coffee cup for a moment, maybe weighing whether or not to drink it now that it had cooled off. Then he, too, set it on the counter and pushed it away. With a startling amount of bitterness, even for him, Ridley said, "Let's just say Kinza and I probably have a few things in common."

"Oh. Sorry to hear it."

"Yeah, well." Ridley made a dismissive gesture. Clearing his throat, he glanced at the empty doorway. "Are you, um, sure I shouldn't leave you to work things out with him?"

"It's up to you," Mahir said. "Sorry things were cut a little short."

This time, Ridley smiled, and it was a warm expression, devoid of bitterness or even the devilishness that had been in his eyes most of last night. "Honestly, I'm just glad we had that little bit of time. Maybe we can squeeze in another night like that. Soon."

"Soon," Mahir said with a nod.

"So, I'll, um . . ." Ridley cleared his throat again. "I'll see you tonight? At the—" His eyes darted toward the doorway. "At work?"

"Yeah. Do you need a lift back to the docks?"

Ridley hesitated. "Yeah, I probably should. Otherwise I'll be wandering aimlessly around Bremerton for a few hours."

Mahir chuckled. "Guess we should get dressed, then."

He drove Ridley back to the docks, and they exchanged a quick kiss in the car. Always paid to be discreet in public, even when they didn't have an "employer" who'd have their heads on pikes if he knew about them. Once Ridley had reached the walk-on entry point, Mahir started the car again and drove home.

Rustling sounds in the kitchen suggested either a family of raccoons had invaded or Kinza was out of his room. Mahir wasn't entirely certain which option he would have preferred. He stepped into the kitchen, ostensibly for a second cup of coffee. A direct, confrontational approach might get too quickly out of hand.

"Where's David?" Kinza asked, distributing half a jar's worth of peanut butter onto some bread slices that covered most of the breakfast bar.

"Back on the ferry." Mahir poured himself a fresh cup of coffee. He dug into the fridge for milk, then spotted the carton near Kinza on the bar. He walked over to take it.

"What kind of colleague is he? A cop or that job you're doing?"

"It's none of your business, actually." Mahir poured milk into the coffee, then stirred it.

Kinza glanced up from his peanut butter legions. "Why did you bring him home?"

"Why do you think? I might be old in your eyes, but I'm not past it."

"Yeah, and I can't see Tyson."

"Difference being I'm an adult and you're not. Also, you don't have any explaining to do if I get caught with a guy." Mahir took the coffee cup. "Which you know well. So why don't you stop jerking my chain and tell me how it went?"

Kinza's dark eyes flashed with annoyance, but then his shoulder sagged. "They want to send me away. Europe, or something. Away from 'corrupting influences,' though they didn't call it that."

Me? Oh, Adil, you bastard.

"Do you get a say in that?"

"They're selling it as this great thing for my career. I don't *want* to be a doctor. Not in Cambridge, Oxford, or Lausanne, wherever the fuck that is. I'm not leaving Tyson."

At least you have your priorities straight. Though, that wasn't fair. It was easy to dismiss a young relationship as a crush, but he had colleagues who'd ended up marrying their high school sweethearts. Telling Kinza he'd get over it wouldn't exactly be helpful. Though, considering his nephew's quicksilver temper, Tyson today could mean Dwayne tomorrow. At that age, some measure of wandering and gathering experience was the sane thing to do. "Did you tell them about the law enforcement idea?"

"Yeah. Didn't go well." Kinza took two bread halves and almost hammered them together. "Whatever. Once I can make my own damned decisions, they'll see what they'll get."

He would run away and live his life on his own terms. Kinza was just that type, and Mahir had very few counterarguments against that. It hadn't exactly damaged him forever, though he sure as hell wished he'd not opted for the school of hard knocks. Or rather, the school of IEDs.

"If it's any consolation," Mahir said, "I don't think they'll send you away."

"Yeah? Why's that?" Kinza tore a giant bite off his sandwich.

"Because you're eighteen in a few months. If they wanted to send you off to boarding school or something, they should've done it when you were younger." Mahir shrugged. "By the time they have the paperwork and payments organized for it, you'll be eighteen, and you can tell them to fuck off."

Kinza almost choked on his sandwich. He washed the bite down with a mouthful of milk.

Mahir shifted. "You, um, might not want to use those exact words, though."

"Why not?" Kinza grinned. "See how purple my dad gets."

Mahir laughed. "Yeah, have fun with that. But seriously, if I know your dad, he's just blowing smoke right now because he knows damn well you're almost an adult and there's nothing he can do to prevent you from living your life the way you want to."

Kinza's humor faded. He stared down at his sandwich, as if debating whether or not he wanted more of the peanut butter with a hint of bread. "So what do I do between now and then?" He lifted his gaze, and suddenly the boy in front of Mahir was the scared, vulnerable kid again. "If he says you have to let me come home, then . . ."

"I'll talk to him," Mahir said.

"When?" Scared, vulnerable kid to angry teenager in one goddamned syllable. "In between booty calls and 'working'?"

Mahir closed his eyes and sighed. He'd had way too little sleep to deal with the teenaged emotional yo-yo. "I'll call him before I go to work tonight. I'm perfectly fine with you staying here as long as you need to."

Except I should be around more. I shouldn't just leave you here. I definitely shouldn't be bringing Ridley here. Fuck.

"What if Dad's not fine with it?" Scared and vulnerable again. "You said yourself, he can make that decision since I'm a minor."

"I did, and he can." Mahir sipped his coffee. Damn. Cold again. "But somewhere under all that yelling and acting like an idiot, your father *is* a reasonable person. He may have a really fucked-up way of showing it, but in the end, he wants what's best for you."

"Which means not being gay," Kinza growled.

"In your dad's eyes . . ." Mahir said with a sigh. "Yes. That means not being gay."

"It's not my damned fault, though, is it?" Kinza crossed his arms in front of his chest and drew up his shoulders. "I've always been gay. It's not like I do it to piss him off."

"I know that. I guess it goes way back. Longer than you've been alive, to be honest."

Kinza looked up with interest, some of the bluster deflating. "What happened?"

"Well, before you were around, I was. Your father never forgave me for being gay. He couldn't exactly stop me, so he's taking it out on you. Eventually he'll have to work through his issues, and I'll do what I can to help you. And maybe even him—to get through this. It's not easy. He is concerned, and from his point of view, that makes sense."

Kinza stared at him. "My father's just a douche, and you're making excuses for him?"

"Once you get into law enforcement, you'll see that there are very few truly evil people in the world. Trust me, your father isn't."

Lombardi, on the other hand—

"You're not under Dad's thumb," Kinza said.

"You'll just have to hold out a little more. It's just a few months now. I know that's forever, but we'll get there. We just have to play our cards right, and I'll have a talk with your mother. She might calm him down enough that he'll see some reason."

Kinza didn't look convinced. He broke eye contact and took another giant bite of the sandwich. Once he'd washed that one down, he said, "So are you going to work tonight?"

The aches and twinges in Mahir's body all sided with the unspoken plea in Kinza's voice: *Please stay here tonight.* Could he blame the kid? He'd been here by himself more often than not recently, and he needed allies.

But then there were the kids carrying coke out of the club and into God knew where. Kids disappearing, condemned to fates Mahir didn't even want to imagine. The sooner he and Ridley cracked the case, the fewer kids left the club with coke pellets and didn't come back.

He sighed. "I have to."

"I figured," Kinza growled without looking up. "Whatever. Tell David I said hi."

"I have to *work*."

"Yeah." Kinza picked up his other sandwich and his glass. "And I'll bet you're crashing with David when you're off work, aren't you?"

He didn't wait for confirmation, just took his food and stormed out of the kitchen. Mahir slouched against the counter. One of these days, he'd explain everything to Kinza. When the case was over and the details were no longer on a need-to-know basis, he could be honest with him.

But not today.

Mahir called Khalisah that afternoon, and she confirmed what Kinza had said about the peace talks breaking down. At least she was more reasonable than her husband. For that matter, she agreed that the Europe threats were utter bullshit.

"Will you talk to him, Mahir?"

"He won't listen to me any more than he'll listen to you," Mahir said. "But I'll try. For now, though, I think it's best for Kinza to stay with me."

"Yes," she said. "I agree. He's doing well there? Keeping up with his studies?"

"Yeah, he's fine." *Maybe not too happy with me, and lonelier than any kid his age should be, but at least he has a roof over his head.*

"Thank you for keeping an eye on him," she said. "He's got his father's stubbornness, so it's best they stay apart for now."

"Anytime." Mahir resisted the urge to mention it wasn't Adil's—or Kinza's—stubbornness causing all the issues now. That was a fight for another day.

After he'd hung up, he knocked on Kinza's door.

"It's unlocked."

He pushed it open, but didn't cross the threshold. "Hey, I'm getting ready to go to work."

Lying on his stomach on the bed, nose in a book, Kinza didn't look up. "Whatever."

"You'll be all right?"

"Do I have much choice?"

Mahir rolled his eyes. "I'll be home tomorrow morning."

"Mmm hmm."

Mahir closed the door and went into his own bedroom to change clothes. Out of the casual Saturday-afternoon comfort and into the suit with the suffocating tie. Out with Mahir, in with Saeed. The day when he could retire that persona couldn't come soon enough—provided it involved solving the case. The case was more important than his having to dress like a thug, think with a thug's mind, and act like a resentful, bitter asshole. It could have been him, but it wasn't, and as long as he remembered that, he'd be fine.

And damn him, but he was looking forward to seeing Ridley again, despite the danger and all the other shit piling up on his shoulders. While the case was going, he'd be close to Ridley. Maybe it kept them together—whether it would outlast the pressure of being in the worst place imaginable for two cops was another matter. He'd try, but—

He passed Kinza's bedroom door, made sure Kinza could hear him leave, but Kinza did not emerge from his room. So he left, took the car and drove back to the ferry. He spent most of the time on board trying to clear his head and get into his role, leaving his real life behind on one shore and gradually easing himself into the darkness awaiting him on the other side.

He quickly checked in at the crash pad, but nothing was amiss—nobody was waiting for him there, no letters that might have given away that he hadn't actually slept there. He psyched himself up more and walked to the club.

It was still early. Staff was trickling in, but there was no urgency to any of it. Even in a dangerous business like this, routine eventually set in. Mahir went straight through to Ridley's office, hoping the man would be there. He knocked.

"Enter."

He opened the door and stepped through. Ridley smiled at him from behind the desk—an oddly warm, unguarded expression that

Mahir hoped would never escape while witnesses were around. Or his answering smile. "Just checking in. Everything okay?"

Ridley nodded. "How are you?"

"A bit stiff." Mahir grinned. "Like I've had a really good night."

"Oh, happy accident," Ridley said, and though it sounded sarcastic, it wasn't. In Ridley-speak, it meant *me too*.

Game face, though it was unwieldy to pack the grin back in and try for Saeed's *I don't give a shit* attitude. "Anything special going on today?"

"No, you'll work in the basement, after you've filled in for one of the guys in the lounge. Dentist appointment, apparently he's still high as a kite."

"Ouch."

"Just a couple hours." Ridley stood and walked around the desk, came closer, and *closer*, giving him one of those cold, hard stares, which oddly helped Mahir sober up and slip into his own role. "Ready to work?"

Mahir nodded. Grinning slyly, he said, "Put me in, coach."

Ridley let go of one of those quiet, subtle laughs, the ones that could just as easily unnerve Mahir under the right circumstances. Gesturing at the door, he said, "Let's go."

They both paused, like actors getting into character before going on stage, and then Mahir opened the door. Ridley went first, and the two of them walked out into the club.

"We've had some drunks getting out of hand up here lately." Ridley was definitely back to strictly business, his tone sharp and his gait fast. He got louder as they approached the lounge and its thumping music. "Few of them have tried messing with the girls. Be ready to throw them out on their asses if they do."

"Got it," Mahir said. "Is this a—"

He stopped dead. Every drop of blood in his body turned to ice.

Ridley threw him a sharp look. "What?"

Mahir's throat tightened around his breath. He finally managed to choke out two syllables. "Kinza."

Ridley straightened. He turned his head, and Mahir thought he heard the man curse over the music. Mahir was *this close* to launching himself across the room and elbowing his way between Kinza and the pair of security guys, but Ridley grabbed his arm and shoved him back into the hallway.

He pushed Mahir up against the wall and forced him to look him in the eye. "Keep your head together, Saeed."

No. No games. No acting. That was his nephew out there. He—

"Listen to me," Ridley hissed.

Mahir looked him in the eye, wondering if this part of Ridley really was a separate entity altogether, one completely incapable of realizing Mahir's *goddamned seventeen-year-old nephew was out there.*

"You go out there and make a scene," Ridley said, calmly and evenly, "and you're risking drawing attention to—"

"I don't fucking care," Mahir snapped. "That's my—"

"Shut up," Ridley snarled, shaking him hard. "Listen to yourself." He gestured toward the lounge. "Lombardi is in there. He's in the fucking lounge right now. And what do you think will happen if you go marching in, make a big goddamned scene, and someone calls you Mahir?"

Mahir's whole body froze.

"Because that's what he'll do," Ridley said, gentler now. "One little slip. And when Lombardi asks how you two know each other?" Ridley raised his eyebrows and inclined his head.

Mahir sagged against the wall. "What do I do?"

"Nothing." Ridley let him go and took a step back. He tugged at the cuffs of his jacket, then straightened the lapels. "Let me handle this."

"But he's seen you, too."

"Once." Ridley slipped on his dark sunglasses. "At least, he *thinks* he's seen me before."

Mahir swallowed. He didn't like this. Not one little bit. But he trusted Ridley, and in this dark hallway with the music throbbing against his eardrums, he realized he even trusted him with Kinza. Not that he had much choice.

"Just get him out of here, okay?" he whispered.

"I will." Ridley started toward the lounge. "Stay out of sight."

Of course, curiosity was an evil thing, and Mahir had to know what was happening. He knew the lounge well enough to find a discreet vantage point.

From there, he could see everything.

Kinza. Two of the security guys.

And Lombardi. Fuck. The man had noticed Kinza and had sidled up to him, his Armani-clad arm slithering around Kinza's shoulders. He gestured with his drink, speaking with a smile that might have been charming if Mahir hadn't been fully aware of the things this man was capable of.

Ridley stood between the two security guys, arms folded across his chest. His expression was as blank as it always was, the sunglasses obscuring his eyes.

Now Lombardi spoke to Ridley. More smiling, more gesturing. Was he drunk?

Ridley made a sharp gesture toward the front door. He reached for Kinza's elbow, but a slight twist of Lombardi's torso pulled the boy just out of Ridley's reach. A flicker of . . . of something crossed Ridley's face. An *oh shit* look like the situation wasn't as in his control as he'd hoped.

Lombardi herded Kinza away, toward the back of the lounge. Toward the stairway. The one that led up to his office.

Fuck. Fuck. *Fuck!*

Ridley swept past Mahir with a terse, "Let's go," and they damn near sprinted back to Ridley's office. The second the door was shut, Ridley tore off his sunglasses. He threw them, sending them sliding across his desk before they landed on the floor with a *crunch*. Raking a hand through his hair, he started pacing.

"What happened? What the fuck? What is he doing with—"

"Lombardi just recruited Kinza as a courier."

"I'm going to kill him," Mahir ground out, his heart beating so hard it hurt.

Ridley stopped in his tracks, put both hands on Mahir's arm, gripped him tightly enough that Mahir couldn't immediately free himself, which forced Mahir to lock eyes with Ridley.

"I swear, I'm going to kill him. There won't be enough left of him to have a trial."

"He sure deserves it." Ridley sounded calm. Much too calm, given the situation. If Ridley meant to act as a lightning rod, he wouldn't enjoy the experience.

Ridley's grip tightened. "Nothing has happened yet. Relax."

Relax!? Mahir glared at him. "He's my nephew. If Lombardi touches so much as a hair on his head . . ."

"He's here for a reason."

Mahir paused, wondering if that was meant as an accusation. *You weren't careful enough—he followed you. Your fault.* But it didn't seem that way. Didn't mean he wouldn't sweat bullets over it until he'd freed Kinza from Lombardi's spiderweb.

"We have to do something. Find a way to make him unsuitable. Anything. We can't let him use Kinza as a fucking drug mule." Just saying it made him want to throw up. His brother would have his head. Pickled. And wouldn't he be right, in that leaving his son with Mahir wasn't safe? That this whole crazy idea of living your life the way you wanted meant danger and crime and madness and throwing away a young, promising life on a whim? Damn, he would never be able to look into Adil's eyes again.

"From Lombardi's point of view, Kinza has a stomach and legs, so he's suitable."

Mahir groaned, trying to keep his own stomach where it belonged. "I can't let him do this."

"You don't have a choice at this point."

In a heartbeat, rage replaced nausea. Mahir shoved Ridley back, sending him stumbling into the desk. "Don't have a choice, my ass." He stabbed a finger at Ridley. "I'm getting him out of here."

He started for the door. Had his hand on the doorknob.

Then Ridley was behind him and forced him chest-first into the closed door. "Listen to yourself," Ridley hissed in his ear, his voice as quiet as it was dangerous. "Stop. Just stop."

Mahir closed his eyes, exhaling slowly and struggling to keep his fury contained.

Ridley kept him pinned, pressing so hard against him that Mahir struggled to breathe. "You know damn well what'll happen if you get between Lombardi and Kinza right now." He paused and must have decided Mahir wasn't going to fight him because he backed off just a little. "If you want Kinza to get out of this unscathed, and maybe live long enough to explain to him what's going on here, we *have* to tread lightly."

"Letting my nephew pack cocaine is not treading lightly." Mahir hated the way his voice shook just then. "What if he ODs?"

"I . . ." Ridley sighed. His hand appeared on Mahir's shoulder and squeezed gently. "I don't know. We can come up with a . . . a plan of some sort. But we've both got to keep clear heads. All right?"

Mahir nodded.

Ridley stepped back. For a second, Mahir was tempted to make his break after all. Get the fuck out of this office and give Lombardi the hot-lead injection he so richly deserved. But Ridley was right.

Mahir turned around and pressed his back against the door. "What do we do, then?"

Ridley started pacing again. Damn, that man didn't wear nerves well. He'd been caught off guard, thrown off his game, and the more he paced and gnawed on his thumbnail, the more he unsettled Mahir.

"I don't think we have many options," he said.

"What options *do* we have?"

Ridley stopped. Mahir wished he'd start pacing again. At least then he wouldn't be standing there, nervous energy collecting in his muscles, his whole body tensing as his brow furrowed deeper and deeper. Mahir had a feeling he didn't want to know what was on the man's mind, but he pressed anyway. "Ridley?"

Ridley swallowed and looked Mahir in the eye. "I think we can use this . . . situation to our advantage."

Mahir blinked. "Come again?"

"Hear me out." Ridley put up a hand. "You're not going to like this, but just . . . just hear me out."

Oh. *That* was fucking promising.

"Fine." Mahir pressed his shoulder blades into the door.

Ridley rolled his shoulders, then his neck. "We don't know where the drug mules are going. It's the one thing we haven't been able to figure out, along with where they're going when they stop coming back."

Mahir's gut twisted. *Please don't be going where I think you are with this . . .*

"If we let Kinza make one run, then—"

"No. Absolutely not."

"Listen to me, *Saeed*," Ridley snapped. "Yes, it'll be dangerous. Yes, we're putting him at risk. But he's already in the line of fire, and there's no way to get him out without putting him, us, and the rest of the mules at risk."

"That doesn't mean we need to have him swallowing—"

"Yes, it does." Ridley leaned on the edge of the desk, long fingers drumming beside the blotter. "It's either that or we yank him and send him into witness protection. All we need is for him to get to wherever the other boys are going, and we might have enough to crack this case."

Mahir's shoulders sank. So did his heart. "And then what?"

"Then we have the whole thing, and we take it all down. Lombardi goes off to rot in prison for the rest of his life, so does every one of his goons, his buyers. We're taking everything. Clean out the casino."

Don't remind me it's a fucking gamble.

"His father's going to kill me." *If I consent to this, I won't even fight back. I'll deserve it.*

"Yeah, well, we'll cross that bridge when we get there." Ridley fixed his eyes on Mahir's. "It's unfortunate, it's a fucking disaster, but it's also the break we needed, if we're playing this right and if your nephew can keep his shit together for a few days. Beats trying to get to one of the others without knowing whether or not we can trust them. At least we know where Kinza's loyalties are."

"With me." That, at least, he didn't doubt, though he'd done fuck all recently to deserve that.

"Then it's decided, isn't it?"

Just make the damned decision. Don't make me be complicit in this. I'll never be able to forgive myself.

"Isn't it?"

Oh, you bastard.

Mahir lifted his shoulders. He hated himself, and the only word he could get out was "*In'shallah*." God's will. They'd need a great deal of luck to get out of this, and it would keep him awake at night, but now that the rage and despair in his brain started to cool, he saw that it made sense. A horrible, twisted sense, not unlike hacking off your own arm if it were trapped under a boulder, but sense nonetheless.

Ridley nodded. "I'm sorry, but it is the best we can do."

Mahir rubbed his face. "Fuck."

Ridley stepped closer and stopped. He touched Mahir's arm. "We'll do everything we can to keep him safe. If there was any other way to do this, you know I'd never even dream of putting him in this position."

"You didn't," Mahir whispered. "I pissed him off. Left him alone when he needed someone there, and then made him think I wasn't actually working when I said I was." He sighed. "Should've seen this coming, but . . ."

"There's no point in blaming yourself," Ridley said softly. "We'll get him—and ourselves—out of this."

He met Ridley's eyes. "You know damn well you can't promise that any more than I can."

CHAPTER SIXTEEN

Ridley didn't say anything, which only made the cold dread in Mahir's gut even colder and heavier. Yeah, he did know, and he didn't argue when he was called out on it. Damn him. His arrogance could've come in handy right about now.

"So what do we do? We don't work with the mules."

"Kinza will be able to leave," Ridley said. "If he's got a brain, he'll go home. Back to your place. Once he's there, we—"

"Oh shit." Mahir's spine straightened. "What if he talks? Before we have a chance to tell him what's going on? All he has to do is say he knows us, and—"

"Relax," Ridley said. "When I talked to Lombardi, I said, 'How do we know we can trust this kid? We've never seen him before.'" A subtle grin pulled up the corners of his mouth. "Apparently he's a smart kid because I gave him a look, and he didn't say a damned word."

Mahir laughed, a little much-needed relief coursing through him. "Guess that balls-withering look of yours comes in handy sometimes."

Ridley chuckled. "It does." The chuckle died. "You'll have to talk to him. Tell him everything he needs to know. It's too risky for me to go back to your place with you."

Mahir nodded. "All right."

"I want him to wear a GPS tracker." Ridley hesitated. "Except I don't know what security measures the boys go through. They've found the trackers I've planted on them before, and if he's caught with one . . ."

Mahir shuddered.

Ridley chewed his lip. "Much as I don't like the idea, we may have to send him on two runs."

Mahir stared at him.

"Once to feel out the route and the routine," Ridley said. "And once with the tracker."

"He'll be expected to recruit after that. That's . . ."

"Worst-case scenario, it's a good moment to get somebody else in if this doesn't work out. I'm sure we can hustle somebody up who's more professional, but if we're just a little lucky, Kinza's all we need."

"Oh."

"We won't let him recruit an innocent, don't worry. It's stopping right there. I promise."

"You can't."

"Well—" Ridley shifted. "—anything he can tell us is gold for this case. Every bit."

"All right." Mahir closed his eyes and tried to collect his thoughts. "At least I get now why you want to stop doing undercover work."

"Yes. Welcome to my world." Ridley closed the distance again and touched Mahir on the shoulder, looked deep into his eyes, and the tingle was not so much sexual as an odd kind of physical trust. Ridley touched his face, and Mahir relaxed a bit. "You good?"

"A bit better."

They both started when somebody banged on the door from the outside.

Ridley stepped aside, and Mahir pushed himself off the door. They both tugged at cuffs and collars, straightening clothes like they'd been caught in more than a reassuring non-embrace. An exchanged glance, a nod from Mahir, and Ridley reached for the doorknob.

Mahir played it as cool and casual as he could, brushing imaginary lint off his jacket as if he was bored in the office and annoyed with the intrusion. The door obscured the person on the other side—and likely hid Mahir from sight, as well—and Ridley and the intruder exchanged a few terse, hushed words.

Ridley closed the door and faced Mahir. He released a huff of breath, his obvious relief unnerving Mahir even more.

"What's wrong?"

Ridley shook his head. "Oh, that. It—" He waved a hand toward the door. "Just Gray coming by, said I need to check on a few things downstairs. So I'd better get going." He held Mahir's gaze and swallowed hard. "Guess it's a good thing we weren't . . ."

"Yeah. Good thing."

They didn't dare risk so much as a kiss before they left. Mahir was sure even a single hair out of place would give away everything they'd done in that office.

On the way down the hall, Ridley said, "Stay in the lounge for the evening."

Mahir gritted his teeth. He wanted to be downstairs where he could keep an eye on Kinza in case the pimp was giving him the grand tour. But orders were orders. Presumably, Ridley knew what he was doing.

Mahir didn't see Lombardi, Kinza, or even Ridley during his shift. The lounge stayed fairly quiet. He was bored out of his skull the entire time, desperate for something—an unruly drunk or anything, really—to give him an outlet for all this nervous energy. He hadn't been this agitated since the coke, and he needed to do something about it. Soon.

Finally, his break rolled around. He left the lounge and went back into the sparsely furnished break room. There, four of the guys were playing cards at the wobbly folding table. And as Mahir crossed the room to the refrigerator, four sets of eyes followed him.

Great. Just what he needed. More bullshit.

"Hey," one of them said. "Camel jockey."

Mahir rolled his eyes but then turned around, eyebrows up.

"You play five-card draw?" the bald, smoking man asked.

"Not terribly well."

"Good." The man waved a hand at Keith. "Beat it, Keith."

Keith huffed and tossed his cards into the middle of the table. His chair scraped on the floor, and he stood. The other three looked up at Mahir.

"I, um . . ." He cleared his throat. "I only have a few minutes. Break."

"Enough time for a couple of hands." The vague note of menace in the bald guy's voice made Mahir even more nervous. "*Sit.*"

Mahir thought about blowing him off, but that menacing tone and the looks coming from all three players told him he ought to play their game—the one on the table and the unspoken one whose rules he definitely didn't understand yet. Such was the joy of working with volatile thugs. Like Fallujah all over again—never sure who to trust, with sudden reversals that meant all the hard-won progress had gone down the shitter, leaving nothing but soul-deep weariness and an overall loss of faith in humanity.

He took a seat in the folding chair across from the guy who'd summoned him.

While one of the others shuffled the deck, the bald guy took a drag off his cigarette and glared at Mahir.

"Seems like the boss man likes you, haji," he said.

Mahir laughed. "Well, I think it's in all of our best interests to stay off Lombardi's shit list."

"I ain't talking about Lombardi." The bald guy crushed his cigarette in the ashtray with more force than was necessary. "I'm talking about Ridley."

"Ridley? He doesn't like anybody." Mahir leaned back a bit but stopped when the rickety chair groaned.

"Uh-huh." Bald Guy wasn't buying it. After the thing with Kinza and his nervous energy, Mahir's self-control was becoming paper-thin. The only thing that kept him quiet was that, if this degenerated into a five-way brawl, it was likely the haji who'd get his ass fired. And while that seemed like a good option to ensure that Lombardi lived to see his trial, it also meant deserting Ridley.

"Thing is, he likes you," Bald Guy continued. "He's spending an awful lot of time in his office with you."

Mahir shook his head. "Really? Wish he didn't. I get chewed out a lot more than I need."

"Chewing is right," one of the guys muttered.

Mahir glanced over his shoulder at him. "He's got a fine ass on him, but I'm not risking my job for that."

Bald Guy clicked his fingers in front of Mahir's face, and Mahir flipped his attention back to him. "Something's happening in there. He's easier to deal with when he's had you in that office."

Very subtle. "Intimidating the fuck out of me relaxes him?" He shrugged. "I have no idea what game he's playing, but it's not that. I need the money."

"We all need the money." Bald Guy smirked. "Question is, you been earning some bonuses in there?"

Mahir rolled his eyes. He looked at the guy holding the deck of cards. "You going to deal or what?"

The one with the cards glanced back and forth between Mahir and Bald Guy, looking a bit like a mouse between two hissing tomcats. Bald Guy waved a hand, and the dealer started dealing, sharp flicks of his wrist sending cards spinning across the table to each player in turn.

Mahir picked up his cards one at a time, watching the suits and symbols forming a shitty hand between his fingers. Pair of fives. Yeah. That would get him far.

Once the cards had been dealt, they all looked at their hands. Without lifting his gaze, Bald Guy said, "Lombardi finds out you two are blowing each other or whatever it is you're doing, you're both going to be in holes in the ground. You know that, don't you?" This time, he did look up, and the menace in his eyes had intensified dramatically.

Mahir tried to tell himself the guy was holding one of those hands—a full house, four of a kind, a flush—that made any man's balls drop. The most timid, poker-faced player might bluff in his bets and not offer any tells that he was holding a game-winning hand.

"Is that a threat?" Mahir asked, narrowing his eyes slightly and adopting a mocking, singsong tone. "Are you planning on trotting up to Lombardi's office and telling him you think Saeed and Ridley are sitting in a tree, K-I-S-S-I-N-G?"

The other men snickered, hiding behind their cards.

Bald Guy's lips pulled tight. "He'll figure it out on his own."

Mahir laughed in spite of the cold flooding his veins. "There ain't a thing to figure out, my friend. So I guess the question is, shouldn't you be hitting the gym?"

"The . . . the gym?" Bald Guy cocked his head.

"Yeah." Mahir tapped his own biceps, then pointed at Bald Guy. "You're looking a little soft over there. Might want to get yourself back in shape if you'll be digging a hole in the ground sometime soon."

"Me?" Bald Guy threw his head back and laughed. "I won't be the one—"

"You will if you accuse Ridley of fucking a member of Lombardi's staff," Mahir said coldly. "Who do you think Lombardi trusts more? Your idiot ass that can barely be trusted to stand watch over a room full of drunks and three strippers? Or Ridley?"

The other guys didn't laugh. They did duck a little deeper behind their cards, probably praying that they could disappear completely. Fucking pussies.

"I have to get back to work." Mahir stood and tossed his cards onto the table. One of them slid off and into Bald Guy's lap, but the man didn't take his eyes off Mahir.

"You're on thin ice, sand nigger," Bald Guy growled.

Don't mix your metaphors on my account, asshole. "Well, unless you have proof that there's something going on, I think your accusation is on even thinner ice."

"Proof?" Bald Guy grinned, revealing three gaps where he'd lost various teeth. "Fine. Enjoy your evening, Saeed."

That wasn't the response Mahir was expecting. He maintained his own poker face, keeping a smug, arrogant grin in place until he'd left the break room, but his heart was pounding as he headed back into the lounge. What if the guy did have proof? Though, wouldn't he have played his cards differently, then? He'd been too off-balance to be holding all aces, so he likely didn't have anything. Didn't mean that Mahir goading him hadn't set something in motion in his head. Now Bald Guy likely wanted proof and would stop at nothing to get it.

Why was this whole thing feeling like a barbed-wire collar pulling tighter with every breath?

Above all, it meant no more conspirator meetings with Ridley, not in that damned office—bugs weren't that expensive anymore, and Bald Guy likely knew how to use them—not in Saeed's crash pad, since they all knew where he lived, and most definitely not at home, as it would put Kinza even more at risk. That left . . .? Hell, they could hardly slip each other notes like schoolboys.

In the lounge, he kept internally begging for a fight or somebody who'd volunteered his drunken head to be broken for sheer stress relief, but it seemed drunks were a bit like cats and knew too damn well when there was a dark cloud hovering over them, looking for a target to zap with lightning.

The hours crept past, and he couldn't do much more than keep his eyes open and look forbidding. Given his mood, that was easy. But it didn't get any easier when the club closed and he'd seen neither tip nor tail of Lombardi, or even Ridley, for that matter. Again, the noncore staff left early, leaving security to check every nook and cranny to make sure every last passed-out drunk ended up on the street. Normally, he sought Ridley's proximity then—or volunteered—but not doing so at least sent the message he'd understood the warning.

Bald Guy made eye contact with him entirely too often for comfort, too, touching the corner of his eye with that age-old *I'm watching you* gesture.

Mahir forced himself not to show his discomfort. Let the man suspect whatever he wanted. As long as Mahir and Ridley didn't give him any evidence, be it a glance or the lingering scent of sex in Ridley's office, then he'd have nothing but suspicions. And even that snaggletoothed idiot probably knew better than to go running to Lombardi's office with half-baked accusations.

When the shift ended, Mahir left without exchanging so much as a word or a look with Ridley, and hightailed it back to Saeed's crash pad. He hung out there for a short while, giving anyone who might've followed him a chance to get bored and take off.

Then he headed down to the docks. It wasn't a long walk, but he took an erratic route, circling two blocks twice apiece and backtracking down one alley.

Certain he hadn't been followed, he walked onto the ferry amid all the bleary-eyed morning commuters. Their collective Monday morning fatigue should have reminded him of all the aches in his bones, both from his shift and the night before, but he was still too wound up. When he finally slept at some point today, he'd probably pass out for ten solid hours, but for now, he was wide-awake, barely keeping himself from pacing back and forth on the deck while the boat made its slow journey across the Sound.

Eventually, the boat arrived in Bremerton, and just in time to contend with both the ferry commuters waiting on that side and the long line of cars waiting to get through the Navy base's gate. All traffic is finite, though, and finally, he broke free from the snarl and drove—perhaps a little faster than he should have—the rest of the way home.

In the house, he tossed his keys on the table and went down the hall. Kinza's door was shut. With his heart in his throat and a few whispered prayers, he knocked quietly. No movement, no response. He knocked again, louder this time, and to his tremendous relief, someone stirred on the other side.

Kinza opened the door. He was even blearier eyed than the morning commuters, and wearing only a pair of sweatpants. "What?"

"We need to talk."

Kinza rolled his eyes. "I'm trying to sleep."

"Too bad." Mahir nodded down the hall. "I'll put some coffee on."

Kinza wrinkled his nose. "I hate coffee."

"Then you'll have to find another way to wake yourself up," Mahir said. "But this can't wait."

With another eye roll, the kid reached for a rumpled T-shirt on the floor. He shuffled down the hall after Mahir and dropped into a chair at the kitchen table while Mahir started the coffee. Kinza hugged himself, arms folded low on his chest and back hunched over like he was cold, the way he often did when he was awake against his will.

"We need to talk about last night." Mahir pulled a coffee mug from the cabinet.

"Look, I'm sorry I followed you. I was just curious where you were going."

"Yeah, well. I'm not sure you realize what you're tangled up with now." He shot a glance at Kinza, whose sullen expression told him it was completely lost on the kid.

"And you work there?"

"Undercover," Mahir snapped. "So I have a pretty good idea what's going on and what you signed up for."

"I didn't," Kinza muttered.

"You told him you're not interested?" *Good boy,* Mahir thought, though it only changed the tension to a different kind of fear. Lombardi might not look kindly on that. You really couldn't run a drug ring on the moods of teenagers unless you had a very heavy hand and deep pockets. But if buying them didn't work . . .

"I went there to find you, not pick up jobs from shady assholes. Can I go back to bed now?"

"You stay put." Mahir sat down opposite. "What did you tell him?"

"Nothing. Told him I'd be back, but I'm not going."

"Did you tell him anything? Where you live?"

"Gave him a fake address and a fake name." Kinza rolled his eyes, like those were basic high school skills. "He won't find me."

Mahir deflated, though his paranoid mind could come up with a hundred reasons why that wasn't enough to shake Lombardi off.

Scumbags like that always had an ace up their sleeve; it couldn't possibly be that easy. "What did he want to know?"

"How old I was, if I wanted to earn a lot of money, if there was anything I really wanted and couldn't afford."

"And what did you tell him?"

Kinza pulled up his shoulders. "Just that you can't buy people's time."

Ouch.

Mahir rested his elbow on the table. "How much did he tell you? About what you'd be doing if you went to work for him?" He paused. "Did you ask him what the job entailed?"

"Sure, yeah." Kinza shrugged. "I was curious, and he didn't really seem to want to take no for an answer."

Oh shit. "So how much did he tell you?"

"Said I'd be helping him move merchandise."

"Merchandise such as . . . ?"

"He didn't say."

Well, that was good. "And what did he say to do next? To take him up on the job?"

"Said to come by the club this weekend. And to call him if I wasn't going to—"

"Call him?" Mahir's hand thumped the table hard enough to make both of them jump. "He gave you a number?"

"I . . . Yeah." Kinza furrowed his brow. "Why?"

"Where? Did he have you put it in your phone? Or did he give you a card?"

Kinza eyed him like he'd lost his mind. "He gave me a phone, actually."

"*What?* Where is it?" Mahir demanded, heart thundering. "The phone. Where is it?"

"It's in my jacket." Kinza made a lazy gesture toward the hall. "In my—"

"Get it. Now." Mahir realized he was talking to Kinza like a suspect or something. Gentler now, he said, "I need to see it."

"Uh. Okay." Kinza got up and left the kitchen.

Behind Mahir, the coffeemaker dinged, but he didn't think he'd need any stimulants now. Lombardi had money coming out his ass, but even he was too savvy a businessman to hand out throwaway phones to any potential mule. Why this one? Why Kinza?

Kinza returned and held out a phone. It was one of those cheap models that predated smartphones. The kind used exclusively by kids, people who refused to join the twenty-first century, and criminals.

And the kind with the battery, antenna, and casing that went perfectly with a small tracking device. Quite possibly a listening device, too, so anything Mahir did to the phone, or anything he said around it, might be picked up by ears on the other side of the water. His skin crawled. So much for this house being a safe place for him and Kinza.

He put a finger to his lips, which drew a puzzled look from Kinza, but the boy got the message and stayed silent.

Mahir pulled a notepad out of a drawer and quickly scrawled across it.

Let's go get breakfast.

Kinza cocked his head but still didn't say anything.

Mahir wrote, *We'll "accidentally" leave it in a booth.* He gestured at the phone with his pen.

Teenagers did stupid shit. They misplaced expensive things all the time. If anyone gave Kinza a hard time, all he had to do was say he'd lost it, and there was no proof his uncle—his cop uncle—had arranged the phone's convenient disappearance. Even better if somebody pocketed it for the credit on it and then got rid of it when it was used up. It wasn't worth much, but somebody desperate enough might just do it for the few dollars.

Kinza took the pen and chewed on it, as if considering a math problem. Then wrote, *I called Tyson on it.*

Mahir stared at him, then at the words forming on the pad.

My battery was dead.

Oh, wonderful. So the phone vanished, the fake address didn't work out, but they could always show up outside Tyson's door and ask him where Kinza was actually staying. Followed by showing up on *this* doorstep, asking him why he would use a wrong address—and whatever Kinza answered to that likely wouldn't make a lick of difference to hardened criminals who made a lot of people *vanish*. They might hurt Kinza not because he posed a real risk to the operation but because he was inconsequential and a loose end, and because Lombardi didn't like getting messed around.

Kinza looked at him and added, *That bad?*

Mahir rubbed his face, wished he could ask anybody for advice or bounce a few ideas around, check if he was getting paranoid or just damn realistic, given the people and the sums of money involved. Considering those factors, life was cheap.

Mahir took the pad.

Get dressed. Come outside.

A few moments later, he had an overtired teenager sitting with him on the back deck, shivering and downcast, and Mahir wished at least he could hug him close and tell him all would be okay. It wasn't Kinza's fault, just a damn inconvenient combination of factors, bad luck and evil people being too competent at what they did.

Though the throwaway phone was in the house and any listening device it carried wouldn't be able to hear them now, Mahir kept his voice down. "I don't want to get you involved in this, Kinza. Any of it."

"What's going on?" Kinza asked. "What are you doing over there?"

"I can't tell you much now, but that guy who's trying to hire you? He's not someone you want to mess with. At all."

"Okay, I won't." Kinza shrugged. "We'll ditch the phone, and I won't go back."

Mahir blew out a breath. "It may not be that simple."

"What do you mean?"

"Where were you when you used the phone to call Tyson?"

Kinza pointed over his shoulder with his thumb, and Mahir winced. Just what he'd been afraid of.

"I can't let you keep staying here," he said. "I'm going to—"

"You're going to send me back to my dad?"

Mahir avoided the kid's eyes. "I'm not even sure how safe that is. Depends on how much you registered on the guy's radar. If he gave you a throwaway phone when he hasn't even hired you on, considering how many teenagers he *does* hire, you might have piqued his interest."

Kinza paled. "So he'll . . . come looking for me?"

After you called Tyson, he may have already found you.

"He might." Mahir put a hand on Kinza's arm, just the way Ridley had touched Mahir's last night when he'd tried to calm him down. "I'm not going to let anything happen to you, but I might have to move you. Somewhere."

Kinza stared at him. "But he didn't hire me. Why would he be so worried about me?"

"Did you say anything about me? Or about cops in the family?"

"He didn't ask about my family," Kinza said. "And, uh, your boyfriend kind of looked at me like I'd better be careful what I said, so I didn't mention I knew you or him."

"Good. Good." Mahir patted the kid's arm. "The less you're connected to us, the better."

"You really were working." Kinza swallowed. "With David."

Mahir nodded.

"Then why was he here?" Kinza nodded toward the house. "Bringing your undercover work home with you?" Under the taut playfulness, there was a faint accusation. *Bringing him to the place where I'm living, too? Putting* me *in danger?*

"It wasn't a wise idea," Mahir said. "But it's done. And now I need to get rid of this phone and figure out where you'll be safest until everything blows over."

"I can stay with my sister," Kinza said quietly, folding in on himself.

Though that wasn't a bad idea, something in Mahir's gut clenched at the idea of Kinza being away from him. Being anywhere near Mahir put Kinza into some measure of danger now, but logic be damned, Mahir wanted the kid close-by so he could protect him.

"We'll figure it out." Mahir started toward the house. "Let's get rid of that phone. Not a word until it's gone. *Capisce?*"

Kinza just nodded. They went back into the house and into their separate bedrooms to change clothes. Fatigue from last night's shift was starting to catch up with Mahir, but he wasn't going to sleep anyway until that goddamned phone was gone. So the sooner, the better.

He opened his bedroom door and skidded to a halt when Kinza was there waiting for him. The kid was so pale he was nearly translucent and held up the tablet they'd been writing on.

There's someone here.

Where? Mahir mouthed, and Kinza nodded toward the front door. *Stay in your room.* Mahir checked the window blinds. Sure enough, in the joyless gray predawn light, a black car sat in the drive outside, one guy at the wheel, and the other—

A man-sized shadow passed in front of the window, making Mahir recoil and curse their luck. Now would be a great time for Ridley to show up, though he hoped that the goons wouldn't raise hell, not on account of a kid who knew nothing yet. Just why was Lombardi so dead set on Kinza?

He blew out a breath and went back into the kitchen to pick up a pistol. If the goons had come to play hard, they'd bitten off a great deal more than they ever had a chance of chewing.

He traced the goon's progress around the house, maybe looking for an easy way in, but Mahir had made sure the house wasn't that easy to break into when he'd bought it. It didn't offer an obvious entry point, which would dissuade an average burglar. For somebody more determined, however, it wouldn't stop him for long.

Eventually, the doorbell chimed.

Chimed again.

Kinza was smart enough to stay in his room as he'd been told. Of course, they knew somebody was inside. Mahir looked through the peephole, staying to the side of the door.

Two guys in suits, looking just official enough to pull off "trouble at school" for an unwary parent. And a hell of a lot more trouble than that for Mahir and Kinza.

He couldn't open the door. While he didn't recognize the suits, they could very well be on Lombardi's payroll, which meant they could come to the club and recognize him.

"The boss gave you the kid's number, didn't he?" one of them muttered. "Call him up and tell him to get out here."

Mahir's heart dropped. He hurried up the stairs as quickly and quietly as he could and lunged for the phone on the counter, but before he could grab it and silence it, the shrill ringtone pierced the silence of the upper floor.

Kinza appeared in the doorway, eyes wide. *What do we do?* he mouthed.

Mahir hesitated, then thrust the phone at him, mouthing back, *Answer it.*

Kinza's eyebrows rose higher. Mahir nodded toward the phone and shoved it closer to him.

The kid took the phone and, with the press of a button, silenced the screeching tone. "Hello?"

Mahir leaned in close so he could hear the voice on the other end.

"Kinza," came the psychotically cheerful response. "So nice of you to answer your phone."

"Uh. Who is this?"

"My employer gave you this phone for an express purpose." The cheerfulness was gone. The psychotic . . . not so much. "We're a little disappointed in you, kid."

Kinza groped around with his free hand, brushing Mahir's, and then gripped his uncle's hand so hard it hurt. Mahir offered a reassuring squeeze.

"D-disappointed? Why?"

"Well, you haven't called for one thing." The other man had perfected the art of combining *I'm not angry, just disappointed* and *you're a fucking dead man* into the same voice. "But you also didn't tell us you were living with a cop."

Kinza's death grip threatened to grind all the bones in Mahir's hand to dust. Between his own pounding heart and the pain in his hand, it was all Mahir could do to stay calm and collected.

"Living . . . with . . ."

"We know you're living with Detective Mahir Hussain. One of Seattle PD's finest."

Kinza's eyes widened. Mahir's blood turned cold.

"We also know you're home," the man continued. "So why don't you come outside and have a chat with us?"

"I'm . . . uh . . ." He looked at Mahir and mouthed, *What do I do?*

Mahir grabbed the notepad and scrawled, *Your uncle is a cop but doesn't know anything about your employer.*

Kinza repeated it. Then he lowered his voice and added, "He's still asleep. If I wake him up, he's going to get really pissed." He paused, and even more timidly said, "Please don't make me come out there and wake him up."

Mahir blinked. *Nice one.*

There was silence on the other end. Then, "Listen, kid. We don't fuck around with cops. I'm going to drive away now, but my employer will see you in his office at three o'clock this afternoon. Am I clear?"

Kinza lost what little color he had left. "Yeah. Three. Got it."

The guy on the other end must have hung up because Kinza visibly deflated, so much that Mahir gently moved him over to a chair to sit down, then took the phone out of his hand and switched it off. He put an arm around Kinza, and they both sat there, shaken. Kinza looked as green as Mahir felt. When Mahir's heart had stopped racing, he led Kinza downstairs to the furthest part of the house from the phone.

"Well, that means a change of plans." *And so much for making a swift, elegant escape.* That they knew about him—Mahir—jeopardized everything. Would Lombardi truly have the balls to hire a cop's nephew to do his dirty work? Surely, a cop would move heaven and earth to find a member of his family.

Unless, of course, Lombardi had an ax to grind or felt he was untouchable. Most criminals had the good sense to stay out of a cop's hair, but Lombardi might be of the species that considered it a dick-waving contest, showing how badass he was by not even stopping where every other crime lord would think twice to proceed.

"What plan?"

"I'm trying to work that out. They got you, they got me, and they got Tyson."

"Tyson?"

"Yeah, though they don't really need him anymore to find you."

Kinza hugged himself and bent over like he was going to be sick, so Mahir rubbed his shoulder, trying to impart some of that grown-up reassurance that Kinza might still be too young to know was bullshit. Hopefully. "Listen. Lombardi—the man who talked to you? He's smart, and he's resourceful, but he's also pretty damn insane if he messes with a cop's family."

"Doesn't mean he won't."

"Nope. But it is a flaw. The guy's good, but he can be beaten."

Kinza looked up, half-skeptical and half-hopeful, and Mahir already hated himself for what he was about to say. "He can always get what he wants, or at least think he does. The bastard likes a challenge, but he likes winning even more. You can let him win . . . and help me bring him down."

And just how many codes of ethics was he violating right there?

"Help you on your job?"

"Yes. I'm sorry I dragged you into it. I'd never suggest it if there were any other way. I don't want you anywhere near this case, but . . ."

"Because of the missing kids?"

Mahir sighed heavily. "I just don't want you anywhere near Lombardi or that club."

"So, how do I help without going anywhere near Lombardi or the club?"

"I said I didn't want you near them." Mahir rubbed the back of his neck and sighed again. "I didn't say it was avoidable."

Kinza squirmed beside him. "What am I supposed to do?"

"You'll go talk to Lombardi today. Play up what you hinted about on the phone, that your uncle is a volatile bastard and you're itching to get out of here."

"Why would I do that?"

"Because he'll see it as a way to manipulate you into working for him. Offer you a huge chunk of money that'll give you the means to leave."

Kinza nodded slowly. "And all I have to do is move his, uh, merchandise?"

Mahir swallowed. "It's not quite that simple."

"What do you mean?" He paused. "It's drugs, isn't it?"

"Yeah. And let's just say you don't move them by hiding them in your pockets."

"So how—" Kinza released a strangled sound. "*Oh*."

Mahir cocked his head. "You know about this stuff?"

"I saw a documentary on it. The guys who swallow drugs and take them through airports."

Mahir's stomach twisted again. Airports. It hadn't even occurred to him the boys might not be staying local. What if they were flying somewhere? Potentially outside his and even Ridley's jurisdiction? There was, after all, a major international airport a stone's throw from Seattle.

He took Kinza's hand and squeezed gently. "Let's take this one step at a time, all right? Go in and meet with Lombardi like he asked. Find out what he wants, what he's offering. Any information you think might be relevant, you give to me. Even if you see a postcard on his desk from Fiji or something. Anything."

Kinza nodded. "Okay. Yeah, I'll do that." He looked around the room, shoulders hunching as he seemed to shrink in on himself. "Is it still safe to come back here?"

"Yeah. This is probably the best place for you to go, since they already know you live here."

"What about you?"

"We'll play it by ear. If you convince them you have no loyalty to me, and no reason to come tell me about what's going on, they probably won't keep too close an eye on the house. But . . . we'll see."

"Okay." Kinza closed his eyes and released a breath. "I'm sorry I followed you. I made this into such a mess."

Mahir hugged his nephew close. "It wasn't your fault. I didn't give you a lot of reason to trust me. But it's done, and we're in this together." He drew back and looked Kinza in the eyes. "We're in this together, and we're going to get out of it together. Okay?"

Kinza held his gaze, then nodded slowly. "Okay." He chewed his lip. "What about David?"

"What about him?"

"Is he . . . um . . ."

Mahir froze. It was dangerous enough that Ridley had tipped his hand and revealed himself as a deep-cover agent to Mahir. The more people who knew, the more danger everyone—especially Ridley—was in. "He's Lombardi's head of security. Runs everything."

"And he's your boyfriend."

Mahir nodded. "Something like that."

Kinza's eyes widened. "But he's been *here*."

Mahir cringed. Shit. He'd forgotten about that. "Okay. Okay. Look, I . . ." He rubbed the bridge of his nose. "Undercover work involves a lot of deception. The more people know, the more chances they have to accidentally out someone. You understand?"

"Uh, kinda."

"So, I'm . . . Okay, I lied. I'm trying to protect all of us, that's all."

"Lied about which part?"

"David's not one of the bad guys. How about we just leave it at that?"

Kinza eyed him, some of that distrust creeping into his expression.

"I had good reasons," Mahir said softly. "When this is all over, I'll tell you everything. Okay?"

Kinza regarded him suspiciously, but then relaxed. "Okay."

"Good." The thought crept in to ask whether Kinza had liked "David," but that would mean revealing too much of his hand—and felt incredibly premature to boot. Maybe Mahir was just a sucker for harmony and wanted the two most important people in his life right now to like each other. Though, admittedly, right now that "relationship" with Ridley wouldn't really hold up under any closer scrutiny, least of all his brother's assertions that gay relationships were volatile, harmful, and driven mostly by sex and nothing else. No mutual responsibility. No care.

He shook his head and remembered how Ridley had surrendered to him, trusted him. How much Kinza showing up and Mahir's response to it had rattled a man who'd had it together enough for eighteen months to play arch henchman to one of the biggest scumbags in Seattle. That counted for something, didn't it?

He patted Kinza on the shoulder and straightened. "We can rehearse what you're going to say before you go. I think we both need to catch a couple of winks."

Kinza nodded. "If I can ever sleep again."

"Consider it a practical on-the-job exercise. This is the kind of person you're going to stop if you're going to join the FBI. Just possibly even worse."

Kinza lifted a hand, signaling he'd heard enough. "I'll put on some music where the phone is."

"Don't rely on it, but I'd go with something loud and horrible."

Kinza rolled his eyes, and Mahir took that as a small hope that the kid would be all right. The alternative was too bleak to contemplate.

He went up into his own bedroom after another sweep of the house and the street outside. Nobody in sight, which wasn't that surprising, given that most of these people were nocturnal.

He poured the stale coffee away, drank a big glass of water, and went to his own bedroom to catch a few hours of sleep. He had to rely on his brain with everything that would happen tomorrow, and though sleep wasn't easy, he eventually managed it. He only woke when a body joined him in bed, and Kinza slung his arms around him. Given the circumstances, Mahir just pulled him closer and let him sleep there. The kid probably just needed to know he still had someone. Everything going on right now was terrifying enough for Mahir. He could only imagine how it was for Kinza.

CHAPTER SEVENTEEN

Mahir was on duty downstairs again. This was the last place he wanted to be, keeping an eye on the boys coming in and picking up their merchandise for today's run while Kinza was upstairs with Lombardi. It was about as comforting as watching gory autopsy videos while waiting to hear if someone had come out of an emergency surgery.

All the boys took antacids to keep their stomach acid from chewing through the condom-wrapped cocaine pellets, and the more he watched them methodically working the huge pellets down their throats, the more he could have used some of those antacids himself.

Mahir wasn't as devout a Muslim as his family would have liked, but he caught himself sending a few pleas skyward throughout the evening. Acknowledging that Allah's will was good and that Allah knew what he was doing but still trying to bargain for Kinza's safety. That didn't offer much comfort, though. His faith had been shaky enough recently without having to ask himself if Allah's will really was good when a man had to also ask, *but if you could find it in your heart to watch over this poor kid . . .*

He shook his head and tore his gaze away from a pair of boys behind a box of coke-packed condoms and forced himself not to think about them or God or anything else except making sure no one came through that door who didn't belong in here.

You mean like these boys? They don't belong in here.

He scrubbed a hand over his face. No wonder Ridley was done with deep-cover work. This was bullshit.

The door opened. The two boys looked up, and Mahir's head snapped toward the door.

Gray closed it behind him. "I'm relieving you. Boss man wants to see you in his office." A hint of a leer told Mahir exactly who he was talking about, but for the sake of appearances, he asked anyway.

"Which boss?"

Gray sniffed. "Which one do you think?"

Mahir glared at him and didn't move.

Rolling his eyes, Gray said, "Ridley, idiot. Who else would be looking for you?"

This whole *he's sweet on you* shtick could go right to hell. He had no patience for this shit. He didn't respond, didn't even grimace, relieved to get out of there and yet keenly aware that it didn't mean he was out of danger. Not at all. Just a different set of bullets he had to dodge. And he somehow needed to get Ridley to understand that the game had completely changed.

He did not look forward to that.

When he knocked on Ridley's door, it opened almost immediately. Ridley gave him a terse once-over, then stepped to the side only enough that Mahir could enter without brushing him. The door closed behind them with a sound of finality that made Mahir jump despite himself.

"Did you see who's in the club?"

Mahir grimaced now. "Some new courier. Another sand nigger. They already said. That's my business how?" *Academy Awards committee, take note.*

Ridley took a step back, looking genuinely surprised, then tilted his head in question.

And dammit, but they did have rapport—a kind of physical understanding, maybe from all the sex or having to watch other people closely, or from being in the same kind of mind-set. Mahir glanced demonstratively around and tapped his ear and eye, hoping that whoever was trying to trap them had gone for the cheaper option.

"Anything else you wanted?" He sounded abrasive and insolent even to his own ears, but damn, if a little playacting saved all their hides, he could keep that up no problem. "Because if you keep calling me to your office, people will think we're fucking."

Ridley's eyes lit up in understanding. "Really? Who said that?"

"By now? Everybody. And from what I'm getting, there's at least one guy who'd love your job."

"Who?"

"Somebody." Mahir shrugged.

Ridley was on him like lightning, grabbing him by the throat and nailing him against the wall with his body weight, strong fingers around Mahir's windpipe. Hell, he was scary, and he pressed up against Mahir in a weird mix of danger and trust and conspiracy that had Mahir more breathless than the vise around his throat. "Who?!"

Mahir shook his head, then mouthed, *Bald Guy*, running a hand over his head and then over his chin, indicating the man's leather-daddy-type goatee.

Ridley's brow furrowed, and his lip started to curl just enough to make Mahir wonder if he'd pushed him too far. Or if Ridley was so pissed off at Bald Guy, he might fuck up anyone in his path, which right now meant . . . Saeed.

All at once, Ridley released him and shoved away from both Mahir and the door. "Get the fuck out of my office."

"I thought you wanted to see me for something," Mahir said with just the right amount of snark to make sure anyone listening thought there was anything but a lover's quarrel—or lover's anything else—going on in here. "Should I get back to work?"

With his back to Mahir, Ridley waved a hand toward the door. "Gray will take over for you downstairs. Go watch the lounge."

At least Mahir wouldn't be stuck watching the boys swallow coke pellets.

He left Ridley's office and went into the lounge. For a weeknight, the place was pretty crowded. Bachelor party, by the looks of it. Bunch of drunk assholes trying to get one friend extra drunk in between taking incriminating cell phone pictures of him with the strippers. Mahir and most of the guards were usually quick to intervene and tell them photography wasn't allowed, but the other guys were hanging back, smirking as they watched the damning evidence of this oblivious groom-to-be pile up.

Mahir just sighed and took up position where, thanks to the mirrors, he had a panoramic view of everyone and everything.

Maybe an hour into watching the bachelor party photograph their drunk friends, Mahir wasn't just bored, he was annoyed. There were far too many things he needed to be dealing with. Where was Kinza? *How* was he? What had been on Ridley's mind when he'd called Mahir into his office? The last thing he cared to do right now was guess which of the guys crowded around Vanessa's stage would vomit first. Hopefully not on her shoes like last week. Poor girl had damn near broken her—

The air temperature plummeted, and the hairs on Mahir's neck stood on end. He knew before he turned his head that Ridley had walked into the room. When he'd developed a sixth sense for the guy, he didn't know, but there it was.

And there Ridley was.

Heading straight for Mahir.

His sunglasses were on, leaving only the tightness of his lips and the set of his jaw to give Mahir any clue about the man's mood. That and the way Ridley walked with long, fast strides, the gait of a man on a mission. A pissed-off man on a mission, Mahir guessed.

Ridley stopped in front of Mahir and stabbed a finger at him. "We need to talk," he snarled. "Not my office. But we need to talk." The undercurrent of his voice didn't match the rage in his expression and gestures, and Mahir realized it was all a facade. A show for the others. Saeed in deep shit, not getting frisky with the boss again.

"Where, then?" Mahir put his hands up and drew back defensively.

"Same place as the other night." Ridley's eyebrow rose above the edge of his sunglasses.

"Not there." Mahir shook his head quickly, hands still up like Ridley was scaring the hell out of him. "The staff. Some of them know."

Both eyebrows went up this time, and Ridley's facade cracked for a second. Then he schooled his face back to steely fury. "Who? And *how*?"

"It's . . . it's a long story." Mahir shrank back against the wall. "But they know. That's why I'm not the only one who showed up today."

"Fuck," Ridley said, the sound mostly disappearing into the loud music. "We might have to risk it. In my office, I mean."

"And if people suspect anything?"

"Let them suspect anything they want." Ridley grinned, the expression icy even with his eyes obscured. "Every last one of them has sucked my dick at one time or another, so if they really want to run and tell Lombardi they think you've gotten to do it more often than they have . . ." He lifted one shoulder in a subtle shrug.

Jealousy carved a hot path up the center of Mahir's chest, but he reminded himself how he'd gotten on the payroll to begin with. He hadn't really thought he was the only one, had he?

Ridley stepped back and, once again, stabbed a finger at Mahir. "Twenty minutes," he barked loud enough to make the drunk assholes glance their way. "My office. Don't *fucking* be late this time."

He stormed out of the lounge, leaving Mahir up against the wall like a fucking coward. He didn't have to check to know the other guards were looking, too. So were the bartenders, a few of the patrons, and one of the strippers.

Mahir took a deep breath, rolled his shoulders, and straightened his jacket. He made a grand display of trying to collect himself but not quite managing to do so. After about a minute, he went to the bar and asked for a glass of ice water and a shot of vodka.

The bartender—Santiago tonight—filled the water but didn't get him any vodka.

"Come on, man." Mahir waved a hand toward where Ridley had shouted at him. "I've gotta face that fucker behind closed doors, and he's *pissed.*"

"What happened to not drinking?" Gray materialized beside him and smirked.

Mahir threw him a look. "Even Allah would probably have a couple of shots before dealing with fucking Ridley."

Gray eyed him suspiciously, grunted, and gave a sharp nod. "Yeah, he probably would." He clapped Mahir's shoulder. "Nice knowing you, man."

"Thanks." Mahir looked at Santiago. "Please?"

Santiago glanced at Gray, but he must have sympathized, because he finally poured the shot. All the way to the rim of the glass, too.

Mahir threw it back. Fuck, but he'd forgotten how much the hard stuff burned. Grimacing, he shook his head. "Wow . . ."

Gray laughed. "Go get 'im, haji."

Mahir checked his wristwatch. "Any idea what's up?"

Gray shrugged. "Above my pay grade. And I don't want to know." With that, he turned away, hopefully convinced that Saeed had lost what mettle and bravado he possessed. Twenty minutes—that should be enough to sweep the office for bugs. Ridley was a pro, he had to know what he was looking for, and he wouldn't ask Mahir back if it wasn't extremely important. That thought alone made Mahir's knees weak. How could this have gone from a dangerous mission to a hellish mission? Oh, yeah, by putting more than his own life at risk, that's how.

He was genuinely distracted while he waited, checking his watch every now and then. Gray ended up relieving him again a minute or so before he had to be in the office, and he headed to the back, hesitant but too scared to not comply—at least for any onlooker.

He knocked on the door and made his way in. Ridley sat on the corner of his desk. "Tell me."

"They have us by the balls on this. Lombardi's tracked Kinza and knows he's living with a cop. Short of jeopardizing everything . . ." He gritted his teeth. "So we're going with your idea." And he quickly summarized the whole thing, from the phone to the goons to Kinza agreeing to play along. Gradually, Ridley's tension shifted from pissed off to calmer, more in control and predatory.

"Doesn't help that Bald Guy really wants to catch us fucking. The man wants your job bad, and that's the obvious way up."

"Lombardi wouldn't trust a traitor, I don't think." Ridley stood from his perch and came over to Mahir. "Have you briefed Kinza?"

"Much as I could."

"He knows about me?"

"No. I said you were a good guy, but that can mean anything. Including you having volunteered to play witness."

Ridley frowned but nodded. "So it's going well."

Only Ridley could make such a statement right now and actually mean it. The man had balls of brass when it counted, and some of that calm, arrogant confidence bled over to Mahir, settling him down enough to feel a little bit more optimistic about their chances.

Mahir glanced at the door. "I should go soon. I stay in here getting my ass handed to me long enough, people are going to expect me to leave with a bloody nose."

Ridley's expression didn't change. Or rather, it didn't change the way it should have. The way he eyed Mahir's face, lips quirked slightly like he was in deep thought, didn't sit quite right.

"What?"

Ridley shifted his weight. "If we've got something going on the way people think we do, they probably wouldn't expect me to do anything to damage your mouth."

Mahir's jaw dropped. "I . . . *What*?"

Ridley flexed his fingers on his right hand, then tightened them into a fist. "Keep up appearances."

"So you're . . ." Mahir eyed the hand that had done all kinds of things to him at this point but hadn't done *that*. "You want to hit me? To keep up appearances?"

"I don't want to, no." Ridley grimaced. "Last time I punched a guy, I fractured my hand. Do you have any idea how long that takes to heal?"

Mahir blinked.

Ridley laughed dryly but then turned serious. "No, I really don't want to. But we need to finish this conversation, and the fewer suspicions we rouse, the better."

"You said yourself every guy here's sucked your dick. Does it matter what they think at this point?"

"It does if it means we have to deal with Lombardi or the other guys when we need to be focused on Kinza and the rest of the operation. The more we can do to shut down the rumors, the less we'll be distracted by them."

"Great." Mahir idly rubbed his jaw, wondering just how much force Ridley intended to put behind that fist. Because a visit to the dentist to fix some cracked teeth would really make his week. "Let's finish this conversation, then."

Ridley nodded. "Right. You'll be leaving early tonight. Your jaw and me being homicidally pissed at you will give you a good alibi to get the fuck out of here for an evening."

"You're a real pal, you know that?"

"Get home, talk to Kinza. Find out everything he knows or even thinks he knows. When he's supposed to come back. What he's doing and where he's going."

Mahir nodded. "Right. I told him to keep track of any details that might be useful."

"Good. Once we know when he's doing his first run, we can go from there. When he gets back, then I'll figure out what our options are in terms of tracking devices and shit like that."

Mahir's stomach turned. He still couldn't get his head around the idea of sending Kinza out into parts unknown with a stomach full of cocaine.

Ridley touched his arm. "We'll both do everything we can to keep him safe. With any luck, he'll only have to make those two runs. Maybe even just one if we get really lucky."

"Yeah. If we get really lucky."

"If you have any other ideas, I'm open to hearing them."

"Not really, no." Mahir smirked. "What does it say about me when I can't think of any alternatives to sending my nephew on a drug run and letting you coldcock me in the mouth?"

Ridley gave a quiet laugh. "I think it just says how fucked up this situation is." He took off his jacket, and when he went for his cufflinks, Mahir looked away. At least Ridley's nice white shirt wouldn't end up with blood on it.

"So, um." Mahir cleared his throat. "What do you say we make sure this is the only incident of domestic violence we ever have?"

Ridley chuckled as he rolled his sleeve to his elbow. "Deal."

Frozen peas weren't nearly enough to deal with what had happened next. Ridley's shirt, for one, remained clean, but Mahir's didn't. He made pretty much no attempt to stop the bleeding—not that he really could, blinded with reflexive tears and shock, doing nothing but keeping his balance with one hand against the door, nose and lips burning and blood running into his mouth. Didn't seem to be all from the lips, either. Some of that had to be gums, and he quickly ran his tongue along his teeth to make sure they all remained in place. Sore, too sore to want to touch them, but no gaps or hard edges that hadn't been there before.

Through the pain, he felt Ridley's hand on his arm, a firm, steadying grip, while Mahir let the blood run down his chin and throat. At least that kind of injury bled readily, and the rate at which his heart was pumping just pushed more out of the split skin on his lip and his nose, though that hadn't broken.

"How're the carpals?" Mahir muttered.

"Coping."

"Frozen peas," Mahir said, his voice nasal. He wiped at his face, smearing blood onto his shirt cuff.

"I'll look into it," Ridley said calmly, amusement taking the place of concern. Then something shifted in the atmosphere of the room. Being aware of the shift still didn't quite prepare him for Ridley shouting, "And get the *fuck* out of my office."

Mahir clambered away from the door, managed to find the handle and open the door, getting through just a split second before Ridley slammed it hard back into its frame.

Mahir paused, wiped at his eyes, blinking back tears, then did what any guy would do—get to the staff restroom to wash the blood away. Luckily, the restroom was on the other side of the break room, so the goons probably saw him rush there.

His suspicion was confirmed when the door to the restroom opened while Mahir was spitting blood into the wash basin, watching it turn pink in the running water and vanish like diluted paint. He reached for a pile of rough paper towels and placed a wad of them under his nose, tilting his head back as he controlled the bleeding. His stomach turned at the metallic taste running into his throat and down. He hated the taste of blood.

Gray entered.

Mahir raised an eyebrow and looked at him.

"That hurt?"

Mahir gave a snort that was more a nasal groan. "Told you he's pissed."

"What for?"

"Who the fuck knows."

"You can tell me."

What? An answer, quick. "You're not telling? Lombardi?" Extra points for Gray for understanding him through a wad of towels and bruised lips.

"Trust me."

In a million years, when there's no other human around, maybe. And even then I'd only trust you with a pistol at your temple. After the shot.

"Refused to suck him off. I really don't want to lose the job and besides, I'm not that into cocksucking anyway. Not if it's not reci— Mutual." Just turn the whole thing into a nice piece of sexual harassment in the workplace.

Gray moved behind him, peered over his shoulder into the mirror. "Bag of ice?"

"I'll get some painkillers on the way home. Not the worst I've had."

Gray's hand landed on his shoulder, and Mahir closed his eyes. Um. This wasn't happening, was it? The asshole had been ribbing him all the time because he was *interested* in him? What a fucking box of lunatics this place was.

The grip turned firmer, kneading his shoulder as if to reassure him. Mahir's skin crawled—terrible timing, terrible everything.

"You sure you're all right?" Gray held his gaze in the mirror. "You look pretty rattled."

"Bloodstains kind of give everyone that look."

Gray laughed. "Seriously." He leaned in closer and spoke in a conspiratorial whisper. "You're not telling me anything I don't know. Guy's a fucking maniac."

Mahir nodded, exhaling hard under the wadded paper towel. "He is. Fuck, man, he really is."

"Yeah." Gray squeezed his shoulder again before letting him go. "We should get back to work if he's on the warpath tonight."

"He told me to get the fuck out of here." Mahir threw a wary glance toward the restroom door. "Said if he saw me again, we might have to have a longer . . . discussion."

Gray grimaced. "Yeah, you'd better roll, then. You need a lift home?"

Mahir pulled the paper towel away, then inspected his reflection. The bleeding had mostly stopped, aside from a thin trickle from one side of his nose and a little bit that had pooled in the corner of his lips. As much as he didn't want to leave this place with anyone else, he did happen to look like ass. Walking through Seattle with a bloodied face and blood-spattered clothing was, in a word, conspicuous.

"Sure, thanks." Mahir tossed the saturated paper towels and picked up a couple more. "I'll try not to bleed all over your upholstery."

Gray chuckled and headed for the door. "It's a beater. I'm not worried." He held open the restroom door, and the two of them made a discreet exit from the back of the club. Gray paused to let Bald Guy know he'd be back shortly, and Bald Guy looked more than a little alarmed when he saw Mahir's swelling face.

Gray was right about the car. It was a battered Honda, probably twice as old as the piece of shit Mahir drove, and it had enough stains of questionable origin that a few smears of blood probably wouldn't make much difference.

The engine started, though not without a sputter of protest, and Gray drove them out of the small lot and onto the cross street. Evening commuters were already choking the sidewalks as were people heading for dinner and whatever else they did for entertainment, so Mahir was glad he'd taken Gray up on the ride home.

"You probably cost a few people some money tonight," Gray said out of the blue.

"Oh yeah?"

Gray nodded, resting a hand on top of the steering wheel as he waited for a light to turn green. "Pretty sure half the staff had bets going about you and Ridley. I think someone said the long shot bet was that he lets you fuck him up the ass."

Mahir laughed, wincing when he stretched his cut lip a little too far. "That what you all do when you're bored? Speculate on whose dick is going into whom?"

"Well, when we see someone spending that much time in that asshole's office . . ." Gray trailed off, shrugging. The light turned green, and he accelerated. "You two did seem pretty chummy before, um, before . . ."

"Before he redecorated my face?"

"Yeah." Gray laughed dryly. "Something like that." He glanced at Mahir. "Be careful with him, Saeed."

"You don't say," Mahir muttered.

"I'm not kidding. If he is into you, you might want to think twice about turning him down."

Mahir waved a hand. "What the hell? I spend too much time in his office, he's fucking me. I come out of his office looking like this, and maybe I should be a little more receptive. What do you people want?"

"Hey, none of us want one of our own getting involved with that psycho," Gray said sharply. "Too much room for favoritism and all that. But I don't want to see anyone getting hurt, either. And if he wants it that bad, well, then I guess it depends on how well you like your teeth."

Mahir shook his head and looked out the window. And he'd thought Fallujah was a fucked-up work environment. "I'll think on it. Hopefully he'll hire a rentboy and fuck it out of his system. I won't be doing any cocksucking with these lips anytime soon, that's for damn sure."

"Just be careful," Gray said, briefly touching Mahir's thigh.

Oh, hell no.

At least Saeed's crash pad wasn't too far away.

"Painkillers?"

"Should have some upstairs."

"Okay." Gray walked him to the door, though, still concerned. Maybe curious where and how Saeed lived. Gray couldn't possibly hope to get anywhere with that. Or maybe he was just being friendly—chummy in his own way. Mahir'd never thought of himself as irresistible, and a sniffling guy with a swollen face wasn't an ideal date by any means.

"I'll manage, thanks." He fished for his keys, thinking, though that was hard with the headache that was manifesting now that the adrenaline was bleeding out of his system. "Meet for coffee one day?" After all, being chummy with one of the boys would work in his favor. If they thought he and Gray had something brewing, it would further distract from Ridley. And it was hard to hate Gray completely. He was only trying to help.

Gray smiled. "I'd like that."

Bet you would.

"Great. I'll . . . uh, get some pills down and sleep it off. Can you tell the others about this in a way that doesn't make me look like a pathetic loser?"

"Hey, it's Ridley. Nobody thinks you're a loser if Ridley messes you up."

"Good. Last thing I need is people talking about how this sand nigger can't take his punches."

Gray chuckled. "You came out of Ridley's office on your own two feet. The last three or four guys can't say the same." He clapped Mahir's shoulder. "You're good. Don't worry."

The last three or four guys?

He managed a halfhearted smile. "All right. Well. Thanks for the lift."

"Anytime."

Gray left, and Mahir went into Saeed's apartment. He showered, thankful to finally be rid of the last sticky remnants of blood on his face and neck. The shirt probably couldn't be salvaged, but whatever. He put on a clean one and took another look in the mirror.

Ridley definitely hadn't pulled the punch. The earliest signs of mottled discoloration were starting to form, like a Polaroid developing, and by tomorrow, the side of his face would be one hell of a conversation piece. His jaw hurt where the fist had made contact, and it ached all the way up into the joint. He could still move it, though, and later this evening when he was brave enough—or hungry enough, anyway—he'd try eating. Perhaps something soft, just to be on the safe side.

Speaking of the safe side, he couldn't get to the other side of the Puget Sound fast enough. With the blood mopped away and a clean shirt on, he left the shithole apartment and made his way down to the docks.

When he walked in the front door of his house, he was relieved to see Kinza waiting for him. The kid was huddled on the couch under a blanket playing video games on Mahir's flatscreen. He probably intended to look like he was just trying to get comfortable, but the way he kept his knees tucked under him and the blanket bunched against his chest gave away his nerves.

"You doing all right?"

Kinza nodded. "I guess. Whoa, what happened to your face?"

"Occupational hazard. You eaten yet?"

"Not yet."

"I'll make dinner, then. Come in here while I cook."

Kinza paused his game. He left the blanket on the couch and joined Mahir in the kitchen, taking his usual seat at the kitchen table. Funny how he'd become a regular, almost permanent fixture at that table. In the house. They'd barely spent time together since Kinza had started staying with him, but all circumstances aside, Mahir couldn't help liking his nephew's presence.

"So. Um." He cleared his throat as he riffled through the freezer in search of something he could eat without further irritating his jaw. That lasagna would do. He took it out of the box, pierced the seal, and tossed it into the microwave. He was about to ask Kinza a question, but then he took out his phone and mouthed, *Where's the phone?*

Kinza gestured down the hall, where muffled rap music pounded through a closed door.

"Good." Mahir put his cell away and turned to pull some plates out of the cabinet. He kept his voice quiet. "I assume you spoke to the big boss today."

"Yeah." The chair creaked, and Mahir didn't have to look to know Kinza was fidgeting. "That dude is nuts."

"Is he?" Mahir turned around. "What? Did he do something?"

"Well, no. I mean, kind of." Kinza folded his arms on the edge of the table. "He just has that vibe about him like he's about to lose his shit." He snickered. "Kind of reminds me of Grandpa."

Mahir laughed. His father had been fairly temperamental, especially in his waning years, but he'd never been like Lombardi. Mahir had seen *just* how volatile the pimp could get. "So what happened?"

"He told me he'd pay me. A grand for the first run. Fifteen hundred for the second. Two thousand for the third. And ten grand for the fourth."

Mahir eyed him. "Ten grand for the fourth?"

"Yeah." Kinza laughed, shaking his head. "I can see why so many guys sign up for it. Ten grand to take a trip that short?"

"How short?" Mahir closed the refrigerator. Dinner could wait a few minutes. He sat across from Kinza. "Did he give you details about the trips?"

"Not really. Just said I'd need a passport, but he'd take care of that."

Mahir's chest tightened. "A passport. Did he say why? I mean, where you might be going?"

Kinza shook his head. "He did say the first three runs are local. There and back in a day, most of the time. The big one, that's the one where we need the passports."

"Anything about how long that big trip is?"

"He said I'd get more details after I came back from my third run."

Mahir exhaled slowly. The fourth run never happened, as far as he knew. He'd never seen a kid go past the third. "Did he say when he'll have to put in for the passport? Take your picture and all of that?"

"He already did that. Today."

God. That meant Lombardi was having false passports manufactured for these kids. Which meant he could be sending them *anywhere* once he was through with them.

"Oh," Kinza said, keeping his gaze down. "He definitely knows about you."

"What do you mean?"

"I mean, he knows you're a cop. Knows pretty much everything about you. He doesn't know you're there, though. Thinks you're just working some bullshit gig in Bremerton, and the force keeps writing you up for some gambling habit that keeps interfering with your work."

"A gambling habit?" Mahir laughed. "That's rich."

"Yeah, well." Kinza shrugged. "I guess they think you're spending all your free time at the casinos over here, and it's gotten you suspended a few times."

Mahir wondered who at the force had cooked up that little tale and how much they'd enjoyed painting him as a gambling-addicted loser. "And how much does he know about our relationship?"

Kinza swallowed. "I told him staying with you is better than staying with my dad, but you're an asshole, too, which is why I can't wait until I'm eighteen and can leave."

"Good," Mahir said with a nod. "Did he warn you or threaten you about me?"

Kinza's shudder answered the question well enough, but he said, "He told me he's got eyes and ears all over the police forces in this state, and if he catches wind that you know anything about his operation, he'll make sure your next case is my murder investigation."

There were physical punches and punches like that. He definitely felt that one, the sheer baleful evil of that guy. "Maybe at the lower level, he has a few people. But nobody at that level knows anything about what I'm doing. It's going according to plan, and we will take him down." He leaned forward. "You're very brave helping me with this. You really are."

Kinza looked up, his eyes wide, but Mahir meant it; he just sometimes needed to remind himself to praise people and express the good things he thought about them. And Allah knew, but Kinza didn't get a great deal of praise from people who mattered to him.

Kinza smiled. "I want to see him go down."

"That's the spirit. And we will. It's going really well." Not without minor hiccups, but the trajectory was right. More people trusted him, Ridley was with him in this—what a hellish job it would have been if he weren't—and Kinza was strong.

The microwave beeped, so he busied himself with dishing out the food. Should be soft enough to not overly tax his jaw, at least. He poured them both big glasses of water and pondered the new information. He needed to touch base with Ridley about this, but considering how their last encounter had gone, that might be a tense standoff in front of the crew. Maybe planting a suggestion with Gray, his brand-new confidant, would make any need to punch him for real obsolete. He could always just claim he'd gotten Ridley off or taken it up the ass.

"Ewww." Kinza grimaced.

"What? Something wrong with the food?"

"You have that stupid grin on your face."

Mahir laughed, despite himself. "Careful. I can think what I like."

"Not if it's that clear on your forehead you can't. That's disgusting. I'm eating!"

Mahir laughed and almost spit his water out. "Fine. Then go take the food and eat all over the Xbox. See if I care."

Magic formula: *Poof*, the teenager was gone.

Mahir chuckled and took his own food into the living room, eating while he watched Kinza play some frighteningly realistic, though much more cinematic, first-person shooter game that was probably not cleared for under-eighteens, but he figured if he was forced to watch his own nephew turn into a drug mule, at the very least he could be lenient with that kind of thing. Ironically, Adil would probably encourage Kinza to play more of this sort of game. Violent and manly and anything but gay. Naturally.

While Kinza played his game and Mahir gingerly worked his way through his food—damn, but his jaw was not happy—Mahir wondered about their next move. The game plan, as it were. Tonight's fisticuffs would work to his advantage, as much as he hated to admit it. An appearance in Ridley's office would be expected. The prodigal employee given a chance to either acknowledge that he'd reformed his ways and wouldn't cross Ridley again, or the fed-up boss forking over his walking papers. Either way, as long as he looked duly chastened and nervous, he could report to Ridley's office early in the evening.

"When are you supposed to go back to the club?"

"Friday." Kinza didn't look up from his game.

Good. That gave Ridley and Mahir a few days to figure something out. The options were limited, and there was probably little they could do but wait until Friday, and then wait on pins and needles while Kinza made his first run. Lots of waiting. Lots and *lots* of waiting.

He'd often heard that cops on stakeouts secretly wished someone would start shooting, just so they could get out of the car and stop with all the endless waiting. Though Mahir understood the sentiment, he couldn't go so far as to hope for gunfire and explosions to liven things up. Not this time. If he spent Kinza's entire run pacing back and forth, running a million worst-case scenarios through his head—*why* did they have to watch those overdose films at the academy?—and nothing actually happened, he really couldn't complain. As long as Kinza made it back safely.

Safely, and hopefully with the information Ridley needed to figure out how to track Kinza on his second—and please, Allah, please let it be his last—run so they could bring this whole motherfucking ring down. He wondered how much bribery and backhandedness it would take to get the warden at Walla Walla to "accidentally" put Lombardi in with the general population.

Picking at the remnants of his cooling lasagna, debating whether or not he really wanted to make his jaw do any more of that chewing nonsense tonight, Mahir couldn't help thinking about how things would be once this was all over. Kinza would be an adult, no longer under his father's thumb and free from Lombardi's payroll. Chances were, he'd either be well on his way toward a law-enforcement career or doing everything he could to get as far away from anything police related as he could. There'd be no *Eh, maybe I'll go that route* for him.

And what about Ridley? Odds were he had a home and a life someplace else. Probably nowhere near Seattle. After a year and a half in this mess, he'd probably want to get even further away once the case was over. Which left Mahir . . . where? In the sealed box full of things marked *that horrible case I never want to think about again*?

He dug at the lasagna with his fork. Jaw aside, his appetite was gone. At least he'd eaten enough now to take a painkiller, and fortunately, he'd kept a few of those around after he'd had some wonderfully pleasant dental work done a few months ago.

"I'm going to call it a night," he said. "You have school tomorrow, don't you?"

"Uh-huh." Kinza made no move to stop playing his game.

"You, uh, didn't go today right?"

"Nope."

"Then you need to go tomorrow. Get some sleep."

Kinza groaned. "Okay, fine. Let me get to a checkpoint and save my game."

"All right. Have a good night, kid."

"You too."

Once Mahir took one of those pain pills, he wouldn't know or really care if Kinza played a little longer and stayed up a little later. Quite frankly, the boy had a bumpy road ahead of him. If he stayed up late tonight and played hooky from school for a day?

Well, Mahir couldn't really blame him.

If anything, he envied him. Being a grown-up certainly sucked when all of his life—apart from his career—suddenly grew vicious thorns and every move could be the last. At Kinza's age, the full seriousness of everything hadn't sunk in completely. He just hoped that survived the next week or two.

CHAPTER EIGHTEEN

A t least the bruise turned out beautifully. The split lip closed to a very impressive dark-red line at the corner of his lips, which Mahir favored to not open again. His nose still felt tender and raw, but he sounded mostly normal when he spoke.

And a couple of other things had changed with Ridley hitting him. When he came into the break room, no offhanded racist comments. People watched him but didn't challenge him anymore. When Gray showed up with a carrier of paper cups from a coffee shop, miraculously one was left for Saeed—something that had never happened before. Mahir took it with a grateful smile, and a wince when the movement pulled at his lips.

"You're healing up well. In that kind of light, people might not even see." Gray clapped him on the shoulder, his fingers lingering.

"Saves me from claiming I fell down the stairs," Mahir muttered against the rim of his coffee cup.

Gray laughed and kneaded Mahir's shoulder again. It was all still very deniable and buddy-buddy, but there was a clear invitation below the surface. Mahir briefly squeezed Gray's hand but then turned away and let it slip off his shoulders, as if trying to stay professional. Mahir would deal with that complication when it became necessary.

He ended up in the lounge again, clearly out of favor with the head of security. But everything changed halfway through the night when he was relieved. Gray took his place, which was lucky considering he would need the man to tighten up his alibi.

"Boss wants to see you in his office."

Mahir rolled his eyes. "Bet he does. Asshole."

Gray held him back. "Hate to say it but remember, might be easier if you play along."

Mahir bristled at the suggestion, looked toward the back of the club, and deflated somewhat. "Maybe I'll get away with an apology."

"Maybe." Gray looked on with something like compassion, so Mahir pulled himself visibly together and headed toward Ridley's office, making sure to show how displeased he was with the prospect of meeting Ridley again; he even went so far as to move his jaw a few times, like a boxer checking the extent of his injuries.

A few of the guys offered semi-sympathetic, *sucks to be you* glances as Mahir crossed the lounge. He did his best to keep a nervous front, even pausing at the mouth of the dark hallway to roll his shoulders and compose himself. Deep breath, a moment of *I can do this*, and then he continued.

He knocked on the door.

"It's open."

Mahir stepped into the office and closed the door behind him. Ridley was, just as he'd been last night, perched on the edge of the desk, hands resting on his thighs. Mahir wasn't even a little surprised to see some bruising on the man's knuckles.

Ridley grimaced. "You look like hell."

"I look like I got my ass handed to me by the head of security."

Lowering his gaze, Ridley laughed, but it sounded like it took a hell of a lot of effort. "How's Kinza?"

"Nervous."

Ridley looked up again. "So he's really doing this."

"I don't think he has much choice now." Mahir shouldered himself away from the door—and any prying ears on its other side— and didn't wait for an invitation before taking one of the chairs in front of the desk. He sat back, one ankle resting on the opposite knee, and looked up at Ridley.

Their height difference used to bug the hell out of Mahir, used to intimidate him like mad, but it didn't bother him now. Which was bizarre considering Ridley's bruised hand. Bruised from bruising Mahir's face. Somehow their quiet little conspiracy and their charade to divert the other guys' suspicions put them on more level ground than they'd ever been. They had to trust each other more than ever. In a strange way, the marks on Ridley's hand and Mahir's face were like opposite pieces of one of those ridiculous friendship necklaces young girls wore. Two halves of a whole.

Ridley turned a little so he was facing Mahir. "How much does he know?"

Barely whispering, just in case, Mahir briefed him on his conversation with Kinza.

Ridley stroked his chin with his unmarred hand. "So we have until Friday."

"To do what?"

"I'm not sure." One of Ridley's fingertips idly traced the sharp edge of his jaw. "Maybe figure out a plan to follow him. Or track him. Or . . . something." He dropped his hand, sighing as he shook his head. "There's got to be something we can do, dammit."

Ridley's intense frustration-bordering-on-anger was surprisingly endearing. He sensed the ticking clock as acutely as Mahir did and was as determined to find a solution to keep Kinza out of danger. That ticking clock, though, as well as the lack of a solution, kept Mahir from finding much comfort in that or anything else. There seemed to be no real refuge. If he'd known that the night in his own house with Ridley in his bed had been the only opportunity, he'd have made more of it. They hadn't exactly wasted time, but it still felt like there might have been a way to squeeze more from it. Somehow.

He shook his head. "Beats me. I'll keep thinking."

Ridley rubbed over his raw knuckles with the thumb of the other hand and glanced at the door. "Guess so." He still seemed reluctant to let Mahir go, instead placed his hand against Mahir's jaw, gently enough to just feel for the swelling. If anything, that touch asked for forgiveness.

Mahir sighed. "What's that? More sexual harassment?"

"Come again?"

"One of the guys is getting too friendly. Told him you hit me because I refused to suck your cock since you never reciprocate. He told me I should just close my eyes, bend over, and think of America if that means you won't turn me into minced meat."

Ridley huffed laughter. "Painting me as the villain."

"It's what you've been doing with the guys for more than a year. That's what they expect."

"Most of those guys are pretty unsavory characters themselves. So who is he?"

The last bit had contained some definite barbed wire to it. "Gray."

"Really? Interesting." His hand ran down along his jawline, then dropped to Mahir's chest, tracing the line of his collarbone and down his sternum. The touch couldn't have been more intense if Ridley had used a still-hot gun barrel. Mahir shifted. "So you're now making amends for your insolence?"

"In a manner of speaking."

"That's what they expect," Ridley mimicked Mahir's tone. "Personally, I think a blowjob is a great idea."

"I really—" Mahir began, but then Ridley dropped to his knees, pushing Mahir's legs further apart. "Uh."

"You were saying?" Ridley politely enquired while opening Mahir's trousers.

Mahir couldn't help laughing. "Now who's the tease?"

"I never tease." Ridley grabbed his thighs and pushed them further apart, as if only to let Mahir feel his strength. It was enough to restrict his chest, apparently, because breathing was harder than it should've been, and he nearly jumped when Ridley's tongue traced the line of Mahir's cock in his briefs. Leaning back and thinking of America wasn't an option, not when every touch—and yes, he teased—every sound of moving cloth, every breath, the very presence was so Ridley it was impossible to forget that or even push it aside. Mahir just placed his hands in the man's hair when he finally, finally, took his cock in his mouth, and let that pent-up groan escape.

The sound of his own voice almost startled him out of that state of bliss. What if someone was listening? Oh, but he wasn't going to tell Ridley to stop. And he doubted Ridley had any intention of stopping, not with as much as he seemed to savor every inch of Mahir's dick, slowly working his way all the way down to the base before starting back up.

Mahir dug his teeth into his lower lip, holding his breath in part to stay silent and in part because he couldn't remember what else he was supposed to do with all the air trapped in his lungs. Ridley had sucked him off before but not like this. Not even close. Fingers, lips, tongue. He used everything at his disposal to tease Mahir's nerve endings to life, and with every passing minute of this—hell, every passing second—Mahir struggled even harder to keep himself quiet. For all either of them knew, there wasn't a soul within earshot, but it was equally possible that everyone—Gray, Bald Guy, Lombardi, the strippers—were just outside this door with glasses pressed to the wall, listening to every creak of furniture and every sharp breath.

That thought sent a thrill through him. An exhilarating rush. The danger. The possibility of half the club knocking down this door and finding Mahir in the chair, with Ridley kneeling and hungrily going to town on Mahir's very erect dick. Let them catch him. Let every last one of them envy him because he doubted any of them knew what it was like to have Ridley's warm lips and skilled tongue sliding up and down their cocks, or how Ridley stroked with his hand just right to make their heads spin. Only Mahir knew.

He gripped Ridley's hair for something to hold on to. His eyes kept tearing up from the sheer intensity of everything Ridley did, but he blinked them into focus again and again so he could watch.

Ridley's eyes flicked up to meet his. That wasn't a look he could've hidden behind sunglasses. No amount of heavily tinted lenses could have masked that smoldering desire. Then he lowered his gaze and deep-throated Mahir. Easily, skillfully, and so fucking perfectly.

Mahir hooked his feet around the legs of the chair to keep from bucking or pushing, not because he thought Ridley couldn't take it but because he wanted to stay just like this, let Ridley have control and show him what he could do, how he could play Mahir's desire exactly how he wanted. Short of fucking him slowly on their sides that night when Ridley had given him control, it was the most intense thing they'd ever done, and the danger just made it better. Though that was lunacy. It was also strangely way beyond any anonymous blowjob he'd ever received in his life—it was too sensuous for that, too intense. Mahir relaxed one hand and ran it over Ridley's face, too aroused to say anything, share anything in that moment. He just wanted to say something like *Me, too,* or *You're killing me.*

Gradually, the sensations became too much. Ridley was leading him toward climax, and Mahir simply followed, concentrating on Ridley, the sensations that bled into feelings too complicated for the situation, the purely physical need to shed the pressure Ridley was building. No rush at all, the pace set purely by Ridley's skill and devotion to the task and Mahir's need to come. Nobody on the outside mattered just then, and in this crazy situation, that was the only kind of freedom they managed. But it was enough.

Mahir's body tensed—from his toes to his thighs, every muscle in his chest—and Ridley urged him on with a couple of intense strokes on his cock, twisting and turning when he came nearly all the way back up, overloading Mahir with arousal, and just as Mahir was beginning to lose it, swallowing him again all the way to the root so Mahir came in his throat, teeth clenched, the release damn near blacking out his vision.

Ridley eased off him, sat back, and looked up at Mahir.

"Fuck." Mahir swept his tongue across his lips. "Holy fuck . . ."

"For the record," Ridley said with a grin. "You're forgiven for yesterday."

Mahir laughed breathlessly. "Thanks, boss."

Chuckling, Ridley eased himself back to his feet. "You'll have to let me know if Gray's skills compare."

"Gray?" Mahir glanced up from fixing his clothes. "You really think I'd go near that jackass?"

Ridley laughed again, and Mahir swore there was a note of relief in his voice. A hint of jealousy that had peered out of the cave but then drew back into the shadows when the threat passed.

"Is that what this was about?" Mahir zipped his trousers. "Gray?"

"What? No." Ridley's eyes darted downward, then met Mahir's again. "I mean, you didn't seem like . . . I was pretty sure . . ."

Mahir grinned. "You're adorable when you're jealous."

"Fuck you." Ridley chuckled, but the touch of color in his cheeks gave him away.

Mahir pushed himself up and put his hands on Ridley's waist. "I'm serious. Just so you know."

Ridley looked up at him, an unusual glint of insecurity in those crystal-blue eyes.

"I'm serious," Mahir said again and touched Ridley's face. "You are fucking *adorable* like—"

"Oh, shut up." Ridley laughed and playfully pushed Mahir's chest.

Mahir didn't move. He pulled Ridley a little closer. "I wouldn't touch Gray with Bald Guy's dick. Just so we're clear."

"Well, you're not missing anything. I'm surprised he can eat with that mouth."

Mahir's jaw dropped. "What?"

Ridley batted his eyes. "What?"

"I don't even want to know."

Grimacing, Ridley shook his head. "Trust me. You don't."

"I'll take your word for it." He ran his hand up and down Ridley's waist. "So, what now? Now that we've, um, settled our differences."

Ridley's features all sharpened again, the joking and jealousy evaporating in an instant and leaving behind the man all the other guys thought Mahir was meeting in here. "Now we figure out how to keep Kinza safe. And with any luck, keep him from going on more than one run."

"But there's no way to follow the boys without rousing suspicion."

Ridley shook his head again. "I've tried. Part of their route is way too out in the open, so anyone tailing them is too obvious. I've put a whole team on them before, but these kids are damned good at varying their routes and losing tails." He cupped his elbow in one hand and idly ran the backs of his fingers along the edge of his jaw. "And a GPS tracker won't do us any good if someone finds it and chucks it."

"Dammit." Mahir exhaled. He realized then his hand was still on Ridley's waist but didn't lift it away. He liked the contact. The closeness kept their conversation duly hushed in case anyone was listening, but he also just liked it. At this point, he'd take any comfort and reassurance he could get.

"As much as I don't like it," Ridley said, "I think our only option is to put this in Kinza's hands. Let him do a run. We have to know where the boys are going."

Mahir chewed his lip. "What if they're not going to the same place every time?"

"Then we're back at square one." Ridley cocked his head. "You think they're varying the meet-up points too?"

"Maybe. Lombardi told Kinza that he'd be paid per run, and that the fourth run required a passport."

Ridley's eyebrows jumped. "Except none of the boys have done a fourth run."

"Not that we know of, no."

"What do you mean?"

"Considering Lombardi offers to pay them through the nose for that fourth run, it's entirely possible it's just a carrot on a stick to get them to do the first, second, and third. But Lombardi also took Kinza's photo so he could get him a fake passport. We have to consider the possibility that there is a fourth run, and that the boys are being taken out of the country." He paused. "Since I've never seen anyone return from a third run, though, it's probably even more likely that they're being taken out of the country on the *third* run."

Ridley released a breath. "Then let's hope we get the information we need before Kinza winds up testing that theory."

"Yeah." Mahir glanced back at the door. "Okay. All right. It'll all turn out well." It simply had to, though crucial pieces were missing and the associated risks were spiraling out of control. Lombardi would pay for this—for the rest of his life.

"I'll put you down in the basement. When it's Kinza's turn, maybe that'll help him a bit. Afterward, you debrief him at home."

"We should do that together. Maybe you'll think of something I wouldn't. Then we should all plan the next step together."

Ridley seemed to weigh the pros and cons for a full minute, and Mahir cursed him internally for taking his time. It did mean Ridley in his house, and that likely meant in his bed, but Ridley's hesitation was hard to interpret. Was it about the case or the rest?

Ridley's lips quirked. "Should I bring a toothbrush?"

Oh, you bastard. "No." Ridley's face fell. "I have a spare you can use."

"So it's a deal." Ridley turned away and sat back on his desk corner. "Can't wait for this to be over."

"Same here." Mahir adjusted his cuffs and collar. "And maybe talk about everything else. Would be nice to have a meal and relax."

Ridley's expression looked soft—not worried, which was a good sign. Maybe they had something. Maybe it would all play out well, though of course, the case was more important than the mutual attraction or even their personal feelings. With all these unknowns floating around, even a *let's be friends* or *let's keep this to pleasant memories* would be a huge relief. "That we'll do."

Mahir headed back out and toward the basement, keeping his features guarded for any curious glances shot his way. Thoughtful and reserved could be read either way—maybe him scrabbling for some dignity after whatever Ridley had done to him.

Whatever the other guys thought about Saeed or what—or who—must've gone down in that office, none of them said a word.

No one approached him. He went downstairs, took his place in the back room, and tried not to think about Kinza setting foot in here anytime soon.

Friday night came all too soon. Mahir stood guard in the room with the coke and the condoms, and every time the door opened, his gut twisted into knots. It was a busy night, several pairs of boys heading out into parts unknown with God knew how many kilos in their stomachs.

At quarter past eleven, well after the boy should have been home with an Xbox controller in his hand, Kinza followed one of the other couriers in through the heavy steel door.

He looked as nervous as any of the boys did on their first run. His escort was cool, confident, and dressed like he'd been paid as well as Kinza had been promised. Mahir tried to ignore the sick feeling that climbed the back of his throat at the thought of Kinza reaching that level, being the confident one who could show another naive teenager how to earn a paycheck from Lombardi. Kinza wouldn't reach that point. He wouldn't do his three—or four—runs. Over Mahir's dead body would he do more than two.

Kinza's gaze slid toward Mahir. The kid was pretty good at hiding any signs of recognition. He looked at his uncle as though Mahir was just another security guard. No affection, no contempt. Just superficial acknowledgment that there was another person in the room.

Then he looked away and listened to his companion. The experienced kid made gestures and pantomimes that made Mahir want to puke. Tilting his head back as if to make his throat as straight as possible. Running his hand down the front of his neck as Mahir had done when trying to get a pill down a cat's throat. Explaining that the first few times were the hardest, but it got easier with a little practice. That it was totally safe.

And for Kinza's sake, Mahir couldn't do so much as blink, had to try to be reassuring without actually doing anything that a bored guard who didn't know or care about these kids wouldn't do. Maybe another reason to use men who were unlikely to be fathers? Though

Lombardi clearly underestimated how many gay men were fathers or uncles or maybe had a damned *conscience*.

Mahir inspected his fingernails while the kid finished his explanations, though he nearly jumped out of his skin when Kinza touched one of the pellets, then lifted it up in his hand, weighing it. Damn, Ridley had a *lot* more confidence in Mahir's acting skills than Mahir had right now. The visceral horror of Kinza lifting it to his face was nothing short of seeing a toddler play with a rattlesnake. Mahir forced himself to look away, knelt down to tighten his shoelaces to keep from slapping the pellets out of Kinza's hands. If this went wrong, he'd never be able to forgive himself. Even if it went *right*, forgiveness seemed a fragile concept. But hearing Kinza struggle to swallow that vile thing? That would follow him into his dreams.

He managed to not watch, but his imagination possibly made it worse. The sounds weren't helping. Retching. Damn Ridley for talking him into this. It made sense, but then having to do nothing while it happened? Too much. He was about ready to blow it all—the case, the whole damned thing—when Kinza's distressed sounds stopped.

Mahir glanced over. Kinza looked a bit green but seemed to be coping well. As well as anyone could, Mahir supposed. The other kid was doing fine, tilting his head back and dropping a latex-wrapped pellet into his mouth like it was a fry or something. A little bit of a grimace as he worked at swallowing, but he took it like a pro. Because he was a pro. And so was Kinza.

Fuck.

"How many am I supposed to take?" Kinza asked, rubbing his throat.

"We need ten between us, so five."

Kinza turned even greener. He looked at the box in front of them. Then his eyes flicked toward Mahir, and they screamed, *Help me.*

Except Mahir couldn't help him now. Anything he did would have consequences far worse than a gut full of cocaine. There was nothing Mahir could do except watch, and there was nothing Kinza could do except swallow one pellet after another until both boys were carrying enough.

I am so sorry, Kinza. I hope you can forgive me for this.

Twice, Kinza put a hand over his mouth and hunched over the table like he was ready to get sick. The other kid reassured him, telling him to take deep breaths, that it would pass just like it had for him and everyone else. And both times, it eventually did. Kinza composed himself. He kept the coke down where it belonged. He still alternated between various shades of green and pale, but he got the last pellet down and kept it there.

And then, without so much as a backward glance at Mahir, Kinza and the other boy were gone.

As a security guard, Mahir was useless for the rest of the night. For all he was paying attention, the strippers could have come down and started fucking the other guards right there on the tables. Or the guards could have blown each other. Or there could have been a gunfight, a marching band, and a Justin goddamned Bieber concert. Mahir didn't know, and he didn't fucking care.

Kinza and the other boy weren't back when Mahir's shift ended. That much he'd expected. He knew damn well they wouldn't check in until sometime tomorrow. But he was still sick at the thought of leaving the club and heading home, knowing Kinza wouldn't be curled up on the couch playing video games or doing homework, and there wouldn't be any surly comments or food debris in the kitchen or mentions of Mahir's idiot brother. Kinza wouldn't be there. The house would be empty.

"Try to get some sleep," Ridley told him on the way out. "You won't be any good to him if you don't get some shut-eye."

Sleep.

Right.

Easy for him to say. He wasn't the one who'd be dreaming about watching his nephew swallowing condoms full of cocaine.

CHAPTER NINETEEN

Mahir awoke from one of those dreams in a cold sweat and a panic. Not the same panic that had had him hyperventilating after every similar dream he'd had since he'd got home, but a fresh kind. Something else had attacked his senses and brought him out of that nightmare.

Movement. In the house. Someone was here.

Kinza? Mahir glanced at the clock. It was well past noon.

He threw back the covers and jumped out of bed. When he opened the bedroom door, the feelings of disappointment and relief should have canceled each other out, but they didn't.

No Kinza.

Ridley.

"Looks like you managed to get *some* sleep." Ridley offered a thin smile, and the shadows under his eyes suggested his night hadn't been much better.

"Some. Yeah." Mahir ran a hand through his hair, not even sure why he bothered trying to put it in any semblance of order. "Any word on the boys?"

Ridley shook his head. "They weren't back when I left. Probably still aren't." He squeezed Mahir's arm. "They're not late. Let's not panic yet."

"Yet." Mahir laughed bitterly. "Right." He gestured over his shoulder. "I'm going to grab a shower."

Ridley said nothing. He just held Mahir's gaze, and Mahir felt a pang of guilt. He wasn't at his best first thing in the morning, and he needed that shower. Mostly to help shed whatever scraps of nightmare still clung to his brain.

He turned and went to the bathroom, stripped completely, and kept the shower to just over ten minutes—enough to let the hot water relax him somewhat and feel sharper and clearer. It seemed like a short respite from whatever else was going to happen, which he had no control over. He got dressed and smoothed his hair back before he hurried downstairs, half-hoping that Kinza might have arrived in the meantime.

But he hadn't.

Ridley stood in the kitchen, a mug of coffee in his hand, another one steaming right next to him on the counter.

Mahir went to retrieve it, and Ridley used the moment to touch his arm. "The boys have done hundreds, if not thousands, of delivery runs. There's no reason why this one should go wrong."

Nothing but the fact that Kinza was the nephew of a cop and Lombardi had a special interest in him. Nothing but Murphy's Law that things went wrong when they could least afford to. Mahir couldn't decide whether having Ridley here made him feel more on edge or less. Kinza was the one thing devouring his brain, and the worry really didn't allow him to think about all their other unresolved issues. Right now, Mahir resented Ridley for pushing him into this. It was a purely emotional response, his rational mind maybe trying to shift the guilt because it was too heavy for him alone.

"Hey." Ridley moved in front of Mahir's face. He lowered his gaze, unable to meet Ridley's eyes. "It'll be fine. He'll come home, and we'll find a way to stop this."

"I can't let him do that again."

"If we see this through, none of those kids will have to do that again. We'll stop the whole ring. We're close, Mahir."

Mahir looked up. If nothing else reached him, hearing Ridley speak his name did.

"We're almost to the end," Ridley said, nearly whispering.

"And you don't know any more than I do if it's going to be a happy ending or not."

"It *will* be." The fierce determination in Ridley's voice should have eased something in Mahir, but it just brought renewed fury to the surface.

He stepped back, turning away sharply. "You don't know that."

"No," Ridley said. "But I do know that either this ends well or I die trying to make it end well."

Mahir faced him again, eyes wide.

The determination that had laced Ridley's tone was written all over his face. "I'm not stopping until this is over, and this isn't over until Kinza is home safe."

Some of Mahir's anger deflated. "You mean until the case is solved."

"And Kinza is home safe."

"You're in this to solve a case. Don't try to—"

"Getting him out of this is important to me, too."

"Why? Why him specifically? Why the hell do—"

"Because he's *your* nephew," Ridley snapped. He swallowed hard, breaking eye contact. "I'll do anything to get all the kids out of this safely, but . . ."

Mahir's lips parted. "I don't . . . You're serious." He stepped closer. "Ridley, you're . . ."

"Yes, I care about him." Ridley faced Mahir, his expression steel hard as ever but . . . brittle. Like he was forcing himself to stay stoic. But his resolve wasn't going to last. "Because you do. And I . . . care about you. Maybe more than I should under the circumstances, but I—"

Mahir cut him off with a light kiss. His lip hurt, but he ignored it. Ridley stiffened at first, but they both relaxed against each other, wrapped their arms around each other. The kiss deepened but not by much. Mahir's heart beat faster, and he wanted nothing more than to pull Ridley even closer. But it wasn't about sex this time. Things had changed. Somewhere along the line, while Mahir hadn't been looking, they'd gone from adversaries to lovers to . . . this. Whatever this was. Much more than two deep-cover operatives had any business having.

That and, right now, Ridley was the only person in the world Mahir could be absolutely sure was still here. The only one who was alive, and on his side, and not potentially the reason for a *we regret to inform you* phone call. Mahir needed to be sure he really *was* here.

Ridley touched his forehead to Mahir's. "I don't know how this is going to end," he whispered unsteadily. "I don't. I can't know that any more than you can." He touched Mahir's face, stroking his cheekbone with the pad of his thumb. "But I mean it when I say that if I have to, I will spend my dying breath doing everything I can to make sure you and Kinza make it out of this."

"I want you to make it out, too." Mahir ran a hand through Ridley's hair. "This isn't over until all three of us get out alive."

Ridley lifted his chin and kissed Mahir lightly. "I promise, I—"

The shrill screech of Mahir's personal phone startled them apart.

Mahir snatched the phone off the counter, praying it was Kinza calling to tell him he was getting on the ferry. One look at the caller ID, though, and his heart plummeted into his feet.

Adil.

"Yes? Mahir speaking."

The sigh might have meant Adil was close to losing his temper but reined himself in at least for the moment because shouting immediately meant Mahir might hang up. They'd played that game a few times.

"It's Adil."

"How are you?" Mahir had to work to put back up the defenses that Ridley had just torn down. His stomach was still flipping when he looked at the man, so he half turned away. "Why are you calling?"

"It's about Kinza, of course." The *don't be an idiot, even though you did go into law enforcement* voice. "This can't continue."

Great. So Adil was choosing now to push on the matter? "What exactly do you mean?"

"You supporting him in his terrible decisions. Kinza is about to ruin his life, and you're just standing back and letting him do that. No, Mahir. You have no idea what it is like to take responsibility for a child and another person's life. You can go on living your hedonistic, selfish, self-destructive lifestyle if you absolutely must, but don't drag my son into that morass."

Normally, the holier-than-thou tone just merely grated, but some of it actually slipped past because he had placed Kinza in harm's way, had encouraged him to do harmful things. He hadn't meant to, was intending to fix it, had just made the hard decision in a scenario without any right decision, but those were still chinks in the armor that allowed Adil's words to strike true.

"It's not a lifestyle," Mahir choked out. "Being gay is not a choice. We both knew he was going to turn out that way. It took him a little longer to realize, but now that he knows, there is no way to put the cat back into the bag. It's done. He's out of the closet, and you can't force him back in."

"He's seventeen, Mahir. People change. It's a phase. If any man who'd ever fooled around with another turned out a lifestyle homosexual, there would hardly be any straight men left!"

Oh really? "And how would *you* know that?" Attack being the best defense and so on.

"Oh, come on. Are you going to use that against me now?"

"Honestly, I don't care what you think about 'experimentation.' That cuts both ways. I know lots of gay men . . ."

A snort. "I bet."

"*Lots* of gay men who experimented with women. It happens. It's fluid. Between one-hundred-percent gay and one-hundred-percent straight is still a lot of room."

"And Kinza is not going to go into that lifestyle!"

He already is. Complete with boyfriend. "It's not your choice. It's not even my choice."

"You're doing this to get back at me for not supporting your choices!"

Oh, this projection thing was a bitch. "I've made my peace with the fact that I lost my brother when I stopped obeying him."

Deathly silence.

Subtle movement beside him reminded Mahir that Ridley was still here. He glanced at him, and Ridley's eyebrows rose with concern. He put a hand on Mahir's arm, and Mahir rested his own hand on top of it.

Remembering Ridley was here reminded him what they'd been discussing just before Adil had called. About why this acidic knot of sick terror was still coiled in his gut.

And his frustration with his brother turned to something far more venomous.

"You don't know how lucky you are, Adil," he said through clenched teeth.

"Lucky?" A derisive snort. "How am—"

"So your son is gay. He's healthy. He's alive." *Please, Allah, please . . .* "He's a good kid, dammit. You know he is."

"He was."

"For fuck's sake." Mahir exhaled sharply. "Is it really that big of a crisis? Really? In the grand scheme of things, when he could have been a delinquent or had some horrific disease, is your son being gay really that big of a deal? Dammit, Adil, get your head out of your ass and into the twenty-first motherfucking century."

Ridley's eyes widened, and he drew back a little, like the outburst had startled him as much as it had Mahir himself, who was shaking now as much from fury as the adrenaline rush that followed unloading something like that.

Adil sputtered a few times. Even as children, Mahir had never spoken to him this way. "You . . . you don't understand."

"You're right. I don't." Mahir shifted his weight enough to relocate some nervous energy but still keep his arm within Ridley's gentle grasp. "I don't understand how you can be such an intolerant fucking monster that your son feels the need to *leave his own home* and come live with me just so he can feel safe." *And what have I done? He came to me to be safe, and now he's a drug mule.*

Allah, Kinza, please forgive me.

"Safe?" Adil scoffed. "He has never been unsafe in my home."

"Does *he* know that?" Mahir growled.

More sputtering and stammering.

Ridley squeezed Mahir's arm gently, running his thumb back and forth over the top of Mahir's sleeve.

His brother muffled a sharp cough. "You'll send him home to—"

"The fuck I will."

Pause. "*What?*"

"I know he's a minor. I know, legally, you have the right to demand that I let him come home, though I'm certainly not keeping him here against his will. But if I feel he's going back to an unsafe environment, I'm obligated—as both an officer of the law and his uncle—to intervene."

"Is that a threat?"

Mahir mulled it over. "You know what? Yes. Yes, it is. You force him to come home before I'm convinced you've joined the twenty-first century and aren't going to try to beat the gay out of him, I will get Child Protective Services involved. So what'll it be? Let Kinza stay with me until you can settle your differences? Or let him spend his last few months of high school in foster care?"

"You would have him taken from his family?"

"If it means keeping him safe, yes." Mahir flinched at his own words. He ought to have been calling CPS on himself at that point. "I'm trying to look out for Kinza here. He's gay. He always will be. You can either accept that or tell Khalisah to start setting one fewer place at the dinner table."

Silence. Long, drawn-out silence.

Then, calmer than before, Adil said, "Tell my boy to call me. He's not answering his phone."

Mahir flinched. Hopefully that just meant Kinza had—wisely—turned his phone off for the time being. "I will."

And with that, the line went dead.

Mahir tossed his phone on the counter. He rubbed his temples to keep his hands from shaking.

Ridley put an arm around him. "That took some balls."

"Yeah. And you don't know my brother."

"Is he . . . abusive?"

"Depends on how you define the word." Mahir looked at Ridley. "Can't imagine he's done anything worse to Kinza than I have. My rap sheet's looking at a few counts of reckless child endangerment."

"We had no other choice." Ridley remained close, steady and reliable, and Mahir realized with a start that that was probably the real man. Somewhere, Ridley had been shedding more and more of his persona, and what he was now dealing with was the cop and nothing but.

"Once they relieve me, I need to get away from all this and the city."

Ridley nodded. "I'm due some leave."

"Good." That'll work. Getting to know him better in peace and with all the time in the world. It sounded like heaven. "Can't say I'm looking forward to introducing you to my family, though. They're complicated like that. But my brother's easily the worst."

Ridley nodded, lips in a taut line. Well, two families that weren't exactly supportive. Adding the complications of faith and ethnicity, they were probably better off on their own.

Mahir cleared his throat and shook his head. "I would introduce you to my parents, though, and Adil can take it or leave it. And you do know Kinza already. His siblings turned out surprisingly well, considering their father."

Ridley squeezed his hand. "No need to create more friction in your family on my account."

He was being diplomatic and yet not—it wasn't shorthand for *let's not move too quickly.* "I just think it might be time to make more of a stand, stop using the easy way of just shutting them out."

"If and when you're ready." Ridley smirked. "Not when they are."

"Probably won't be tonight, then."

Ridley laughed. "Good. I don't think I can handle trying to impress your family along with all this other shit."

All this other shit.

And there they were, back in reality, the momentary escape gone as quickly as it had begun. Mahir sighed and glanced at the clock on the microwave. Almost one thirty.

"Patience," Ridley said.

Mahir swallowed. "If anything happens to one of the boys, does Lombardi call you?"

Ridley shook his head. "No. I handle security at the club only. He doesn't even talk to me about the couriers."

So much for that.

"Well—" Mahir sighed. "—I guess all we can do now is wait."

Ridley was just starting to doze off on the couch, and Mahir was focused on a rerun of some sitcom from years ago when a key in the front door had them both on their feet.

Mahir hurried to the stairs, Ridley hot on his heels, and they were both on their way down when the front door opened.

Kinza looked exhausted, even a little bit rattled, but physically no worse for the wear. He closed the door behind him, turned the dead bolt, and looked up at Mahir. "I'm home."

Mahir's pulse jumped into his throat. "How do you feel? Are you doing okay?"

"I need a shower." Kinza shuddered.

"Okay. Go." Mahir stood aside, as did Ridley, clearing a path for Kinza to get upstairs. "Are you hungry?"

Kinza grimaced and shook his head. "Not really."

Worry tugged at Mahir's gut, but he didn't argue. "All right. Grab a shower. Do you feel up to talking?"

Kinza released a breath, his shoulders sagging like the mere thought of a conversation exhausted him. "Yeah. Just . . ." He waved a hand toward the bathroom.

Ridley and Mahir watched the kid walk down the hall, a lone figure that seemed unreachable to Mahir. He wanted to follow him but worried he'd be rebuffed. *Let him have space* warred with *It's all your fault.*

Once Kinza was out of earshot, Mahir said, "You think he's okay? Is this normal?"

"Mahir." Ridley put an arm around him and kissed his cheek tenderly. "Think about what he just had to do. I don't know what it's like to be a mule, but just knowing what he did is probably making him feel a bit ill."

"But you don't think he's . . . I mean, it's not a side effect, or—"

"You mean like he got some coke into his system?"

Mahir nodded, feeling sick to his stomach.

Ridley shook his head. "No. He'd be in a world of—" He glanced at Mahir. "He's fine."

Mahir forced himself to at least try to relax a little. The fact that Kinza was home and mobile was a good sign. He had to cling to that.

"You want a cup of coffee?" Ridley asked.

"You're my guest," Mahir said with a halfhearted chuckle. "Shouldn't I be getting you some?"

Ridley laughed. "Well, I was going to be an imposition and get some for myself, so . . ."

"Fair enough, then."

They both went into the kitchen, and Mahir was thankful he'd had the forethought to put more coffee on earlier. Maybe not forethought. More like restlessness. Going through the motions of filling and starting the coffeemaker had been a good enough outlet, and now there was fresh coffee so he wasn't going to complain.

As Ridley poured the coffee, Mahir reached into the dishwasher for a couple of clean spoons. When he stood, the movement of his own reflection in the kitchen window caught his eye, and he startled.

Was there somebody on the other side of the glass? He shook his head. *You* are *being paranoid.*

Until something else moved. This time it wasn't his reflection.

He casually moved away from the window but craned his neck to look outside.

It wasn't his imagination. Someone was in the backyard.

"I think they followed him," he said. "There's somebody in the back. Check the front."

Ridley pulled the pistol from his shoulder holster, and Mahir rushed to the living room to get a pistol, too.

"Anybody outside?"

Ridley turned toward him and nodded. "Tell Kinza to stay in there."

"Right." Mahir ran down the hall and knocked on the door until the water stopped. "Kinza. Stay in there. Do not come out."

Muffled, "Why, what's . . ."

"Our friends are here. Just stay put."

He rushed back down the hall and down the stairs to the landing where Ridley stood watchful and tense.

"Any idea who they are? Club? External guys?"

"I think I saw Bald Guy," Ridley said quietly. "But there are others. At least three."

"I can't imagine Kinza slipped up."

"Maybe it's just because he's living with a cop. No idea."

"Shit."

A shadow fell over the door's peephole from the outside.

"Stay back."

"What are you doing?"

"No time." Ridley pushed him toward the stairs and motioned for him to go up. Grudgingly, Mahir obeyed. At the top of the stairs, he pressed his back up against the wall and held his breath as he listened to Ridley unlock and open the front door.

"What the *fuck* do you think you're doing?" Ridley barked. "Sneaking around like this in broad fucking daylight? Are you out of your goddamned minds?"

"Uh, Ridley." Bald Guy. "What are you doing here?"

Mahir gritted his teeth. Nice idea to try to intimidate the goons, but that was a lot to hang from Ridley's acting talent alone.

Ridley brushed him off. "Nice neighborhood like this, every neighbor around will call the cops."

"I said, what are *you* doing here?"

Oh great. So this was the moment Bald Guy made his play for leadership?

Floorboards creaked quietly, like one of them had leaned toward or away from the other. Mahir hoped it was Ridley using his presence to compel Bald Guy and his cronies to get the hell out of here.

"What did you say?" Ridley's tone was quiet and dangerous.

"You heard me. Both times." A footstep, followed by another creak. "Or have you been spending so much time with the sand nigger, you're forgetting how to understand English?"

"You're an idiot," Ridley snarled without missing a beat. "And you're going to make a scene and draw attention. I'm handling this."

"Oh yeah?" A quiet rustle and a squeak, like a leather jacket protesting slow movement. "Handling *what*, Ridley?"

Mahir gulped. *Don't lose your cool now, Ridley. Keep it together.*

"Last I checked," Ridley said, still calm and collected, "you answer to me. Not the other way around. I'm going to say this once. Get back in the car, and get—"

"You know, I don't think so."

Sharp movement. A heavy smack. A grunt followed by stumbling footsteps. Mahir craned his neck, using the reflection in a picture frame to see what was going on, and he held his breath as Ridley recovered from, apparently, being shoved back a step.

Ridley snatched the lapel of Bald Guy's jacket. "Are you insane? Do you want the cops to come and break this up?"

"Wouldn't have to wait long, would we?" Bald Guy shoved Ridley back another step. "Since one lives here. But you already know that, don't you?" He didn't wait for a response, and Mahir flinched as Bald Guy threw his fist, which meant he fortunately didn't see where that fist connected.

When he looked again, Ridley had stumbled back to the very edge of what the picture frame's reflection could monitor, clutching the side of his face.

"Jesus fucking Christ." Ridley stood, stepping back into Mahir's view and right up in Bald Guy's face. "Lombardi is going to have you—"

"Lombardi is about done with your double-crossing bullshit, Ridley." Another punch, but this time, Ridley blocked it. He grabbed Bald Guy's arm, spun him around, and pinned him against the wall with the guy's arm twisted painfully behind his back. The other men lunged forward, but a look from Ridley halted them in their tracks.

Mahir's heart pounded. Though Ridley was badly outnumbered, he had the upper hand. But for how long?

He crept closer to the corner of the wall, moving as stealthily as he could. Fortunately, he knew every floorboard in this house, which ones squeaked and which didn't, and carefully sidestepped one he knew to be noisy.

He stopped, pressing his back against the wall and keeping his gun at the ready. He glanced at the picture frame, leaning just right so the reflection showed him what was going on.

And for a split second, in the reflection, he made eye contact with the restrained Bald Guy.

"Hey!" Bald Guy shouted. "There's someone upstairs!"

Mahir cursed silently, then heard the unmistakable sound of breaking bones. Ridley must have snapped Bald Guy's arm, and the terrible scream that followed confirmed his suspicion.

Steps sounded. At least two people rushed closer, and a solid *thud* spoke of more blows being exchanged. In the reflection, he saw one guy grapple with Ridley while another squeezed past and headed up the stairs.

There wasn't really anyplace to go unless he exposed Kinza, so Mahir raised his gun and lined it up with the head appearing in the stairwell.

Gray.

A gunshot sounded, almost causing Mahir to squeeze his own trigger in surprise, if nothing else.

Gray turned and looked at him. His eyes went wide, and that was when Mahir knew the game was up. Gray had made the connection, the one piece of the puzzle that the goons had kept missing. Now all covers were blown, and they were rapidly descending into FUBAR territory.

"Put down your weapon!" Mahir barked.

Gray stared at him.

Another shot downstairs and a choked sound of pain. A body going down.

Mahir lost patience and came around the corner. Gray had half turned at the shot—a pure reflex—and when he turned back, Mahir's pistol hit his temple. He went down, crumpled on the stairs, and Mahir grabbed him by the collar and pulled him up, mostly to clear the staircase rather than to ensure he wasn't going to tumble down and break his neck.

"Ridley?" he called down as he yanked Gray's wrist behind his back. "Ridley?"

No response.

Oh shit.

CHAPTER TWENTY

He quickly cuffed Gray, then shoved him face-first onto the stairs. Police brutality, whatever. He hurried down to the landing where three men lay still and bloody.

Bald Guy. The third goon. And Ridley.

Mahir dropped to his knees beside Ridley and felt his neck. The pulse was there but weak. The other guy was half-draped over Ridley's torso—and judging by the piece missing from the side of his head, probably didn't need to be triaged—so Mahir shoved him off.

And then his heart really dropped. Ridley moaned weakly, making a feeble effort to stop the flow of blood from a substantial wound in his side.

"Oh fuck. Ridley, can you hear me?" Mahir pulled off his shirt, wadded it, and pushed Ridley's hand away so he could compress the wound. Ridley gasped, groaned, and tried to wriggle away. "Just hold still. Hold still." Through the open front door he could hear sirens in the distance; a neighbor must have called the cops when they'd heard the gunfire. *Thank you, Mrs. Blunt.*

Just in case, though, he shouted over his shoulder, "Kinza! Kinza, I need your help!"

The bathroom door opened. Soft footsteps came down the hall and down the stairs.

"Oh my God." Kinza halted, all the color slipping from his face. "What—"

"Call 9-1-1." Mahir nodded toward the kitchen. "Hurry."

Kinza seemed paralyzed for a second, but then he rushed back upstairs.

Mahir turned back to Ridley. "Come on. Stay with me. Help's coming." All phrases that sounded so clichéd and empty and meaningless. "Look at me, Ridley."

To his surprise, Ridley managed to open his eyes, though he seemed to be struggling to focus them. He swept his tongue across his rapidly paling lips. When he tried to pull in a breath, he met some resistance with the shirt Mahir had pressed against him and winced.

"Just stay still," Mahir said. "The less you move, the better."

Ridley let his eyelids slide shut, and Mahir thought he'd slipped into unconsciousness, but then Ridley moistened his lips again. "Kinza."

"What?"

"Is . . . Kinza okay?"

"He's safe. He's upstairs calling an ambulance for you."

"Good." Ridley relaxed a bit. Too much for someone in his condition.

"Hey." Mahir patted his face. "Stay with me, all right?"

Ridley just groaned.

Mahir felt around and found Ridley's hand, which was wet and sticky with blood, but he gripped it anyway. Ridley's fingers twitched a little. When Mahir squeezed gently, Ridley squeezed back. Weakly, but Mahir would take what he could get.

The sirens outside were getting closer. Mahir prayed over and over that they got here in time. He didn't like the way Ridley was paling or the way his chest didn't seem to rise quite as much after each breath.

"Come on, Ridley," he whispered. "This isn't over. I need you to help me finish it."

"Think . . ." Ridley winced. "Think I'm gonna . . . be outta commission for a while."

Mahir laughed, sounding almost hysterical. Maybe he was. At this point, anything was possible.

The sirens were really close by now.

"Kinza," he called up the stairs. "Make sure the ambulance finds the house."

"Will do."

Kinza trotted down the stairs and past Mahir, out into the front yard. For a split second, Mahir had visions of more goons waiting outside to finish this, but he knew better. Once the bullets started flying, they'd have joined in, and there'd be no one left to put pressure on Ridley's wound.

"The ambulance is almost here," Mahir whispered, not sure if he was trying to reassure himself or Ridley. "You can make it. I know you can."

I need you to.

He was terribly tempted to kiss Ridley, but it would have felt too much like good-bye, so he just touched his face and pulled back when the EMT crew rushed through the door. As much as he would have wanted to stay around, they needed all the space they had to stabilize Ridley. A shudder raced through Mahir's body, and he turned around and stepped outside to wait for the police. Kinza stood there, too, looking forlorn, and Mahir placed an arm around his shoulder.

"You've been very brave," Mahir said.

"What now? Is Lombardi going to get away?"

"I should hand this over to my colleagues." He wasn't looking forward to that messy debriefing by any means.

"You mean, you're just . . . waiting? Rather than going to get Lombardi?"

"It's not quite like in the movies, Kinza."

And still, nobody knew yet what had happened. Rather than this being the epic fuck-up that put the case out of his hands and into those of the department, nothing really had happened. Not in Lombardi's version of reality.

But he had to make up his mind quickly, before the cops showed up and gave him a hard time, even despite his own badge. Staying here just meant getting grilled and then maybe spending the rest of the night waiting for Ridley to come out of the OR. "Okay. Listen. When the cops show up, you'll just go with them. You're the only one who can tell them a mostly coherent story, so that'll help a great deal."

Kinza's eyes lit up. "You're going to get Lombardi?"

"Wouldn't miss it." Mahir stepped back and checked his pistol. His jeans were bloody, but that would only give him more credibility when he showed up. If he played this well, he'd still bring the case in, and in less of a tattered, horrible mess.

"Good luck," Kinza said softly.

"Thanks." Mahir squeezed his arm. "Just cooperate with the police, okay?"

His nephew nodded.

Mahir's car was in the garage, blocked in by the ambulance that had backed into the driveway, but the car Gray and others had driven in was still out on the curb. He went back inside, squeezing past the paramedics and not letting himself look at Ridley's still, bloody form on the floor.

He grabbed the scruff of Gray's neck. "Where are the car keys?"

"Fuck you," Gray spat.

Mahir gripped his neck harder. "The fucking keys. Someone needs to tell Lombardi all this shit hit the fan."

Gray stared incredulously at him. "What do you care? You're a fucking—"

"Shut the fuck up," Mahir snapped. "I'm *not*, and I almost had everything in the bag, including Ridley, before you idiots showed up."

Confusion contorted Gray's expression.

Mahir shifted impatiently. "I need the fucking keys. You want me to tell Lombardi you made this mess even worse?"

Gray scowled. "My left front pocket."

Mahir reached into the front pocket.

"That what it takes to finally get you in my pants?" Gray asked dryly.

"Shut up." Mahir took the keys and stood. Out front, flashing blue lights had joined the flashing red ones. He slipped back up to the top floor, then sneaked out the back sliding glass door onto the deck. Creeping as quietly but as quickly as he could, he hurried back down to the ground level. He went around the side of the house, pausing a few times to make sure no one was coming to check the backyard.

Most of the officers were in the house now, except for a pair outside talking to some wide-eyed bystanders. Mahir took advantage of their collective distraction and casually made his way to the shiny black car by the curb.

It wasn't until he was out of the cul-de-sac and on his way down the main road that Mahir released his breath. Now to get back to the club. He debated skipping the ferry and driving around via the Narrows Bridge, but even if he drove at reckless speeds, the distance and the traffic would hinder him; he'd never make it before the ferry docked on the other side. Ferry it was.

He drove on this time. The attendant at the ticket booth didn't give him a second look—fortunately, the shadows obscured his bloody slacks, and his shirt was dark enough the stains weren't obvious—and sent him to get in line with all the other cars.

Panic rattled him straight to the core. The ferry was approaching, but it would take a good ten or fifteen minutes for it to unload. There were several lines of cars ahead of him, and a quick mental count put him in that gray area where he *might* make it on this boat, and he *might* have to wait for the next one. Drumming his thumbs on the wheel, he hoped this evening's crew was made up of Tetris experts, the ones who could wedge an extra dozen cars onto a deck that was full by anyone else's standards.

The ferry unloaded. One by one, the rows of waiting cars were directed to board. *Please, please, load this row.* If he didn't get on this one, it would be at least another hour before the next one came. That gave Lombardi a good two hours to work out that things had gone wrong.

Mahir's row started moving. With his heart in his throat, he followed the slow line of cars toward the orange-vested crewman who waved each vehicle in turn onto the boat. Up ahead, the car deck was almost full. Maybe enough room for three more cars, and Mahir was fifth in line.

Come on, come on.

The crewman let the car ahead of Mahir get on board but put a hand up and halted Mahir.

No. No! Shit, no!

But then the crewman nodded and gestured for Mahir to go ahead. The car just fit into a small pocket of space, and as the other crewmen put wedges under his tires to keep him from rolling backward off the boat, the gate went up.

He was the last one, but he'd boarded.

Now, all he had to do was wait until he reached the other side.

Please don't let this be the run where they decide to stop mid-Sound and do an evacuation drill . . .

As the boat pulled away from the dock and began its glacially slow journey to Seattle, Mahir debated his options. He'd be in deep shit for leaving the scene. No doubt about that. If he called ahead now, and they sent SWAT in, Lombardi might have a chance to lock down the basement and dispose of some of the evidence—human and narcotic alike—before anyone got close.

His best—and riskiest—bet was to go in alone. Phone into James's office just before he entered, and then hope he could pin Lombardi down before SWAT showed up. Given the club's location and the traffic at this time of night, he'd have twenty minutes at best.

And then he just had to hope he didn't get caught in the cross fire.

Just a few weeks ago, he wouldn't even have hesitated, but with Kinza and hopefully Ridley waiting for him, catching a bullet was a lot less enticing. But he didn't do waiting very well, and just the thought that Lombardi might be able to clean up made his stomach roil. After sending everybody else into danger, maybe now it *was* his turn.

The crossing was an exercise in torture. Mahir fiddled with his cell phone, tempted a few times to check in with Kinza, half-expecting his brother to call and fire accusations at him. But the fact that it remained silent was maybe even worse.

He closed his eyes and played through several scenarios in his mind—angles, visibility, and how much resistance he'd encounter. Most of all, though, he had to rely on improvisation. There was no telling how Lombardi would respond, though his arrogance was a known factor.

Mahir drummed his fingers on the steering wheel, then noticed the faint reddish shadow of Ridley's blood on his right hand. Guilt slammed into him, and he sent a quick prayer to Allah, hoping the operation would be successful and he'd get to tell Ridley what he actually felt. That, too, was a terrifying prospect, though in his mind and heart, it was all clear. Not just work, not by far, and maybe, if Ridley was on the same page, they could find a way to—

He shook his head and pushed those thoughts away. All in its time.

The ferry stopped. Fortunately, being the last car on meant being one of the first ones off. Within minutes of docking, he was off the boat.

Heart racing faster, he made his way down the dock and to the main road. The club was only a few minutes away. Before he knew it—though it still felt like an eternity—he'd pulled into the parking lot behind the club. He took a few deep breaths to collect himself.

Then he took out his phone and called James.

"Hussain," his superior said. "What's up?"

"I have to make this fast." Mahir glanced at the club's back door, which was still closed. "Some shit's about to go down at the club. Covers have been blown, and some of Lombardi's men are dead."

"*Shit.*"

"Yeah. Once he finds out, he's going to start doing damage control. I'm going in now to stall him as best I can."

"You want to take him down *now*?"

"What choice do we have?" Mahir paused. "There are kids involved. Getting sent to God knows where. How soon can your boys be here?"

"I, uh . . ." James stammered. "Twenty. Maybe a few minutes longer. Are you there now?"

"Yes." Mahir checked his pistol again. "I'm going in. Get here as soon as you can."

"You're not going in there alone! Are you insane?"

"He doesn't know who I am. And I can stall him."

"Mahir, you're out of your fucking mind. He even catches the scent of a pig on you, he's going to blow your head off."

"I'll take my chances. See you in twenty." He hung up and slipped the phone under the driver's seat. Then he got out and headed inside.

One of the guys by the door did a double take. "What the hell happened to—"

"I need to see the boss," Mahir said sharply. "Now. It's an emergency."

The guy's jaw dropped.

"*Now!*" Mahir barked.

The guy hurried toward the stairs leading up to Lombardi's office. Mahir followed, but he walked. By the time he made it to the top, he'd have Lombardi's attention; no point in running up so he could stand by a closed door for a minute or two.

Just as he'd predicted, when he reached the top, Mahir was greeted by an open door and two wide-eyed bodyguards ushering him inside.

Lombardi looked him up and down, his jaw slowly falling open. "What the fuck are you doing in my club looking like that?"

"I didn't have a choice." Mahir put up his hands. "Shit got crazy."

"What happened?" the pimp bellowed, slamming his fist down onto his desk. "Tell me. Now!"

"I will, but there's something more pressing than that."

"What? What are you—"

"Can we have some privacy?" Mahir asked, eyeing the other men in the room. They all looked at each other warily.

"Just talk, haji," Lombardi growled.

"This isn't something you want the whole crew to know about, sir." Mahir deliberately injected a panicked waver into his voice.

Lombardi regarded him silently, then waved a hand, and everyone else vacated the room. When the door was closed and locked, he said, "Now talk before you've got your own blood on those pants."

Mahir came closer. He leaned over the desk and lowered his voice. "We've been compromised. The operation downstairs, it's—"

"*What?*"

"Ridley tried to stop the snitch, but he went down, and—"

"Snitch? Ridley? Went down?" Lombardi shook his head. "Are you telling me Ridley's dead?"

Mahir nodded gravely and gestured at the blood on his clothes.

Lombardi paled, leaning back in his chair. "Fuck . . ."

"Someone knows, Gene," Mahir said quietly. "Not just about what the couriers are carrying." He inclined his head and lifted an eyebrow in a silent bid for Lombardi to read between the lines.

It must have worked because the color left in Lombardi's face evaporated. "What? How do you know about—"

"It doesn't matter," Mahir snapped. "But there are cops headed for the clients from the last three runs. You need to contact them before they get busted." He prayed his bluff would work. Prayed *hard*.

"And how do I know the cops aren't headed here?" Lombardi asked.

"Ridley managed to throw them off," Mahir said. "Sent them looking for a warehouse in Olympia. But the snitch got the locations of the buyers, and he knew down to the last detail who they were, what they'd bought, and where they'd be. They've got feds getting ready to bust their doors in." Mahir thumped a knuckle on the desk. "If they get caught, they're going to believe it was you who sent in the feds."

"That's bullshit." Lombardi waved a hand. "Everyone knows I wouldn't cooperate with cops."

"You willing to gamble with your entire operation that one of the undercovers didn't tell a different story?"

Lombardi swallowed.

"Call them," Mahir said. "Tell them the feds are on their way."

Lombardi cast him a baleful look but reached for his cell phone. Mahir straightened up and stepped back—not much, just to no longer be right in the man's face. He couldn't be too interested in the calls, either, so he found a box of tissue on a side table, pulled out a few, and wiped at his trousers, accomplishing exactly nothing. The phone bill would be interesting. The books Ridley had mentioned. Surveillance tapes.

But if he'd hoped that Lombardi's calls would give him anything at all, he was sorely disappointed. He was speaking Italian, and Mahir only understood the occasional word, which was just as well.

Lombardi spoke fast, impatiently, but didn't have much of his arrogant bluster. He was worried, possibly scared. He ended that call and quickly made another, this exchange very quick, rushed and one-sided, too.

Mahir doubted very much that the guys on the other side got even a word in, which was all as planned. If they kept running, they wouldn't stop and ask questions or start to doubt what they thought to be true. And with every minute that Lombardi spent wrapping himself deeper into the spider silk, he'd make a pretty parcel by the time SWAT arrived.

Third call. This time, Lombardi's voice was different again. Plaintive? So he'd had to build up courage to call this one. Perfect. Mahir gritted his teeth to keep from smiling, betraying anything he felt when he heard Lombardi very clearly scared. Begging. Maybe a boss. Maybe a step up in the hierarchy, some shady capo or don who was normally untouchable because all he did was collect cash envelopes on Christmas. Whatever it was, it sounded very promising.

Lombardi ended the call and leaned forward on his desk, hands folded in front of him, neck bowed. Looking beautifully defeated. Mahir kept his eyes on him, but for a few moments, Lombardi did absolutely nothing.

"So, tell me the whole story. What happened?"

Mahir straightened, and just as he was about to tell a version of events that would keep Lombardi busy asking question for ten more minutes, Lombardi's cell phone vibrated on the desk, the sound unnerving and irresistible. Lombardi glanced at the display, then back at Mahir.

Mahir lifted an eyebrow. "One of the customers?"

"No. Unknown caller ID." Lombardi had to be rattled if he simply answered the question.

The phone kept buzzing, wandering an inch or so to the side. Lombardi's hand fell down on it like he was squashing a bug, but then he answered. "Yes?"

Mahir watched him, and he did not like how his expression shifted. Surprise, then something not unlike amusement, then his features darkened again. "Tell me what happened."

It took every bit of self-control Mahir had—calling on every ounce of Saeed he still had—to keep his expression blank. To not swallow nervously as he heard the faint buzz of someone on the other end of the line, speaking quickly and frantically. Especially since Lombardi didn't have that unfocused, distant look of someone listening intently to the information coming through the phone.

Oh no.

He was focused.

Right on Mahir.

As he stared at Mahir across the desk, murmuring the occasional "uh-huh" and "I see" as the rapid speech from the other end continued, his eyes narrowed a little. Then a little more.

Mahir stared back, stoic and unmoving in spite of the panic coiling beneath his ribs. This wasn't part of his plan. Whatever Lombardi was hearing, this wasn't part of Mahir's plan.

You call that a plan? Keep him busy making incriminating phone calls until SWAT shows up? Great plan.

"Interesting." Lombardi was looking so intently at him, Mahir almost thought the comment was directed at him. "I'll have a car sent for you. Someone will post bail."

Oh. That wasn't good.

Lombardi casually ended the call and set the phone on the desk, facedown, the plastic casing making a quiet but somehow menacing *click* on the polished surface. "That was a fascinating phone call."

"Have you called the other clients?" Mahir asked, making an obvious gesture of checking his watch. "The feds are going—"

"How did you get that blood on your shirt, Saeed?"

The note of suspicion attached to his pseudonym didn't help with Mahir's already-pounding heart. "Sir, with all due—"

"I asked you a question." Lombardi opened a drawer on his left. He reached into it, and with all the agitation and animation of someone taking out a checkbook or a pen, he withdrew a glossy nickel-plated handgun. He laid it on the table beside the phone, the metallic *clink* even more menacing than the sound the phone had made a second ago. "How, Saeed, did you get the blood on your shirt?"

"Do you really think we have time for this?" Mahir shifted in his chair and glanced first at the gun, then at the door behind him. "You've got clients who—"

"I've got ears in this building who don't belong here." Lombardi folded his hands on the desk behind the phone and the gun, both items laid out like Exhibit A and Exhibit B of a trial Mahir hadn't known had begun. "It turns out you're right, and Ridley's dead, which is unfortunate."

He may as well have kicked Mahir in the gut just then, and Mahir fought not to show it.

"You'll find I have a tremendous amount of patience when it suits me," Lombardi said in a low, even growl. "When the information I want is worth the wait, and the effort it takes to extract it, I assure you, my patience will last a lot longer than your blood supply."

Mahir swallowed. "I was—"

"That Arab kid is the nephew of a cop," Lombardi snapped. "Now, maybe I'm just being an ignorant wop, thinking all you camel jockeys look the same, but I can't help but wonder why you were at the kid's uncle's house when I certainly didn't send you. You *or* Ridley." He stroked his chin thoughtfully, glaring at Mahir. "I send my boys to check on a kid I don't think I can trust, and instead of his uncle showing up, you do. Along with Ridley." He leaned forward over the desk. "After I've heard the boys talking about you and Ridley being awfully chummy these days."

Gray, I will fucking kill you . . .

"I don't understand, sir." Mahir shook his head. "Ridley asked me to come with him to—"

"You take your orders from *me*!" Lombardi shouted, slamming his fist down hard enough to make both phone and gun bounce off the desk. "I didn't give the order. I didn't authorize Ridley to be in that sand nigger cop's house. You have one chance, Saeed." Lombardi snatched the pistol off the table, and in a heartbeat, Mahir was looking down the barrel. "Tell me why you and Ridley were in that house."

What had Gray seen? What exactly would he have said? The man wasn't stupid, but he'd seen nothing that connected Mahir with Saeed or Saeed with Kinza. But thinking under that amount of pressure wasn't easy, not with *Ridley's dead* echoing in his head. "He called me as backup, said he had a suspicion the kid might be talking and feeding information to a snitch on the security team."

"Really?"

No, I made this shit up with a gun pointed at my face.

Mahir blew out a breath. "It's not like he told me anything. He needed backup. He knew I served in Fallujah and would keep my shit together if people started shooting. Then Gray and the others showed up."

"And?"

"One of them started shooting. I didn't see who it was." Mahir forced himself to look beyond the gun right into Lombardi's eyes. "And Ridley was gone." He forced himself to keep the emotion out of his voice, but it hurt saying it aloud. "Tried to bring him back to get rid of the body, but there were others, and I figured I should get back and warn you. Maybe if we got here quickly . . . ah, no. Gray's in custody? He wasn't dead." Losing the plot somewhat, which was only understandable with all the stress.

"So that's Ridley's blood."

"Can anybody trace the bodies here?"

"You're answering *my* fucking question."

Mahir shook his head as if to clear his mind. Those ten minutes by now felt like ten hours. "Yeah."

"So you guys were fucking." Lombardi didn't look surprised.

"I'm sorry, sir. Gray was . . . very persuasive. But I realize I shouldn't have done that. He's not even my type."

"Gray?" Lombardi leaned forward. "Who the fuck is talking about Gray?"

"You didn't . . . Oh. See, Gray thought I had something going with Ridley, even though that bastard punched me in the face so hard

I almost broke a tooth. I was getting annoyed until I realized he was jealous, so I fucked him. Gray, I mean."

Lombardi arched an eyebrow, and Mahir couldn't tell if he was confused or just disbelieving at the gay soap opera Mahir was unfolding for him. "I hire cocksuckers for my security team so they don't fuck my girls." The eyebrow came down, and Lombardi clenched his teeth. "Not so they'll fuck each other."

Moving slowly to avoid startling Lombardi's itchy trigger finger, Mahir put his hands up and showed his palms. "I didn't know what else to do. I just didn't want to get fired. Or, uh, killed." His eyes darted toward the muzzle of the pistol, then back to Lombardi.

Lombardi sighed. He lowered the gun and put it back on the desk beside the phone. Mahir didn't dare breathe a sigh of relief. Not yet. Volatile as this motherfucker was, he could've planted a stick of dynamite under Mahir's chair or something.

"Ridley will be a bitch to replace," Lombardi grumbled. "But if he's going to complicate simple fucking orders . . ." Trailing off, he shook his head.

"Simple orders?" Mahir furrowed his brow. "He was never clear about why we were—"

"It was simple enough a goddamned retarded kid could've handled it," Lombardi said. "That's why I sent Gray, Keith, and Curly, for God's sake."

Something cold and prickly crawled up from the base of Mahir's spine.

"You have a gun, Saeed?"

Mahir gulped. "Yes. Ridley gave me one when I started."

"Good. Because you'll have to finish the job he botched."

C'mon, SWAT. Where the fuck are you?

Lombardi eyed Mahir with one of those weird, baited looks that always unsettled him. "Can you handle that?"

"What's . . . what's the order?"

"The kid." Lombardi tapped his forehead, right between his eyes. "Make it clean."

Mahir's throat constricted. "You . . ." He almost choked on his own breath.

"Is there a problem?" Lombardi folded his hands and cocked his head slightly. "My workforce has just been downsized rather abruptly." He smiled a creepy smile. "I need some of my remaining employees to pick up the slack until I can fill the gaps. You understand, don't you?"

"He's just a kid."

"He's a *cop's* kid," Lombardi said, the smile vanishing. "He is a liability to my business. And I'm a businessman, Saeed. I don't like getting my hands dirty." The smile returned, this time even creepier than before. "You like working with your hands, don't you?"

Mahir swallowed. He had no idea how to respond to that.

"I also have to cut my expenses." Lombardi was way too calm right now. Especially for a man who'd been shaking in his boots five minutes ago. Something wasn't right.

SWAT? Guys? Anytime now. Seriously. Any-fucking-time.

"I have to cut my expenses, and gas is getting terribly expensive." Lombardi had adopted an incredibly earnest voice, like he was really very worried about the price of gas, not the fact that the feds might be sniffing out his human trafficking ring. "So I'd just as soon you do the dirty work locally, if you know what I mean."

Someone knocked on the door. Mahir jumped as though a gunshot had gone off. SWAT must have arrived. Someone had seen them. Had come up to tip off Lombardi. That meant Mahir was a dead man, but maybe the operation would—

"Come in."

The door opened, and one of the guards outside said, "Darren is here, sir."

What the hell? Was Lombardi going to kick him out and continue with business as usual? A meeting with an associate?

Lombardi gave the man a nod. His smile turned to one of those grins that made Mahir's skin crawl. He folded his hands behind the pistol and the phone again, and looked right at—right *into*—Mahir. "Fortunately, you won't have to go far."

Before Mahir could put the pieces together, a commotion caused him to turn around, and he faced the door just in time to see Kinza stumbling through like someone had shoved him.

Behind him, smug and smirking in a state patrol uniform, a cop entered the office. "Found him at his uncle's house, all alone and waiting to talk to us." The man's eyes narrowed, and his gaze slid toward Mahir, but there was no overt recognition. A new haircut and different shaving habit surely couldn't change him so much? The cop must have had access to Mahir's file. Now, nobody really resembled his photo on file, but it seemed almost too much to ask for. "Seems his uncle had to take off and take care of some more . . . pressing business than the shoot-out in his hallway."

Surely he knew? Was he playing a game? Or the least bit reluctant to be responsible for the death of a colleague? Mahir met the gaze but forced himself to look away before the dirty cop had enough to get suspicious about. "Saeed." There were several levels of dirty, from small irregularities to complete corruption. But even in that hierarchy there was a special place for cops who'd hand over a kid to be executed.

Forget Gray. I'll kill you first. Slowly.

Kinza stared at Mahir, but he didn't let on like he knew him. He just looked suitably shocked and frightened, which was normal, given the situation.

Ironically—well, almost, if he'd had enough emotional energy for humor—up to now Mahir hadn't really expected to walk out again. Getting caught in the cross fire, getting outfoxed by Lombardi, all that had kind of figured in the back of his mind.

With Ridley dead, walking back out was less important than making sure he took Lombardi with him. But right then, looking at Kinza, that flip-flopped, and nothing else was more important than getting his nephew out in one piece. He owed him that much, but it went deeper than even that.

"Ah, I like the far-reaching arm of the law," Lombardi said with glee.

"Speaking of which, somebody ordered a SWAT raid on these premises." The cop polished his fingernails on his uniform. "Took the liberty of calling the head of the department to call it off. The things dirty cops will do when they run out of options, huh?" *James, and you believed him?*

Mahir was fighting full-fledged panic now. One handgun, two armed men, and Kinza right in the middle. This wasn't going to end well.

Lombardi slid the nickel-plated gun into his waistband and slowly came around the desk toward Kinza, who stood off to one side on shaking knees. The closer Lombardi came, the smaller Kinza seemed, like he was truly shrinking and not just cowering like any terrified kid would.

Standing right in front of him, Lombardi looked him up and down, eyes narrow and lips quirked. Mahir wanted to lunge at him and choke the fuck out of him for even *looking* at his nephew. Mahir's heart beat faster and faster with every tense, silent second as Kinza stared up at Lombardi, his eyes wide and his face paling.

His hands go near that gun, I swear . . .

Mahir casually shifted position so his hand was a little closer to the gun on his hip. The movement tugged the fabric of his blood-saturated shirt, the stickiness against his skin reminding him that he'd already lost one person today.

Out of nowhere, Lombardi backhanded Kinza across the face, hard enough to send the boy down to one knee.

Before he could think twice, Mahir was halfway across the room, and by the time he realized he'd moved, he was between Lombardi and Kinza.

Lombardi smirked at him. "Well, well. So I can get a reaction out of durka durka here."

"He's a kid," Mahir snarled.

"He's a liability."

Another sudden movement and the cold nickel-plated muzzle was pressed to Mahir's forehead.

"He's a liability," Lombardi said in a low, dangerous tone that rivaled Ridley at his most terrifying, "and so are you, apparently."

Mahir gulped. "He's just . . . a kid." Quiet sounds behind him told him Kinza was slowly getting to his feet, wisely backing away in the process.

"He's a kid," Lombardi acknowledged, "but he's spoken to the cops. I can't have that on my payroll. And if I just fire him, then he's out there, out in the world, with my sensitive information in that pretty little head of his." He pressed the gun harder against Mahir's head, grinding the muzzle against his skin. "Which is why I need you to blow it right out of his skull. Understood?"

"I think you've scared him," Mahir said. "He won't talk. Will you, kid?"

"N-no," came the timid half whimper from behind him.

Lombardi's face was getting redder by the second. "Do I look like an idiot to you? Really? He's not going to—"

The lights went out.

Mahir didn't miss a beat. He hit the gun away with his forearm. Lombardi must've pulled the trigger because a shot near his head deafened him. A fist went into his gut.

He punched blindly, hit Lombardi. He sensed the vibration of something hard and solid hitting the floor near his feet. Both of them dropped, scrambling in the darkness for the gun on the floor as well as any purchase on each other.

Mahir sensed movement all around him, but he didn't dare let go of Lombardi. No way was he losing him in the darkness.

He couldn't find the gun. It had been there a moment ago. Then it was gone.

Something flashed in the corner of his eye.

Then something else, bigger and brighter, turning the darkness to nonsensical green shapes as his retinas struggled to adjust.

A tremendous force hit his shoulder. Then Lombardi tensed in his arms. Sagged, squirmed feebly.

There was light. How much, he couldn't tell. He still couldn't focus.

Strong hands lifted him away from Lombardi, and searing pain under his arm brought a cry out of him. At least, he thought it did. He still couldn't hear a damned thing.

Someone slammed him down on his back. He blinked a few times. The shadow above him slowly took shape. Black. All black.

White.

White lettering.

Seattle S.W.A.T.

The guy's lips were visible, and moving, but Mahir couldn't hear anything. He just closed his eyes and tried to figure out why his side hurt. Why it was wet.

Kinza. Where's Kinza?

He turned his head in the direction his nephew had been a moment ago, and in spite of his fucked-up vision, he found the boy. Kinza was huddled against the wall, a SWAT officer's hand on his shoulder. He was shaking. Crying.

The officer's gloved hand tugged at Kinza's and finally freed what he'd been holding.

The nickel-plated pistol.

CHAPTER TWENTY-ONE

Hazy delirium took over his consciousness. Sometimes he was awake. Sometimes he thought he was. Darkness faded in and out. There was silence, there was noise, the most annoying *beep-beep-beep* lurking almost constantly in the background. Faces hovered above him. Needles. Painful prodding at his side.

Sometimes he convinced his parched mouth to speak, and whenever it did, he sounded miles and miles and miles away, saying either *"Ridley?"* or *"Kinza?"* Then there would be noncommittal responses from the hovering faces.

"He's fine."

"You need to rest."

"Just relax."

At some point, Mahir opened his eyes, and he was at the other end of that haze. Back on terra firma, his brain processing things the way it hadn't in . . . Fuck, how long had he been out of it?

He tried to sit up, but a sharp pain under his right arm made him think better of it. That arm was pinned against his side, and now that he was aware of it, the thick bandaging between his arm and his side was irritating as hell. He felt it tighten around his chest every time he breathed, which stung deep in his lungs.

Closing his eyes, he exhaled slowly. Maybe being semiconscious for a while wasn't such a bad thing. Whatever was hurting now had probably been worse before, so hooray for heavy drugs and sweet oblivion.

Though he was thankful for the gap in his coherent memory, he didn't like the idea of not knowing how much he was missing. A few hours? Days? Weeks?

They've probably already buried Ridley.

The thought drove itself deep into his chest, far beneath the injuries and straight to the core. He squeezed his eyes shut and told himself the ache in his throat was from whatever tubes and crap had probably been shoved down it.

Ridley. Fuck, Ridley . . .

I never even knew his real name.

And deep-cover agents had a way of disappearing into thin air. Once an investigation was over, and the persona was no longer needed, the name and the face vanished, hopefully leaving behind some incarcerated felons and ruined trafficking rings.

Mahir never had asked what they told the families of agents who died during long deep-cover ops. Did they tell them anything at all? Maybe it was best if they never learned the truth. Ridley's mother would probably have enough trouble sleeping without knowing he'd died in a gunfight.

Footsteps nudged him out of his thoughts, and he blinked his eyes into focus as a nurse walked into the room.

"Well, good morning," she said with a smile. "You're looking a little more bright-eyed and bushy-tailed today."

Mahir moistened his lips as best he could with a mostly parched tongue. "How long . . . how long have I . . ."

"You've been here almost seventy-two hours."

Three days. Gone. Just like that. Wow.

"My nephew, he—"

"Must be the one named Kinza?" Her smile brightened a little more. "He's been trying to come in and visit you since you were admitted."

"And he's okay? He's not hurt?"

"He's been pretty rattled." She checked monitors and fussed over tubes and wires. "But he's just fine. Sweet kid, too."

"Yeah. He is." Mahir closed his eyes and exhaled. Kinza was uninjured. Mahir still physically ached with grief for Ridley, but at least Kinza was all right. He'd never have forgiven himself if the boy had been hurt or killed. Right then, he'd take any silver lining he could get.

Once the doctor making his morning rounds had checked Mahir over, it was determined he was in good enough condition to move out of the intensive care unit. And he'd barely settled into his new room when a nurse asked him if he was ready to receive visitors.

"Who?" Mahir asked, hoping it was Kinza.

"He said his name is"—she glanced at the note in her hand again—"Adil Hussain."

Mahir's heart skipped. Shit. His brother worked in this hospital. Mahir was lucky the man hadn't just barged in.

"Sure." He reached for the cup of ice chips on the tray beside the bed. "Send him in."

The nurse left, and Adil came in. He was on shift, dressed in his white coat, looking every bit the professional. He approached without a word, not looking Mahir in the eyes. The chair legs squeaked on the hard floor. Then Adil eased himself onto the seat. From there, he inspected all the readings on the monitors as if he was Mahir's doctor instead of his brother.

Mahir swallowed the ice chip he'd been playing with. "I'm sorry, Adil."

Adil turned to him, his face unreadable.

Mahir cleared his raw, dry throat. "I never intended for Kinza to get into harm's way. I swear to you."

Adil's expression didn't change, but he looked down at his hands, which were folded in his lap.

The unnerving silence went on with that damned beeping heart monitor in the background. Mahir pulled in a breath, trying to keep himself composed. At least the sharp pain in his side was intense enough to distract him from the lump in his throat, so he concentrated on that. When he was sure he could speak, he said, "I promise, I—"

"The blame is mine."

Mahir blinked. "What?"

Adil gnawed his lower lip, an uncharacteristically nervous gesture for that man of steel. "I don't approve of what he is. Of what either of you are." He slowly lifted his gaze and met Mahir's eyes, and Mahir had never seen his brother looking so lost before. "But I would rather my son be . . ." He paused, swallowing. "I would rather my son be gay than dead."

Mahir winced. "I'm so sorry."

"No." Adil lifted a hand from his lap and reached for Mahir's arm. He hesitated, hand hovering over Mahir's wrist for a moment, then let it settle. He squeezed gently. "No. What happened, it wasn't your . . ." He swore in Arabic under his breath and shook his head. "Kinza told me everything. Why he followed you. How he got involved in that, that group of criminals." Adil's shoulders sank. "He was alone. Frightened. He should have been home with his parents, but . . . I drove him away." He sighed. "He's just a boy."

Mahir gingerly brought his other hand over, careful not to jar the IV, and squeezed his brother's hand. "You couldn't have known he'd get tangled up in something like this."

"No, but what father sends his boy away?" Adil looked at Mahir, and Mahir swore there was the *faintest* hint of tears in his eyes. "I don't approve of him, but he's still my son. He should be safe and well in my home."

"You can't separate who he is from what he is," Mahir said, biting back his frustration. "He's gay. Just like I am. But he's still your son just like I'm still your brother, and if you want to keep him at home where he's safe and part of the family, you have *got* to let this go."

Adil set his jaw, but the pain in his eyes trumped the stubbornness, and his jaw relaxed. "Tell me what to do. I don't . . . I can't just pretend he's—"

"No, you can't. Because it's part of who he is. Maybe the two of you can agree to not talk about it for the time being. Just, you know, settle back into being father and son again. Maybe get a therapist."

Adil bristled. "A therapist?"

"Whatever it takes." Mahir almost shrugged but remembered just in time that his right side wasn't ready for any kind of motion. "But he's not going to change, and you can either accept that or not. So whatever you have to do to get back on an even keel with him . . ."

His brother moved his jaw, as if chewing on the idea. Finally, he nodded. "I'll talk to him. We can . . . we can work on it."

"Good."

It shouldn't have taken his son dodging a bullet to rattle Adil into considering this, but at least now he was.

Mahir swallowed. "Is he doing all right?"

Adil nodded. "He's well. He'll be better once he's been to visit you."

"I'm looking forward to seeing him."

Especially since he desperately needed to see Kinza in the flesh so he could truly know that the boy was all right. After everything that had happened, he needed proof that Kinza had really come out of all of that unscathed.

As unscathed as could be expected, that was. The showdown in Lombardi's office was slowly coming back to Mahir, but the final moments of it, chaotic as they may have been, were seared into his memory. Especially the last thing he'd seen just before he'd passed out, that shining silver gun in his nephew's shaking hands.

He looked at Adil. "Kinza saved my life, you know."

"I know." Adil smiled, though it seemed to take some work, his expression finding an odd tipping point between fatherly pride and guilt. "I'm glad he did."

"Yeah." Mahir smiled, too. "Me too."

Adil's pager went off and he glanced at it, but he was already standing up. "I'll check on you, make sure the colleagues have sewn you up well. But Khalisah insists you come for dinner once you feel up to it."

Wow, now that was a reversal. Ever since his coming-out—as tastefully as he'd done it—he'd only ever met his brother's family at his parents' house. Though it went outwardly unacknowledged, Mahir had known why, but he'd refrained from accusing them or telling them what he thought of it.

"I'd love to," Mahir said honestly. He was still wary; Adil could always relapse. Though some reason for the lack in contact must have been that he thought Mahir might somehow contaminate Kinza with gayness, like transmitting the flu, likely via handshake.

"Good." Adil glanced down at the pager, then pressed Mahir's hand again. "Let me know if you need anything. I've instructed the nurses."

And likely put the fear of Allah into the whole station in that they might earn the enmity of the most prestigious heart surgeon in the entire hospital, if not all of Seattle.

Mahir watched him leave, feeling oddly exhausted after his brother's intensity. He'd have preferred to rest a bit, but the door opened again, and seeing Kinza alive jolted him awake.

Kinza's face brightened with a smile, and he hurried over, plunking down on the chair that was likely still warm from his father. "You saw Dad?"

"I couldn't really escape. It's all a conspiracy." Mahir lifted his hand.

"I could help you escape?"

Mahir started to laugh, then stopped himself because it still hurt too bad. "I've had enough adventures for a while." Though he was not looking forward to getting debriefed in this state—or even when fully healed.

Kinza pouted, then reached for Mahir's hand. His fingers were cool and clammy, but if a little nervousness was the only thing wrong with him, that was quite all right. "Does it hurt a lot?"

"Just when I laugh . . . That gets through the drugs." Mahir closed his fingers around Kinza's hand. "How are you? What happened?"

Kinza looked around as if worried about witnesses. "I talked to the police. Your boss, I believe. I think I . . . didn't make a great impression. Sorry."

Oh, Kinza. "I'd have been a wreck. I'm sure you did just fine."

"Uh-huh." Kinza looked down at his feet.

Mahir squeezed his nephew's hand. "Kinza, look at me." When he did, Mahir said, "In that office, you handled yourself better than most kids your age—hell, most guys *my* age—would have."

Kinza eyed him skeptically. "I didn't do anything." He shrank back against the chair. "Besides shoot you."

Chuckling, Mahir patted his hand. "Considering that was literally a shot in the dark, I'd say you did pretty damned good."

Kinza laughed but not even halfheartedly. "I could have killed you."

"Lombardi could have, too."

Kinza shuddered.

"It took a lot of balls to pull that trigger at all," Mahir said. "And to keep yourself together during all the shit you've been in since this started. I'm proud of you, kid. I really am."

Kinza lifted his gaze and searched Mahir's eyes for a moment. "Really?"

Mahir nodded. "Yeah."

"Even if I . . ." Kinza shifted in his seat, staring at their still-joined hands. "I blew your whole case. Lombardi never would have—"

"You didn't know what you were getting into. Look, I'm trained for all this. I've been through more simulations and worst-case scenarios than I even want to think about. And I still barely kept it together there toward the end. You haven't had a bit of training, and you still managed to keep a level head, and even help defuse the situation right before SWAT showed up."

Kinza chewed his lip and kept his gaze down.

"And I want you to know that I'm sorry for leaving you alone. I know you came to me because you needed someone, and that's why you followed me that night. That wasn't your fault. That was mine."

Kinza swallowed but still didn't look up.

"If I had to do it over, I would have taken myself off the case or found some other way to help you." Mahir flinched at his own words. "I don't know exactly what, but I'd have done something other than just leaving you alone."

Kinza pulled in a breath, then let it out slowly. "You really would've left the case?"

"I'd have done something different. The case was important, but so are you."

His nephew continued staring downward. Finally, he spoke so softly Mahir barely heard him. "I'm sorry, Uncle Mahir."

"For what?" Mahir squeezed his hand again. "This wasn't your—"

Kinza's head snapped up. "If I hadn't screwed up and gotten involved, David would still be alive."

Mahir couldn't stop himself from visibly flinching.

"He's dead because Lombardi's guys followed me." Kinza looked on the verge of tears. "Because I fucked up and—"

"You didn't know. None of this was your fault." Mahir reached out and pulled a tissue from the box on the nightstand, then handed it to Kinza. "And you know what the last thing David said to me was?"

Kinza shook his head slowly and scrunched up the tissue in his hand.

Mahir swallowed, struggling to keep his own composure. "He asked if you were okay. He knew you were important to me, and he wanted to protect you as much as I did. And he wanted to know that you were okay."

Kinza exhaled, his shoulders sinking. "I'm sorry . . ."

"I'm sorry you got roped into this. You never should've had to see or hear any of this, and anything I can do to make it up to you, I will."

Shaking his head, Kinza rose. "No. You don't need to." Then he leaned over and gently hugged Mahir.

Mahir wrapped his one mobile arm around Kinza. "You're a good kid. You know that, right?"

Sniffing sharply, Kinza nodded. "Thanks for being there when I needed you."

"I'm always here for you. I promise."

"Thanks." Kinza held on a little tighter. "I love you, Uncle Mahir."

"I love you, too, kiddo." He pretended to not notice that Kinza's eyes were a bit wetter when he let him go, and Kinza found enough tact—or was just embarrassed himself—to not comment on Mahir having to blink a few times himself. A very manly agreement to keep their mutual dignity intact, which almost made Mahir chuckle. "Visit me when you're bored, all right? It's not like I can run away to work anytime soon."

Kinza pursed his lips. "Can I bring Tyson?"

"You guys still going strong?"

"Well, yeah. I can't see him much or anything. He has to study harder so he doesn't fail some classes."

"Maybe you could study together?"

"Uh. We'd just get distracted." Kinza colored a bit.

"Invite another guy or a girl? Girl might be safe?"

"Yeah, I'll think about it." Which was family-speak for *not in a million years*. Kinza was walking backward to the door already. "Text me if I should bring you anything."

One-handed, that would be a challenge, but Mahir nodded, struggling now to keep his eyes open. He must have fallen asleep because when he looked up, Kinza was gone, and some nurses were bringing him soup.

He ate, then rested, exhausted from just swallowing and lifting his arm—at least that much he could do. At some point, the door opened again, and James walked in with a middle-aged lady. He turned to her and said, "I'd like to speak with him alone for a little while," and she nodded and withdrew. She did look kind of official, and Mahir racked his brain to work out where and if he'd seen her before. James pulled a chair closer. "Well, the doctors said I can't exhaust you, but we do have some urgent questions about some details. How are you feeling?"

"I'm good, sir." Mahir cleared his throat. "And I'm sorry for all the things that went wrong and the mistakes I've made. I've had a little time to think about it."

His boss waved a hand. "We'll deal with that when you're back on your feet. IA and the chief aren't happy about a few things, but the fact that you and that DEA agent managed to bring down Lombardi's ring? Well, they're willing to overlook some indiscretions."

"You knew about the DEA agent?"

"One of the higher-ups contacted me after the op went south. Gave me the rundown since the whole thing was over and it wasn't necessary to keep the agent's cover." He shook his head. "Sounds like you could've used him during that last little meeting."

"Yeah, well. Shit happens." Mahir sighed. "Believe me, if I could've stopped anything from happening to him . . ." *I'd have done it. Anything. Anything at all.*

"Well, as you said, shit happens." James sat back in the chair, thumbing the edge of a thick file folder. "He'll be out of commission for a few months, but by the time—"

"Wait, what?" Mahir straightened just enough to remind him why he wasn't supposed to move much. He winced, then slowly released his breath as the pain took its sweet time receding. "What do you mean he'll be out of commission for a few months?"

James cocked his head. "He took two to the gut, detective. You don't bounce back from that overnight."

"Bounce . . . I . . ." Mahir blinked a few times. "I thought he was dead."

"He's a lucky man." James grimaced. "It's a damned good thing they made the call to airlift him to Harborview, or he might not have made it."

"Harbor—" Mahir stopped. "He's *here*?"

His boss nodded. "Yep. Left the ICU around the same time you did." He uncrossed and then recrossed his legs. "I'm sure the two of you will want to compare war wounds, but we need to discuss a few things first."

"Sure," Mahir said. "Right."

The boss made him run through all the details he could remember, from the day he'd started in the club until the showdown in Lombardi's office. Then he updated him on the status and condition of everyone who'd been involved that day. Mahir wasn't sure how he felt about learning that Lombardi was still alive—and *also* in this hospital—but whatever. Hopefully he'd end up in the general population when a jury sent his ass to Walla Walla. Considering the recent calls on his cell phone had linked him to buyers on a massive child-trafficking ring, Lombardi would be very high on the lists of some of the other violent offenders in that pen. And both Ridley and Mahir, as well as Kinza, would be expected to testify.

Gladly.

Eventually, James had what he needed. There'd be more questions, and probably a very thorough and painful investigation by IA, but for now, the case was considered a success. Lombardi would be behind bars as soon as he was released from the hospital. The employees were either dead or in jail.

And more important than anything else in Mahir's mind, Ridley was alive.

"Hey, can you do me a favor?" he asked when James went to leave.

"Hmm?" James lifted his eyebrows.

"That DEA agent. I'd like to see him."

His boss nodded. "Get some rest for now, but I'll arrange it."

"Thank you."

That night was some of the best sleep Mahir had managed to get in recent memory. The drugs helped, of course, but his mind was more at ease than it had been in a long time, and not long after James had left, he was out cold.

He didn't dream. He just slept.

CHAPTER TWENTY-TWO

A nurse who was entirely too chipper for someone working an early shift came in as Mahir was finishing his breakfast of green-flavored Jell-O. He thought she'd come in to draw blood or take his blood pressure or something, but then another detail registered.

She was pushing a wheelchair.

"Ready to go visit your friend?" she asked in a perky voice that bordered on shrill.

He wasn't about to be annoyed, though. "Yes, thank you."

He'd been up and around a few times, fortunately, and had gotten a little more adept at maneuvering himself—with some help—to his feet. He was half-tempted to insist he could walk, but . . . no. He was still light-headed whenever he was vertical, and just walking to and from the bathroom had exhausted him before. Wheelchair it was.

She wheeled him out of the room, his IVs and monitors hanging from the rack that rolled alongside him. He was surprised the heart monitor hadn't picked up his elevated pulse. Or maybe he was just imagining it. His heart sure felt like it was racing as they went down the hall and into the elevator. He didn't even notice if they went up or down a floor. He was just too damned focused on one simple thing: Ridley.

The nurse stopped outside a room. "I'm just going to make sure he's awake and ready to see you, okay?"

Mahir nodded.

She disappeared into the room. He could hear her voice and thought he made out the faintest familiar edge of Ridley's voice, but it was so quiet, he couldn't be sure.

She returned, and Mahir's heart rate jumped again when she pushed the door all the way open and wheeled him in.

And there he was.

He looked like hell. Pale, even for a white guy. He had IVs in both hands and one of those oxygen tubes across his upper lip and in his nose. It was impossible to tell if the shadows under his eyes were bruises from the brawl on Mahir's stairs or just a side effect of being at death's door for a few days.

But he was definitely alive, sitting up and looking at Mahir with those familiar, if exhausted, blue eyes. His pale lips pulled into a smile. "Hey."

Mahir returned the smile. "Hey."

Ridley glanced at the nurse. "Would you excuse us?"

"Of course." She pushed Mahir's wheelchair up to Ridley's bed, double-checked that both of them were all right for a few minutes, and then left, closing the door behind her.

For a long moment, they just looked at each other.

Finally, Mahir said, "Up until last night, I thought you were dead."

Ridley laughed the way only Ridley could: dryly, a little sarcastically. "Up until yesterday morning, I was kind of wondering the same thing."

Mahir swallowed, remembered the flashing lights and Ridley's fingers weak around his. Walking into Lombardi's office soaked in Ridley's blood. At least it had felt that way. "Next time you tell me you'd be willing to die for Kinza, you really don't have to go and prove it." It was the only thing he could say to keep things light and still say what he meant.

Ridley arched an eyebrow, but the expression didn't last. He relaxed into the pillow, looking frail, though still sharp. Intelligent. Perceptive. "What happened?"

"It's a long story, but I pretended to be Saeed and went back to safeguard the evidence. Lombardi got so spooked he called some of his customers. They were selling the *kids*."

"Mother of God."

"It was kind of obvious. Or would have been, if they'd been pretty, underage girls." Mahir shook his head. "Talk about a blind spot."

"How's Kinza?"

"Rattled a bit, but he did well. He ended up shooting me, but that was the lesser evil."

"Shot you?"

"Lombardi tried to get Saeed to execute him. Test of loyalty. It all went south from there, but SWAT came in and saved the day. I still caught a bullet. Seems we were both getting operated on at roughly the same time."

"Now, that's romance." Ridley smiled weakly.

Mahir suppressed the laugh. Damn, they weren't in any shape to even laugh about their exploits. "I prefer roses or a candlelight dinner myself, but whatever gets you off."

Ridley chuckled but then grimaced. Yep. No state to share the mirth. They were some fucked-up battle horses for real. "Now that we've tried my idea of romance, maybe give yours a shot?"

A shot. "Haha. I see what you did there." Mahir lifted a warning finger, and Ridley smiled at him tiredly. "I don't think I'll ever have Italian again."

"With my guts, I'm off pasta myself. I think I can have some soup in a week or so."

"You're missing nothing with the Jell-O. Trust me."

"And now you've dashed the one glimmer of hope I had left."

Mahir smirked. "Sorry. The candlelight dinner is still on offer, though."

Ridley lay there perfectly still, eyes searching Mahir's face, and Mahir cursed himself for not being more straightforward about it. Maybe he still feared he'd get rejected, or maybe it was because they'd both just survived and were not exactly in the best shape of their lives. Bad enough to be physically vulnerable, but emotionally?

"I'd like that," Ridley said quietly, voice breaking down to little more than a whisper.

"Good. I mean. Thank you. For that and for everything you've done. For being there." *For surviving.* "For being a damned good cop, too."

Ridley nodded. "Likewise."

Mahir grinned. "You know, I still don't even know your real name."

Ridley gave one of those soft, barely there laughs. "Actually, you do."

"I do?"

"My name's David."

"Ah."

"And I'm assuming Kinza was using your real one when he called you Mahir?"

"Yeah." Mahir nodded. "It'll probably take me a while to stop thinking of you as Ridley."

Ridley lifted his hand off the blanket and carefully, gingerly, reached for Mahir's. His hand was cool, his grip weak, but he curled his fingers between Mahir's. "There's no rush to get used to it. I'm planning on sticking around for a while."

Mahir's heart fluttered, and he gently squeezed Ridley's hand. "Good. I was just starting to get used to your bullshit, so you can't leave now."

They both chuckled quietly.

Mahir cleared his throat as he stroked the side of Ridley's hand with his thumb, carefully avoiding the IV. "I should let you get some rest."

Closing his eyes, Ridley nodded. "Yeah. I don't want to fall asleep on you."

"You want me to come back and see you?"

Ridley tightened his grasp. "As often as you can."

EPILOGUE

Four months later

"I just have one question." Kinza set a box down with a heavy *thud* on Mahir's counter. He turned around and faced Mahir and Ridley, who sat at the kitchen table. "If you two still aren't allowed to lift more than twenty pounds at a time, why did you pack all the boxes so they're more than twenty pounds apiece?"

"What?" Ridley put a hand to his chest, looking hurt. "Are you suggesting we don't want to do any of the heavy lifting?"

Mahir scoffed. Shaking his head, he picked up his beer bottle. "Kids these days. No respect whatsoever."

Kinza glared at both of them in turn. Then Tyson came in behind him and dropped another box on the counter.

"Jesus fuck," he said. "Do you own anything that weighs less than half a ton?"

Ridley shrugged. "Yeah, but I packed it all in with the heavy stuff." He made a shooing gesture. "C'mon, boys. Back to work."

The boys groaned, picked up their boxes, and continued down the hall.

Mahir chuckled. "If we weren't paying them twenty bucks an hour for this, I'd actually feel a little guilty."

"I wouldn't." Ridley shrugged. "They're kids. It builds character."

"Uh-huh."

Ridley grinned and took a sip from his beer.

"So you don't think we'll get sick of each other?" Mahir leaned back in his chair. "We're going to be tripping over each other left and right now."

Ridley set his beer down, then reached over and took Mahir's hand. "If we didn't get sick of each other during the investigation, I think we'll be fine. Besides, at least we know damn well we can work together even under the shittiest conditions."

"No kidding." Mahir grimaced. He turned his hand over beneath Ridley's. Considering they hadn't gone to blows—much—during that period, they'd be fine working as partners now. The part he didn't say aloud was that even if their personalities did clash from time to time, all it took was a reminder of how close they'd come to losing each other—a glance at one of the impressive scars they both had now—to remember there were worse things than differing opinions.

Ridley cleared his throat. "By the way, we're supposed to report into the boss's office on Monday. He wants to brief us on our new assignment."

Though the idea of going back undercover made Mahir's stomach turn, he couldn't help grinning. "A new case. This should be fun."

"Should be." Ridley grinned. "And hey, at least this time we both know from the start that we're on the same team."

"Finding out we were was hot, though."

"Yeah, it was. Though it'll be hotter to learn everything else about you. Waking up together is not as overrated as you think."

"Never said that."

"Well, you sure didn't make it a habit." Ridley winked at him. Just ribbing. Though he was right, even more so about other guys. Mahir had been a hit-and-run kind of lover who just didn't hang around for fear of maybe getting in deeper than he could afford in his job, his family, or maybe just life in general.

But that could be different with Ridley. Dating each other still meant keeping things discreet or they couldn't work together— something Mahir wanted. In the new department, he wasn't ready to go through all the settling in, learning about colleagues and which ones were possibly racists. Getting to partner up with Ridley meant he knew his place, knew one guy had his back, knew there was one man he could trust unconditionally.

Anyway, he hadn't planned to be anything less than professional while on duty—and observed—so keeping their relationship quiet would work fine. If people wondered why they lived together, that was a different matter. Maybe it was telling them without telling them. Deniable and completely clear—not a shameful secret.

"I think I'm good at forming new habits. Will they put us straight to work?"

"From what I heard, it's going to be a briefing on an ongoing thing with the option to pull us in deeper if they have to, but right now it looks more like support."

"Are we getting an office together?"

"Desk is ready for you, though you'll have to promise you'll treat my plants with respect."

Mahir laughed. "Okay. I'll even water them."

Ridley gave him a speculative once-over that made Mahir's skin tingle. Damn, this familiarity felt nice. Making plans together, all the little jokes that long-term couples developed. Khalisah and Adil almost spoke their own language, and he and Ridley were a few steps down that road already. "I'll give you instructions."

Oh, yeah, and Ridley being bossy at times sure didn't hurt the attraction.

"That's because you love me," Mahir tried.

"That's because I love my fucking plants. And you." Ridley grinned. "All fifteen of us will get along just fine."

ALSO BY L.A. WITT

Static

A Chip in His Shoulder

Something New Under the Sun

O Come All Ye Kinky

Left Hand of Calvus

Finding Master Right

Unhinge the Universe, with Aleksandr Voinov

Conduct Unbecoming

From Out in the Cold

Tucker Springs Novels

Where Nerves End (coming soon)

Covet Thy Neighbor

After the Fall

Coming Soon

Noble Metals

Precious Metals

For a complete list, please see www.loriawitt.com.

ALSO BY ALEKSANDR VOINOV

Scorpion (Memory of Scorpions, #1)
Lying with Scorpions (Memory of Scorpions, #2)
Skybound
Incursion
Gold Digger
Country Mouse, with Amy Lane
City Mouse, with Amy Lane
Unhinge the Universe, with L.A. Witt
Dark Soul Vols. 1–5
Break and Enter, with Rachel Haimowitz
Dark Edge of Honor, with Rhi Etzweiler
The Lion of Kent, with Kate Cotoner

Coming Soon
Counterpunch
Suckerpunch
A Taste for Poison (Memory of Scorpions, #3)

For a full list, go to www.aleksandrvoinov.com/bookshelf.html.

ABOUT L.A. WITT

L.A. Witt is an abnormal M/M romance writer currently living in the glamorous and ultra-futuristic metropolis of Omaha, Nebraska, with her husband, two cats, and a disembodied penguin brain that communicates with her telepathically. In addition to writing smut and disturbing the locals, L.A. is said to be working with the U.S. government to perfect a genetic modification that will allow humans to survive indefinitely on Corn Pops and beef jerky. This is all a cover, though, as her primary leisure activity is hunting down her arch nemesis, erotica author Lauren Gallagher, who is also said to be lurking somewhere in Omaha. L.A. can be found at www.loriawitt.com, as well as exchanging irreverent tweets with Aleks as @GallagherWitt.

ABOUT ALEKSANDR VOINOV

Aleksandr Voinov is an emigrant German author living near London, where he is one of the unsung heroes in the financial services sector. His genres range from horror, science fiction, cyberpunk, and fantasy to contemporary, thriller, and historical erotic gay novels.

In his spare time, he goes weight lifting, explores historical sites, and meets other writers. He single-handedly sustains three London bookstores with his ever-changing research projects. His current interests include special forces operations during World War II, preindustrial warfare, European magical traditions, and how to destroy the world and plunge it into a nuclear winter without having the benefit of nuclear weapons.

Visit Aleksandr's website at www.aleksandrvoinov.com, his blog at www.aleksandrvoinov.blogspot.com, and follow him on Twitter, where he tweets as @aleksandrvoinov.

Enjoyed this book? Visit RiptidePublishing.com to find more romantic suspense!

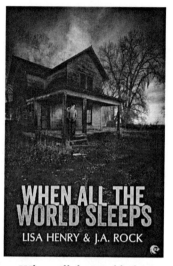

Catch a Ghost
ISBN: 978-1-62649-039-0

When All the World Sleeps
ISBN: 978-1-62649-079-6

Earn Bonus Bucks!

Earn 1 Bonus Buck for each dollar you spend. Find out how at RiptidePublishing.com/news/bonus-bucks.

Win Free Ebooks for a Year!

Pre-order coming soon titles directly through our site and you'll receive one entry into a drawing to win free books for a year! Get the details at RiptidePublishing.com/contests.

CPSIA information can be obtained at www.ICGtesting.com
Printed in the USA
LVOW12s1841300914

406572LV00006BA/655/P